A SILVER
SEASON

LINDA HUDSON-SMITH

A SILVER
SEASON

A SILVER SEASON

A New Spirit Novel

ISBN-13: 978-1-58314-585-2
ISBN-10: 1-58314-585-0

www.kimanipress.com

Printed in U.S.A.

This novel is dedicated to all the
beautiful 40+ people throughout the world.

This novel is also dedicated to the sweet,
loving memory of my dear aunt:

Josephine Arlene Grinage-Jenkins

Sunrise: September 6, 1917

Sunset: April 13, 2005

Your unconditional love for your family and
friends will be forever missed!

Chapter 1

As Savannah Richmond looked around her totally empty View Park home, tears brimmed in her sable brown eyes. Moving about from room to room brought to mind many of the memorable events that had occurred inside the home Savannah had once shared with her husband, Geoffrey, and their two children, Kenya and Kevin.

Savannah and Geoffrey, a beautiful couple, with matching personalities, had met while attending neighboring colleges in Atlanta, Georgia. Geoffrey had graduated from college with a degree in engineering and Savannah had earned a degree in nursing. Both bride and groom were employed in the state of California, in the colorful city of Los Angeles. Savannah worked for the Los Angeles County Department of Mental Health. Before his demise, Geoffrey had worked for a division of NASA in El Segundo.

After forty-five years of living on the planet, twenty-five years of an extremely happy marriage, and two pregnancies, Savannah had managed to maintain her natural beauty. She possessed a smooth-as-silk honey-brown complexion and a stunning five-foot-six figure boasting plenty of exercise and a healthy diet.

Savannah had recently cut off her long brown hair and had it shaped into full-bodied layers that fell slightly below her ears. The chic new hairstyle made her look much younger than her actual age. The broad gray streaks in her tresses had once been a striking feature against her skin but were now tinted with golden-walnut cellophane, making her hair appear frosted.

Widowed for well over two years, and with her two children both grown and gone, Savannah felt terribly alone the majority of the time. The drastic changes in her life had been hard to get used to, especially when most of her time had revolved around her loving family. Savannah was a great mother and had been the best wife any man could ever hope for.

Kenya was now married to a wonderful doctor, Cole Standiford, and Kevin moved up north to the Bay Area approximately a year ago, where he'd landed a job as a pharmacist with a well-established pharmacy chain. Kenya was a spoiled daddy's girl. Had always been one. Kevin and Savannah had an extremely close relationship, as he was her firstborn. Savannah also doted on Kenya while Kevin and Geoffrey had been practically inseparable. In hopes of raising Kevin to be a fine young man, Geoffrey had been much tougher on his son, expecting far more out of him than he had from Kenya.

The dreadful loneliness had prompted Savannah to make a few radical changes in her life, including selling her home. All of her precious memories had been packed up and shipped off to her newly built home in Fontana, located in Southern California's Inland Empire, approximately fifty-five miles east of downtown Los Angeles.

With the crime in Los Angeles constantly rising, Savannah had given much thought to Geoffrey's idea of moving farther east. As an avid golfer, his first choice had been Palm Springs. Since she now had to make the move alone, she had decided to only go as far as Fontana, the same city where one of her close friends resided and who'd also made the move from Los Angeles.

Recently taking an early buyout retirement from her twenty-year job as a registered nurse with the Los Angeles County Department of Mental Health, Savannah thought her income would stretch a lot further up in San Bernardino County. When the California real-estate market unexpectedly soared sky-high, she had viewed the sudden rise in her equity as an excellent reason to sell her home. Not only would she make a huge profit in the process, there'd also be enough money for Savannah to maintain a comfortable nest egg without taking a full-time job.

After Savannah dropped down on the carpeted floor to wait for Kenya to come over to say her farewells, she opened her wallet and took out a picture of her loving husband. Two years of mourning was enough, she'd been telling herself lately, but she wasn't sure she'd ever stop grieving Geoffrey. Savannah desperately needed a fresh start in her life as a single woman and she also desired an opportunity to meet other people and possibly forge new friendships.

Savannah's grief had been terribly unmanageable at one time. Then, on one sad, extremely lonely night, she had pulled out all the pictures, videotapes and love letters, along with every other exciting memory of her marriage to Geoffrey. Shortly after reliving all the wonderful memories she had had in her life with Geoffrey, Savannah had finally begun to come to terms with his untimely death.

A massive heart attack had claimed Geoffrey's life rather swiftly. One moment they were in the speeding ambulance on their way to the hospital. In the next moment he was gone; they'd only been minutes away from the closest emergency care facility. Up to the point when the chest pains had begun on that fatal day, Geoffrey had been physically fit, had never suffered from anything more than an occasional cold and a bout with the flu a time or two.

Savannah and Geoffrey had had a very good life together. Their marriage had been an extraordinary one, the type that many people had envied. Practically every moment of their life together had counted for something. Geoffrey had been a vibrant man, an incurable romantic, as well as a wonderful son, brother, friend, husband and father. Geoffrey had also been a very humble Christian man, one who proudly talked the talk as he walked the walk. Geoffrey had lived and died upon the righteous path that had eventually led him home to be with the Lord.

After Savannah pushed all her grievous thoughts to the back of her mind, she arose from the floor, having decided to wait for Kenya outside in her Lexus. Despite the fact that the house was completely empty, just as it had been on the day she and Geoffrey had first moved into it, the countless memories were still there to overwhelm her. There wasn't a room in the entire house that didn't hold for Savannah some sort of sentimental memory of Geoffrey.

Once Savannah had put the security alarm on, she stepped outdoors, taking a quick glance at the Magnum Realtor's Sold sign stuck down into the grass on the front lawn. Knowing she'd miss her old home like crazy, she locked up the place for the last time ever. She planned to take a slight detour to drop off the extra set of keys to the realty office on her way to the freeway. The closing to finalize the sale of the house had already taken place.

2222 Victoria Court was where Savannah had lived, laughed, and had loved with her husband, the same place where they'd raised their two children. It was a warm home where many social and fun events had taken place. It had always been a safe haven to the family, as well as a welcoming refuge where other relatives, friends and neighbors could drop in unannounced.

Once Savannah dropped down on the top step to continue waiting for Kenya to make a showing, she looked up and down the street at the houses of all her neighbors. Theirs was a great neighborhood. With the exception of one or two grumpy folks on the street, most everyone else got along and they all looked out for each other. Many of their kids had grown up together and had remained friends into adulthood. Life had been very good at 2222 Victoria Court.

Friends and family had told Savannah that she was giving up a lot in moving so far away from the area, but she didn't see it that way. As long as she could drive, and owned a good set of wheels, she could come back to the neighborhood to visit as often as she liked. It wasn't about what she was giving up. Savannah believed she had a lot to gain in starting a new life.

This old place would always hold sweet memories of her life with Geoffrey, which would make it hard for her to make new ones inside of it with someone else. Savannah wasn't looking to ever get married again, but she was hoping to one day have a really nice male companion. Savannah didn't do loneliness very well. It had never really suited her.

Surprised to see Savannah outside the house, Kenya Standiford pulled her silver Toyota Camry into the driveway, rolling down the window just before she cut the engine. The painful expression on her mother's face told her that Savannah was having a hard time of it, just as she was. She hated to see her mother move out of the same city she herself resided in, but she hadn't been able to talk Savannah out of the idea no matter how hard she'd tried.

The Inland Empire wasn't all that far away from Los Angeles, but Kenya was used to reaching her parents' home in about ten or fifteen minutes. It would now take her at least an hour and a half to get to her mom's new place, and that was only if the traffic was good. Kevin had thought the move was a great idea, so Kenya hadn't been able to rely on her brother as an ally.

After Kenya got out of the car, she smoothed down her denim jean outfit, hoping she looked presentable. She then walked over to her mother and dropped down on the step beside her, giving her a warm hug. "What are you doing out here, Mom?"

Savannah shrugged. "Memories just kept on getting to me, threatening my sanity. There are times when it's hard for me to believe that I've actually sold our home."

Kenya's expression was pensive. "Second thoughts, Mom?"

Savannah shook her head in the negative. "Not at all. This is a good thing I've done. Eventually everyone will come to see it. I have no regrets, Kenya. Not a one."

Kenya closely studied Savannah. "Is this move an attempt on your part to forget Dad? Are you trying to erase twenty-five years worth of memories?"

Surprised by her daughter's question, as well as somewhat dismayed by it, Savannah looked right into Kenya's eyes. "Forgetting Geoffrey is utterly impossible for me. I don't know what prompted such a question…and I'm not sure I want to know. Moving away won't erase a single memory, nor would I want it to. My memories with your dad are etched in granite."

"But, Mom, all your memories are right here. How can you just leave them behind?"

Savannah smiled at Kenya with understanding. She knew that selling the home where her daughter had grown up had been extremely hard for Kenya to witness. She could only hope that her daughter would one day understand why the sale had been necessary. "Leaving this house is all about preserving those precious memories, while also giving myself the opportunity to make new ones. You can't possibly know how much your father and I discussed this very issue. In the event of death we both agreed that we shouldn't ever allow our grief to rob us of the beauty of living. He'd be happy with my decision to move forward with my life. And, if I had been the one to go first, I'd be happy for him. Geoffrey is smiling down on me with approval, Kenya. I need you to believe that."

Kenya smiled weakly. "Speaking of moving on, Mom, are you going to be out there looking for another man?"

Savannah thought that Kenya's question was a strange one, but she understood it as well as the other weird queries her daughter had been voicing lately. She turned down her mouth at the corners in a gesture of thought. "I can't say that I'll be checking out places in hopes of finding male companionship, but I'm surely not opposed to meeting someone nice. I'm very much alive, Kenya, at forty-five. I can't imagine being this lonely for the rest of my life."

Kenya looked unhappy with Savannah's response. "I don't know that I can accept another man, Mom. Just the thought of seeing you with someone else makes me feel sick."

Savannah took Kenya's hand, squeezing her fingers gently. Kenya being a daddy's girl doesn't give her the right to try and run my life, Savannah mused, figuring that she'd better nip her daughter's problem right in the bud. Savannah took a couple of seconds to think about what to say. Then it dawned on her that there was no nice and easy way to tell someone to butt out. Savannah loved her daughter every bit as much as her father had loved her, but there were times when their relationship was like oil and water. Bitter battles between them often occurred.

As Savannah once again made direct eye contact with Kenya, she gave her a wry smile. "You're not the one who has to be accepting of anyone else in my life, Kenya. This *is* my life—at least I thought it was. My being alone is not going to bring your father back. Like I said, your father and I had discussed things like this, long before his death. Continuing to live our life to the fullest was the conclusion we'd come to if and when death ever pulled us apart. If I can come to accept having another man in my life, you won't have much say in the matter. Let's be clear on that right up front, Kenya. I won't allow you or anyone else to run what's left of my life."

The sigh coming from Kenya's mouth was long and hard. Her mother being so insensitive on a sensitive subject like this was difficult for her to swallow. "Don't you think it's kind of soon for you to be talking about dating another man, Mom?"

Savannah looked taken aback by Kenya's snippy tone. "If I'm not mistaken, Kenya, you're the one who brought up the subject. I only mentioned meeting someone nice." Savannah got to her feet. "You came here so we could say our farewells. I think we should do that right now so I can be on my way. I have no intention of getting into a verbal disagreement with you."

Savannah reached down and extended her hand to Kenya. "Come on, Kenya. Let me help you up. I need to move on up the road before it gets too late."

Looking rather sullen, Kenya reluctantly took hold of her mother's hand. As she got to her feet, she stiffened her upper body, more so when Savannah pulled her into her arms.

Savannah instantly felt the tenseness coming from her daughter, which prompted her to hold Kenya at arm's length. "Honey, I love you. I'll call you right after I check into my hotel. I'm looking forward to seeing you and Cole at the end of the week. Give that handsome doctor of yours a big hug for me. I'm sorry he wasn't able to come over here with you today."

Kenya forced a smile to her generous mouth. The

mention of her husband's name always brought joy to her heart. Dr. Coleman Standiford was the love of Kenya's life. "He was sorry, too, but duty called. You know how much he loves you, Mom. Cole also hates that you're moving so far away from us." Kenya sighed. "At any rate, we'll be up in Fontana at the end of the week to help you get all moved into the new place. See you then. I love you, too, Mom."

Savannah hugged her daughter again and kissed her on the cheek. "Until then, Kenya."

The unexpected right turn onto Prairie Avenue didn't surprise Savannah in the least. Her Lexus always seemed to have a will of its own whenever she was in this particular part of town. Although it hadn't been her intent to stop by the Inglewood Park Cemetery, one more visit to Geoffrey's grave site wouldn't hurt, especially since she wouldn't be visiting his resting place as often. Savannah had already made arrangements for periodic flower deliveries to the grave.

After Savannah pulled the car past the black iron gates, she followed the road around to the right and then parked in front of the cemetery's florist shop. Hustling out of the car, she ran up the few steps and rushed inside the shop, where she purchased a large bouquet of colorful spring flowers. Once she'd signed the credit card receipt, she made a mad dash back to the car.

Arranging the flowers in the permanent water well only took Savannah a couple of seconds. As was her normal routine, she sat down on the ground in front of the El Sereno grave site to have a last-minute chat with her beloved.

Involuntarily, Savannah's tears began to flow. "Hey, big

guy. It's me, Savannah. If you've been looking down on me, as you promised, you know that our house is sold and that the few precious things I decided to keep will be delivered to the new house on Friday…."

Savannah's sobs began to come so hard that she had to take a minute to regroup. She'd had countless conversations with Geoffrey since his funeral service…and all of them had been just as emotional. It was hard for her to think of her beloved husband stuffed in a decorative box and planted permanently in the ground. Moving into a brand-new home without him was even harder for her to conceive, yet she knew it was necessary. Time waited for no one.

The sweet memories of their lives spent in the old house were theirs to forever keep.

"Okay, let me try this again. I know you always hated to see me cry, but it is hard living in this cruel world without my lover and best friend. But you're not coming back, so I have to start my life over without you at my side. Long ago we discussed what we'd do if one of us went away, so I know I have your blessings in moving on. However, a small sign would be helpful."

Savannah removed a wad of tissues from her pocket and then blew her nose. "Kenya is having a hard time with all of it, but I'm hoping she'll eventually come around. Kevin is excited for me. He knows you wouldn't want me to remain sad and lonely. Our son understands that life has to go on. He constantly tells me that we either live in the present or we will eventually die trying to relive the past. I know you agree with your son.

"As you probably know, I've moved a good ways from

here. That means I won't be coming to visit you as often, but you won't ever be abandoned. Kenya and Cole will see to it that your resting place is kept in good condition. I've arranged for you to have fresh flowers quite often. All the kids are coming to help me get settled in. Kevin will be flying in from San Francisco on Thursday. He'll spend one night at the hotel with me. Kenya and Cole will be coming up on Friday. The moving van will also arrive on Friday. All the new furniture will be delivered late the same evening.

"Everything will be okay, Geoffrey. If everything goes as well as the closing, I'll have an easy time of it. I know you and God are having a grand old time telling your life stories, even though He already knows all of yours. Mention me to Him every now and then. I love you, my darling. Continue to rest in peace. Please remember me always, your one true love."

With her tears flowing like the River Jordan, Savannah leaned forward. She then lowered her head and kissed the cold marble. Once she got to her feet, she began backing away from the grave site, blowing into the wind soft kisses all the while. Her heart usually broke even more, every time she had to go away and leave Geoffrey behind, but today was different.

Today was just the beginning of Savannah's new tomorrow.

As Savannah looked up into the sun-filled heavens, she opened her arms wide. When the heat from a beaming sun ray suddenly kissed her face, she realized that this was the kind of sign she'd been looking for, a sign that would give her the courage she needed to move forward.

Instead of accepting that the sun ray was responsible

for the warmth she'd felt, Savannah chose to believe that it was Geoffrey's warm smile beaming down on her face, because that's what would get her through. That sweet touch of her husband's tender love had shored her up. Geoffrey had just reiterated to Savannah his heartfelt blessing. Of that she was sure.

Savannah's laughter danced on the wind as she reentered her car.

Savannah used extreme caution now that she was in the downtown area of Los Angeles, several miles from the grave site and the realty office. Savannah directed her car onto the I-10E Freeway, heading toward San Bernardino. The hotel she'd chosen to stay in for the rest of the week, Airport Hilton, was located in the city of Ontario, only a few miles from her new home.

Somewhat familiar with this route, since she'd been going back and forth on a regular basis to tend to business concerning the house, Savannah relaxed and began to enjoy the long drive. Unlike so many of the roadways in California, the I-10 Freeway was in pretty good shape. Had she not beaten the rush-hour traffic, the driving circumstances just might be very different. Although there was always heavy traffic on the highways, hitting them after three o'clock could turn out to be a nightmare. Savannah was so happy that she'd gotten off to an early start.

As Savannah's thoughts turned to Kevin, she smiled. Her handsome son had been an extremely good boy, a manageable teenager, and he'd turned out to be a fine young man. He'd made his family proud on so many occasions. Kevin was strong both academically and athletically. He had earned an academic scholarship to the University of San Francisco, where he'd majored in chemistry. He'd also attended the school of pharmacology at Howard University, but not long after his graduation he'd returned to San Francisco, the city Kevin had come to love.

Fried chicken, mashed potatoes and applesauce were Kevin's absolute favorite foods. Soul foods came in at a close second. Once all the appliances were hooked up, and a few pots and pans and eating utensils were unearthed from boxes, Savannah hoped she could fix her son his favorite meal before he had to return home. He loved being pampered and catered to, much like his father had. Kevin had taken a week of vacation just so he could help his mother out.

In many ways Kenya was the complete opposite of her brother, but there were areas where the two siblings were also a lot alike. At twenty-one years of age, Kenya was three years younger than her big brother. Both children were very outgoing and had great personalities. Their senses of humor had the tendency to be a little over the top, but they each loved to laugh and have loads of fun. She was also strong in academics, though she'd dropped out of nursing school with only one more year to go. Kenya constantly talked about finishing up the work needed for her degree, but so far it had just been nothing more than a topic of conversation.

Once Kenya had married Cole it seemed to Savannah that her daughter had put on hold all her own dreams and aspirations. Kenya's world now revolved around her husband. That concerned Savannah quite a bit, but the young couple seemed extremely happy. Their love for each other was irrefutable. There'd been no talk of them planning to have children, thus far, which Savannah was glad of. She'd really like to see Kenya finish school and join the workforce for a few years before settling down into motherhood, a full-time job by itself.

Kenya was a constant challenge for Savannah. If Savannah said it was white, Kenya would argue that it was black, knowing her mother was right. Rebellious couldn't begin to describe Kenya's teen years. The constant battles, bitter ones, between Savannah and Kenya had kept the entire family on edge. Savannah wouldn't want to go back and relive those frustrating times, not even if she was promised a million dollars to do so.

Normally it was the mother who had a tendency to be jealous of the relationship between father and daughter, but it was not so with Savannah. Kenya had been the envious one. Whatever Kenya could find to do to pull Geoffrey's attention away from Savannah, naughty or nice, she'd never think twice about it. It was all about Kenya being the center of her father's world.

Once Geoffrey had recognized the problem with Kenya, he'd done his best to keep his daughter in check, but for him, it was difficult at best, especially when she would pout and refuse to talk to anyone in the house for days at a time. She'd lock herself in her room and dare anyone to try and gain entry. Geoffrey had been the only one who could bring her out of her dark moods.

Kevin got along real well with Kenya now, but he hadn't been able to tolerate her as a teenager. Unlike her parents, Kevin had completely ignored Kenya when she was being difficult, rarely allowing her to engage him in all-out warfare. To be disregarded was what Kenya hated most. Daily troubles in the Richmond household hadn't calmed down until after Kenya went off to college. She had eventually changed some of her downright evil ways, but Kenya still liked to challenge her mother whenever the opportunity arose. Since her father was no longer around to give her all the attention she required she now demanded it from her husband and Savannah.

Savannah didn't think Kenya had truly understood the demands on Cole's time as an ob-gyn resident when she'd agreed to marry him. When Cole was too busy to tend to Kenya's needs, which was quite a bit of the time, Savannah was often tagged *it* by her daughter. While the two women had grown much closer, Savannah had to constantly stay on guard with Kenya.

All in all, motherhood was everything Savannah had ever hoped it would be. In recognizing that her two children were completely different individuals, with their own patented personalities, parenting them had become much easier. Kevin and Kenya would always be her adorable babies. Savannah loved them equally, though she had loved Kevin the longest.

Glad that there hadn't been a long line at the hotel check-in desk, Savannah went about getting herself situated in the nicely decorated suite. She'd only brought along a couple of bags, which were packed with just enough clothes and toiletry items to last her for the rest of the week. Both the queen beds and the sofa looked comfortable, making her think that a short nap might do her a lot of good. She'd only been up since 5:00 a.m. A quick glance at her watch told her that it was now twelve-fifteen. It had taken her a little less than an hour and a half to make the drive to Ontario, which she thought was pretty good timing.

After Savannah stored her hang-up bag in the closet space, she unpacked her other clothing items and laid them neatly in the dresser drawers, with the exception of the toiletry items she planned on placing in the bathroom. She then plugged her cell phone charger into the electrical outlet closest to the nightstand.

Once Savannah stepped into the bathroom, she placed the toiletry items on the granite countertop. She had to laugh at the miniature bath and body items provided for the hotel guests. It was barely enough for one person, yet the same amounts were used even when there were two guests in the same room. She checked out the condition of the bathtub, making sure it was thoroughly cleaned. She hated it when hotel tubs were shabby-looking or when the enamel was cracked and rusted. Savannah loved to take long, leisurely bubble baths, but she'd only use the shower if the hotel's bathtubs weren't up to her standards.

Satisfied that everything was up to snuff in the bathroom, Savannah walked back into the living area, where she sat down at the round mahogany table to peruse the guest book. It listed the hotel's amenities, including choices for dining within the facility. She was starting to feel a bit hungry. The nearby Ontario Mills Mall had a large food court, but after the long drive Savannah wasn't too eager to get back into the car anytime soon. The surcharge for room service was ridiculous, but she had promised herself not to pinch pennies when it came down to pampering herself. Geoffrey used to tell her she was worth every penny he'd ever spent on her; he had spent plenty of money on the things he'd thought his wife might like to have.

As Savannah perused the room-service menu, she thought hard about what she'd like to eat. Once she'd finished examining the very palatable food choices, she didn't see a thing on the menu worth the exorbitant amount of money the hotel was charging, let alone paying the tacked-on surcharges. She wasn't a cheap person by any stretch of the imagination, but she wasn't a darn fool, either. Despite her earlier thoughts about pampering herself, getting back into her car right about now was looking real good to Savannah.

Standing before the mirrored closet doors, Savannah surveyed her appearance, trying to decide if she should change out of the crisp denim jeans and simple white shirt and slip into something a little less casual. After several minutes of twisting and turning before the looking glass, she decided that she looked just fine with what she had on. Savannah was also pleased with her figure. Two babies and twenty-four years after finishing college she still had it going on. Routine exercises had kept her body tight and fit. She was actually only three to four pounds over what she'd weighed in college. Savannah was proud of how well she'd maintained herself.

As Savannah grabbed a hold of her purse, a brightly colored magazine stationed on the nightstand caught her eye. A closer look at the publication revealed the title. *Crossroads.* Curious as to what kind of articles were inside the magazine, Savannah picked it up and then sat down on the side of the bed. It didn't take her long to learn that the periodical was about the midlife years, thus the name *Crossroads*.

Just as Savannah flipped over to the next page of the magazine, a coupon in large print slipped out. Upon examining the mail-in postcard, she saw that it was an invite to receive information in the mail about the Golden Age Senior Center. Her interest in volunteering at a senior center or a similar-type establishment was instantly aroused. Since the address of the Ontario center was given, she decided to just stop by and see if she could get a quick tour.

Although Savannah had thought she could do justice to a full-course meal, the smoked turkey sandwich and tomato soup she'd consumed at a small Ontario deli had satisfied her completely. There was no doubt in her mind that by late evening she'd probably be ravenous.

Savannah had already parked her car in the parking lot of the senior center, but now she wasn't sure this was something she really wanted to do. She had often accompanied her mother to the senior center when she was alive, but did she want to be in the company of seniors on a regular basis? Her hopes of getting her mother interested in life again, after her father had passed away, was the reason Savannah had frequented the senior center.

Savannah was very proud of her age, especially since she saw just waking up every day as such an extraordinary blessing. She had taken a special interest in the elderly because she knew for a fact that some people had the tendency to treat older folks quite differently, as well as disrespectfully. Seniors were often discriminated against and targeted for all sorts of malicious acts and outrageous scams. Savannah had done her best to protect her parents against those evils.

God forbid that someone should try to get over on her in a malevolent way when she became a senior, Savannah mused, because they'd definitely be borrowing big trouble. Although she saw herself as a very good Christian woman, and as someone who'd help anyone in need, she wasn't an easy prey. As she was involved in many service organizations in her church, she purposely avoided all types of confrontation like the plague. However, Savannah would aggressively defend herself and others if the need arose.

Savannah had been the neighborhood helpmate. Everyone knew that they could call on her in a time of dire need. All her neighbors had to do was let her know that there was some sort of a need in their household. If it was something within her power to grant, the need became a done deal as soon as she could see to it. If she couldn't do it, she tried to find another way to get it taken care of. Her family, church family and friends were also the recipients of her benevolent spirit. Considered an angel of mercy by many, Savannah was loved by all who knew her.

After deciding that it couldn't hurt to just do a quick tour of the senior center, Savannah got out of her car, set the alarm and then made her way to the entrance of the gray-and-white brick building. On her way inside the huge place, she took notice of the exemplary way the grounds were tended to. Signs of spring could be seen everywhere. An array of colorful flowers, shrubs and trees brought the property to life. If the indoor atmosphere was anything like the outside, Savannah figured it was more than likely a nice place for older people to spend time in.

Once inside the building Savannah made up her mind to take a quick look around the facility on her own before she asked to speak with anyone. She had to like the overall atmosphere of a place before she'd ever consider spending her precious leisure hours there. Surprised to find that no one was milling about, although most of the day *was* gone, Savannah went on about her explorations without interruption. As a very observant person, she could take quite a lot into her line of vision with quick glances here and there.

The place was immaculate enough, Savannah considered, liking that the various furnishings were very modern. She easily guessed that the facility was a fairly new structure. The large room she came upon next looked as if it may serve as a recreation area. She then saw that the library was right next door. This was a place where she just might enjoy volunteering her time. Before she could do any further exploring, she heard footsteps coming up behind her.

Savannah quickly turned around to face the person approaching her. The moment her eyes connected with the tall, dark man she heard something akin to bells going off inside her head, making her feel extremely weird. It took Savannah a minute to pull it together. God forbid she should make a fool of herself in front of a stranger.

The stately gentleman looked very familiar to her, but she was sure she'd never seen him before in her life. Perhaps he just had one of those familiar faces, yet she got the sense that there wasn't anything ordinary about him.

He appeared dignified and quite self-assured. Savannah had a hard time taking her eyes off him. The handsome man had a very commanding presence.

The broadly smiling man extended his hand to Savannah, his eyes covertly making acquaintance with her shapely anatomy. "Mr. Antonio Delabay," he said, shaking her hand briefly. "I'm the executive director of the center. How can I be of help to you?"

"Savannah Richmond," she said politely. "I'm here to take a tour of the facility." Savannah had only made contact with Antonio's hand for a second or two, but it was long enough for her to feel the softness of his palm. His skin had felt so pliable, not to mention warm and tender. Holding on to his hand too long might've given her a heat rash, she pondered, fighting the urge to laugh at her provocative thought process.

Antonio wished he could reach up and wipe off the dumb-looking smile on his face. He felt as if he were acting like a hormone-raging teenager. At forty-eight years of age, he wasn't supposed to have these types of juvenile reactions. He'd seen plenty of beautiful women in his lifetime, many who were even better-looking than Savannah. But by his overwhelming reactions to her good looks, he wouldn't be able to prove it to a single soul. Attractive or not, Savannah Richmond was way too young for him, he considered. He liked more mature women, those much closer to his own age group. No one could ever accuse him of being a cradle robber.

"Welcome to the center, Ms. Richmond. My administrative assistant normally does the tours, but she took off early today for a doctor's appointment. So it looks like you're stuck with me as your tour guide, since I'm the only one in the building. Are you perhaps checking out our facility for a senior family member or maybe an elderly friend?"

Savannah actually blushed, chuckling lightly. "I guess we could say both. I'm a family member and a friend to myself." She chuckled again, nervously so.

Antonio angled high his left eyebrow. "Are you sure you're in the right place? This is a center for senior citizens, Ms. Richmond. The age requirement for membership is fifty-five."

If Antonio hadn't looked so genuinely surprised by her revelation, Savannah would've thought he was trying to flatter her. But she really hadn't gotten a false sense about him. Antonio had seemed so sincere to her in his state of shock.

Savannah smiled, pulling out her California driver's license. She then handed the laminated document to Antonio. "I'm definitely the one interested in learning about the center, but not as a member. I'm not too old, but neither am I all that young. I may be interested in volunteering some time or landing a part-time job as an events coordinator. Golden Age Senior Center appears to have a lot to offer."

As Antonio looked at Savannah's birth date, he shook his head in amazement. "Lady, I never would've guessed your age. I had put you in your late thirties, but nowhere near forty-something. Nature has been extremely kind to you. Youth is truly an ally of yours." He handed her back the license. "Ready to take the dime tour?"

Savannah smiled sweetly, tamping down her desire to be openly flirtatious. "Ready as can be. More ready than anyone can ever imagine." Wishing she'd left off that last bold statement, Savannah bit down on her tongue to punish herself for being too forward.

As if Antonio thought there'd been a double message in Savannah's comment, he looked closely at her. He then cast his dark brown eyes down at her hands. No wedding rings, he thought, but that didn't mean she wasn't married. Antonio was about to offer Savannah his arm, as he would with a date, but he caught himself just in the nick of time. This isn't a date, he told himself, nothing akin to one. "Is your husband interested in volunteering his time as well?" Well, he mused, that cleverly posed question should get me an answer about her marital status. "Most of our members are singles, widows and widowers."

Savannah sucked in a few calming gasps of air. "I'm a widow, Mr. Delabay. No one else will be volunteering with me. I still have a few other senior centers to check out to see what they have to offer. I'm staying at the Hilton Hotel here in Ontario until everything is delivered to my newly built home in Fontana, which is only a few miles from here."

Too much information, Savannah thought, scolding herself inwardly. She had noticed that Antonio wasn't wearing a wedding band, but that wasn't a true indicator of his marital status. Men didn't always opt to proudly advertise their marriages like women did. There were also religions that disallowed jewelry.

That she was telling this man so much about her personal business had Savannah a bit concerned. Admitting an attraction to Antonio wasn't that hard for her, but she wasn't sure she should entertain any romantic notions about him, or anyone else, for that matter. Despite her desire to move on with her life, coupled with Geoffrey's blessings for such, Savannah still felt a little guilty about actually doing it.

Antonio gestured for Savannah to follow him down the long corridor. "I'm quite familiar with Fontana. We're practically neighbors. I live right next door in Rancho Cucamonga. I love living in the Inland Empire. I moved up here several years ago, about a year or so after my wife passed away. Like you, I'm a widower. It seems that we have at least that much in common."

As much as Savannah tried to ignore Antonio's last comment, she had to wonder exactly what he'd meant by it. Was he also having romantic notions about the two of them? Loneliness had a way of making a person go crazy; especially those who'd lost their lifelong partners. Being widowed wasn't a good thing to have in common, at least not in Savannah's opinion.

While Antonio guided Savannah through the senior center, he gave her all the pertinent information he thought she'd need to make an informed decision on becoming a volunteer. The membership was only ten dollars a year, which seemed utterly ridiculous to Savannah, but she was sure that it was a real treat for those folks who might not be financially secure.

From computer classes to yoga, the large variety of activities offered at the center was astounding to Savannah. Savvy instructors also taught line dancing and Tai Chi. Acting and art classes were offered as well. Day trips and out-of-town trips to Las Vegas and other interesting places were scheduled every couple of months. The media room, recreation room and library were the areas most used by the members. However, Antonio told Savannah that the newly built facility wasn't being utilized nearly as much as those in the city government had hoped for.

There were quite a few regular senior members at Golden Age, but many of them only participated in a couple of the activities. Cards were played a lot, bridge, bid whist and pinochle being the all-time favorites. Bingo was also much loved. The male members mostly enjoyed the chess club, but there were also a few ladies who knew how to play the complex game very well. "Unfortunate for everyone, the woman members greatly outnumbered the males," Antonio said.

Antonio then mentioned to Savannah that he was looking for someone to hire for the activities department, a person who'd know exactly how to light a bonfire under the participants. As the executive director, Antonio wanted this brand-new center to become the hottest spot for the Ontario seniors, desired for it to become the most talked-about center in the Inland Empire. He was also interested in bringing in nonseniors as members to participate in various social activities. Antonio had his sights set on the forty-something crowd.

After a visit to the large dining room and the executive offices, the very informative tour came to an end. Savannah was very impressed with everything she'd seen and all that she'd heard. Antonio had sold her on the place, but she still wanted to explore the centers closest to her home before making her final decision. His future visions for the center were awesome and Savannah was sure he'd make a success of it. To her Antonio seemed like a determined man.

Savannah extended her hand to Antonio, thanking him for the very enlightening tour. She hated that it was over already, but she'd never let him know that. Going back to sit up in a lonely hotel suite wasn't very appealing to her. In fact, the thought was downright daunting.

Savannah now wished that she had taken Kenya and Cole's offer for her to stay with them until the end of the week. Out of the blues she had suddenly begun to feel was sparked the idea for her to visit her longtime friend Bernice Saunders, who was one of her dearest friends, the one who'd moved up to the Inland Empire from Los Angeles.

Looking as though he had a lot on his mind, Antonio studied the odd expression on Savannah's face. He'd often seen the type of deep sadness he saw in her eyes. Every time he'd looked into the mirror he'd seen it. Long after his wife had died it had still been there, a look of darn near hope-lessness. Antonio had wallowed in his grief for the better part of two years.

Then, one night, in the haze of a horrific nightmare, Antonio's precious Sylvia had come to him, telling him that life was impatiently waiting for him to reenter the arena of the living. She had said that she was very happy and con-tent, with no more pain to bear, and that she'd always be waiting for him to come to her. Then she'd said this to him: "Antonio, the Lord told me to tell you that now just isn't your time to meet up with death. Live life to the fullest while you have the opportunity. Death will come for you all too soon. That's a given, my beloved. Live in peace."

Antonio began to reclaim his life the very next day.

Since Antonio didn't know how long Savannah had been

widowed, he thought she might still be grieving. He wanted to ask her out to dinner, but if her husband had just died, he knew that would be downright insensitive of him. Wishing he could sweep away Savannah's grief, Antonio also knew exactly how terrible she felt. Grief was very hard to overcome.

Antonio quickly snapped himself out of his deep thoughts. "Let me walk you out to the entrance, Mrs. Richmond. I'm thrilled that you enjoyed the tour and I hope you'll consider joining us here in some capacity. We'd love to have you as a volunteer or as an employee of the Golden Age Senior Center. I enjoyed meeting you."

Savannah immediately noticed how Antonio had gone from calling her Ms. to Mrs., which was just another indication to her of how respectful he was toward others. "I enjoyed meeting you, too, Mr. Delabay. Thanks again for the tour. I really enjoyed it. If I decide to volunteer at this center, which has so much to offer, you'll be seeing me again."

Antonio felt like he just couldn't let Savannah's last statement pass him by. He saw it as the perfect opportunity to see exactly where she was in her grieving process. Nothing ventured, nothing gained, he mused. "Speaking of seeing you again, I'd love to, but not necessarily as a volunteer of the center. Is it still too soon for you?"

Savannah looked puzzled, wondering what Antonio was talking about. In the next second, when lighting struck hard the soft tissue inside her head, she had it figured out. Yet she decided to play coy. If he weren't talking about what she thought he was, then she'd truly feel like an idiot.

"Think you might clarify your question for me? I'm a bit confused over here. Too soon for what, Mr. Delabay?"

Antonio suddenly looked nervous. That Savannah hadn't gotten his exact meaning was rather embarrassing to him. But if he wanted to see this woman outside of this center, he'd better stop acting like a silly schoolboy and come off like the confident man he was, he mentally scolded. It had been his life experience that women liked men who were downright sure of self.

With all that in mind, Antonio knew he had to grab the tiger right by the tail. "I'd like to take you out sometime, Ms. Richmond. While I'm very mindful that you've lost your spouse, I have no way of knowing how long it has been, not without asking. However, I don't want to be insensitive to you in any way. As I mentioned to you earlier, I've lost a loved one, too, so I really do understand the grieving process. I was asking if it's too early for you to have a date."

Savannah thought of pretending that she was incensed by Antonio's question, but she wasn't, so she knew she probably wouldn't pull that act off too well. "Oh, I see," she said, stalling for a little time to think. Her mind was already speeding at an uncontrollable rate.

Antonio was attractive and very charming, she mused, but was she ready for someone strong and powerful like him? She was sure there was more to him than what had already met with the eye. Besides, this was a man she could really get into, which might not be too safe for her under the circumstances. What circumstances, she asked herself? *You're a widow, Savannah. Yeah, but… But what? There are so many things to consider… Consider what?*

Warding off her challenging demons, Savannah smiled warmly at Antonio. "I think I'd like to go out with you sometime, Mr. Delabay. It'd be really nice to have a friend who truly understands what a person goes through when they lose their significant other. I've been widowed for over two years, but there are times when it seems like it happened just yesterday."

Antonio felt that stupid smile pasted on his face again, but this time he wasn't worried about it, since just the opposite of smiling could've been the outcome. Only he knew how much disappointment he may've suffered through had she turned him down cold. Even though he'd only spent a short time with her, Antonio already knew that he liked Savannah a lot. Though he'd thought her to be much younger than himself, he wasn't sure it would've mattered one way or the other now that he'd gotten to know a little bit about her.

Antonio blew out a breath of relief. "I'm delighted to hear you say that. Since it looks like we're going to become fast friends, mind if I call you Savannah?"

"If I can call you Antonio. The word 'friend' has a nice ring to it." Savannah was trying to make sure Antonio understood that friendship was all she was looking for. Anything more than that would have to come down the road a bit, way down the road.

Antonio chuckled. "I'm reading you loud and clear, Savannah. You'll come to learn that I'm not a pushy man. If friendship is all you'll ever want, that's all you'll ever get from me. I promise. Now, when can we get this friendship started? My calendar is completely open."

Savannah looked hesitant as she put her fingernail up

to her lip. "Well, I really don't know. I haven't moved into my home yet, so I don't have a place for you to pick me up."

"You mentioned the Hilton in Ontario." He looked down at his watch. "What about dinner in one of their restaurants this evening? The food is excellent. I've eaten lunch there numerous times. How about seven-thirty, Savannah? Will that give you enough time to do whatever you might need to accomplish before then?"

Not knowing what she should say to his request, Savannah looked rather confused. She hadn't expected an invitation for an outing this soon, certainly not for this evening. She actually liked a man who was resolute, but Savannah still wasn't sure how to respond.

Go ahead, throw caution to the wind, said the little voice inside her head. *What could it hurt to have a harmless dinner with such a charming man, especially in a very public place?*

Savannah gripped Antonio's hand, but only for a brief second. "You know what, Antonio? I kinda like your idea. There's no use in me dining alone tonight when I can dine with a new friend. Seven-thirty is fine by me. I'll meet you in the lobby of the Hilton."

Although Antonio wanted to jump up and down with joy, he gave Savannah a reserved smile. "The lobby it is. Oh, one more thing." Antonio reached into his pocket and pulled out a business-card holder, plucking one free. He then took out his pen. After palming the card, he wrote down his personal numbers and then handed the card to Savannah. "I'm just a call away."

Chapter 2

No matter how hard Savannah tried to calm herself down, the mad-hatter butterflies in her stomach just wouldn't go away. She thought it was silly of her to be so darn nervous. It wasn't like she was entering into a romantic liaison with Antonio. They were only going to sit down and have a nice meal together. Yes, she mused, she was very attracted to him, but that didn't mean she was going to end up swooning at his feet. She'd also made it clear to him that she was only looking for a friend, something Antonio had readily accepted.

Because Savannah hadn't packed any evening clothes, she hoped the simple black dress she had put on was appropriate for dinner in the hotel dining room. It would have to do. There were no other options available to her. She certainly wasn't going to run out and buy something new. Then she had to stop and think about that one. If there were enough time left to do so, she'd probably go for it. Antonio was expecting her to be down in the lobby in approximately thirty-two minutes and twenty seconds, so she'd better hurry up.

Timing their imminent meeting down to the second made Savannah laugh. What she was feeling now was certainly better than what'd she'd felt on the drive back to the hotel. It seemed to her that her conscience had tried to beat her down, making her feel as if she'd done something terribly wrong by accepting Antonio's invitation to dinner. She had soon figured out it was only her own guilt at work. *How could she move on with her life when her husband no longer had one?* That was the one question she'd asked of herself over and over again. It seemed so unfair to Savannah, but that's just the way it was.

Savannah would still love to have Geoffrey right by her side, at every waking moment, but that was utterly impossible. And if she wanted to be true to herself, she'd go ahead and admit that she simply wanted to be happy again. She actually missed the sound of her own laughter. She wanted to wear upon her lips a constant smile and to also have someone smile back at her. In order for those things to occur, she was the only one who could change the course of her life. Taking charge of her destiny was a must. Savannah had to find a way to do just that.

The emptiness Savannah always felt inside was a real bummer and she eventually wanted to have that void filled all the way up to the top. She knew that she couldn't begin to feel anything if she continued to cut herself off from the world. Life was created for the living. And Savannah wanted to feel very much alive again, the way she used to feel with Geoffrey.

Geoffrey would definitely want her to stop putting herself through hell over every little decision she made that couldn't possibly include him. How many times did she have to remind herself that her beloved husband wasn't coming home again, not ever? What they'd had was over, kaput. As painful as it was, death was final. And Savannah had to learn to accept that fact, no matter how hard it was to do. The flesh and blood Geoffrey was laid to rest for all eternity.

Looking into the mirror, Savannah wiped the tears from her eyes with a tissue, glad that she hadn't put on her makeup yet. Another quick glance at her traveling alarm clock let her know she had burned up fifteen minutes with just her thoughts, which only left her seventeen to finish up everything. Since she didn't wear a lot of makeup, fixing her face wouldn't take much time at all. Savannah's hands moved rapidly as she applied her creamy MAC foundation, sealing it with a few brushes of corn silk. A few strokes of dark brown mascara to her lashes came next. A dab of blush to her cheeks and a generous amount of Ornamental lip gloss to her mouth, also by M.A.C., were the perfect finishing touches.

With Savannah knowing she had no choice but to be satisfied with her appearance, since she had packed nothing else nice enough to fit the occasion, she grabbed her purse and left the room. The thought of seeing Antonio again made her smile, causing her to make a silent vow to have a really good time in his company. This date didn't have to be difficult.

Savannah knew that she deserved to be happy…and happy is what she planned on being.

* * *

As if Antonio had known exactly which elevator Savannah would arrive in, he had stationed himself right in front of the one she eventually got off of. They exchanged warm smiles and cordial greetings before Antonio ushered her over to the entrance of the hotel's main restaurant. He loved the way Savannah looked in the stylish black dress, with its simple elegance. Antonio was also very proud to be seen in the company of such a striking woman.

Savannah really liked the navy blue sports jacket and matching slacks that Antonio had changed into. The lavender shirt, opened at the collar, was a nice accent. The designer suit he'd worn earlier had been tailored to perfection on his lithe body, but the sportier look made him appear younger and more relaxed. She had always viewed the button-down look as rather stuffy. That style of dress was okay for the business world, but she didn't care for too austere a look when having an evening out on the town. Savannah thought Antonio looked so handsome.

Once Savannah had made her dining choices, Antonio had given both their orders to the not-so-friendly waitress. He didn't know what to make of these young people who took jobs in the service industry, but then refused to be of any service. The waitress had rubbed him the wrong way from the moment she'd approached the table. Her gum chewing, as she talked, was the most annoying to him. Then the impatient sighs had come, as if she'd wanted them to hurry up and make up their minds. Yet he'd said nothing, only because he hadn't wanted to make an issue of her bad attitude in front of Savannah. However, Antonio's feelings would definitely reveal themselves at the end of the evening in the not-so-generous tip he planned on leaving behind.

Antonio felt that the silence between him and Savannah was sort of awkward. But most first dates were most always abnormally strained. He was usually a man who had a heck of a lot to say, even when he thought he should shut up, but Savannah's obvious nervousness had him at a loss as to what to say to break the ice.

Antonio had his opening when Savannah picked up her glass and drank from it.

"How's your iced tea, Savannah?"

"Really good. It's not too strong, which is how I like it. Is the tea to your liking?"

Antonio shook his head in the negative. "I prefer mine much stronger than this, but I can live with it. Do you prefer tea over coffee, Savannah?"

Savannah turned down the corners of her mouth. "No, not really. I like them equally as well. I only do coffee in the mornings, otherwise the caffeine keeps me up all hours of the night. What about you? Which of the two drinks do you prefer?"

"Without a doubt, it's coffee. Used to drink it all day and throughout most of the evening, but I've cut back considerably. Two cups a day is all I consume now. What do you think of the restaurant? Is it okay with you, Savannah?" Antonio suddenly realized that he actually loved saying Savannah's name. It sounded like sweet music to his ears. He thought that her name fit her to a tee. She reminded him of a sophisticated but genuine southern belle. Antonio couldn't help wondering if she might even be a native of the south, as he was.

Savannah nodded. "Very nice, Antonio. It's quite warm and cozy in here. The candlelight is nice also. I hope the food is as wonderful as the atmosphere. But I guess there's not much you can do to ruin grilled lemon chicken and steamed vegetables, other than burn them to a crisp."

Savannah went on to tell Antonio how she'd wanted to order from the room-service menu until she'd seen the ridiculous prices and added surcharges. Her pulling a face to make her point made Antonio laugh, which caused her to suck in a deep breath of air. The sound of his laughter was intriguing to her, to say the least. Savannah then let Antonio know that she wasn't cheap, that she just knew how to practice frugality.

Savannah and Antonio both had a good chuckle over her comical remarks.

After sobering up a bit from his bout of laughter, Antonio took a folded sheet of paper from his breast pocket. He then handed it to Savannah, hoping she wouldn't feel that he was being too presumptuous. He hoped she wouldn't be offended by the gesture either.

"This is a list of the activities that I love to do in my spare time, Savannah. If you don't mind, I'd like you to check off the things that you feel we might have in common. If we should continue seeing each other beyond this evening, I'd like to also know the things you're interested in doing. This way is easier than me trying to guess at your likes and dislikes. I have to warn you, though. I'm a very active man, one who requires very little sleep. I stay on the go. Staying busy keeps me from being too lonely. There are times when I'm in a room full of people, yet I still have the tendency to feel just as lonely as ever."

Antonio hadn't dated a lot since he'd begun living again, but he had yet to go out with someone who'd held his rapt attention like Savannah did. She'd stirred up inside of him all sorts of crazy emotions. He thought her to be both witty and charming, loving her great sense of humor. If Savannah didn't agree to see him again, Antonio knew he'd be terribly disappointed.

Offended wasn't at all what Savannah felt after reading the sheet of paper, but it made her more nervous than she already was. It looked to her as if this handsome man had come there prepared to sweep her right off her feet. His gesture was surely a thoughtful one. She liked the idea of him wanting to find out what she liked and also that which she didn't care a bit for, but she couldn't help thinking he might be moving a little too fast for her. Then she smiled, remembering his earlier promise to her. *If all she ever wanted from him were friendship…*

"Wow!" Savannah laughed lightly. "If you do just a few of these activities on a regular basis, I can see why you're so busy. 'Staying on the go' wasn't an understatement, Antonio."

Savannah paused a moment to collect her thoughts. She then made eye contact with Antonio. "It's not that I'm not open to seeing you again in the near future, but I'm afraid at the moment I can't think past this evening. I have so many must-do things on my plate right now, with the move and unpacking at the top of the list. If you don't mind—" and even if you do, she added in her thoughts "—I'd like to see how the rest of the evening goes before I commit to another outing. I'd also like to learn more personal details about your life after we've eaten."

Antonio smiled gently. "You won't get any opposition on either of your requests."

Savannah blushed, hating her cheeks for coloring up on her. "Thanks, Antonio."

Once the meals were served and the waitress had gone on her way, Antonio asked Savannah to bow her head for a few moments so that he could voice a prayer of thanksgiving. Glad to know that he at least believed in the Almighty, Savannah quickly obeyed his request. Since they hadn't gotten into any conversation on spirituality or religion, Savannah didn't know where Antonio stood on either issue, yet she'd be willing to bet that he was a man of God.

People didn't necessarily have to be religious for Savannah to make friends with them, but she preferred to align herself closely with those who were somewhat spiritual. However, she knew that someone was always seeking God, as well as a righteous way of living, and she would never turn away someone because they didn't share in her beliefs. Her belief and trust in God was very strong, but it wasn't up to her to decide how or when other folks worshipped the Master. An individual's personal relationship with God was between no one but the two of them.

In Savannah's opinion the food was incredibly tasty and very well prepared. The lemon chicken was tender enough for her to cut with a fork and the steamed vegetables were both tender and crunchy. By the look of utter pleasure on Antonio's face, she guessed that his prime rib, cooked medium well, had been prepared to his satisfaction. The baked potato, garnished with all the fattening trimmings, was larger than any she'd ever laid eyes on, making her wonder if he'd be able to eat the whole thing. Big man or not, Antonio had lots of food on his plate.

With no room left in her stomach for dessert, Savannah declined the offer of such. Antonio had ordered apple pie à la mode, which astounded her, since he'd eaten every bit of food on his plate, along with the large garden salad and fresh vegetables. He then explained to her that he only ate one large meal a day. If he ate a big lunch, he skimped on food at dinnertime, and vice versa, rarely eating more than a bran muffin or a bowl of oatmeal for breakfast. Plenty of exercise kept him slim and trim. Jogging at least five miles a day had become habitual to him.

Twenty minutes later, all finished with his delicious dessert, Antonio slightly pushed back his chair from the table. Talking had been held at a minimum during the meal, but he was ready for him and Savannah to engage in an enlightening conversation. She had earlier expressed her desire to learn more about the personal side of his life and he was quite eager to oblige her. Antonio also had quite a few personal questions of his own that he'd like to pose to Savannah.

Since it was just a little before nine o'clock, Antonio hoped that he and Savannah would have plenty of time to try and get to know each other a little better. The restaurant closed its doors at ten, but there was an abundance of cozy seating areas out in the lobby. The hotel lounge was also open until eleven-thirty.

With the order for tea and coffee already placed by Antonio, he sat back in his chair, smiling affectionately at Savannah. "Okay, Savannah, I'm ready to answer all your questions."

All, Savannah mused, seriously doubting that statement. Telling *all* up-front might just come back to haunt, she thought. "And I'm ready to ask them. Have you always worked in the type of business you're in now?"

Although Antonio was quite aware of the etiquette no-no, he rested his elbows on the table anyway. "Before landing the job I presently have I was in the United States Air Force for twenty-four years. Was commissioned as an officer right out of college, at the age of twenty-two. Retired two years ago with the rank of colonel. I'm a forty-eight-year-old man who's had an illustrious military career and I'm still going strong in the workforce. Next question, please."

Savannah laughed at his request. "You're widowed also. How long has it been?"

Antonio's eyes briefly clouded with pain. "Four years, Savannah. The first couple of years were very long ones, then I got the courage to begin my life over. But only after my wife appeared to me in a dream, encouraging me to get back into the game of living."

Unwittingly Antonio had just given Savannah proof that she wasn't the only one who communicated with a deceased loved one. For whatever reason, the revelation comforted her.

"Children, Antonio. Do you have any?"

Antonio began to beam like a bright ray of sunshine. His children were his life before and after his wife's death, his towers of strength. "Two, a son and a daughter. Both of them are all grown up and have long ago flown the coop. They both live in Atlanta, both are very successful. My son's a doctor and my daughter is an English teacher."

Savannah smiled gently. "I'm sure you're proud of them, and I bet they're just as proud of you. How often do you seem them?"

"Pride can't begin to explain how I feel about my children. I see them quite often, but still not regularly enough for me. The kids can't come home that much because of their busy careers, but I travel to Atlanta whenever I can. My daughter used to take off the summers, but now she only takes a month of vacation, which she uses to travel to exotic locales all over the world. As a matter of fact, I'm getting ready to limit my hours at the center so I can also travel more. I'm even considering retiring altogether. I'm already financially set."

"Sounds like you have a wonderful family, Antonio. I'm surprised to hear you say you're ready to hang up your work boots. Have you given this second retirement a lot of thought, or are you just toying with the idea so far?"

"It doesn't take much thought when you start to get restless at what you do, Savannah. I love my work at the center, but there are still voids that need filling. Loads of travel could do that for me. As a military man, I'm used to traveling all over the world. My wife and I were going to do just that, but she took ill before we could put our retirement plans into action. I took the job at the center as a temporary measure, until I could start to make sense of my life again. But when I accepted the job offer, I also vowed to make it the best senior center in the nation. I haven't abandoned that vow, but I am thinking of bringing someone else in to help fulfill the set goals."

Savannah couldn't help but be impressed with Antonio and the life he lived. She liked how genuine he was, how easy he was to converse with. He seemed to have loads of integrity. That he dearly loved his family was also a huge plus. There wasn't anything about him to dislike. Antonio Delabay seemed to be a good person, a gentleman in the true sense of the word.

Savannah looked down at the list of things Antonio had written down on the paper. "Out of all the things you've listed here, which is your favorite pastime?"

Antonio knew that he couldn't tell Savannah his very favorite pastime, which wasn't on the paper, not without stirring her emotions. Catering to his wife's every need and want was what he had loved most. Seeing that Sylvia was happy every waking moment was what had made him feel like he was on top of the world. The benefits of being a husband and a father were far greater than any riches untold, as far as Antonio was concerned. Sylvia had been his main hobby.

After taking a swallow of coffee, Antonio set his cup down. "Golf is my favorite pastime. I play every Friday afternoon. I put in extra hours during the week so I can have that time off. Have you ever played golf, Savannah?"

No, she hadn't, but Geoffrey had loved to play. Golf had also been his favorite activity. Not wanting to tread onto memory lane, Savannah turned off her thoughts of her late husband. "No, I don't play. Have never had any desire to learn to play. Golf seems downright boring. I only started watching it on television after the extremely talented Tiger Woods emerged."

"Ah, Tiger Woods, the master. I like that kid a lot. He's a winner. Now that I've answered your questions, do you mind answering a few of mine?" Antonio asked Savannah.

Savannah smiled softly. "That's only fair, Antonio."

Antonio started out asking Savannah pretty much the same questions she'd asked of him. He was impressed with her career as a nurse. With his son as a committed doctor, he knew how very dedicated to public service were the majority of folks who opted to make their living in the health-care profession. Antonio thought Savannah's was a highly commendable career choice.

Then, when Antonio learned that Savannah's son was a pharmacist, and that her daughter was close to becoming a nurse, he was doubly impressed. He knew that it took a lot of compassion and patience to work in the field of health care. He himself was a very sympathetic man. All the horrific, darn near inhumane things Antonio had had to endure during his wife's fatal bout with colon cancer proved that his compassion was endless.

The senior couple continued their personal fact-finding conversation until the restaurant closed down on them for the evening. The suggestion by Antonio to move into the lounge was declined by Savannah, who then cited that she'd had a long day and expected the next one to be even longer. There were still a lot of things she had to do to get ready for her move into the new place. A shutter company was sending out someone to measure for shutters, the telephone had to be turned on, and the home fitted with extra phone jacks, as well as turning on the other utilities.

Antonio had offered to help Savannah get all moved into her new home, but she wasn't comfortable with that suggestion. Her kids would be there to help and she didn't think it was the right time to introduce them to her new friend. Yet Savannah had promised to see Antonio again.

* * *

As Savannah dressed for bed, she thought back on the evening. In her opinion her first date with the opposite sex had been a very good one. Antonio was a great conversationalist, which was a very positive attribute, since she herself loved to talk up a storm. His ability to speak with authority on various subject matters had showcased his immeasurable intelligence. He was truly authentic and his sensitivity had come through in spades. That she had been the focus of his attention throughout the evening made Savannah feel that Antonio was really tuned in to her.

Extremely impressive and quite admirable was how Savannah had summed up Antonio, the man, though she felt as if she'd only seen half of what made him so interesting and such a delight to be in the company of. The evening, from beginning to end, had been lovely.

The one thing Savannah had noticed was that neither of them had mentioned the actual names of their spouses. She couldn't help wondering if that was just a coincidence or had it been by design. She saw it as an interesting thought to say the least. However, she wasn't sure what it meant, nor was she sure if it was a positive sign or a negative one, she mused, kneeling down.

After Savannah got up off her knees, she slipped into bed, and then reached over and picked up the Bible off the nightstand. Her hands roved the red soft leather bound book before she opened it up to peruse it. When Geoffrey was alive, the couple had had morning devotion and had always ended their day the same way, in prayer. This ritual had also been followed when their children had lived in the home with them.

Savannah missed the wonderful fellowship she once shared with her husband and family. Now her morning and nightly rituals, after prayer, were to read a few of the scriptures she loved. Psalms, Proverbs, Song of Solomon, and I Corinthians were her favorite books of the Bible.

The Girl: "Kiss me again and again, for your love is sweeter than wine. How fragrant your cologne, and how great your name! No wonder all the young girls love you! Take me with you; come, let's run!" Song of Solomon, 1:2–4.

King Solomon: "My beloved is a bouquet of flowers in the gardens of Engedi. How beautiful you are my love, how beautiful! Your eyes are soft as doves'. What a lovely, pleasant thing you are, lying here upon the grass, shaded by the cedar trees and firs." Song of Solomon, 1:14.

The Girl: "My beloved is mine and I am his. He is feeding among the lilies! Before the dawn comes and the shadows flee away, come to me, my beloved, and be like a gazelle, or a young stag on the mountain of spices." Song of Solomon, 2:16

Smiling both inwardly and outwardly, Savannah closed the Bible, and then put it back in its place on the nightstand. The Song of Solomon was only comprised of eight short chapters in the Bible, but Savannah thought Solomon's writings were something every woman and man should read. King Solomon also wrote the book of Proverbs, just another of his amazing literary works.

"A date!" Bernice Saunders's mouth fell open. "I'm so happy for you, Savannah. Tell me about it, all of it, girl. Don't you dare leave out a single detail! First of all, what's his name?"

Savannah set down her cup of tea on the round hardwood table in Bernice's cheerful, Rancho Cucamonga kitchen, boasting bold colors of sun yellows and a variety of bright blues and leaf greens. "It was just a friendly outing, Bernie. Nothing serious. You know I'm not ready for anything more than what we had last evening, just a casual date. His name is Antonio."

Hoping Savannah wasn't talking about the infamous Antonio, Bernice's brow furrowed. "Antonio who, Savannah? Where'd you meet this Antonio fellow?"

"At the Golden Age Senior Center in Ontario."

As her dark brown eyes grew wide with disbelief, Bernice slapped her hand down on the table. "Lord, have mercy," Bernice shouted. "Friend-girl, you are in serious trouble!"

With no clue as to where this conversation was heading, Savannah appeared stunned by Bernice's loud outburst. "What are you talking about, Bernie? What kind of trouble?"

Bernice rolled with laughter. "I can't believe you're sitting here in my kitchen talking about the man of every woman's dreams. Delabay is only one of the most sought out bachelors in the Inland Empire. He has even caught my attention…and you know how hard it is for a good-looking man to even get a nod from me. You know I still believe the majority of the fine ones are outright evil. Girl, you're gonna be one hated sister when the word gets out about this!"

Savannah wanted to laugh at Bernice's comments, but she was too worried about the things that had been said. All of Bernice's friends knew that she preferred an ugly man to a handsome one, believing that the unattractive ones were more the stay-at-home type. Savannah disagreed with her friend on that issue. Good-looking men didn't have a monopoly on evil ways, not by a long shot. *Iniquity resided within the heart of man, not in the outward appearance.*

Was Bernice suggesting that Antonio was some kind of womanizer, or what? Savannah had to wonder if her basic instincts had been all wrong about one Mr. Delabay. "You've met Antonio? If so, why haven't you mentioned him?"

Bernice shrugged her shoulders. "I haven't seen you since then, but I guess I could've mentioned it over the phone. But, Savannah, you know you've been severely down over the past two years. I didn't think it was in good taste for me to gush to you over the phone about some handsome stranger. Clara, Janice, Marie, Madge and I began to accept our single status a long time ago. You weren't ready to move on yet, Savannah. At least I didn't think you were. How quickly things change. I guess you're now eligible to join our Secret Singles Club."

Looking as if she'd been hit by yet another thunderbolt, Savannah gasped loudly. A portrait of pain had quickly appeared in her eyes. "Secret Singles Club! Is that really a legitimate club, Bernie? When and who started it up?" Savannah suddenly felt left out of something that might be important to Bernice, but she didn't know exactly what it was.

As dear friends, Savannah thought she and Bernice shared all the important stuff in their lives. That was the main reason she was seated at Bernice's kitchen table. The date with Antonio had been a very important event in Savannah's life, a milestone so to speak—therefore she'd wanted to share all the details with Bernice, both the positive and the negative.

After seeing the painful look on Savannah's face, Bernice felt really bad over the way she'd handled this conversation with her dearest friend. She certainly hadn't meant to cause her any pain. Savannah was the last person she'd want to hurt. If there was a time when too much information was given all at once, this was it, Bernice mused.

Bernice reached over and patted Savannah's hand. "I think I've blown it here, Savannah. You can always count on me to let my big mouth run away from me. You look as if I've dropped a ton of bricks on top of your head. Am I right?"

Savannah sighed deeply. "I guess you can say that. First of all, let's get back to the subject of Antonio. Are you saying he's not someone I should involve myself with? Has he dated anyone that you know personally, or someone that you may have some knowledge of?"

Knowing she had unwittingly sent Savannah all the wrong signals, Bernice shook her head from side to side. "None of that, Savannah. That's the problem. He hasn't paid an ounce of attention to the women I know, but they're all vying for it. Antonio is a member of my church, where there are more single women than any man could ever imagine. He's friendly enough to all the sisters, but from what I've heard, he's hasn't shown a personal interest in a single one. Savannah, that alone should tell you something about the man. I think he's very decent."

Savannah eyed Bernice with open curiosity. "Are you interested in him on a personal level, Bernie? If so…"

"Don't even go there, girl." Sucking her teeth rather

loudly, Bernice waved off Savannah's concerns. "Antonio is not my type…and you know it. The heartbreak I endured at the hands of one pretty-looking devil was enough pain to last me a lifetime. It doesn't matter that my broken heart occurred when I was only twenty. The scars are still there."

"But what about Jacob? He wasn't a bit ugly, Bernie."

Standing five foot six, possessing rounded curves in all the right places, with a gorgeous smile to die for, Bernice was a very attractive forty-eight-year-old woman. Unlike Savannah, she had no biological children, but Bernice was a surrogate mother to every boy and girl child in her church. It always bothered Savannah that her close friend didn't see herself as the beautiful creature she was. Bernice had a heart of gold, but she just didn't see her own glowing light.

Bernice looked over at the windowsill, where she kept a picture of her late husband, Jacob Saunders. "He wasn't the least bit pretty either, at least not on the outside. I fell in love with Jacob's beautiful heart, Savannah. You know what kind of man he was—simply the best."

"Yeah, I *do* know. And Jacob also fell in love with a pure heart. Hearts don't come any purer than yours, Bernie. 'Simply the best' is a phrase that goes double for you."

Bernice again waved off the comments. She didn't like it when folks made a fuss over her, including her dearest friends. All she saw herself as was a child of God; as if that wasn't everything she needed to be. "Cut the sentiment, Savannah. You know I cry at the drop of a hat. Anyway, thanks for the nice compliments. Honestly now, I think Delabay is one of the good guys, handsome and all. He's very distinguished and he always carries himself as a gentleman at church. After being out with him last night, what is your opinion of him?"

Savannah wished she had been able to hold back her smile, but it had come naturally. If felt good to smile again; she wasn't sure she should be trying to control it. "I have no complaints about Antonio, Bernie. He acted pretty much the same way with me as how you say he conducts himself at church. He was very respectful toward me. But now I'm worried. If he's so sought after by so many women, I'm not sure I want to be in the mix. I don't relish being hated by anyone. I know how some women can act when they think another woman is kicking up her heels in their wading pool. Bernie, you know how I try my best to avoid confrontation."

The smile on her friend's face had not gone unnoticed by Bernice. It was good for her to see Savannah smiling again. Savannah had cried so many tears since Geoffrey had gone home to be with the Lord. For all the tons of help Savannah gave other people, no one had been able to help her get through her grief. If Antonio could do that for her dear friend, Bernice was all for it.

Bernice leaned across the table and gave Savannah a quick hug. "This is not about how other women act, Savannah. This is all about you and Antonio. It's obvious to me that you and him had a grand time last night. That's a big change in your life, you know. Your lovely smile is back in place. I'd like to see it stay there on your pretty face. Antonio chose *you* to go out with, not any of the women who've been running behind him like they've never had a man before. Don't let anything I've said put you off the discovery path you're on. It's time for you to start living again, honey. Geoffrey would want you to be happy. I think you know that already."

Holding back the tears, Savannah smiled again. "I truly know that, Bernie. Geoffrey has always wanted the absolute very best for me. There's no doubt there."

"Good. Any man worth his salt, dead or alive, wants his woman happy when he can no longer be there for her. Are you going to continue seeing Antonio?"

"Antonio asked me if we could see each other again. I agreed to go out with him, but we haven't scheduled anything yet. I want to get all moved into my new home before I make any other social plans with him. Besides all the ladies you've mentioned, I'm also very concerned about Kenya's reaction to me seeing Antonio socially. Daddy's little girl will be none too happy. Oddly enough, we just had a conversation about me dating before I left L.A. yesterday. Kenya has already said she can't accept another man in my life. How do I deal with that?"

Bernice gave a mighty harrumph. "By telling little Ms. Kenya to mind her own business. No beating around the bush is the most effective way to get through to your daughter. You have always shown your strength as an assertive parent, Savannah. I can't imagine you letting your kids start to run your life now. I'd be surprised if you told me Kevin feels the same as Kenya."

Savannah chuckled under her breath. Bernice had just stated her very sentiments, but she didn't want to be insensitive to her daughter, who was still having a hard time without her dad. Kenya was living her life just as she saw fit, hardly ever taking any advice from anyone, but Savannah knew Kenya would put in her two cents as to how her mother should live hers. She had gotten a headache just from thinking about how bratty Kenya might act toward Antonio.

"You're right about Kevin, Bernie. He will be happy if I'm happy and he'll do his best to like and respect whomever I'm happy with. Kevin has never required much from his dad and me. He's so secure within himself, unlike Kenya, who needs constant reassurance from all of us. I plan to tell Kevin about Antonio when he gets in on Thursday. He knows how to handle his little sister pretty well, but I don't want my kids to get into it over me. I'm eager to see my son's reaction to me having had my first date, though I'm sure his attitude will be positive."

Bernice got to her feet. "Everything will be okay, Savannah. You'll see. If you're not in a hurry, I'd like you to come outside and see the flower and vegetable gardens I recently planted."

Savannah glanced at the clock on the stove. "I have a little time before I need to meet the phone guy at the house. But before we go outside, what's up with the club you mentioned?"

"Oh, that," Bernice said, plopping back down in the chair. "The club was actually started by Marie. It has been astounding to her that she and I lost our husbands within a year-and-a-half span. Then you ended up losing Geoffrey fifteen months later. The club was started only a few months ago. There are currently eight members. A few of them are divorced. Janice brought into the group a couple of other ladies from her church. We just get together and hang out. We take turns hosting a meeting. Each of us gets to choose a special place for our social outings."

"Very interesting concept, but I wouldn't have joined. I can't imagine joining right now, though it sounds like you all might have a lot of fun at the meetings. Maybe I can be a guest."

"We do get crazy, Savannah, but we also have a ball. This is going to blow you away, but Madge Jacoby is one of the members. She's been compiling a list of eligible widowers in the IE for us to check out. If Antonio's name makes the list, I'll make sure we take it off. We didn't ask you to join the club for the reasons I've already stated, but you can read our bylaws."

Savannah jumped to her feet. "I'll see them another time. I want to see the gardens now."

With the day's end upon her Savannah was pleased with all of her accomplishments. The phone, gas and electricity were now turned on in her new place. The man had come to measure the majority of the windows for white plantation shutters and to also take the measurements for the bay window in the kitchen to have cell shades fashioned. Savannah loved plantation shutters; the rich white wood gave a southern comfort to a home, making it cozy and warm.

As Savannah stood before the bathroom mirror in the hotel, she closely studied her face. From the days of her youth her features had changed, but gracefully so. Changed by the slender streaks of gray, the color of her hair was no longer a rich dark brown. Even her sable eyes had faded a tad in color, but the brightness of life had started to shine through again. Being at peace had a way of rolling the burdens away. Just as the angels rolled away the huge boulder from in front of Jesus's tomb, Savannah felt as if she'd suddenly been freed from her prison of grief.

There was a time when Savannah had feared aging, had seen it as a death sentence. Now she could look upon the age process as seasonal changes, a *silver season*. She had successfully survived the spring and summer of her life, which had served as the days of her youth.

The age of autumn was now upon Savannah, the season when most everything green turned a striking array of colors. No longer the green kid she used to be, Savannah proudly wore the brown, gold and orange hues of autumn. God had well seasoned her, making her spicy with color, strong with conviction, showering her with the kind of wisdom only shared by the aged. She hoped for a long autumn, so that she was prepared to step into the final winter of her life, where everything would become shiny as silver. No longer the little girl who had big dreams, Savannah was a woman who'd achieved many goals, who was now in the season of giving back.

The interesting visit with Bernice came to mind as Savannah slipped into bed. Although she had given thought throughout the day about the things said about Antonio, she wasn't as troubled by it as she had been at first. He couldn't help it if women were chasing him down. Nor was it a fault that he was so darn good-looking. A woman would have to be half dead not to feel something stirring inside her when he stepped into their vision.

Savannah had to laugh, since Antonio had certainly made her feel alive again. In fact, she felt like singing. Spring was in full bloom, which had been evident in

Bernice's colorful flower garden. Even the green leaves of the vegetable garden had been a beautiful sight for eyes that had been dulled through pain and suffering. It seemed that everything was coming back to life right before her very eyes. How she had sorely missed the colors of the world!

The bedside phone rang, jarring Savannah out of her delicious reverie. Thinking that it might be Antonio, even though she hadn't given him the hotel number or the one to her suite, for that matter, she took in a few calming breaths of air. She then picked up the phone.

"Hey, Mom. It's Kevin. Sorry to call you so late, but I hadn't talked to you in a couple of days. I missed chatting with you. How are you?"

The bright smile on Savannah's face extended from ear to ear. "Kevin, I'm just fine, darling. How are you, son?"

"It's all good. Looking forward to coming down and hanging out with you for a few days. All ready for the big move?"

"More than ready, son. I can't wait to get settled in. I've only been out of the house two days, but I already feel like a vagabond." Even though he called her on a regular basis Savannah sensed that something out of the ordinary was up. His voice was kind of strained with hesitancy.

"Yeah, I know that feeling. Been there and done that a few times. Uh, Mom, I have something to ask you. I need you to hear me out before you say anything. Okay?"

"Okay." *I was right. Here it comes. Lord, please let it be something I can deal with.*

"I'd like to bring a guest home with me, Mom. I know stuff is going to be all over the place, but Madison is a worker bee. She's willing to do anything we need her to. Is it okay if I bring my new girlfriend with me? This relationship is the most serious one I've ever been in."

Savannah sighed with relief. That there wasn't something heavy going on with Kevin had her tossing up silent thanks to the Lord. "Kevin, I think you already know the answer. Your friends have always been welcomed into our home. I'd love to meet Madison. Does she have a last name?" Savannah joked, laughing lightly.

"It's Bonet. Madison Bonet. You know, just like the actress Lisa Bonet. Madison just finished law school, but she hasn't taken the California bar exam yet. I know you'll like her, since she's a lot like you. You two are made up of the same gooey, sweet stuff."

Savannah smiled at that, recalling all the times Kevin had told her he wasn't going to get married until he found a woman just like his mama. For him to tell her this relationship was serious meant that it really was something special. Kevin didn't say things like that, not without a lot of thought. He was a very private person, but he shared most everything with Savannah.

"That's so sweet of you to say, Kevin. Thanks. You made this old lady feel pretty good with that sentiment. Are you still coming on Thursday?" Savannah then thought about the fact that Kevin was supposed to stay one night with her in the hotel. She had gotten the suite to accommodate him, but she couldn't imagine her sleeping in the suite with him and his friend.

"The schedule hasn't changed. I already called the hotel and made a reservation for Madison. I hope you don't mind, but I got a room for myself, too. Madison might think it's kind of weird for a man my age to be sleeping in the same hotel suite with my mom. But after she gets to see how close you and me are, she'd understand it then. Besides that, the one room was a money-saving venture to begin with by my very frugal mother." Kevin chuckled over that.

Savannah was too choked up to speak. Kevin's deep respect for women made her so proud of him. Here she had assumed that he and Madison would want to share the same bed, but he had proved her wrong. *How special was that?* Too special for words, she mused. His dad's teachings had certainly paid off. Geoffrey had taught his son to always respect women and his elders and all others. Then he had shown Kevin how to show respect to everyone through leading by example. Kevin had never seen Geoffrey disrespect Savannah in any way.

"Mom, are you still there?"

"Yes, darling boy, I am still with you. Just had an emotional moment to get through."

"Are you okay? You're not feeling down, are you?"

"Kevin, I've never been better. I'm so proud of how you respect the women you date. You are such a fine young man and I couldn't be prouder of you. Can't wait to see you."

"Mom, you sound more optimistic than I've heard you in a long time. I'm glad to hear the joy back in your voice. Has something happened to you? Have you met someone special?"

This man-boy of hers was too intuitive for words, Savannah realized. "Let's just say that I've decided to put my playing piece back on the game board of life. Now I've got to get used to moving it around cleverly so I can figure out how to win at life again."

"Welcome back to life, back to reality, Mrs. Richmond! See you on Thursday. Good night, Mom. I love you."

Chapter 3

While Savannah held her arms out to Kevin, she covertly surveyed the stunning-looking woman whose hand her son was holding on to rather tightly. Several inches shorter than Kevin's six-foot-two frame, Madison Bonet was an absolutely gorgeous female who possessed a beautiful head full of brunette and bronze-tipped Shirley Temple–style curls.

It appeared to Savannah as if her toasted-almond-complexioned man-boy had picked out a rare beauty. By the looks of the young woman's girlish figure Savannah guessed that she couldn't weigh more than a hundred and ten pounds, if that. If Madison was anything like Kevin had said, she had a beautiful heart to match. Savannah wondered if Madison was *the* one.

Kevin rushed into his mother's arms, hugging her tightly. "Aren't you looking mighty pretty, Mom," he said, appreciating the sunny yellow top and slim white pants she wore. "I love how you look in the bright spring colors. You've even colored your hair. When did you do that?"

Savannah hugged her son back, kissing his slightly unshaven face, which was a new look for him. Her son had always been the clean-cut type, but it only took Savannah a minute to decide that she liked his trendy look. Savannah planned to answer all of Kevin's queries about her, but with Madison looking a little left out, she first wanted to put the beautiful young lady at ease. Savannah hadn't before noticed Madison's unusual grayish-blue eye color, a stark contrast to Kevin's ebony eyes. "You must be Madison!" Savannah didn't hesitate a bit in taking the slip of a woman into her warm embrace. "It's so nice to meet you, Madison. Welcome to my neck of the woods. I'm so happy you could join Kevin on his home visit. This is a real pleasure for me."

"Same here, Mrs. Richmond," Madison voiced with genuine enthusiasm, her eyes sparkling like a million flecks of diamond chips. "You are as pretty as Kevin has said. He talks about you all the time. I'm glad I could come home with him, too. I was honored by his invite."

Kevin gave each of the women a light kiss on the forehead. "Wow! You two even look a lot alike. Madison could easily pass for your daughter, Mom."

Savannah smiled at that remark, hoping Kevin didn't slip up and say that in front of his sister. Kenya would throw a fit upon hearing him say something like that. She had never really liked any of her brother's girlfriends, but it had very little to do with the character of the women he dated. Kenya was plain jealous of anyone who got attention from any of her family members.

"Madison, you stay here with Mom while I get our bags off the carousel. I'll be right back, honey." Kevin kissed his girlfriend lightly on the mouth before strolling away.

Madison blushed heavily. "I hope that didn't embarrass you, Mrs. Richmond. Kevin is so affectionate with me. I love that about him. He never tries to hide his feelings."

Savannah gently pulled Madison to her and gave her another warm hug. "Ours is an affectionate family, Madison. Kevin got it honestly. We hug, touch and kiss each other all the time. I hope we don't end up embarrassing you before the week is over."

"I doubt that. I wish my family were more touchy-feely with each other. My mom is a little bit affectionate, but my dad only gives out the hugs and kisses on special occasions." Madison laughed nervously. "I guess you can't give out what wasn't given to you. I've actually learned from Kevin how to be more open with affection. I like how it makes me feel inside."

Madison's willingness to share a piece of her personal family information was a tad surprising to Savannah, since they hadn't yet begun to get to know each other. But Savannah liked that quality in a person. It showed her that Madison had no problem being open and honest with her, which meant that she was probably open and candid with Kevin.

Kevin came back to where the two women stood waiting for him. "Mom, where are you parked? The bags haven't come around yet. I hope they haven't lost them."

Savannah turned and pointed out the large plate-glass window in baggage claim. "I'm right across the street in the short-term parking lot. Why do you ask?"

"Since this is the first time I've flown into Ontario International, I thought you might be parked in one of their remote lots. I was going to suggest that I go get the car while we waited for the bags. But if you're just across the street, I don't see a problem." He then turned to Madison, smiling at her in a flirtatious way. "Doing okay, hon?"

As Madison looked at Kevin, her eyes softened and sparkled at the same time. "I'm fine, Kevin. Things are just like you said they'd be. Your mom and I are getting along famously."

The loving way in which Madison looked at Kevin nearly took Savannah's breath away. This relationship *was* very serious, she mused. This woman loved her son, undeniably so. These two young people appeared to be deeply into each other. Savannah then realized that she could be standing there with the woman who may one day become the mother of her grandchildren. Savannah had an idea of why Kevin hadn't told her about Madison before now. He liked to see if his relationship was going well before he got the family involved. It wasn't unusual for Kevin to date someone for several months before he'd tell his mother all about the woman he was involved with. But he really didn't need a reason for not telling her about Madison, Savannah mused; but it wasn't the least bit odd for him to have kept her a secret either.

Kevin walked away again and Madison and Savannah resumed their conversation.

"Kevin tells me you just finished law school. Congratulations! You must be excited."

Madison nodded. "Thanks. I am very excited. Now all I have to do is pass the bar exam. I'm very confident I can

pass it, but it's still a little scary. There are a high percent-
age of law students who don't pass it on the first try. I'm
scheduled to take it at the end of the month. Please keep
it in prayer if you don't mind. I know God didn't bring me
all this way to let me fail now."

Kevin interrupted the conversation once again, but this
time he had the bags in tow. "Looks like we're all set. Lead
the way, Mom. I'm hungry as a bear so I hope we can stop
off and get something to eat."

Savannah began walking slowly, her heart swelling at
Madison's mention of prayer and God. "There's a wonderful restaurant in the hotel, or would you rather eat somewhere else?"

Kevin hunched his shoulders. "You know the area, Mom.
Whatever you suggest."

Seated comfortably at the popular Mimi's Café, the
threesome had already received their chosen meals.
Between bites of food, Savannah, Kevin and Madison con-
versed with relaxed ease, laughing and joking with each
other. Although Savannah and Madison had just met, they
seemed like old friends. Each woman had already gained
great respect for the other. Kevin was very pleased with the
way his two ladies were responding to each other, but then
again, he'd already known the outcome. His mother was
one fantastic woman and so was Madison.

Savannah's ears perked up at the intriguing laughter she
heard from somewhere nearby.

She'd heard it before, just recently. Her cheeks grew rosy
with color as she remembered where she'd come into
contact with that enchanting melody. As she took a covert

look around the restaurant, Savannah spotted the silver-haired fox whose laughter gave her a barrel of thrills.

Antonio was seated only a couple of booths back. Savannah saw that there were three other men at his table. When she thought of what might happen if he saw her, the joy of seeing him was short-lived. There was no way he'd ignore her if he noticed her. She was sure he'd come over to her and say hello. *How was she to explain Antonio to Kevin if that were to occur?*

As though Antonio had somehow sensed Savannah's presence, he got up from his seat. Then he openly surveyed the restaurant before heading toward the back of the place, which meant he'd have to pass right by Savannah's table.

Seeing Antonio coming toward her caused Savannah to darn near panic. Their eyes connected just before he reached her booth. It was as if their eyes had partnered in a slow dance. The bewildered glances passing between them were probably covert to everyone but them. Savannah wondered if she had the right to feel this breathless. Was it an insult to her husband's memory for her to want to really get to know Mr. Delabay? She quickly scolded herself for that foolish thought. Those issues had been long since settled in her mind. *Moving on*, she mused.

Savannah tensed up the moment Antonio stopped in front of the table, praying that she'd handle everything appropriately. She never dreamed that Kevin and Antonio would meet this soon, but neither had she dreamed she'd even meet Antonio. *Was this fate, or something fatal?*

"Hello, Savannah," Antonio said with far too much enthusiasm for her liking. "Fancy seeing you here. I was on my way to the men's room when I spotted you." He then glanced at Kevin and Madison. "Are these your children? I remember you saying they were coming up to help you get moved in."

Kevin got to his feet and politely extended his hand to Antonio. "I'm Kevin Richmond, Savannah's son. This is my girlfriend, Madison Bonet. We're visiting from San Francisco."

Antonio shook Kevin's hand and then released it. "I'm Antonio Delabay, Kevin and Madison. It's a pleasure meeting you both. I recently met Savannah when she came to the Golden Age Senior Center to take a tour of the facility. Well, I'd better let you all get back to your lunch. I hope we'll get the opportunity to see each other again, before you leave town."

Antonio then looked at Savannah in a very knowing way, wondering why she hadn't spoken a word. Not even a *hello* had come from her generous mouth. Her silence bothered him.

Sensing that there was something intriguing going on between his mother and this distinguished-looking man, Kevin pointed at the empty bench space next to Savannah. "Why don't you stay and join us for lunch, Mr. Delabay? That is, if you're dining alone."

Antonio smiled broadly. "Thank you, Kevin. I'd love to take you up on your offer, but I'm actually dining with a few of my colleagues. Business luncheon. But what if I take you all out to dinner this evening? It would be my pleasure and my treat. Of course."

Kevin looked to his mother for her input. "How do you feel about that, Mom? We'll be working hard the rest of the weekend, so this might be our only chance to have a relaxing evening out. There probably won't be much to do at the hotel later in the evening."

Fearful of what was happening here, Savannah nervously wrung her hands together. Suspicion would be aroused no matter how she responded. Kevin was already looking at her with curiosity. He definitely suspected something. "If you and Madison want to go out to dinner this evening, I'm fine with it. What time should we be ready, Mr. Delabay?"

Antonio raised his eyebrow at Savannah's formal use of his name. Was she trying to hide their friendly connection from her son? Perhaps she hadn't had the chance to mention to Kevin anything about their first date, Antonio mused, hoping he hadn't caused any sort of trouble for Savannah. "How does six-thirty sound to everyone?"

Savannah and the others nodded in agreement.

"Then it's settled. I'll meet you all in the Hilton lobby at the designated time." After bidding everyone a good afternoon, Antonio continued on toward the back of the restaurant.

Savannah had cringed at Antonio's last statement. That he knew where she was staying was a dead giveaway. He had unwittingly let the cat out the bag, even though Kevin had probably already figured out everything for himself. Waiting for the inquisition from her son to begin, Savannah settled back in her seat to await the rapid-fire questions.

Kevin eyed Savannah closely. "Who *is* that guy, Mom? It looked to me as if he has a thing for you. Is that why you're sounding so optimistic and why you've changed your hair color? Something tells me he's not a stranger to you. Am I right?"

"Kevin," Madison protested, "you shouldn't be getting into your mom's personal business like that. She already seems like she's embarrassed by the man's sudden appearance."

Laughing, Kevin kissed Madison gently on the lips. "You have no idea how close we are. We don't have any private business. Mom and I talk about everything."

Madison raised an eyebrow. "Everything!"

Kevin chuckled. "Everything but *that*, Madison. Mom would tell me 'that's too much information' if I tried to get into anything akin to *that* with her."

Savannah knew exactly what *that* was. "Okay, guys, let's cool it off in here. Mr. Delabay and I only met that one time. But then we had dinner the same night. I also call him Antonio. So if you picked up on how I had addressed him, the way I'm sure he did, I'm sorry for not acknowledging him the way I do in private. I hope I didn't offend him too badly. He's really very sensitive. One date is all we've ever had so don't let your imagination go wild. Antonio has shown himself to be a really nice man thus far. He's shown me nothing but the utmost respect."

"I'm glad to hear that, Mom, but you wouldn't ever deal with anybody who didn't respect you. By the way, you didn't answer me about the hair color and the joyful tone of your voice."

Savannah chuckled softly, wishing her son wasn't so darn observant, but he'd inherited that from her. She herself paid very close attention to detail. "My hair is just rinsed, Kevin, not permanently dyed. It seems to make me look a couple years younger, but I don't think I'll get it colored again. I earned those strands of silver. I just had my hair done yesterday. I found a new stylist, a man, and I love the way he does my hair. I'm glad that I won't have to go back to L.A. for salon appointments. His name is Tessell Jones. He's another genuinely nice guy."

Savannah put her forefinger up to her right temple. "As for the optimism, it's nothing new—just lost it for a while. The old mom you knew is finally making her way back. But, yes, I have to admit that Antonio is partly responsible for some of the joy I feel. He makes me smile."

Kevin beamed at his mother. "That's great, Mom. He also seems nice enough to me. I strongly sensed something was happening between you two. You really like him, don't you? Has he been married before? If so, does he have any children?"

Savannah saw the need to go ahead and tell Kevin everything she knew about Antonio, which wasn't a heck of a lot. She had expected her son to be understanding of her situation, but he'd shown her so much more than that. There were no signs that he thought it was too soon for her to begin dating. Her son loved his father dearly and he was just as fair about everything as Geoffrey had been. That Kevin was handling everything so maturely made her very proud.

As Savannah finished up her and Antonio's story, she suddenly realized that Antonio hadn't told her the names of his children, just as neither of them had uttered the name of their deceased spouses. Oddly enough, she couldn't remember if she'd shared with him her children's names or not, but she had mentioned their professions, and he'd done the same.

"With Mr. Delabay being a widower, I imagine he knows

exactly what you've had to go through, Mrs. Richmond. If you don't mind me saying it, I think you two will be good for each other. Grief is a tough thing to get through alone. I lost my grandmother several months ago, but I really haven't been able to share my true feelings with anyone in my family. Our family is so different from yours. We just keep everything bottled up inside. It makes me crazy. Since I've only known Kevin for a couple of months, I didn't want to heap my grief onto his shoulders."

Kevin looked troubled by Madison's confession of feeling grief. He had no idea she'd lost her grandmother. Maybe she hadn't told him because he'd told her about the death of his father first, he figured. "I'm sorry for your loss, Madison. I didn't know you were grieving." He gave her a warm hug. "I'm here for you, honey. Don't ever worry about heaping anything on my shoulders. They're pretty strong. I can't comfort you if I don't know you need that from me."

Madison leaned into Kevin, bumping him playfully with her shoulder. "Thanks for that, Kevin. I won't forget what you've said, or your powerful shoulders. It means a lot to me."

The length of time that Madison and Kevin had been seeing each other explained to Savannah why Kevin hadn't mentioned her to him before he'd done so over the phone a couple of nights back. It must've been love at first sight for these two kids, because there was no doubt in Savannah's mind that these two were in love. Cupid also knew how to work instant magic.

Savannah reached across the table and placed her hand over Madison's. "I'm also deeply sorry for the loss of your grandmother. If you ever need to talk about her, I'll be here for you, too. Talking about our loved ones who've been lost to us in death is a way of keeping them alive in our hearts and spirits. It's only natural to want to talk about the people we love dearly."

"Thanks, Mrs. Richmond. You guys are very understanding. I like being around you."

Savannah smiled warmly at Madison. "We like having you around, Madison. Would it be okay for you to call me Ms. Savannah? Mrs. Richmond sounds way too formal for friends."

"I'd really like that," Madison expressed with joy. "Thanks for making me feel so welcome, Ms. Savannah. I can't wait to meet Kenya. I'm eager to get to know all of Kevin's family. He hasn't met mine yet, but that's going to happen when we get back up north. I know my parents are going to like him. I have two brothers, who I think he has a lot in common with."

"Well, Madison, you'll get to meet the others tomorrow," Savannah enthused. "Kenya and Cole are expected to arrive well before noon. Cole is only scheduled to work four hours in the morning. Since his workday begins around 4:00 a.m., he should be all through by eight."

All finished with her little speech, Savannah moaned inwardly. Meeting Kenya might not be as pleasant an occasion as Madison seemed to hope for. Then Savannah decided to give her daughter the benefit of the doubt, hoping that Kenya would like Madison every bit as much as she did. Madison was an endearing young woman and Savannah prayed that Kenya would be drawn to her just like she and Kevin were.

Savannah had the sneaking suspicion that Miss Madison Bonet was going to become an important part of their lives. Kevin wouldn't have brought her home on such short notice as this had Madison not been very special to him. In fact, Savannah could only remember Kevin bringing home one other young lady. That relationship had fizzled before it had really had a chance to begin. Kevin couldn't stand demanding, overbearing women, which was what Yvonne had eventually shown herself to be like. Kevin had quickly removed himself from that situation.

Now that everyone was finished eating lunch Savannah summoned the waitress with a slight wave of her hand. "Oh, before the waitress gets here, is anyone interested in dessert?"

Both Kevin and Madison shook their heads in the negative. It seemed to Savannah that everyone was as full as she was. She didn't have room for another bite, but she was sure by the time six-thirty rolled around her stomach would be on empty. Hopefully she wouldn't be too nervous around Antonio to eat. Another interesting evening with him was close at hand. Once the waitress presented Savannah with the bill, she carefully perused it. Then Savannah handed her Visa check card to the young lady for payment.

Once Kevin and Madison were all checked in at the hotel desk, the threesome took the elevator up to the twelfth floor, the same floor Savannah was staying on. Two rooms right down the hall from hers had been available when Kevin inquired about the possibility of being on the same wing where his mother was staying.

Kevin dropped his duffel bag in front of the room he was assigned to and then he carried Madison's bag to her room, which was two doors down from his. Kevin then walked his mother to her room, telling her that he'd come back to chat with her after he freshened himself up. He also told her that he needed a bit of motherly advice, so he wouldn't bring Madison with him. But he then said he'd phone Madison to come on down after they had their one-on-one chat, if that was okay with her. Savannah told Kevin she didn't mind at all. Having settled that, Kevin kissed his mother and then started back toward Madison.

Before letting herself into her suite, Savannah waved another farewell to her son's beautiful girlfriend, whom she liked very much. Madison didn't have to do too much more to win Savannah's heart; she'd already earned her respect and trust.

Upon entering the suite it didn't take Savannah but a split second to realize she didn't have anything else nice to wear to dinner this evening. Antonio had seen the best dress that she'd brought with her, certainly a far cry from her finest. Savannah moaned loudly. Moaning and groaning would do her no good; hitting the Ontario Mills Mall would.

Wondering if Kevin and Madison would like to make a quick run to the mall with her, Savannah sat down on the side of the bed, intent on calling Kevin's room to make the inquiry. Before she even reached for the telephone, she heard the knocking. Savannah jumped up from the bed and headed for the door. Knowing it was probably Kevin, she opened the door without asking who was there.

Finding out that it wasn't Kevin at the door, Savannah's

eyes stretched with disbelief. The young man standing before her held in his hands an elegant crystal vase filled with a beautiful bouquet of spring flowers, wrapped in a huge purple-and-red bow.

"These flowers are for you, ma'am. Where would you like me to put them?"

Savannah pointed at the coffee table. "Right in the center, please." She then grabbed her purse to pull out a tip for the delivery guy, aborting her mission upon hearing another knock, though the door was already open. This time it *was* her son.

Kevin held out three one-dollar bills for Savannah to take. "Looks like I'm much quicker on the draw than you are, Mom," Kevin joked. "The money's for the tip."

Savannah accepted the money from Kevin. She handed it to the young man, reading his name tag at the same time. "Thanks so much, Brian."

Brian nodded, smiling gratefully. "You're welcome, Mrs. Richmond! Thanks for the tip." Now that his delivery mission was accomplished, Brian quickly left the room.

Savannah turned to Kevin and smiled, fighting off the wave of emotions threatening to engulf her. She then gave her beloved son a big hug. "I have you to thank, too. That was so thoughtful of you to send me flowers. I'm impressed. They're simply beautiful, Kevin."

Shrugging his broad shoulders, Kevin looked totally perplexed. "I wish I'd thought of it, but the flowers aren't from me, Mom. Maybe you'd better read the attached card. Before checking it out, care to make a bet as to who the flowers are from?"

Not daring to allow her mind to go where Kevin's obviously had, Savannah shook her head in the negative in regards to the wager. "They're probably from Kenya," she said, knowing that nothing was further from the truth. Since Kevin wasn't the bearer of beautiful gifts, that only left Antonio. Savannah suddenly felt breathless again.

Kevin cracked up. "Yeah, right. Had you said Cole could've sent them, I might've bought into it. Kenya wouldn't think to be this nice to anyone."

Savannah laughed. "I'm not just anyone. I'm Kenya's mother. She's my daughter."

"Okay, Mom. Have it your way. But we both know where the flowers came from. Go ahead and sit down so your knees won't buckle on you when you read his mushy sentiment."

Savannah walked over to the coffee table and removed the small greeting card. Her hands trembled as she opened the tiny envelope. "Just to let you know I'm thinking of you," she read. "I hope we can arrange to see each other real soon." The card was signed: *Fondly, Antonio.*

Simply because Savannah *was* overwhelmed by Antonio's altruistic spirit, she took Kevin's advice by dropping down on the sofa. As she read the card again, it then dawned on Savannah that Antonio had ordered these flowers before their recent encounter at Mimi's Café. As she slapped her open palm down hard on her thigh, her laughter filled the suite.

"What's so funny, Mom?"

Savannah ran her fingers through her hair. "This entire scenario. It seems that Antonio had already ordered the flowers when we saw him earlier. Since I didn't mention I'd received them, he probably thinks I'm ungrateful. Will wonders never cease?"

"How were you to acknowledge something you had no knowledge of? You can thank Mr. Delabay at dinner. Mom, did you feel pressured by me to go out with him this evening, or are you really okay with it?"

"How do you think I should be with it, Kevin? The dinner date was prompted when you asked him to join us for lunch. Maybe you should be asking yourself if you're okay with it."

Kevin rapidly crossed the room and stopped in front of the sofa. Leaning over, he placed his hands on her shoulders. He then pulled her up to him and gently pressed his lips into her forehead. Kevin had to search for the right words to let his mother know that she shouldn't worry about going out with Mr. Delabay. He was even positive that his father would approve of his wife finally starting her life over. Kevin had to wonder how he could convince his mother that she wasn't doing a thing wrong. In fact, she was absolutely doing the right thing.

Kevin lightly squeezed Savannah's shoulders. "This isn't about me, Mom. I only did what I did because I sensed that you two had a special interest in each other. As for me being okay with it, I couldn't be happier about it. Mom, Dad would want you to do whatever it takes to make you happy. I miss the old Savannah, the one who used to brighten up everyone and everything around her. We all need to feel on our faces the sunshine from your warm smile, Mom. Seeing you happy again is what I need most in this world."

Savannah wiped the tears from her eyes. "Son, I can

always count on you to lift me up when I'm down. But honestly, Kevin, I'm really not feeling the least bit low. I'm happy. The decision to start living my life anew was made before you came home. Knowing that you're okay with me resuming a social life, especially one that includes the opposite sex, means a lot to me. I expect to get a lot of resistance from Kenya over this, but having you as a silent ally will make it easier for me to deal with her. I don't want you to have any unpleasant words with Kenya. Eventually it'll all work out and she *will* come around. She'll have no choice."

Kevin dropped down on the sofa and then patted the cushion next to him for Savannah to be reseated. There were a few things he needed to run by her regarding his relationship with Madison. Kevin was in need of some good advice, the type only a wise mother could give.

Looking a little worried, Savannah heeded Kevin's summons by reseating herself next to him on the sofa. "What's on your mind, son? How can I help you?"

"It's about my relationship with Madison. We've only known each other for a very short time, but Mom, I'm already in love with her. I'm so sure of it that I'm entertaining the idea of asking her to marry me. What do you think?"

Savannah was flabbergasted over the marriage part. However, she had already guessed that Kevin and Madison were in love. At least that's how things appeared to her. "Honey, getting married is a very serious undertaking. Have you two even discussed how you feel about marriage in general?"

"We've tossed the *M* word around a time or two. Mom, I know what type of relationship I want with her and I don't see why I need to cool my heels. I don't want to wait around and let her get away either. I want the kind of love life you and Dad had."

"Have you and Madison verbally confessed your love for each other?"

Kevin shrugged. "I've said 'I love you' to her, but all she ever says in response is 'me, too.' I don't know if she's referring to me or to herself when she answers like that. I feel that she loves me, though. Her actions tell me what she feels for me. She's so darn sweet, Mom."

"While you're talking about asking her to marry you, you'd better be darn sure of her feelings for you. If she's never said she loves you, then maybe she's not where you are in the relationship. How're you going to feel if she turns down your proposal of marriage, Kevin?"

"Like an idiot! So, Mom, it sounds to me like you're saying I'm moving this relationship too fast. Is that it? Should I slow my roll?"

"Once again, it's not about what I think, Kevin. But I do believe you should give the relationship more time to develop. If you love Madison already, chances are you'll still love her a couple of months from now. You think?"

Kevin grinned. "I'm sure you're right, Mom, as you are most always. It's just that I've never felt this way before about anyone. You know how much I love my space, but I can hardly stand to be away from Madison for any length of time. I remember Dad telling me he felt that he had to snatch you right on up before someone else came along and swept you off your feet."

Savannah chuckled. "Trust me, your dad took his sweet time in asking me to marry him. And he was much too sure of what we had to worry about someone else taking me. Daddy loved to exaggerate, so don't make any decisions in your relationship with Madison based on any of his silly boastings. Daddy was pretty scared of the *M* word. Take it from one who knows."

Kevin looked a little sheepish. "I hear you loud and clear. I guess I'd better get back to Madison before she starts to think I brought her here just to abandon her. Thanks for the sound advice, Mom. Are you going to lie down before *our* dinner date this evening?"

Savannah liked that Kevin had put emphasis on *our* when speaking of the date. Since the evening outing did include both him and Madison, Kevin had used the word appropriately. "Actually, what I'm going to do is run out to Ontario Mills Mall and buy me something nice to wear. Antonio has already seen the one decent dress I brought along to the hotel with me. I was wondering if you guys wanted to go with me, but I'm sure you two need some time alone."

"Are you kidding? If Madison finds out I didn't tell her you were going out to a mall, she'll throw a tantrum. She loves to shop. I'll go and ask her if she wants to tag along. I'll ring your phone with the answer in a couple of minutes."

Savannah, Kevin and Madison sailed in and out of one store after another at Ontario Mills Mall even though Savannah had purchased a classy outfit in the second shop they'd entered. Since spring was in the air, Savannah had settled on a lavender-blue straight skirt and a frilly low-cut top done in foam-green and lavender-blue flowers. The lavender crepe jacket matched the shirt. Savannah had later found a pair of lavender pumps and a matching purse.

Madison bought a spring outfit as well, which was very similar to Savannah's, but was fashioned in several different shades of yellows and oranges on filmy silk. As hard as Madison and Savannah tried to get Kevin to purchase a new shirt and tie, he refused, saying he'd brought along an outfit appropriate for the evening festivities. However, after Savannah and Madison had thrown a fit over a striking lavender shirt and iridescent tie, done in swirled shades of purples, lavenders and blues, he hadn't been able to resist the two ladies' begging and prodding. After hitting a few more stores, they'd all left the mall, each one happy with their new purchases.

Antonio couldn't believe how much younger Savannah looked in the bright spring colors she wore. A fresh breath of air was the first thing that had come to his mind when he'd seen her getting off the elevator. The black outfit she'd previously worn on their first date had been stunning, but it had also made her look a little older and more sophisticated. He positively loved the brighter colors against her smooth honey-brown complexion. Antonio felt that he'd be forever indebted to Kevin for making their second date possible.

With Kevin and Madison running a bit behind the scheduled time, Savannah and Antonio had taken seats in the lobby, where they'd made small talk until the younger couple had arrived. The time spent alone hadn't been the least bit awkward for either of them. Each had found the other easy to converse with, just as it had been on the first date.

* * *

The scenery from Crescendo's, a popular mountaintop restaurant, was absolutely breathtaking to Antonio and his guests. The city below was alive with hundreds and hundreds of lights shining out from homes, businesses and numerous moving vehicles. Jazz was the music offered for the diners' entertainment, performed by a local, well-known jazz combo.

Savannah was very pleased with Antonio's choice for dining. He'd earlier told her that he wanted to take her to places he'd never been before. Since he knew full well that they both had a lifetime of memories with their spouses, he thought it might be awkward for them to revisit those memorable places together. It wasn't that he was trying to erase the memories of their deceased loved ones; he just believed that old stomping grounds would produce feelings of guilt and make it hard for them to move forward.

Savannah had agreed wholeheartedly with Antonio's assessment of the situation. She had then told him how much she appreciated him being so open and honest about his feelings. Not many people would've thought things through so completely, as he had obviously done.

Once the waiter had taken down everyone's drink and meal orders, he started to leave, but Antonio summoned him back. Antonio then asked the waiter to give them some time to feel the atmosphere before serving the meals. Antonio also wanted his companions to have some time to enjoy the music before dinner was served. The waiter nodded as he took off.

"How did the rest of your day go, Savannah?" Antonio asked.

"Very well, Antonio. Once Kevin and Madison were all

checked into the hotel, we slipped off to the mall for a short while. After making a few purchases, we went back to our hotel rooms and rested up. I did some quiet reading before I fell off to sleep."

Antonio's eyes embraced Kevin and Madison. "How's your visit going so far?"

Madison looked to Kevin to speak first. "Time spent with Mom is always good. I enjoy being with her. We always have a lot to talk about." Kevin nodded for Madison to take up where he'd left off.

Madison smiled warmly. "I'm having a great time so far. I can't imagine it getting any better than it has been. Ms. Savannah is such a nice person. I've never met anyone who can manage the role of parent so well, while also being a very good friend. When Kevin told me that his mother was his best friend, I had my doubts. But after seeing them together all day, I now know that it's absolutely true. I wish I had the same type of relationship with my parents."

Grateful for the sincere compliments, Savannah smiled as she winked at Madison.

Kevin leaned over and kissed Madison on the mouth. "Never doubt me, girl," he joked.

"My mother also taught me to always be honest, no matter what."

"Honesty *is* the best policy," Antonio weighed in. "I like hearing that everyone had a good day. I hope this evening will be just as satisfying. I've never been to this restaurant before, but I've heard nothing but great things about it. What do you think of the music, Savannah?"

Savannah nodded. "Very relaxing. I've also heard a lot of nice things about Crescendo's. The name is certainly fitting. It's nearly at the apex of the mountain. Great atmosphere."

Antonio pointed to a dimly lit alcove. "Would you like to have one dance before the meal is served, Savannah? I really like the song playing. 'At Last,' by Etta James is a very old hit."

Appearing very nervous, Savannah didn't seem to know what to do. Since 'At Last' was a slow song, that meant Antonio would have to hold her rather closely. That frightened her somewhat. After one glance at Kevin, who gave her a reassuring nod, Savannah began to relax. She took hold of Antonio's extended hand. This would be their first dance, she noted.

"Madison, let's join them," Kevin said, wanting to put his mother further at ease. When Savannah gave him a knowing smile, Kevin knew he'd accomplished his mission. There was a time when Kevin thought he'd be opposed to his mother in the company of other men, but after seeing her so down for over two years, he'd completely changed his way of thinking. Seeing her looking so beautiful made him happy. Hearing her laughter again thrilled Kevin to no end.

Antonio led Savannah to the dance floor. When it was time to take her in his arms, he held her at a respectable distance. He had sensed her reluctance to slow dance with him, had seen the fear in her eyes. Antonio didn't need to be a genius to guess that being in such close proximity to him was an issue for her. Respecting Savannah's issues was very important to him. It was Antonio's desire to please Savannah, not have her constantly on pins and needles.

Savannah was very happy with the safe distance Antonio

had put between them, but she thought he could've held her a little closer. She had to laugh at how scared she'd been only a few minutes ago that he'd be holding her, period. *How could a grown woman act so childish?* This was all so new for her, she told herself, hoping she'd get used to it. Savannah had to wonder if she and Antonio would become exclusive or if they needed to explore other options as well.

The idea of dating more than one man at a time gave Savannah a sudden jolt of heartburn. Even when she was younger, she had never dated more than one guy at one time. Many of her girlfriends wouldn't think of dating only one guy, but she'd always thought that the juggling process would be much too difficult for her to handle. Savannah could see herself getting all tangled up in a web of lies, because she wasn't a liar. So how could she be a convincing one?

As soon as the song ended, Antonio escorted Savannah back to the table. Kevin and Madison stayed out on the dance floor to enjoy the next tune, which was a more upbeat tune with a faster tempo. The younger couple wasn't into jazz, but they really seemed to enjoy the veteran combo who knew exactly how to please audiences of all ages.

Antonio reached over and briefly covered Savannah's hand with his own, intrigued by the engaging sparkle in her lovely eyes. "Are you having a sentimental moment or two? You look as if you're recalling something very special."

Looking in the vicinity of where Kevin was dancing, Savannah smiled broadly. "I was thinking of my dear son. It seems like only yesterday that he was a babe in my arms. He's all grown up now, no longer the little boy who used to follow me all over the house. There was a time when I couldn't even go to the bathroom without Kevin thinking I'd left him. He used to sit outside the bathroom door to wait for me, crying his tiny heart out. How quickly things change. My only son tells me he's in love. Imagine that."

Antonio smiled. "Madison seems like a lovely girl. I'm surprised that Kevin has never been in love before now. When we're that young, we often believe ourselves in love at least a dozen times before we eventually find the right one. Does Kevin think Madison is *the* one?"

Savannah's eyes misted up. "He does. We had a heart-to-heart about it this afternoon. They've only been seeing each other a few months, but he's convinced that she's the right one for him. I advised him to slow down a bit. Kevin has always been very responsible with his relationships, so I know he'll do only what he thinks is best for the both of them. He's a very unselfish young man and he deserves a selfless mate. I already like Madison. She's very sweet."

"And what about you, Savannah? Are you ever planning to marry again?"

A little caught off guard by the question, though it wasn't an offensive one, Savannah took a couple of seconds to ponder it even though she'd had occasion to think about it in depth. She couldn't help wondering why Antonio had posed such a provocative question as that. "Marriage isn't something I'd even consider at this point in my life. To be totally honest with you, Antonio, I'm really just finding my sea legs again. Let's say I'm a lonely widow who'd like nothing more than to have companionship every now and then. You know—movies, live theater, concerts and other fun activities that a woman might hate to attend alone."

Pleased that he and Savannah were on the same page, Antonio smiled with compassion. "I do know, Savannah, all too well. I'm also looking for companionship. I'd love to attend some of those fun things with you from time to time. You just to need to let me know when and where. Dating isn't easy, Savannah. Getting to know someone is harder than hard. It's nothing like it was when we were so young and carefree. Putting yourself out there and baring your heart and soul again is even scarier for those of us who are widowed."

"I don't know if I've told you this or not, but you are my first date. How's that for stepping out of the dark shadows of grief? I never thought this time would come."

Antonio couldn't remember if Savannah had mentioned him being her first date or not, but it sure made him feel warm inside. It didn't matter to him if he was her first or fiftieth, he felt special just being with her. "I'm flattered, Savannah. Am I the first to ask you out?"

"Oh, heavens no. Men who don't even know me ask me out on dates all the time. However, there were a few brothers in my church who called themselves giving me enough time by waiting six months to ask me on a date. I must admit that I was surprised by a couple of them since they were acquaintances of my late husband. Antonio, it seems to me that we haven't mentioned the names of our spouses. Is that a problem for you?"

Antonio shook his head in the negative. "It isn't. What I don't want to get into is making comparisons. We both know that there isn't a single person on this earth who can match up with the mate we once had. There's too much history there, but that doesn't mean widowed people can't find something very special with someone else. I'm not looking to fill anyone else's shoes, nor do I expect anyone to walk in Sylvia's. Sylvia is my late wife's name."

Savannah really liked what Antonio had had to say. It was very wise and healthy for him to think that way. Lord only knew that no one could ever fill up Geoffrey's big old shoes. She also was aware of the potential for widowed folks to do comparisons. She'd done that already with other suitors, those who hadn't gotten to first base with her. After listening to what Antonio had said, she now understood that no other man had ever appealed to her simply because she had been unwittingly comparing them to dear Geoffrey.

Savannah had a thoughtful expression on her face when she directed her gaze right at Antonio. "My late husband's name is Geoffrey. And I do know what you mean about comparisons. I can now make a promise not to do that, but that would've been impossible for me just a short time ago. I'm glad we have that out of the way. Here come the kids, so I guess it would be wise to choose another topic, one that they might enjoy discussing."

"The waiter is also coming this way, Savannah. I'm sure he thinks we've had more than enough time to relax and get settled in," Antonio responded. "I love talking with you. I hope there are many more positive conversations to come. I think communication is everything, especially when building new friendships."

Savannah lifted her water glass and gestured a toast. "I agree with you one-hundred percent. Cheers, Antonio!"

Chapter 4

With all the moving in of furniture and the unpacking of boxes occurring in her new home, Savannah found herself wishing for a quiet place to slip away to. The moving van had arrived at 7:00 a.m.; it was now early afternoon, time for her to feed her hungry brood as well as all the workers. Fast food was the quickest and only solution to getting the crew fed. Kentucky Fried Chicken was a favorite for most, but she didn't want to spoil the special fried chicken and mashed potato dinner she'd planned to cook for Kevin before he retuned to San Francisco. Keeping her son in mind, Savannah finally decided on purchasing the meals from the local Subway.

Kenya and Cole had arrived earlier than she had expected them to, which had been a pleasant surprise for Savannah. Kevin was thrilled to see his sister, and she him; that is, until she'd found out that he'd brought a woman along with him. Kenya had been polite enough to Madison, but Kenya's displeasure over the situation was obvious to all those who knew her well, which included everyone but Madison. Kenya had later complained to Savannah that this weekend should've been family time, since it was pretty much a new beginning for all of them.

After Savannah announced her plans to pick up sandwiches at Subway, she passed around the Subway take-out menu she'd earlier removed from the glove compartment of her car, along with a sheet of paper for everyone to write down their food choices on. The moving men were certainly surprised at such a generous offer, but not one of them was about to turn down the generosity of the lady of the house.

When Madison quickly expressed her desire to ride along with Savannah to help her out, Savannah cringed at the look of utter dismay on Kenya's pretty, but now distorted face. A second later an envious Kenya said she was also riding along with her mother, with her bad attitude easy to discern through the language of her body.

Savannah was so relieved that her son wasn't in the room to witness his sister's outrageous display of jealousy. She was in no doubt that Kevin would've checked Kenya on the spot. Then it would've been on between the two siblings. Cole, tall, dark and handsome, had immediately given his wife a chilling glance, but being her usual stubborn self, Kenya had given her husband a cold, defiant stare in return.

Just before Savannah and her riding companions left the house, Savannah looked around for Kevin, wondering where he'd gone. It wasn't like him to disappear without saying a word to anyone about where he was off to. As she headed out the front door, she saw exactly where her son was. Kevin was out on the street, bent over, with his head stuck inside the back door of Antonio's late-model Mercedes-Benz.

When Savannah finally spotted Antonio, she saw that he had two large brown shopping bags, one in each hand. Since she hadn't given Antonio her address, she figured that he and Kevin had cooked up something between them at dinner the previous night. It wasn't surprising to her that the two men had gotten along so well. Kevin had later told her that he genuinely liked Mr. Delabay and that he thought Antonio would be a nice person for her to hang out with.

Although Savannah was thrilled that Kevin and Antonio had taken a shine to each other, she wished they'd let her in on their plans for seeing each other today. She wouldn't have invited Antonio over simply because of how Kenya might react. In view of how rude Kenya had begun to act with Madison, Savannah expected her to treat Antonio the same way. There was never a time when Savannah wanted to fight with her daughter, but if Kenya got out of hand she would instantly set her straight. Kenya would not be allowed to disrespect anyone in Savannah's home.

Kenya flashed her mother a disturbed glance. "Who's that man with Kevin, Mom?"

"Mr. Antonio Delabay is a friend of mine, Kenya. I just met him a few days ago."

Kenya jerked her head back and forth. "Excuse me! Met him where?"

Before Savannah could respond to Kenya, the men were coming up the driveway, laughing and talking. Kevin also had several brown bags in his hand. Savannah was so fearful of what was happening right here and now, but there was nothing she could do about it. She was in no doubt that Antonio was there at Kevin's invitation. Savannah only wished that one of the two men had given her a clue. Kevin had to have known it wasn't a good time for all this to occur.

"Mom, Mr. Delabay brought lunch for everyone. He cooked it himself. Where are you and your sidekicks rushing off to?" Kevin leaned over and kissed Madison on the forehead, causing Kenya to look like she wanted to throw up.

"Back into the house, since we were on our way to Subway to get lunch. Hi, Antonio," Savannah warmly greeted, "this is such a nice thing for you to do for us." She then turned and slipped her arm around Kenya. "This is my lovely daughter, Kenya. Since you've already met Madison, no introduction is necessary. Come on in the house and meet my son-in-law, Cole."

There was no way Antonio could've extended his hand to Kenya, since they were full of bags, but his bright smile and gently voiced sentiment showed his absolute pleasure at meeting Savannah's daughter. "You're beautiful, Kenya. Just like your mother."

The hard warning look coming from Savannah was not lost on Kenya, so Kenya halfway smiled at Antonio, though she'd would've preferred to demand answers as to why he was at her mother's home, bringing her a home-cooked meal, no less. Kenya wasn't afraid to ask Antonio just what his intent was toward her mother, but she knew that Savannah would instantly snap her head off and then hand it to her if she dared. Kenya was also hoping that she'd jumped to all the wrong conclusions—and that Mr. Delabay didn't call himself romancing her late father's wife.

Kenya thought Antonio also needed to know that his attempt at flattery hadn't worked one bit with her. It really rankled her to the bone that Madison had already met the man she hadn't even known existed until now. The nerve of her mother to insult her only daughter in that manner had Kenya incensed. She could hardly wait to tell her family exactly how she felt, but she'd just have to wait until after the falsely charming Mr. Delabay finally took his leave. If Kenya had had her way, this refined-looking gentleman wouldn't ever make it inside the house.

The others trailed Savannah inside her home. Once Savannah introduced Antonio to Cole, she asked everyone to follow her out to the huge country-style kitchen. Savannah loved to cook and entertain her friends and family, so the large room had been a must-have on her housing amenities list. Bright and shiny with all stainless steel-appliances, ceramic tile flooring, and backsplashes done in earth tones, granite countertops, breakfast bar and four stools, and a large round hardwood table and six chairs, her island-style paradise had been designed with all the finest in home décor. Savannah also had an extra stove and refrigerator in her three-car garage and two barbeque grills, gas and charcoal, on her back patio.

While Savannah's guests joined her in opening up all the bags, helping to set the table with the disposable dinnerware and putting out the meal, Kenya was seated at the table looking like she could take a huge bite out of something other than the delicious-smelling food.

Biting down hard on someone in her family was more like it, but Kenya wasn't sure whether her mother or brother was to blame for the latest unwanted guest. It wasn't enough that Kevin had brought in some strange woman for what should've been a family-only event, now some other bozo had shown up to add to her grief. At any rate, Kenya knew that the sinking of her teeth into someone would certainly be felt before this miserable day was over.

Aware of the violent storm brewing inside her daughter, Savannah thought it was in everyone's best interest for her to continue to keep a watchful eye on her pouting offspring. However, she was hoping that Kenya had the good sense to keep a lid on the tempest in the teapot until after Antonio and the movers had left. The reason why Kenya saw fit to try and ruin this special day for the family was beyond Savannah, who believed her daughter would've found something else to be difficult about even if Madison and Antonio had not been present.

Cole came up to Savannah and put his around her shoulder. "Mom, can I see you in private for a moment or two?"

Savannah got a strange feeling from the expression on Cole's face, but she let him guide her away from the others. "What is it, son? You look troubled."

Cole sighed hard. "I'm thinking I should take Kenya on home. I don't know what your relationship to Mr. Delabay is, but Kenya looks ready to explode over him just being here. I can read my wife pretty good, you know. What do you think I should do?"

Savannah brought Cole to her and gave him a warm, reassuring hug, as she'd done on many other occasions when he hadn't known what to do about Kenya's dark moods. "I think you should do absolutely nothing, Cole. We can't continue to allow Kenya to control the tempo of every family gathering. She can't always be the center of attention."

Cole shrugged, shoving his hands deep in the pockets of his pants. "Yeah, but I'm sure you know where this is all headed, Mom. Her dark-thundercloud look is just a preamble."

"I understand, but we've let her get away with it too many times already. Since this is my home and Kenya's my daughter, you let me handle everything. This is a new day for all of us. She may as well get ready for the new changes. Kenya will not control this day or me. Now let's get back in there so we can sit down and eat the food that the good Lord has blessed us with."

Cole looked rather skeptical, but without further protesting Savannah's decision, he followed his mother-in-law back into the kitchen, where everyone had already taken a seat. Kevin had even set up the card table for the four movers to eat upon.

Antonio had surely thought of everything when he'd decided to prepare a delightful Italian feast. Spaghetti with huge meatballs, a pan of lasagna, and a large vegetarian pizza were the mainstays; complemented by a large bowl of garden salad; there was a variety of dressings to choose from, French sourdough bread, and freshly grated Parmesan cheese. Antonio had even brought along a couple of bottles of fine wine and a case of soft drinks. Savannah was very pleased with his thoughtfulness, so much so that she asked Antonio to pass the blessing over the meal.

In Savannah's opinion the food was as delicious as it looked. Antonio was a marvelous chef. She respected a man who knew his way around in the kitchen and wasn't ashamed to show off his culinary skills to other males. Savannah had friends who had husbands who knew how to cook, but these men wouldn't do it simply because they felt the kitchen was a woman's place. Antonio's favorable quality points were adding up rather quickly.

In only a few days of her knowing him, Antonio had scored high marks with Savannah. Although she planned to talk to him about coming to her home without giving her prior notice, she actually held Kevin responsible for the surprise visit. Even so, she believed that her son had meant well. The invite was a very nice gesture, but knowing how difficult his sister was Kevin should've taken Kenya's feelings into consideration. Savannah thought it should've been her own decision as to when and where Kenya and Antonio would meet.

The hot, soothing bath felt so good to Savannah's tired, aching body. She had obviously used muscles that she hadn't known existed before today. All the stretching and lifting had worn her completely out. With everyone else already off to bed, Savannah was glad to have this down-time to herself. Despite Kenya's dark mood it had been a very exciting day.

Antonio had left Savannah's home not long after helping to put all the heavy furniture and large boxes in place. He had taken his leave so that she could enjoy the evening alone with her kids. Before departing, he'd told Savannah that he'd only come there at Kevin's insistence;

that he wouldn't have come had he known she objected. Kevin had assured him that his mother would welcome his visit. Still, Antonio had taken full responsibility for not having first checked out things with Savannah, promising never to allow something like that to happen again.

It was unbelievable to Savannah how much had been accomplished in a single day. Everyone who'd come there to help her out had worked his or her buns off to whip her new place into shape. Other than the few personal boxes of items she had yet to unpack, everything else that had been assigned a place was now in its designated space. The movers had hauled away the bulk of the trash, including the larger empty boxes. It had been their way of thanking Savannah for the very nice meal she'd shared with them, not to mention the great tip they'd received.

A light knock on the bathroom door gripped Savannah's attention, causing her to moan with displeasure. The timing couldn't be worse, since she had just gotten totally relaxed.

"Mommy, can I come in?" Kenya had asked the question in a soft, shy voice.

Savannah instantly banged her eyes shut. She knew what that tone of voice meant, had heard it all too often. If she allowed Kenya access to her peaceful haven, she may as well just go ahead and toss her serenity right out the window. That little shy voice Kenya had used was just one of numerous devious tactics she often used to try and get her own way.

Calling Savannah Mommy was just another of Kenya's obvious ploys. Because Savannah had earlier refused to get into a conversation with Kenya over Antonio, Savannah was

almost sure that her daughter wanted to resume her inter-
rogating style of questioning.

"Can you wait until I get through taking my bath, Kenya?
I really need this time alone."

Totally ignoring Savannah's wishes, Kenya opened the
door and stepped into the room. "I can't believe you're still
refusing to talk to me, Mom. What's up with that?"

"Young lady, I am not denying you anything. I simply
want to finish my bath. And if I'm correct in my assumptions, you came in here just to start a silly argument. I'm
not up for it, Kenya. I'm extremely tired and all I want to
do is get into my bed and go to sleep."

Savannah wrapped a large bath sheet around her body
as she stepped out of the tub. The relaxed state of mind
was gone and the tension was already back, so she saw no
use in trying to recapture her serenity. Savannah's piece of
heaven had already been stolen out from under her.

The way in which Kenya was rolling her eyes at her
mother had Savannah wanting to order her daughter to get
out of her bedroom—and in no uncertain terms. Instead,
Savannah went about the business of thoroughly drying off
her body and then slipping into her silk nightgown and
robe. Ignoring Kenya had always worked very well for
Kevin, so Savannah thought it just might work for her, too.
With that in mind, Savannah began to massage lotion into
her feet.

Kenya haughtily positioned herself on the love seat in the
alcove of her mother's bedroom. "I'm not leaving this room
until you tell me what's going on with you and that man."

Hating that Kenya insisted on pushing her testy buttons,
Savannah sighed hard. "That man has a name, Kenya. And

it's none of your business what's going on with Mr. Delabay and myself. If I were you, I'd go back into the guest room and slip into bed with my husband."

"Is that what you would've done with Mr. Delabay had your family not been here spending the weekend with you? Is it already like that with you and him, Mom?"

"Kenya, you're way out of line!" Savannah shouted pretty loudly. Feeling as though her world had been snatched right out from under her, Savannah dropped down on her bed. Burning tears stung her eyes, but she refused to let Kenya see her cry. Never before had she felt this close to slapping her obnoxious daughter right across the face. This move had bothered Kenya from the very beginning, but now Savannah could see how much it was really affecting her.

Savannah's bedroom door suddenly burst open and then Kevin practically fell into the room, looking rather shaken. "Mom, are you okay? I heard you shouting." Then he saw Kenya, which explained the sickening look of defeat on his mother's face. "What are you up to now?" Kevin shouted at Kenya. "You never stop being nasty and mean, do you?"

"Kevin, please don't," Savannah warned in a gentle tone.

"No, let *Mr. Man* have his say," Kenya said, practically snarling at her brother. "I'd like nothing better than to tell Kevin Richmond what I think of the awful stunts he's pulled off on this family. All of them have been in bad taste."

"Kenya, I'm not even trying to hear you. You've been disruptive ever since you first arrived at the house early this morning."

As if everyone in the house had heard Savannah shouting, Cole made a sudden appearance. "What's everyone doing in here? Is someone sick?"

"Yeah, bro, your evil-butt wife," Kevin responded. "You need to take her on back to bed. Or better yet, take her trifling behind back to L.A. I don't know what she's said to Mom, but you can make a safe bet that it wasn't very pleasant."

Trying to ease the pain in her head, Savannah rubbed her temples with her fingertips. This was not how she had expected her moving day to turn out. So much for new beginnings, she mused. She had a new home, and wanted a new life, but her family was still the same.

"I just said what you all were thinking. If no one else is concerned that Mom may already be sleeping with that horrible man, I am. She's out here in Fontana alone and vulnerable, an easy prey to the likes of the smooth-talking Mr. Delabay!" Kenya shouted, rolling her angry eyes.

The only thing that kept Kevin off Kenya was Cole lodging his body in between them, yet Cole himself wanted to shake his wife as badly as Kevin wanted to knock her silly. "Kenya, go get our things together. We're going home. Right now."

Kenya gave Cole the back-and-forth and all-around-and-about head action. "I'm not going anywhere, Dr. Standiford. I came up here for the weekend and I'm not leaving until it's over."

"Kenya, I think you should listen to your husband. You've said some things to me that would be unforgivable to someone who didn't give a flying fig about forgiveness. I love you, Kenya, but I don't like you very much right now. This was supposed to be a happy weekend, but you never wanted it to be anything but what you've made it, a complete disaster. You should go on and allow Cole to take you home. I'm all moved in now and I won't be alone, not with Kevin and Madison here. By the way, I'm not as vulnerable as you'd like to think," Savannah said.

Kenya got to her feet in a hurry. "Now that you've used up my husband and me you want to throw us out. If you insist that we leave, Mom, we won't ever darken your doorstep again."

Savannah felt so sad within, but trying to reason with Kenya in her conflicted state of mind was impossible. "Suit yourself, Kenya. You always do. Now if all of you will please excuse me, I'm going to bed. I know I thanked you earlier for helping me out today, but I sincerely thank you again for all that you've done. I love you. Good night. Everyone!"

Kenya stormed out of the room, with Cole right behind her. Savannah felt sorry for Cole, who didn't stand a chance of getting through to his wife, at least not on this night.

Kevin pulled his mother to him and hugged her tightly. "That girl gets worse every time I see her. I can't believe what she implied. Exactly what *did* she say to you, Mom?"

"You heard her, though she was a little more vulgar with her earlier statement." Savannah went on to tell Kevin Kenya's exact words, the excruciating insults that she'd never forget.

Kevin winced, sighing audibly. "I'm sorry, Mom. If I had known inviting Mr. Delabay over here would've caused all this, I wouldn't have. But I guess I should've known. Daddy's little girl didn't even like your own husband to be around you. Isn't it normally the son who acts like this about his mother? It seems that I'm an exception to the rule. Are you worried that Kenya will never speak to you again, since you didn't beg her to stay after her stupid statement?"

Savannah reached up and smoothed her palm over Kevin's hair. "I am worried, Kevin, but not about Kenya never talking to me again. She'll get over it the minute she needs me to do something. I'm concerned about her, period. I know the death of your father has been hard for her, but I don't think I fully realized until today the devastating impact it has had on your sister. Kenya's always been a problem child, but the way she's been acting lately is really scary to me. I believe she might need professional help to get through this difficult time in her life."

Kevin sucked his teeth. "Mom, Dad has been dead over two years so it has to be something else that's bothering Kenya. Maybe her marriage is in trouble. She seems so unhappy. I don't know how Cole has managed to stay with her this long. She rags on him all the time."

Savannah shook her head from side to side. "Kevin, don't say things like that. She's your sister. We have to be sensitive to whatever's going on with Kenya."

"Like the sensitivity she's shown toward you? I don't think so, Mom. But the thing is, I'll be out of here on Wednesday morning, and you'll be stuck here with no one but Kenya if you play into her hands and stop seeing Mr. Delabay. Mom, don't do that. Kenya has to accept that you have a life to live. You've experienced enough sadness. Please don't start backpedaling."

Savannah smiled weakly at her son. "I don't plan to, Kevin. I'm much stronger now. I need to live, son. I desperately want to be happy again. And I will be. I promise you that."

Kevin grinned. "That's the spirit, Mom! Feel like having a cup of herbal tea?"

"That would be nice, Kevin. Would you mind fixing the tea and bringing it in here? I need a few minutes of quiet to try and regroup."

"Don't mind at all. Just name your poison, Mom."

"Orange spice just might hit the spot. Thanks, Kevin, for being my hero today."

The Richmonds and Standifords were seated at Savannah's kitchen table, but very few words had been spoken among them. Savannah wasn't surprised that Kenya didn't go home like she'd requested, nor was she stunned that Kenya had prepared breakfast for the family. Her daughter almost always tried to do something nice for everyone to make up for when she'd behaved badly. Rarely did anyone get a straight-up apology from Kenya, so the later niceties didn't mean a whole heck of a lot to them, especially in the absence of regret.

Kevin could tell that Madison felt all the tension, too. Her sparkling eyes had been darting from one family member to another ever since she'd sat down at the table. She only knew what had gone down the previous night by what Kevin had told her when she'd awakened that morning. Kevin had warned Madison to expect the possibility of more fireworks from Kenya, after he'd learned that the Standifords hadn't gone back to L.A.

Since Madison had already given him numerous clues by the things she'd said about her family, Kevin wasn't too surprised when she told him that they also went off on each other quite often. It was the constant clash between her father and brothers that kept her family in an uproar. The same as it was with Kenya, the males all vied for attention from Jennifer Bonet, the mother and wife. From what Madison had told him before they'd come into the kitchen, her mother wasn't nearly as strong as Savannah. At any rate, Kevin had told his mother that he'd hated placing Madison in the uncomfortable setting Kenya had created.

"Mom," Cole said, "do you want me to get started on your garden for the backyard? I've already located the box that has all your gardening tools inside. I set it aside for Kevin and me to go through it this morning. Once we unpack the tools, you, Kevin and me can run out to Home Depot or Lowe's to get the evergreen plants and annual or perennial flowers you'd like to have planted in the garden. Are you feeling up to it?"

Savannah smiled broadly. "I'm feeling just fine and it sounds like a great idea to me. I saw Ms. Bernice's beautiful garden earlier in the week. The beauty of it gave me spring fever."

"Do you have any idea of what you want to go back there, Mom?" Kevin asked.

"While staying in the hotel I made a list of the plants and flowers that I want for the back. I just have to find it, but I think I have an idea of where I stuck it."

"That'll make the shopping much easier if you already know what you want," Cole said.

"Since the sod for the backyard was a standard item offered by the builder, I was thinking of hiring a land-scaper with the money I didn't have to use for what would've been a big expense. But if you really want to do the yard, Cole, I'd prefer to have you landscape it for me."

Savannah looked over at Madison. "Not only is Cole one of the best doctors around, our boy has mega-landscaping skills. Once I put the kitchen back in order, we can be on our way."

"I can take care of the kitchen, Mom," Kenya offered sincerely, even offering a smile.

For the first time during this morning Savannah made direct eye contact with Kenya. "I thought it would be nice if we all went plant shopping, Kenya, but if you're not interested in going I understand. What about you, Madison? Would you like to come with us?"

"Would love to. I've got a pretty good green thumb also. I love to plant things and watch them grow. So I hope you'll let me help out with the gardening, too, Ms. Savannah."

Kenya eyed Madison with curiosity. "Why don't you stay and help me out with the kitchen, Madison? Then we can hang out afterward and get to know each other a little better."

"Madison is a guest, Kenya. No kitchen duties on her first visit," Kevin commented.

There was no way Kevin was going to leave Madison alone in the house with Kenya. His sister most assuredly had an agenda that included more than just cleaning the kitchen. If the truth was known, Kenya wanted to get all up in Madison's personal business. He was willing to bet his last dollar on that. Besides that, Kevin just wanted Madison to hang out with him.

"With everything settled, let's hit Lowe's first. They normally have the best prices," Kevin said. "I also saw several nurseries on our way from the airport, Mom, if you decide you want to go that route."

"Okay, kids. Let me go back to the bedroom and get my purse. I'll meet you all outside. Cole, are we taking your Suburban?"

"Sure thing, Mom. It's the only vehicle we have that'll hold all of us and the purchases."

Kenya got to her feet. "You know what, the outing is starting to sound like a bit of fun. I think I'll tag along, too. I can take care of the kitchen when we get back."

Laughing inwardly, Savannah saw that not one of the family members seemed surprised by Kenya's sudden change of heart. Could it be that Kenya had become far too predictable?

As Savannah arranged the dirt around a waxy leafed gardenia plant, the cool soil felt good beneath her hands. Cole had designed and landscaped the areas for planting and had strategically piled the mounds of mixed rich soil all around the backyard, but far away from the pool area. Savannah loved the great design job he'd done for her. Cole sure knew his stuff.

Kenya was busy planting the pink-and-white azalea bushes and Madison looked as if she was having a ball handling the various shades of pinks and deep red bougainvilleas, which would eventually climb up and then take over the back fence. Kevin had already placed into the ground a variety of miniature palms and was now working on placing decorative borders around the areas he'd finished. The scalloped cement stones made a nice finishing touch.

Because Savannah had wanted to purchase so many plants, flowers, and shrubs, she had ended up renting a Home Depot truck for them to haul everything back to the house in. The rose garden was Savannah's special project so she had chosen a variety of rosebushes in vibrant colors to grace the property. Yellow roses were her very favorite.

Two dwarf magnolia trees had also been selected for shade trees. Kevin and Cole planned to work together on getting them into the ground, since they needed a little more attention than what the plants and flowers needed. Orange and lemon trees were a consideration, but Savannah hadn't yet decided on them for sure.

Although Savannah definitely planned on having a vegetable garden, she'd decided to also save that planting for another time. A variety of tomatoes, green onions, and a few herbs were the only plants she desired to go into her vegetable garden. Kevin wanted her to get a few collard plants, but greens were a lot of work, as far as Savannah was concerned.

Glancing down at her wristwatch, Savannah saw that they'd been working for several hours now. She felt that it was time for everyone to take a break for the day. Having stopped off at the grocery store, she had purchased all the items she'd need for making sandwiches, along with a variety of snack items. She'd also picked up all the ingredients for Kevin to have his special fried-chicken dinner the next day, which was the Lord's Day. Madison had expressed a desire to bake the devil's food cake this evening for tomorrow's dessert.

The entire family had planned to go to church first and then come back home and get dinner on the table.

Savannah had been invited to Bernice's church, which just happened to also be Antonio's place of worship. With Bernice having mentioned all the churchwomen who were running after Antonio, Savannah wasn't sure it was a good idea to attend service there, but she had already told Bernice that she would do so.

Savannah would also love to invite Antonio over for the Day of Worship dinner, but she felt that enough turmoil had already occurred over his presence in her life. She really didn't want to add any more fuel to the fire if she could help it.

Then Savannah thought of what she'd promised Kevin and herself. It only took her a couple of seconds to decide to give the idea of having Antonio as a dinner guest a little more serious thought. The handsome gentleman had certainly shown himself to be kind and thoughtful enough toward her. Savannah didn't believe any of Antonio's good deeds were just an act.

"I think we should all go in and get something to eat," Savannah announced. "Is anyone as hungry as I am?" Loud affirmations broke out from all her houseguests. "After a quick shower, I'll get the sandwiches made. Kenya and Madison, if you want, you two ladies can help me out in the kitchen. Kevin and Cole, if you could just store the rest of the plants and the unused soil at the end of the patio, I'd appreciate it. Kevin, if you don't mind, you and I can spread the red mulch around on Monday morning."

Kevin grinned. "Sounds like an okay plan to me, Mom. I'll send you my itemized bill when I get back to San Fran."

Kenya laughed heartily, drawing the attention of her mother. Savannah loved it when her daughter was in a good mood, but Kenya's dark moods had been coming on more frequently as of late. Before the Standifords left to go home, she hoped to have a heart-to-heart chat with Kenya. Savannah didn't want to see her kids leave with their relationships in a state of unrest.

The hot shower had Savannah feeling pretty much rejuvenated, although she'd probably fall asleep if she'd lain down in her king-size sleigh bed. Since the weekend was almost over with, she realized how quickly the time had gotten away from her. Savannah was going to miss the kids terribly when they left, but she was also going to bask in the first-time experience of being alone in her new home.

There were times when Savannah wished Kevin would move back down to Southern California, but she'd never voice that to him because he'd more than likely consider it, especially if he thought she needed him. He was always such a big help to her—and mother and son truly enjoyed spending lots of time together. Savannah hated that she and Kenya wouldn't get to shop together or have lunch and take in a movie as often as they normally did, but they weren't living so far apart that an outing couldn't occur at least a couple of times a month.

After stepping into her cavernous walk-in closet, Savannah looked through her wardrobe to find something comfortable but stylish to wear. As jeans and loose-fitting tops were her favorite articles of clothing to wear around the house, she pulled out a pair of white denims, matching them up with a bright red V-necked sweater. Then she decided on her white tennis shoes over the red-and-white sandals. Figuring that her guests were waiting for her to reappear, she quickly dressed and then slipped on her sneakers.

Just as Savannah was about to exit the bedroom, her telephone rang. The caller ID revealed to her that this call had been made from a private number. She started not to answer it, but then she thought better of it. Upon hearing Antonio's voice, she was glad that she'd taken the call. "Hey, Antonio, how are you?"

"Fine, Savannah. I was just calling to see how you were, as well as how the kids are doing. How are things going over at your new place? Still a lot of unpacking to do?"

"You won't believe how much we've accomplished over here. The kids have been working so hard. I never dreamed we'd get this much done. All that's left to unpack are a few boxes containing personal items. We've even started on the landscaping for the backyard. Cole is an expert on designing yard space. By the way, everyone's doing just fine. Thanks for asking."

"That's good to know. Another reason I called was to ask you to join our church congregation for tomorrow's service." Antonio went on to tell Savannah the name of his house of worship, The First Shepherd Community Church, and its location.

"I already know of your church, Antonio. My good friend Bernice Saunders goes there. She's been singing the church's praises since she first started attending there."

"Ah, sweet Bernice. I don't know her all that well, but she has a very good reputation for helping others." Antonio grew silent for a moment. "I can't help but wonder if Bernice has ever mentioned me to you. Has she, Savannah?"

"Is there any reason that she should have?"

"Many reasons. Since I'm touted as the most eligible bachelor around the halls of worship that gives me a cause to wonder. Have you possibly mentioned me to Bernice?"

"I have mentioned you to her and she has talked to me about you, nothing unfavorable though. I *am* worried about attending your church if you're so sought after. Don't want to ruffle any female feathers."

"Not to worry, Savannah. I'm not a promiscuous man, dear girl." Antonio chuckled after that statement. "There's not one female member of my church that I've ever asked out. Does that make you feel any better about attending tomorrow's service?"

"It does, for some strange reason. I'd love to attend, but I don't think we should sit together. I'll probably sit with Bernice."

"Not to worry about that either. I'm singing in the choir tomorrow, so I'll be in the choir box for the majority of the service. I promise to sit rows and rows away from you. I won't even speak to you if that'll make you feel more comfortable. Is that okay?"

It was Antonio's last couple of remarks that made Savannah realize how juvenile she was once again acting. It would also hurt her feelings to have him see her and not even bother to acknowledge her presence. Putting the other issues aside, Savannah was very impressed with the fact that Antonio actually sang in the choir. "A men's choir, Antonio?"

Antonio chuckled again. "All men, Savannah. Most of the members are forty and over. However, there are more women than men. I'm sure you already know that you ladies outnumber us men considerably. Men just can't seem to outlive the lively girls. Of course, I'm an exception to that one, since Sylvia passed before me. But that's certainly not the norm."

Hoping she hadn't caused Antonio any unpleasantness, Savannah felt bad for how the conversation had turned a wrong corner. His voice had dropped a couple of decibels, making him sound a bit sad. Although she knew that it was impossible for them to always get around the deaths of their spouses, she still didn't want to make it the focus of every conversation.

"Well, as for tomorrow, I'm going to give it some more thought. I promised Bernice that I'd attend her church for worship service, and I'm not one who normally breaks promises. If you see me there, please don't be surprised by it. As for speaking to me, please don't hurt my feelings by not doing so. What are your plans for after church, Antonio?"

"I haven't made any, Savannah. Do you have something in mind?"

"Dinner at my place?"

"I'd love that. Are you sure it's okay with everyone?"

"The only person it has to be okay with is me, but why do you ask?"

"Your daughter, Savannah. I don't think Kenya is too happy about having me around. The last thing I want to do is cause trouble between you and your children. I know how girls are about their fathers. My daughter is the same way about me. She still doesn't think I should be dating anyone. So it seems that jealous daughters are something else we have in common."

"Unbelievable, yet so very believable. To borrow a few words from you, not to worry, Antonio. I can handle Kenya in my own way. She isn't very happy about us seeing each other, but it's not you per se. The problem would arise no matter who the male was. Now that we have that out in the open, what about joining us for dinner after church tomorrow?"

"I'd be delighted. Can I bring something, Savannah?"

"Just yourself, Antonio."

"It's a date." Another few moments of silence ensued. "Savannah. Would it be okay if I call you late this evening, after you're all wound down? I enjoy talking to you so much."

Blushing heavily, Savannah was glad that Antonio couldn't see the expression on her face. "I think that would be a perfect ending to a busy day. I'll look forward to hearing from you, Antonio. I hope the rest of your day is filled with pleasure. I enjoy talking to you, too."

"Later, Savannah. Enjoy your family."

As Savannah hung up the phone, she smiled brightly. That Antonio wanted to talk with her later made her happy. She laughed, realizing she still didn't know the names of his children.

A small box caught Savannah's eye, as she was about to leave the room. Walking a few steps away from where she was, she bent over, picked up the box, and carried it over to the bed, where she sat down and opened it up. Her breath caught at the pictures of her husband, many of them included her.

When Savannah had packed this particular box, she had wondered if she should hang the pictures in her new home.

She wasn't trying to act like Geoffrey never existed, but she worried that seeing the pictures every day would be a constant, painful reminder of what was no more. Not to hang them could be seen as her being disrespectful to his memory.

Someone knocked on the door at the same moment Savannah closed up the box. Without inquiring as to who was on the other side of the door, Savannah yelled for them to come in. Upon seeing Kevin, she smiled. "I guess everyone is wondering where I am. I'm coming now."

"Yeah, we *were* wondering. Everyone complained about being hungry, like they don't know how to make a sandwich. Madison is taking care of it for you, Mom. What's in the box?"

"Pictures of your father. I'm in quite a few of them with him. Maybe you can give me some advice. I'm having a hard time deciding if I should hang them up or not."

Kevin shook his head from side to side. "That could be very painful for you. Besides, you'll never forget what Dad looks like no matter what."

"Are you saying I should get rid of them?"

Kevin shook his head again. "I'm not saying that. If I were you, I'd put them all into photo albums. Then, whenever the mood hits you, you could thumb through them. But to put them on the walls is going to keep you from moving forward. Take this for instance. Say you have a date bring you home, and he wants to kiss you good-night, but then you look up and see the loving images of Dad staring back at you. You get what I'm trying to say here, Mom?"

Savannah was laughing and crying at the same time. "I get it, Kevin. I really do get it. Thank you, son, for being my voice of reason. These are very hard decisions for me to make, but they have to be made. I like the idea of the albums. I'd never be able to get rid of the photos altogether. They represent twenty-five years of my life. Thanks for the great suggestion."

Kevin hugged Savannah. "Let's go eat now, Mom. My stomach is growling."

"Mine, too, Kevin. Very loudly, I might add."

Arm in arm, smiling warmly at each other, mother and son left the room.

With Kenya seated on the floor in front of the sofa in her mother's bedroom, Savannah was seated on the divan. Once lunch had been consumed, mother and daughter had left the rest of the crew in the living room playing board games, while they'd escaped to the back of the house for a brief chat.

Savannah took hold of Kenya's hand, squeezing it momentarily, and then releasing it. "Kenya, I know that the death of your father still weighs heavily on you. I understand your feelings more than you could possibly know. Geoffrey's death has taken its toll on all of us. Your behavior this weekend has been outrageous and totally unacceptable to me. You've been extremely rude to my houseguests and that's why I thought we should have this little talk. What are you objecting so vehemently to, Kenya?"

Kenya looked up at Savannah and rolled her eyes. "As if you don't already know, Mom. You don't even know this Delabay guy, yet you seem so taken with him. Are you so needy that you have to jump at the first man who looks your way?"

So much for wearing the kid gloves, Savannah mused, wishing she could soften the blows she was about to throw Kenya's way. "As a matter of fact, Kenya, I'm very needy, but not for a man. Your mother is very lonely. I told you when we last saw each other that I'd like to have male companionship. It just so happens that I met Antonio when I least expected it. What don't you like about him?"

Kenya gave a haughty harrumph. "He seems sly, slick and wicked to me."

"In what way?"

"He's just a little too charming for my taste. He meets me one second and is calling me beautiful in the next one. I can't believe Kevin can't see through him, too."

"Why does Antonio have to live up to your expectations rather than mine, Kenya? Why is it your taste that we have to be concerned with over what's tasteful to me? There aren't too many women that I know of who'd object to respectful compliments. You *are* beautiful, Kenya."

"He doesn't have to do a thing for me. I'm just making observations. Besides, you asked me my opinion, Mom. If you didn't want the answers, you shouldn't have asked."

"I can see that seeking your opinion was my first big mistake. What makes you think I should live out my life as a lonely old woman? God forbid, but if you were to lose Cole, are you saying you'd never, ever have interest in a man again?"

Kenya sucked her teeth. "Don't be absurd! I'm still very young, Mom. You're much older, though you're not acting very mature these days. How can you just meet a guy and then have him over to your house without giving it any thought? If I were to do something like that, you'd throw an absolute fit. Then you'd go on to question my morality."

"First of all, your brother invited Antonio to the house, not me. I thought it was very nice of him to go to the trouble of fixing a meal for us to enjoy. You're the only who seems to have had a problem with his visit. Kenya, I hope we can come to some amicable solution to this. I intend to continue seeing Antonio. I like him a lot. I've also invited him to dinner tomorrow, right after church. I hope you don't insist on making me choose between your company and that of a friend. I don't want to do that. Nor should I have to."

Kenya eyed Savannah with disbelief. "It seems to me as if you've already made your choice. I still believe that this should've been a weekend for family only. These other people shouldn't have been invited in. Kevin and Madison are mooning over each other like two sick lovebirds, which makes me wonder what was their real reason for coming here this weekend. I'll tell you this now. If Mr. Delabay is coming here for dinner tomorrow, Cole and I'll be leaving first thing in the morning. We'll just have to skip church this week."

Savannah's eyebrows furrowed. "Kenya, what is *really* going on here? None of what you're saying makes any sense. Have you forgotten how you and Cole used to moon over each other in the very same way? I just can't believe that my forging a friendship with someone is causing you this much trouble, honey. Is there something going on between you and Cole? Whatever it is, can't you and I talk about it?"

Kenya leaped to her feet. "Oh, no, I won't allow you to make this about Cole and me. Cole has nothing to do with my feelings on this matter. He's too busy siding with you and Kevin to care how I feel. I think you're being down-right disloyal to my father. And I don't like it a bit."

Disillusioned was an understatement for how Savannah felt. How could she be disloyal to someone who was no longer alive? Kenya was acting as if her mother was having an illicit affair on her spouse. Savannah could still see that there was no rhyme or reason to her daughter's off-the-wall comments, yet Kenya had accused her of being immature. Not wanting to fight with her daughter, Savannah got to her feet, and then pulled Kenya into her arms.

Tears fell from Savannah's eyes as she rocked Kenya back and forth in her arms. "Sweetheart, I'm sorry for the way you feel and I do wish I could change it, but I know I can't."

"I'm not asking you to change my feelings. Just respect them, Mom."

Savannah kissed Kenya's forehead. "I do respect them, Kenya."

"It doesn't seem that way to me. I feel totally disrespected by you, Mom."

Savannah saw that Kenya wasn't ready to let go of whatever she was holding on to. There was more to her feelings than what she was letting on, but until Kenya decided to come clean with her mother, Savannah knew that her hands were tied and that she could only pray for the situation to be resolved as soon as possible. This was one for God to work out.

Savannah once again gently pressed her lips to Kenya's forehead. "I'd love for you and Cole to attend church with us in the morning and stay for dinner, but I'll have to leave that up to you. Just know that I want you here. No one is trying to take your father's place, nor am I trying to replace him. That can't be done. No one can ever take from us what we had. However, what we had is over now. We kept our vows—until death us do part."

"Yet you're already involved with someone else. Why does it have to be that way?"

"Because I have no intentions of spending the rest of my life alone. I have a very big heart. I hope you'll come to understand that no man is an island. I love you, Kenya, and I know you love me. Please don't deprive either of us of all the good things love still has in store for us." Savannah thought of calling Antonio to cancel out the invitation she'd made to him, but she saw it as a big step in the wrong direction. Nor would it help Kenya to come to terms with things.

Chapter 5

As Mrs. Anna Clifford cheerfully gave a tour of Fontana's Silver Wings Senior Center to Savannah, Kevin and Madison, Savannah's mind was busy meandering through the last couple of days. A lot had occurred in the past forty-eight hours, most of which had caused her to sleep rather poorly. Savannah wouldn't have wished on her worst enemy all of the upsetting things that had gone down in her home. New beginnings had turned into the same old endings—sad bitter endings, the troublesome type of endings that Kenya seemed to thrive on as of late.

The Lord's Day service at Bernice and Antonio's First Shepherd Community Church had been wonderful, but all that had transpired afterward had been anything but.

Antonio *had* come to dinner at Savannah's place; Kenya *had* acted up. The young woman had insulted Savannah's guests something awful by outright accusing them of being an unpleasant intrusion on the family weekend. Madison had left the dinner table in tears. Then an argument had instantly ensued between Kevin and Kenya. When Cole had thought that Kevin was coming down too hard on his wife, the two men had gotten into an ugly verbal altercation.

As though the arguing was to never come to an end, Cole had ended up giving his wife a rather cutting piece of his mind for being the one to start the entire mess in the first place. Kenya had then bitterly accused Cole of being insensitive toward her and of never taking her side on any of the family issues—her usual, woe-is-me type rhetoric. Kenya calling Cole a traitor had thoroughly incensed him. Seconds later Kenya had demanded that Cole take her home and he'd been only too happy to oblige her. Immediately after Cole had agreed to take Kenya home, she had told him that he should go home alone, that they needed to put some space between them.

Savannah had heard enough by then, nearly gagging on Kenya's intent to stay behind. That's when the mother in her had stepped right on in, telling Kenya that if Cole had to leave, she had to go on home with her husband. Savannah wasn't about to start harboring her daughter in a time of marital discord, especially during a conflict that Kenya had caused single-handedly.

What had most amazed Savannah about the whole scenario was that Antonio hadn't seemed one bit bothered by all the pandemonium. He had waited a reasonable amount of time after Kenya's outburst to take his leave, explaining to his hostess that he hadn't wanted Kenya to think she'd run him off, as she'd done with Madison.

Savannah was happy that Antonio hadn't given Kenya the satisfaction of knowing she'd slightly injured his feelings.

When Antonio had later explained to Savannah that the same types of bitter conflicts went on periodically within his small family circle, she then understood his composure during it all. In fact, it had seemed to her that he had been somewhat amused by the craziness of the entire situation. The astute little grin Antonio had worn on his face had indicated his amusement to her.

The names of Antonio's children had also been revealed to Savannah during their late-evening phone conversation. She had assumed that Antoinette and Sylvan had been given names close to those of their parents, although Antonio hadn't mentioned anything like that to her. The adult siblings were two years apart in age, Sylvan being the oldest child.

After Antonio had told Savannah that his kids were due to pay him a visit in early May, she couldn't help wondering if they'd react to her in the same way Kenya had reacted to their father. Then she thought that was pretty presumptuous of her since Antonio hadn't said a thing about introducing her to his family. Theirs was only a friendship, which may never blossom into anything more than that.

Kevin nudged Savannah hard with his shoulder. "Where's your head, Mom? We've been trying to get your attention for several seconds now. Are you okay?"

Savannah looked embarrassed. "I'm sorry for going off into the thereafter. What is it you were saying?"

"Mrs. Clifford was asking if you so far liked what you've seen of the center, Mom," Kevin said, eyeing his mother with concern.

Looking thoroughly confused, Savannah sighed hard. "I'm sorry, but I haven't been paying much attention since we left the recreation room. But, yes, I do like what I've seen. Please forgive me for being distracted, Mrs. Clifford. I'm afraid I have a lot on my mind."

"Recently widowed?" Mrs. Clifford asked Savannah.

Puzzled by the question, Savannah blinked her eyes hard. "How did you know? Is it that obvious, Mrs. Clifford?"

Mrs. Clifford smiled sympathetically at Savannah. "I'd know that look anywhere. I'm still where you are. Grief is a hard thing to deal with."

"Mrs. Clifford, I'm sorry if I gave you the wrong impression of what I'm currently feeling. Grief isn't playing a part in my distraction here and now. Although I believe I'll always feel the absence of my spouse I've made the decision to finally rejoin the real world. That's one of the reasons I'm looking for a senior center to volunteer in. I need a little social action, so to speak," Savannah said on a chuckle. "I've allowed my life to become rather dull these days."

Mrs. Clifford laughed. "I know what you mean, but I'm not sure you'll get much action here. The members don't seem as interested in partaking of the activities compared to the folks in some of the other centers I've visited. This group seems content to just come here and chat with each other, normally congregating during the lunch hour and early afternoon. The women outnumber the men, of course. I've tried to get them a bit more involved in things around here, but I guess I don't have what it takes. It'll take a special someone to offer some motivation."

A lightbulb suddenly came on in Savannah's head. For

whatever reason, she felt that she just might be the special person the center needed. It somehow felt as if the Holy Spirit had led her to this place. In helping motivate the other members, she would in turn be helping herself to get back into the swing of things. She'd led many church activity groups before, so why couldn't she take the lead in this endeavor if the opportunity presented itself?

Savannah had the idea that the first step was for her to become a volunteer at the center and then she could see firsthand where her people skills would best fit in. Getting herself involved in this way was probably the exact prescription her doctor would order, she quietly told herself, admitting inwardly that she strongly desired to feel needed again.

Savannah recalled that Antonio had said he was looking for someone to help run his center, but this particular center seemed more of a challenge to her…and it was much closer to her home. With her mission planted firmly in her mind, Savannah felt that it would behoove her to pay much closer attention to everything being said by the animated Mrs. Anna Clifford.

Dusk had already fallen from the heavens as Savannah entertained Kevin and Madison in her family room. This was their next to the last night in her home—and she was highly aware of how much she was going to miss them when they left Wednesday morning. Savannah had become quite fond of the lovely Madison Bonet, believing the feeling was definitely mutual.

Madison had told Savannah enough times how much she loved being around her and that she couldn't wait until Kevin brought her down to visit her home again. Savannah had truly gotten the impression that Madison's family wasn't all that the young woman desired them to be. Madison had talked freely about the lack of open love and affection between her and her family members. Despite Kenya's bad attitude toward her, Madison had told Savannah that the Richmonds were what she considered to be a real family. She had also forgiven Kenya.

Madison smiled sweetly, setting her teacup down on the coaster. "Have you given any more thought to volunteering at the first senior center we saw today, Ms. Savannah?"

Seated on the sofa, across from where Kevin and Madison sat on the love seat, Savannah curled her legs up under her. "I can't stop thinking about it, dear heart. As opposed to the last few centers we toured, I think I'll fit in nicely at Silver Wings. Let me tell you all the dizzying thoughts that have been going on inside my head," Savannah enthused.

Beaming all over, as she began speaking about her mission, Savannah enthusiastically told Kevin and Madison about the spirit-driven feelings she'd experienced at the center that morning. Savannah truly believed that she could make a huge difference there.

Kevin blew his mother a kiss. "I know you can make a difference, Mom. I remember all the things you were involved in at the church and at our school. I recall everyone wanted to sign up for whatever group you were offering a class or program to. I was most proud of you for being a big part of the teen summit. Many of my friends used to tell me how they wished their moms would listen to what they had to say without judging them. Madison, all my friends respected my parents. Our house was always full of Kenya's and my buddies because everyone liked how my parents treated them. The food Mom served them was also the best in the hood."

Vividly remembering those special times, too, Savannah laughed heartily. "Those were the good old days in our home, Madison. Geoffrey and I thought it was better for our kids to have their friends inside the house where we could keep close tabs on them. We provided quite a bit of entertainment for them. Our talent shows were very popular in the neighborhood. Most everything we did was spiritually based, but they were allowed to do other things as well, within reason. We never wanted them to feel deprived. Communication was always encouraged by us."

The sudden sad expression on Madison's face made Savannah wonder if the topic of conversation might be disturbing to her. If she didn't have a good family life, Madison might not want to hear the flip side of what her teen years might've been like, Savannah considered.

"Sounds like a very fun place to visit and hang out," Madison said. "Were the guys and girls allowed to have sleepovers at the same time?" Madison's eyes were wide with curiosity.

Savannah thought Madison's question was a strange one, but she decided not to ask her why she'd asked it. "I have a real simple answer for that," Savannah responded. "No."

Kevin put his arm around Madison's shoulders. "If Kenya's girlfriends were sleeping over, my friends couldn't and vice versa. I don't know exactly why that was, but it was."

"Appearance sake, Kevin. Dad and I didn't think it

would go over too well with the parents to have guys and girls here overnight at the same time, although our rules would've been strictly adhered to. Adequate adult supervision at any youth gathering is very important."

Looking as if she were deep in thought, Madison folded her hands and placed them in her lap. She had done her best to hold back her tears, but a couple of drops escaped from her eyes and ran down her cheeks. "Hearing about your wonderful family life is really emotional for me. Everyone doesn't have it like that. I know I didn't. I often wished for what you all had."

Kevin gently squeezed Madison's shoulder. "You're crying, honey. What's wrong?"

Madison's shoulders shook as she shrugged them. "I just feel sad. I know you all have disagreements, which has been evident a few times during my visit. But you all at least talk to each other. Happy or sad, we exercise very little communication in my family. I can't tell you how many times I've tried to communicate with my parents, trying to get them to open up. The problem lies with them. They are very closed-mouth people. It's almost eerie at times."

"You have to keep on trying, Madison," Kevin said. "Maybe your parents don't know how to communicate with each other, so that would make it hard for them to talk to their kids."

"Kevin, we're all grown up now. If it hasn't happened in all these years, I can't imagine things ever changing. I'm sorry. I don't mean to make our conversation an unpleasant one. Our time is short and I don't want to waste it away on painful matters."

"Please don't feel that way, Madison," Savannah pleaded.

"It's okay to share with us whatever you need to, honey. Don't ever think what you have to say is a waste."

"Thank you for saying that, Ms. Savannah. What about those movies we rented? I'm eager to watch them if you two are ready."

Savannah figured that the subject of the movies was a way for Madison to change the tide. She was only too happy to accommodate the young lady. Family matters were often hard to deal with, even in the lives of some of the most well-adjusted families. In adding up all the clues Madison had given out during the long weekend visit, it appeared to Savannah that Kevin's girlfriend had a lot of family issues that had been left unresolved. It was amazing how childhood problems had a way of carrying over and then insinuating themselves into the lives of the same folks who were now adults.

Savannah got to her feet. "I'm going to let you two young people watch the movies alone. I'm feeling a little tired. I'll take a short nap and then get up later. I hope you don't mind."

Madison jumped to her feet, too, running over to stand in front of Savannah. "No, we don't mind at all. But are you feeling sick, Ms. Savannah?"

In a loving gesture Savannah smoothed Madison's hair back from her face. "I'm fine, sweetheart. Just a bit tired. I'll see you all in little while. Have fun," Savannah said wearily, seriously wondering if she'd be able to get back up at all. Her body felt completely worn out.

Kevin moved to the edge of his seat on the sofa. "Mom, do you want me to walk you back to your room? You look like you might tip over before you get there."

Hoping to put Kevin at ease, since he looked so concerned, Savannah threw her head back and laughed. "I think I can manage that minor feat on my own, Kevin, but thanks anyway."

Savannah was tired, but more than that, in recognizing their budding love, she had wanted to give Kevin and Madison some time alone. Since their arrival, the three of them had been together constantly. Besides that, she wasn't sure she could've sat through a romantic comedy, or anything else to do with love-filled relationships. The yearning to love and be loved seemed to never go away. The tense, nagging, aching feeling deep down inside her plagued her both day and night. Although there'd been people all around her over the past week, the loneliness had always refused to be left out in the cold.

After pulling back the comforter and top sheet, Savannah lay down in bed, and placed a plump pillow up under her head. She then closed her eyes. Young love was such a miraculous thing, she mused, smiling softly. The older folks got, the richer were their experiences with loving relationships. It was only the ageless love that endured the test of time.

Love often made lovers of all ages feel as if spring were in the air every single day of the year. Summer love was always filled with fun, intrigue, and picnics and concerts in the parks. Amusement parks came alive and beaches were swarmed with water lovers and sun worshipers.

Then fall danced into play, bringing to couples in love a variety of warm, delicious experiences, as they prepared themselves for the festive holidays. Autumn leaves provided a colorful backdrop for long evening strolls and exciting drives through the countryside.

As winter arrived on the scene, sweeping the world with its cooler temperatures, fireplaces were lit and soft music played while couples snuggled up closely with each other. Popcorn was popped and shared between lovers as they watched dozens and dozens of movies. Savannah imagined that more babies were conceived in the winter months than at any other time.

Savannah fought hard the urge to take a trek down memory lane. She knew that visiting those wonderful places would only increase the painful longing she already felt deep in her heart. The feelings of euphoria often left her drained afterward. It hurt so much to reflect on her life with Geoffrey especially knowing the end of the fairy tale had already come for them. Prince Geoffrey and his beautiful Princess Savannah had had their forever after.

The End.

The sound of the phone ringing awakened Savannah from a peaceful sleep. A glance at the clock revealed to her that it wasn't quite yet 10:00 p.m. One of Antonio's phone numbers was showing on the caller ID. Savannah propped herself up in bed at the same time she picked up the receiver. If she had to be awakened, she couldn't think of a more pleasant way for it to happen. Antonio's phone calls had a way of lifting her spirits. "Hello," she greeted drowsily.

"Sounds as if I woke someone up. If we hang up, would you be able to go back to sleep?"

"Not a chance of that. Besides, I'm sure I don't want you to hang up."

"That sounds mighty encouraging. How's your day been?"

"Busy as usual. The kids and I visited several senior centers today. We had lunch and then did a little shopping. I left Kevin and Madison in the family room watching a movie. I came back here to lie down so I could give them some time alone. I hadn't intended to nap this long, but it had occurred to me that I might not get back up, as promised. How was your day?"

"Every day is beautiful for me, Savannah, and busy, too. When I wake up in the mornings, I'm so glad to be alive to experience another day. I've never been one to mope about the house. But as I get older, I find myself more tuned in to the real meaning of life. I think when you experience the death of a loved one you really start to understand how short life really is. I know your kids are leaving day after tomorrow. I've been wondering how you're going to handle their departure, seeing that you're in a new place and all. You seem so happy with them around."

"I've been wondering that myself. But, as we both know, all good things must come to an end. I really hate to see them go. However, Kevin has promised to fly down again in the next few weeks to make sure I'm all settled in, but I can't see him coming back home without Madison."

"Is Madison coming home again with Kevin a problem for you, Savannah?"

"Oh, heavens no! I didn't mean to imply that. I'm so taken with her, so much so, that I'm worried about how I'll take it if she's not *the* one. Madison is too adorable and so darn sweet."

Antonio chuckled. "That's interesting. I have the very

same impression of Madison. The father in me wanted to run after Madison and comfort her when Kenya hurt her feelings so badly. By the way, have you talked with Kenya since she left?"

"Not a word from her, but Cole had called to say they'd made it home safely. Kenya will pout for a few days and then she'll call me. I used to be the one to make the call first, whenever troubled visited us. But I learned long ago that that only makes matters worse. We just have to give Kenya her space when she's like that. My daughter will come around in due time. I'm so happy to know that she hasn't put you off by her actions. I was really worried about that."

"It would take a lot more than what Kenya can ever muster up to put me off. She's a daddy's girl, plain and simple. I have one of those, too, so I know what it's all about. Toni has to do an attitude adjustment quite often when the three of us get together, yet she's wonderful with her students. I think I allowed her to get away with too much when she was growing up. Sylvia was the same with Sylvan, who's a momma's boy from his head down to his toes."

"I'm glad you're so understanding, Antonio."

Antonio cleared his throat. "Now what's this about you visiting other senior centers? I had high hopes of you working with us at Golden Age."

"Golden Age is the crown jewel of the Inland Empire senior centers I've seen thus far, but Silver Wings is the one I have set my sights on...and for more than one reason. Your center has so much more to offer than all the others, but I can see great potential for the one here in Fontana.

Let me tell you exactly why I think I should work at the center closest to my home."

Savannah enthusiastically shared her reasons for being so excited about volunteering at Silver Wings. She couldn't help smiling inwardly as she told Antonio about how she was so sure that she had the kind of skills that could help make the center a huge success.

"I see what you mean," Antonio said. "You do have the right credentials. When I mentioned to you that I needed an assistant, why didn't you offer your services to me? I'd love to interview you and consider you for the job opening there at my center. What do you think?"

"That it might be quite awkward for us to work together. I know we're just friends, Antonio, but we've already been out socially. Am I wrong in assuming that we're very attracted to each other? If so, that alone is enough for us to keep our business and pleasure separate."

Savannah knew it was too late for her to bite her tongue off, but that didn't stop her from wanting to. Since when had she become so dang daring? Is this what loneliness and desperation did to folks? Had she come across as crass? She craned her neck to look into the mirror on her dresser, wondering if someone other than herself had voiced those bold comments. The woman staring back at her was definitely not a stranger, but this was a side of her she hadn't seen lately.

Antonio rarely found himself at a loss for words, but that was the case at the moment. He hadn't expected Savannah to put it to him in such plain terms, but she had; he couldn't be more thrilled about it. Her opening up to him this way could mean that she really trusted him. His chest swelled at just the thought of having her trust. This was too unbelievable to be true, but who was he to shun good fortune when it came a knocking?

Antonio smiled broadly, hoping Savannah could feel it right through the phone. "You aren't wrong in your assumptions about our attraction to each other, Savannah. I've been drawn to you from the start, even when I thought you were too young for me. Although I see your point, I still wish it were possible for us to work together. I think we could accomplish great things. However, I'll be more than willing to help you pull together your plans for the Fontana center once you see if there's a need for your services. If you need any advice at all, please feel free to call on me. I believe you're on to something good. Just know that I've got your back."

"Thanks for the vote of confidence, Antonio. About the attraction thing, please forgive me if you think I came on too strong. I'm really rather tame, you know."

What a shame! "You handle yourself just fine, Savannah, like the wonderful lady you are. I don't want to press you too hard, but I'd like to know when we might get together again. I'd really like to have you over to my place for dinner. As you know, I'm an excellent chef."

Savannah really didn't want to come off too eager to see Antonio again, but she didn't want to play too hard to get, either. They weren't teenagers. At their ages time certainly wasn't on their side. One of them was close to a half century old and the other was near to it. Ugh, she thought, wishing her thoughts hadn't taken her there. Age was supposed to be only a number.

"The kids are leaving on Wednesday morning so any

time after then would be just fine, Antonio. Outside of knowing how to do wonders with pasta, what is the chef's specialty?"

"A prime rib that'll melt in your mouth, Savannah. Are we on for Wednesday evening?"

"With prime rib as one of my favorites, I don't see how I can turn down your invitation. Wednesday evening works for me. I'm going to bring the dessert and I won't accept no for an answer. So don't even try it. Where should I come and at what time?"

"I'll pick you up at seven-thirty. My place can be a little hard to find if you've never been here before. I'll give you my address so that you can tell someone exactly where you'll be."

Savannah loved the thoughtful gesture Antonio had just made to her. His concern for her safety garnered another point in the plus column. Thus far, there were no check marks for the negatives. He had shown her nothing less than positive attributes. She was sure he had a few flaws, as all humans did, but she really didn't feel that there would be anything glaring.

"I like that you're so thoughtful, Antonio. It's nice to know I can trust you with my safety. My kids normally know where I am and how to reach me. This is the era of unbelievable means of communication. Sometimes I wish I'd never purchased a cell phone. It's rare that it doesn't ring when I'm out and about. At times it's downright annoying."

"That only goes to show how popular you are. Think you can go back to sleep now?"

"Hardly. I'm going to go and see what the kids are up

to. I promised them I'd come back out after a short nap. They're probably not expecting me at this point. But I will check on them."

"Savannah, you have a good night. One more thing before you go. Why don't you and the children stop by Golden Age tomorrow around noon? We're serving up a great lunch for our members. You three can be my special guests."

Savannah laughed inwardly at how she and Antonio always referred to their adult offspring as kids or children. But that's exactly what they were to them. No matter how old the children got, they'd still be babies to their parents. "We just might do that, Antonio. I'll check to see if the kids are okay with the plan. Should I call you in the morning to let you know?"

"That's not necessary, since the luncheon is going to happen anyway. I'll just look out for you. If I don't see you at noon, or shortly thereafter, then I'll know something else came up."

"You're too sweet, but I'll call you in the morning. I don't want to deprive myself of hearing your cheerful voice. You're always so upbeat, and it's kind of contagious."

"In that case, maybe we shouldn't hang up," Antonio joked. "If this conversation gets any more encouraging, I might not get to sleep tonight." Antonio sighed hard. "Savannah, I know this is all so new for you. You can rest assured that I'm not a man who hurries through life. Each delectable moment should be savored. I make it a point not to rush headlong into anything I do. However, you should know that I believe we can build up a very meaningful relationship. What I'm already feeling with you is so different from anything I've felt since I've been widowed. On that last note, I'm going to say good-night to you, Savannah. Sleep tight."

Without further ado, Antonio disconnected the phone lines.

Still holding the phone in her hand, Savannah marveled at the amazingly warm sensations coursing through her. She once again admitted to herself that she hadn't felt this alive in a long time. Antonio's last statements had left her in somewhat of a mystical daze.

As Savannah thought about what she was feeling, she made a conscious effort not to compare it to anything she'd ever felt before. In regards to Antonio being the only man she'd dated as a widow, there was no comparison, period, since there'd been no one before him.

Wondering if the kids were still awake, because at least another hour had already slipped by since she'd last checked the time, Savannah got up and then put her slippers on. She wasn't dressed for bed yet, but she decided to hold off on her nightly rituals until after she saw what Kevin and Madison were up to.

The television could be heard playing as Savannah made her way up the hallway. She always found it hard to believe that there were so many people in the world who could watch television for hours on end. She wasn't that much into the boob tube, but she did love listening to the radio and her CDs. She could remember a time when her parents only had one television, but now everyone seemed to have a set in every room in the house, including her. All the bedrooms in Savannah's home were equipped with television sets; a big screen was located in the family room.

A small thirteen-inch TV was mounted up under one of the maple cabinets in the kitchen.

No sooner had Savannah stepped into the family room, than she stopped dead in her tracks. Her emotions immediately bubbled up at the sweetly innocent sight before her. Seated in an upright position on the sofa, with the sides of their heads joined together at a tilted angle, Kevin and Madison had dozed off. Savannah then noticed that their hands were also entwined.

The two young adults looked so beautiful to Savannah. Kevin held this girl in such high esteem, as Madison did him. In that very instant Savannah prayed for their union and she also asked the Lord that one would never find cause to disappoint or hurt the other. With no desire to wake the sleeping couple and send them off to their guest bedrooms, though she thought she should for the sake of their comfort, Savannah started to back out of the room.

It was then that Kevin awakened and saw Savannah about to retreat. Carefully, he cradled Madison's head and rested it upon his shoulder. His arm then went around her shoulders. "Sorry we fell asleep on you," he whispered. "I guess we missed the last part of the movie."

Savannah smiled sweetly, looking a tad guilty. "You have that all turned around, Kevin. I fell asleep on you two. Don't you remember that I went back to the bedroom to lie down while you and Madison watched the movie?"

Kevin nodded in the affirmative. "I do now."

"Well, I'm just now getting up. I was down longer than I had anticipated. Then, just when I was about to return to the family room, Antonio phoned. That conversation lasted for an hour."

Madison awakened with a start. She then looked up at Kevin, as though he were her hero. "Gosh, what time is it, Kevin? How long was I asleep?"

Kevin put two of his long, slender fingers under Madison's chin, tilting it up slightly. A light kiss to her lips came next. "It's a little after eleven. Since we both fell asleep, I don't know how long it's been. But my guess is that it had to be an hour or more."

Savannah walked across the room and seated herself in the leather recliner. "It looks like we all fell asleep, Madison, yet I'm still ready to go back to bed for the night. We've had a busy weekend, not to mention how hard we've all worked on getting the house in order. Does anyone want a late-night snack?" Savannah inquired of her two houseguests.

"None for me," Kevin responded. "What about you, Madison?"

Madison shook her head in the negative. "All the popcorn I ate earlier did it for me."

"In that case, I'm going back to bed. Before I go, I need to run something by you." Savannah began telling Kevin and Madison about Antonio's invitation.

"It's cool with me, Mom. It should be fun getting to see what happens when a bunch of old folks get together."

Savannah gently scolded Kevin by wagging her finger back and forth in the air. "You're never too old for me to wash out that mouth of yours with soap and water. I don't think I like being referred to as 'old folk.' Besides that, you'd better be careful with your insults. You *will* be one of those old folks someday. That's a given, Kevin Richmond."

Kevin laughed, looking a bit sheepish. "Sorry, Mom. I didn't mean to offend you. I apologize for being disrespectful."

"I accept your apology, Kevin." Savannah stood. "Good night, guys. See you in the a.m."

Savannah smoothed down her cream-colored dress slacks after she got out of the car. The lime-green sweater set she wore was right in tune with the colors of spring. The strapless leather sandals she wore were nearly the same tone as her sweater. As she'd carefully dressed for the luncheon, she had found herself hoping that Antonio liked whatever she wore.

Kevin came around the car and held out an arm for each of his stunning companions to take hold of. Madison looked adorable in her frilly lavender, white and cornflower blue flowered top and a pair of white pants. Madison and Kevin were practically matching since he'd opted to wear his new lavender shirt; his pants were light beige.

Kevin began moving toward the door of Golden Age. "I hope lunch is ready to be served. I'm starving."

Savannah looked at her son in astonishment. "After all those pancakes you gobbled down this morning? Amazing!"

Kevin frowned. "That was at six o'clock this morning, Mom. It's now ten minutes to twelve. I'm also over six feet tall. This big old boy needs a lot of fuel to run on."

Savannah laughed at the expression on Kevin's face. "I guess. But please mind your manners. And don't ask for seconds."

"What if it's buffet style?" Kevin asked Savannah.

"You still need to be mindful of how much you take. They're feeding an entire host of people, not just you."

Madison reached up and stroked Kevin's cheek. "If you don't get full, we can always get something else to eat after we leave here, Kevin. You do require a lot of food, but you don't want to run the risk of embarrassing your mom in front of Mr. Delabay. Okay, Kev?"

Smiling broadly, Kevin eyed Madison adoringly. "I get it, Madison. But I'd never intentionally embarrass my mom or you. Since everyone has straightened me out, and I have retained the lessons on proper etiquette, let's please go inside."

The two women in Kevin's life laughed heartily at the funny face he pulled.

Antonio was standing right inside the door when Savannah and her guests arrived, but he hadn't seen them yet. The middle-aged woman he was talking to was quite attractive and dressed very smartly in a designer pantsuit, Savannah noted. The way the woman was smiling up into Antonio's face, in a knowing way, gave Savannah an uneasy feeling in the pit of her stomach.

Praying that this wasn't going to be an awkward situation for her and her family, Savannah grabbed a hold of Madison's hand, as if she needed comforting. Upon feeling the tension in Savannah's grip, and then seeing the look of uncertainty on her face, Madison squeezed Savannah's hand in a reassuring manner.

As though Antonio had somehow felt Savannah's presence, he rushed right over to where she stood, leaving the other lady's side without any explanation. "My dear Savannah, I'm so glad you all made it," Antonio enthused, taking Savannah into his arms for a brief but tender hug. "Let me finish up my business with Ms. Baker and I'll be right back." Antonio hugged Savannah again, whispering something into her ear that caused her to blush.

Curious as to what had Savannah glowing like a Christmas lightbulb, Madison leaned in to her. "What did he say to you? You're blushing from head to toe."

Savannah smiled mischievously. "I could tell you, Madison, but then I'd have to kill you," she joked, laughing softly. "Just kidding, Madison. 'You look absolutely ravishing. Thanks for making my day by just being here.' That was all he said to me, honey."

Kevin looked over at his mom. "Looks like we're having a social hour before we eat. I hope no one but me can hear my stomach growling."

Savannah gave Kevin a mildly scolding glance. "Behave yourself, Kevin. Please."

Antonio was back in a flash, smiling all over himself, holding out his arm for Savannah to take. "Let me escort my special guests to the table reserved for us. Lunch will be served in about five minutes."

A covert glance over her shoulder allowed Savannah to see the look of utter displeasure on Ms. Baker's pretty face. *Uh-oh, it appears as if somebody's toes have been stepped on.* Savannah hoped that she hadn't caused any unrest for the other woman, but there was no other explanation for Ms. Baker's disapproving expression. Savannah had to admit to herself that she was highly curious about the woman Antonio had been talking to upon their arrival.

"I hope you guys are good and hungry," Antonio mentioned.

Kevin moaned lightly. "You have no idea, Mr. Delabay," he said in a joking manner.

Savannah immediately shot Kevin another warning glance.

The tables were decorated beautifully, dressed with linens done in soft pastels. Crystal bowls of colorful spring flowers and floating rosebud candles served as center-pieces. The china and silverware were of fine quality, as well as the crystal drinking glasses.

Savannah had to wonder if something special was going on today at Golden Age, although Antonio hadn't mentioned any special occasion to her. She just couldn't imagine this kind of table finery being used for a regular lunch day at the senior center. Everything was elegantly decorated and had been created in such remarkably good taste.

The table that Antonio had directed his guests to was up in the front, positioned in the very center of the room, facing the stage and podium that overlooked the entire dining area. Once he saw that everyone was seated comfortably, Antonio excused himself, assuring his guests that he'd return to the table in a matter of minutes.

Savannah was curious about the fifth chair at their table. As she looked around the dining room, she saw that all the other tables were outfitted with at least six chairs. No sooner than she grew comfortable with the fact that only her family and their host were to occupy this table, Antonio came back with none other than the attractive Ms. Baker hanging on to his right arm.

After Antonio pulled out the remaining chair for Ms.

Baker, he made all the proper introductions. Everyone then gave a polite greeting to each other. Then he left the table again, once he'd politely excused himself again. This time Antonio headed toward the stage.

Savannah eyed Antonio with deep curiosity as she watched him go up on stage and then pick up the microphone. It was hard for her to relax in the presence of the other woman, though she wasn't exactly sure why she suddenly felt so tense. Savannah could only hope that Antonio wouldn't dare to seat her and her family at the same table with a woman that might also have a romantic interest in him. If that was the case, Antonio Delabay was already a man who'd merely held a minuscule time frame in Savannah's history.

Antonio tapped the microphone to see if it was on. Satisfied that it was in good working order, he began to speak. "I first want to thank you all for showing up for this very special occasion. It is a pleasure to have you here and to serve you on this beautiful day, another day that the Lord has made. I'd also like to introduce you to my special guests." He then called Savannah and her family by name, asking each to stand for a brief moment so that everyone could see them. After Savannah and her crew were reseated, Antonio asked that all other visitors stand so they could also be acknowledged. A round of applause followed the acknowledgments.

"As all of our members are aware, at Golden Age, we do a celebratory luncheon for those who have birthdays within the same month. Today we are celebrating our April birthdays. Ms. Veronica Baker is our sole honoree. She is our only member with a birthday this month. Ms. Baker, please stand up as we all join our voices together in singing happy birthday to you!"

Savannah let go of a huge sigh of relief, yet she still felt that the birthday girl might have a very special interest in the man she herself was definitely romantically interested in. Savannah knew that her suspicions would just have to remain to be seen for now.

Chapter 6

Savannah had been sitting in her car for about twenty minutes. After dropping off Kevin and Madison in the Southwest Airlines departure area, she'd had to find a safe place outside the perimeters of the Ontario airport terminals to pull over and park her car. Seeing Kevin leaving for San Francisco had been more painful than she'd anticipated. Alone again was how she saw it. Madison was one of most delightful young persons she'd ever had the pleasure of meeting. Savannah had grown very fond of Madison and she'd miss her son's girlfriend, too, like crazy.

Kenya had yet to phone her mother since her visit. That issue only added to Savannah's sadness. She'd been so sure that Kenya would've called long before now. It was not above Savannah to break down and call Kenya, since she had always been the one to take the bull by the horns; she had hoped that Kenya might extend the olive branch for a change. Kevin had tried to call his sister before they'd left for the airport, but he'd only received the answering device.

Savannah wiped her tears and nose again and then deposited the wet tissue in the small plastic trash liner she kept in her car. Although she now felt emotionally stable enough to drive, she thought she'd continue to sit for another few minutes. There were several more hours that she had to get through before Antonio was to pick her up for dinner at his place.

As Savannah thought about the things that had transpired during the luncheon yesterday, she had to laugh. Just as she'd suspected, the widowed Veronica Baker did have a serious crush on Antonio. As for Antonio's part in it, his place in Savannah's history had been graciously extended, right after she learned that all the birthday folks sat at Antonio's table.

Veronica had flirted openly with Antonio, making him feel very uncomfortable. She had also made mention of him being the most eligible bachelor in the Inland Empire. It had blown Savannah's mind when he had corrected Veronica in a very comical way, telling her that he had taken himself off the auction block from the moment he and Savannah had had their first date.

Veronica's claws had come unsheathed the moment Antonio had revealed his romantic intent toward Savannah. Savannah had later wished that Antonio had held off his announcement about them dating each other until the end of the luncheon. Veronica had gone out of her way to put Savannah on notice once she'd found out. As far as Veronica was concerned, until Antonio remarried he was still fair game; she made sure Savannah was aware of her intent to continue to pursue Antonio. The lady wasn't one to mince words, telling Savannah just how she felt.

Antonio had told Savannah that he wasn't aware of the names on the April birthday list when he'd invited her and the kids to the luncheon. He had assured her that he would've thought twice about it had he known it was Ms. Baker's birthday, let alone the only one for the month. He was very aware of the attraction she still felt for him, but he'd done nothing to encourage her. Antonio had then thought some good might come out of her meeting Savannah. Perhaps, when Veronica realized his personal interest lay elsewhere, she'd finally stop her hot pursuit of him.

Unfortunately, Antonio's thoughts hadn't panned out.

After removing her cell phone from its brace on the dashboard, Savannah dialed Bernice's home. With so much time on her hands, she thought it would be nice to pay her old friend a visit. Although she had recently seen her friend at church, they had only talked on the phone twice since Savannah's last trip to Bernice's home. When Bernice's answering machine picked up the phone, Savannah disconnected the call and then dialed Bernice's cell number.

Savannah smiled upon hearing Bernice's voice. "Don't you ever stay at home? You have to be one of the busiest ladies in San Bernardino County."

"Hey, Savannah, what's happening with you, girl? This is so funny. I just left your house. I'm in your hood and thought I'd stop by to see the new home. Where are you?"

"Just left Ontario Airport, headed home. Are you still in the vicinity of my place?"

"I'm about midway down your street. Just pulled out of

the driveway a minute ago. I can go back and wait for you if you'd like. I really don't mind waiting until you get here. I'm really eager to see how you've decorated everything."

"I'm rolling, Bernice. Be there in less than fifteen minutes."

"Okay, Savannah. See you then. Be safe."

Savannah noticed right away that Bernice had several passengers crammed in her car. That surprised her because Bernice hadn't mentioned having anyone with her. Savannah didn't mind the extra company, but it would've been nice had she been informed. Savannah easily dismissed her thoughts since it was no big deal. Clara White, Janice Morris, Marie Clayton and Madge Jacoby, all of them widows or divorcees, got out of the car at the same time Bernice did.

Instead of pulling into the garage, Savannah parked her car right next to Bernice's.

After warmly greeting each of the women, Savannah led them into her home. She then gave her guests a thorough tour of her humble abode, starting with the formal areas, where the sofas and matching chairs were fashioned in a silky-satiny material boasting a beautiful white rose pattern. Much to Savannah's pleasure, genuine compliments flowed freely from her guests, along with several loud *oohs* and *ahs*. She'd done a lot of hard work in decorating her new home and it was a pleasure for Savannah to have people admire her handiwork.

Marie pointed to the set of black dolls dressed in stunning, colorful African attire. "Where'd you get these beauties, Savannah?" Marie asked.

Savannah gently fingered a doll's rich silk dressing gown.

"At an international bazaar held in L.A. several years ago. I purchased quite a few of my African artifacts at the same place. The African paintings were obtained from a variety of studios and art shows."

"The dolls and the paintings are very beautiful, Savannah. Everything in your home is exquisite," Janice said.

Savannah smiled. "Thank you."

Once the tour was over, Savannah directed the women into her spacious kitchen, where she planned to brew up a pot of tea and set out a few snack items. She loved playing hostess to her family and friends. In fact, Savannah loved to entertain in her home, period.

"Please have a seat when you're ready. I'm going to whip up something for us to munch on. Is hot tea okay with everyone? I have other beverages if you'd like something different."

Everyone but Marie agreed that the hot tea would be fine; Marie preferred a soft drink.

Bernice stood at the French doors, looking out at the large backyard. "You sure have a lot of land back here, Savannah. Have you made a decision on the pool yet?"

Savannah laughed lightly, busily making her way around the kitchen. "They start the dig in a couple of weeks or so. That's why you only see plants, flowers and shrubs at the very edge of the perimeters. The pool company also has to take part of the fence down to get the equipment inside the yard. The job would've been much easier had the builder not made us wait until after the closing to start on the pool. The sod was a standard item for this particular floor plan, but it would've been a total waste of money if my friend's niece hadn't been able to use it in her yard. The

Miller-Brown family came over and dug up the amount of sod needed."

Bernice looked at Savannah and chuckled. "I'm surprised you decided to do the pool. You didn't seem to care too much for the one you had in L.A. What made you change your mind about having one put in, Savannah?"

After filling up the teakettle with bottled water, Savannah set in on the burner and turned on the gas flame. "Oh, I thought long and hard about it. It was actually Kevin who convinced me to go ahead and get the pool. The newer ones are also more energy efficient. Every feature, including the Jacuzzi, can be controlled from a panel that'll be installed inside the house. It's also self-chlorinating and I'm having an automatic water fill line installed. Unlike the older one, this pool will pretty much be maintenance free."

Bernice nodded her head up and down. "That should take the guesswork out of it for you. I remember that you wouldn't even touch the controls on the other one."

Savannah laughed as she carried the teapot and cups over to the table. "Never learned how to work the equipment, period. That pool was Geoffrey's baby."

Once Savannah set out on the table a port-wine cheese ball, spinach dip and chips, a tray of crackers and a platter of cookies, she joined her guests. Upon Savannah's request, Janice passed the blessing over the food. Every head bowed for the prayer of thanksgiving.

Conversation began to flow at a steady pace among the six women. Current news events were discussed, along with a brief chat on the subject of politics. The ladies had a lot to say about the horrific things going on in and around the world of today.

"Savannah, I hear you're dating," said the widow Madge, smiling with sheer devilment.

Bernice's eyes widened. The expression on her face let Savannah know that Madge hadn't heard a thing about Savannah's private affairs from Bernice's lips.

Savannah stroked her chin thoughtfully. She wasn't thrilled that the subject had come up, but she wasn't going to shy away from it. She and Antonio hadn't so much as shared a kiss yet, but Savannah had to admit that she looked forward to the day they'd share a bit of intimacy. "Yeah, I am dating, Madge. Nothing serious between us, though. Since you felt comfortable enough to ask me abut it, I guess it won't hurt for me to ask you the source of your information."

As if to dismiss any concern Savannah might have, Madge waved her hand in the air. "Sister Baker mentioned it to me early this morning at our civic breakfast meeting."

Clara, a widow also, grunted loudly. "Sister Baker! That nosy heifer's always up in somebody's personal business… and she can't even take care of her own affairs. You're crazy for repeating anything she has to say. If her lips move, she's lying. She's such a busybody…and too busy running up after Antonio Delabay."

Madge sucked her teeth. "Don't you think I already know all that," Madge huffed. "He lost interest in her shortly after they'd first started dating."

"Ladies," Bernice said, "this isn't something we should be discussing."

Madge looked puzzled. "Why not? Everyone knows how nosey Veronica Baker is."

Savannah laughed nervously. "Because Antonio Delabay is the man I've been out with a few times. Are you saying

Sister Baker didn't mention that to you as well, Madge?" Savannah was really upset over the revelation that Antonio and Ms. Baker had been dating, but she wasn't going to show it. Antonio certainly hadn't given off that impression. It seemed to Savannah that Madge Jacoby just might have a hidden agenda in springing the news on her the way she had.

Madge didn't even look embarrassed. "No, she didn't mention it. I'm so sorry, Savannah. I had no idea you were seeing Antonio. Forgive me for bringing this up. I really didn't know."

Savannah felt that Madge was lying through her teeth, but she had no proof. This thing had gotten messy and she didn't like messes, especially the kind jealous women created. Savannah couldn't be positive, but Madge seemed to have a little jealous streak running right through her back. For the life of Savannah, she couldn't figure out why she'd be envious of her.

"Antonio is a great catch. Savannah, you're very lucky," Janice chimed in.

Savannah looked nonplussed. "*And I'm not?* But as far as him being a great catch, I'm not looking at him as a fish in a pond. I'm not out to catch anything, especially not a chill."

Recently divorced, Janice looked abashed. "You are a good catch, and he's very lucky, too. I didn't mean to offend you, Savannah."

Savannah shrugged, deciding to bite back the acid on her tongue. Janice didn't seem at all like a troublemaker to her. "No harm, no foul, Janice. I know you didn't mean any harm. Antonio and I are only friends, but we're both hoping for more. Our conversations have turned a little flirtatious lately."

Bernice looked intensely interested in the subject matter. "Girl, I think that's so great! How is Kevin with everything?"

Savannah's thoughts warmed instantly. "Just as I'd expected. He was fine with it." She then told the women how Kevin had invited Antonio over to her house without her knowledge.

"How'd all that turn out?" Marie queried, her eyes wide with curiosity.

Savannah smiled weakly. "It was good, for the most part, until my Kenya decided to show off. She clearly doesn't like Antonio. It's her head doing the talking, not her heart. Kenya hasn't even given Antonio a ghost of a chance, so none of this can be flowing from her heart."

"Do you think she'll come around, eventually?" Bernice inquired.

Savannah shrugged with nonchalance. "Who knows? I'm not going to worry myself to death over what Kenya thinks or feels. She's my daughter. Not the keeper of my castle."

Laughter once again rang out among the ladies.

Marie sighed hard. "I don't know why our kids try to interfere in grown folks' business. Carter Jr. vehemently opposes the idea of me dating. Not that anyone has asked me out yet. But Carter Jr. is going to give me the absolute blues if it ever comes to pass. You all know how close he and my ex-husband are. Carter Jr. is a carbon copy of Carter Clayton Sr."

"It'll happen for you—and Carter Jr. will come to accept

it. Your son is crazy about you, too," Bernice told Marie. "He just happens to love both his parents, as it should be."

Janice frowned. "The shortage of eligible men is the real culprit. The majority of black men are incarcerated, gay, or already married. Trenton Morris was always the only man for me—never dreamed I'd be interested in ever meeting anyone else. But I am! More than any one of you could ever know. When Trenton left me, it shook me to the core of my being. Loneliness is the pits. I'm active enough, but the joy of male companionship in my life is sorely missed."

All the women shouted out a hearty amen.

Savannah folded her hands and placed them on the table. "Help me out here, ladies. Do any of you feel that there's something wrong with me seeing Antonio? I think, that as my peers, you all should come clean with me. Am I making a fool of myself by going out with him? Do you all know something about Antonio that I should know, good or bad?" Savannah appeared eager to hear a response from any one of the women, except for Madge.

Since Madge had started in on this particular subject, she thought she should be the one to address Savannah's concerns. Madge smiled at Savannah, reaching over to briefly touch her hand. "There isn't a single thing wrong with Delabay. What's wrong is with all the women who've pegged him ripe for the picking. I happen to know he's a very good man. He served in the military with Branch. My late husband thought the world of him. Military folks always refer to each other by last name. Branch called Antonio 'Delabay' and Antonio referred to Branch as 'Jacoby.' Branch had nothing but good things to say about Antonio. He deeply respected him."

Savannah raised an eyebrow, still very suspicious of Madge's hidden agenda. It was like she was suddenly trying to clean her mess up. "So you all knew him before he was widowed. Were you good friends with his late wife?" Savannah asked Madge, eager to hear her response.

Madge shook her head in the negative, though she looked a bit too sheepish for Savannah's comfort. "That wasn't the case. I only saw Sylvia when we attended the yearly military unit reunions, which came about after both our husbands had retired from service. Branch and Antonio kept in pretty close contact, but we didn't socialize as couples. Why it was that way, I don't know, especially since we once lived in the same area."

"I see," said Savannah, believing Madge knew exactly why it was that way. "Do you all think I should be worried about all these women? As I told Bernice, I don't want to be just another someone in the mix."

"From what I know," Marie offered, "there is no mix. Delabay keeps pretty much to himself at church, other than being heavily involved in many activities. I envy you, Savannah, but only because I wish I'd been blessed enough to meet a man of his caliber. Hearing that you are dating him comes as a real shock to me. Although he has been touted as *eligible*, that's not the impression Delabay gives off. I don't miss my ex, one bit, but I'm lonelier than lonely. Time seems to be running out on this girl. I don't want to be alone when that happens."

Clara shook her head from side to side. "You're not alone in your thinking, Marie. Time is running out on all of us," Clara said on a huge sigh. "When Montgomery passed away, the end of my world came in a flash of blinding light. We'd had our problems in the early stages of our marriage—the few infidelities on his part—but we eventually worked everything through. I can honestly say that the last twenty years of our twenty-eight-year marriage were the best ever. I think the boy suffered greatly through our first seven years, instead of waiting for the seven-year itch to visit him." Clara had to laugh at that. "By year eight he had settled down considerably."

All of the women but Savannah were aware of Montgomery White's infidelity issues. Clara found no shame in sharing her past marital woes. Talking about it and getting advice from others was what had helped to make her so strong throughout her ordeal. She had eventually learned to take the bitter with the sweet. Clara had also learned how to truly forgive.

Forgiveness for Clara meant to never revisit a past issue and continue to throw it up in the face of the perpetrator. In Clara's opinion, to do anything other than let bygones be bygones, were not signs of true forgiveness. She also liked to offer advice to young wives who'd found themselves in the same predicament she'd once found herself in as a newlywed.

"We've all had trials and tribulations in our marriages," Janice remarked. "No matter how sad it is all of our marriages are now a thing of the past. We're lonely women, though not desperate, yet. Admitting our need for male company is a part of the solution. As for our children, we need to be strong in telling them to tend to their own."

"I'm past desperate," Madge joked. "No, not really, but I have to say that I'm getting pretty bad. When a woman my age has to get her passion from between the pages of a romance novel, she's definitely on the verge of desperation. I read a least five steamy novels a week. So, with all that said, Savannah, you have to get your needs met. If Antonio can help do that for you, don't worry about what anybody says, does, or thinks. You have my blessings."

Savannah nodded in response to what Madge had had to say, but the jury was still out on the final analysis. If there was malicious intent on her part, Savannah knew it would come out eventually. It always did.

For the next half hour or so the women continued to discuss Savannah's concerns, with everyone being extremely supportive of the relationship. By the time all was said and done Savannah felt quite comfortable in continuing to date Antonio Delabay, but she also planned to dig further into his relationship with Veronica. It was one thing for him to sit them at the table together, but if he and Ms. Baker were dating, that was another matter entirely.

Savannah didn't know how she could continue getting together with Antonio if he was involved with another woman at the same time. If any other obstacles should arise in their budding relationship, she had decided she'd deal with them at that time. Savannah simply wasn't into borrowing trouble, especially someone else's.

Antonio's companionship and loyalty was something Savannah deeply desired.

Antonio's grayish colored stucco home was a rather large one: six bedrooms and five full baths from what he'd told Savannah. Unlike her, it appeared that he possibly hadn't downsized when he'd moved up to the Inland Empire. Of course she didn't know the square footage of his previous home in L.A., but she couldn't imagine that it had been any larger than this one, which included both formals, a spacious study and a country-size kitchen. An Olympic-size swimming pool, a pool house, and pea gravel decking graced the vast property on the backside of his home.

The ultramodern furnishings and accents were quite elegant; not nearly as manly as Savannah had expected, except for Antonio's humongous all-leather furnished upstairs den, burgundy in color. Of course, a sixty-five-inch Sony big screen filled one entire wall, along with all the other state-of-the-art audio-visual equipment he owned. The hardwood entertainment center was done in cherrywood, as well as the magnificently designed coffee and end tables.

Savannah was impressed with the way Antonio had so beautifully set the table for the evening meal. The man seemed to know all about fine linens and proper place settings. The china, crystal and silverware were extremely refined, much like he himself was. His culinary skills had also been proven by the delicious Italian dinner he'd prepared for her previously. The glowing candlelight lent such a nice, romantic ambiance to the spacious room.

Savannah was very happy that her peers hadn't given her any derogatory information on Antonio, the kind that may've had her changing her mind about getting better acquainted with him. She didn't even want to think about how unhappy that would've made her feel, but she knew she had to watch this thing with Ms. Baker. Bernice had later assured her that she'd had no knowledge of them dating ever, which had also made her wonder why Madge had brought it up.

Antonio pulled out Savannah's chair and then patiently waited for her to be seated at the dining room table. Deep appreciation glinted in his eyes for the stunning red silk dress she wore.

The stylish article of clothing hugged her sensuously in all the right places. Since he'd complimented her earlier, he didn't want to overdo the flattery bit. Despite her having carried two children, she still had a college-girl figure. He even liked the matching red pumps she wore on her small feet. Antonio saw this graceful woman as a very precious work of rare art.

Savannah's gentle beauty and sincere sweet nature continued to astound Antonio.

Antonio tenderly placed his hand on Savannah's shoulder. "Would you care for a glass of wine, Savannah? I've chosen a fine red one to go along with the prime rib."

Savannah tingled all over at the lusty way in which Antonio had said her name. He seemed to take such pleasure in just letting it slip slowly off his tongue. "That would be nice, Antonio. Thank you. But only if you're having a glass, too," she added.

Antonio grinned. "Just one glass for me, Savannah. I have to drive you home later on."

Savannah smiled sweetly. "I appreciate your cautiousness. One glass of wine is all I ever have at any given time. It's a rare occasion for me to have a drink, period. Moderation is the key to everything, Antonio."

Not everything, Antonio mused, knowing how hard it was for him to practice restraint when he was in Savannah's company. There was nothing moderate about his desire to spend every waking moment with her. It was as if he couldn't get enough of her. Ever since he'd met her she was the first thing on his mind when he awakened in the mornings and his last thought before closing his eyes at night.

Antonio had tried hard not to focus so much of his attention on Savannah, but he'd failed miserably at it. This beautiful woman had taken him over by storm. Antonio didn't know what tomorrow held for them, but he sure hoped his future days included many hours spent with her.

"You should only drink the amount you're comfortable with. Too many folks do things to try and fit in with someone else's game plan." Antonio walked away, but turned and came right back. "Please excuse me, Savannah. Think you can deal with a little bit of Miles Davis?"

Savannah smiled warmly. "A man after my own heart. Miles knows how to do it for me."

In a matter of seconds the heady jazzy notes from Miles's trumpet swept into the dining room like a warm summer breeze. The melodic music was relaxing and soothing. If this wasn't the perfect setting for a romantic interlude, then she didn't know what one was. Savannah liked the subtlety of it all. She didn't feel as if she was being outright seduced, yet she felt seductive. Remembering what Antonio had said about him never being in a hurry made Savannah smile.

This quiet evening shouldn't be rushed, not under any circumstances, Savannah mused.

Antonio was back in a flash, carefully placing before Savannah a crystal glass half-filled with the dark red Merlot. "Don't think I'm being cheap with the wine. I thought you might prefer to start out with a little rather than a whole lot. The other half glass is just chilling out."

Savannah laughed softly. "I love your sense of humor. Thanks for being so thoughtful."

Antonio winked at Savannah in a knowing way. "I'm glad I can make you laugh and smile. Laughter is a great antidote for whatever ails us. Smiles are also healing."

Savannah's lovely smile showed Antonio that she was in agreement with his remarks. Antonio excused himself again. After making several trips between the dining room and the kitchen, he'd managed to bring in all the food and set it on the table. Antonio then took the seat at the head of the table. Savannah was seated to the right of him, close enough for him to reach over and touch her delicate hand, which had him hoping for an opportunity to do so. Touching Savannah also brought Antonio great pleasure. A prayer of thanksgiving came next.

The fresh garden salads, complemented by Antonio's specialty homemade buttermilk salad dressing, were consumed first by Savannah and Antonio. The variety of mixed salad greens was crisp and tasty and the vine-ripe cherry tomatoes were firm and garden sweet.

The first bite of prime rib had Savannah closing her eyes to savor the delicious taste of it. Slowly roasted to absolute perfection, the expensive cut of beef was tender enough to simply melt against the palate. The fresh asparagus was as tempting as the meat and was just as tender, though each stalk was crispy through and through. Slightly cooked carrot and celery straws and thinly sliced mushrooms had been sautéed into the fluffy white rice. Homemade yeast rolls, fresh, soft and warm, made by Antonio himself, were butter filled and tasted utterly divine.

By the delightful expression on Savannah's face Antonio

didn't have to ask her if the meal had been prepared to her satisfaction. She looked as if she had just sampled a magnificent slice of paradise. Savannah hoped the delicate peach and cherry tarts she'd baked for dessert would bring Antonio's palate just as much pleasure as the main entrees had brought to hers.

Antonio couldn't help wondering what Savannah might look like after a passionate lovemaking session. He could only imagine the angelic afterglow that would undoubtedly soften her pretty face even more. Her hair would probably be in beautiful disarray and her lips would more than likely be swollen from his soft but ardent kisses. Knowing that he shouldn't be thinking of wondrous moments such as these, he instantly stopped himself from conjuring up any more vibrant images of a passion-filled Savannah.

Over dessert Antonio told Savannah about his military career as a helicopter pilot. He had seen combat in both Desert Storm and Desert Shield. Antonio's job had required him to operate VIP flights, which entailed him flying high-ranking officials from one base to another. Flying in itself was a dangerous enough occupation, but when flying in, through and around combat zones, the ever-present dangers increased greatly. The skills of the best of military pilots were constantly tried and tested, more so during war than at any other time.

Savannah found herself respecting Antonio even more. It took a very special man or woman to make a career in the military. Service to one's native country wasn't for everyone. Courage figured in as well. Fighting in a war was surely a scary thing for the young men and women who made up the armed forces. Fighting in a senseless one had to be even scarier.

The admiration for Antonio burned brightly in Savannah's gaze. "Sounds like you had an exciting but dangerous career, Antonio. I thank God you survived it all. There are many of you who didn't, and many who still aren't surviving the war today in Iraq."

Antonio looked grim faced. "Too many, Savannah. Way too many young folks dying."

Savannah pursed her lips. "During Desert Storm and Desert Shield it was our friends dying young, now it's our children who are being killed in foreign places like Iraq. The reasons for countries declaring war elude me. Military service is such a thankless job. Many civilians still have no clue about what's sacrificed on their behalf by members of our armed forces."

Antonio nodded in agreement. "Some folks will never get it. Too many people take military service for granted. Being on alert twenty-four hours, seven days a week is unimaginable to most. Dedicated members don't complain. They just get the job done as quickly and as effectively as possible. You seem so passionate about what you were saying. Are any of your family members or close friends enlisted or commissioned into the armed forces?"

Savannah battled with her emotions. When her first cousin, Darren Mitchell, was killed in Desert Storm it was one of the worst days of her life. The two of them had been very close. Darren had been drafted into the United States Army back then. "There have been several, Antonio, both family and friends. Also, as a nurse, I have seen the ravages to the bodies of young men and women, casualties of war and everyday military service. Many folks aren't aware of the numerous accidental deaths that occur as a result of just being in the service."

Savannah went on to tell Antonio about her cousin's untimely death.

Although Darren had been proud to serve his country, the days before his departure had been fearful for him, as if he'd had a premonition that he might not return home. Darren had told Savannah all about his fears, making her promise not to reveal his grave concerns to his parents or his siblings. Her father and her two uncles had also served their country in World War II, but no physical harm had come to any of them. Several of Savannah's male high school classmates had also died in Desert Storm. Gone too soon while fighting in a war none of them understood.

"I'm deeply sorry for your loss, Savannah."

"What made you want to go into the service, Antonio?"

Looking thoughtful, Antonio shrugged. "There are numerous reasons, Savannah. For one thing, I wanted to continue my education beyond four years of college. I accomplished that under the GI Bill, at Uncle Sam's expense. Becoming a pilot was a dream come true. As a veteran, buying a home was made possible for me by low interest rates and with little or no money for the down payment. Lifetime health-care benefits were also a consideration. I did not fear going to war at the time I was commissioned, although I should have. I just saw the endless possibilities offered to servicemen and women. When we're young, we think we're invincible, anyway."

Savannah was impressed with everything Antonio had had to say. She admired him more than he'd ever know.

His courage was highly commendable. "I'd love to hear about your family and how you grew up, Antonio. That is, if you don't mind sharing."

Antonio grinned, relaxing back in his chair. "It would be my pleasure, Savannah."

Antonio Delabay had been born and raised in Macon, Georgia. His late father and mother, Langston and Murietta, had been good parents to him and his two brothers, David and Carmichael. The Delabays, as God-fearing folks, had reared up their sons in the church, having taught them good Christian and moral values. The Lord had been the head of their household.

The loving couple had owned a couple of convenience stores, which their sons had worked hard in as teenagers to help make them a success story. The young men were taught that hard work never hurt anyone. Several years after both parents had passed away, Antonio and his brothers had sold the stores to another independent store owner. The decision to sell the stores was later regretted by all the brothers, but the realized profits had been much greater than what each of them might eventually achieve through a lifetime of hard work. However, the Delabay sons still owned the prime Georgia property that the stores had been built upon.

Antonio's two brothers lived in Atlanta and both were very close to Antonio's children. Each sibling had two offspring, a boy and a girl. The six cousins were also very close, but the three young women had an occasion to clash every now and then, mostly about insignificant, silly stuff, the kind that didn't leave permanent scars. Their love for sports kept the young men connected, but not always on the same page. Family was important to all of them. Antonio told Savannah that the Delabay get-togethers were always off the hook, but not always without contention. Theirs was a typical loving-one-minute and fighting-the-next-minute type of family.

When asked by Antonio, Savannah shared with him how her desire to become a nurse had come at an early age. A couple of visits to the doctor's office had aroused inside her a deep intrigue for the women and men in starched whites. Then, with a weeklong hospital stay, after she'd had her tonsils removed, all Savannah had been able to talk about was becoming a nurse so she could help people and feed little kids ice cream, the alleged cure-all for tonsillectomies.

After Savannah finished up her story, Antonio got to his feet. "I'm going to clear the table so we can move into the family room, where we can sit back and relax for a spell."

Savannah stood. "I'll help you out, Antonio."

Antonio took hold of Savannah's hand. "That's not necessary, Savannah. You're a guest in my home. Besides that, cleaning up after myself is something I'm quite used to."

Savannah waved off Antonio's remarks. "This guest ate until she was stuffed and she enjoyed every delicious bite. With that said, Mr. Delabay, we're going to work side by side to get this place back in shape. Four hands can work much faster than two."

The expression on Savannah's face brooked no argument so Antonio didn't give her one.

Twenty minutes later Savannah and Antonio were comfortably seated in his family room, side by side. A crackling fire burned in the marble fireplace despite the season being spring. Close to the mountain range, Rancho Cuca-monga had the tendency to get rather cool at dusk.

Quincy Jones had taken up where Miles Davis had left off, the chords of his jazz music just as sweet and heady as always. The various vocalists Jones often used on his albums all had excellent, soul-stirring voices. Savannah loved both jazz and rhythm and blues. Love songs from the seventies and eighties were her very favorites.

Careful not to come on too strong, Antonio slipped a gentle arm around Savannah's shoulders. As she looked up at him and into his eyes, his heart felt as if it was melting right inside his chest. Wanting to feel her soft skin against his own, he tenderly pressed his forehead into hers. The soft scent of her perfume caught his nose by surprise, causing him to inhale and then rapidly exhale. Savannah smelled so darn sweet and she looked just as delectable.

Savannah felt comfortable enough with Antonio to allow herself to completely relax and lay her head on his strong shoulder. Loneliness was a thing of the past, if only for this one night. Tomorrow was of no concern to her, especially since it wasn't promised. Being at the center of his undivided attention made her feel so special. Antonio had warmly welcomed her into his home and had prepared for her one of the best meals she'd ever eaten. Savannah couldn't have asked him for more. This wonderful evening held so many promises.

Antonio had taken extra care to create for Savannah a subtle, romantic setting, one that she could truly appreciate. As well as the fireplace being lit, glowing candles also burned here in the family room. It had been important to him that he make this special evening everything she could ever hope for. He knew that all too often the over-forty and near-to-fifty crowd found themselves in a deep rut, bored stiff, with nothing to do but watch television and go to bed. Antonio was a romantic at heart and he would go to any lengths to make happy the woman he was interested in. "Savannah, I trust that everything has been to your liking."

"Everything has been superb." Savannah looked thoughtful for a moment. "Would you mind too terribly, Antonio, if I took my shoes off and put my feet up? I'm feeling pretty tranquil right about now." Showing Antonio her deep appreciation of all that he'd done for her would come easy for Savannah, not to mention the pleasure it would give her.

Antonio's heart swelled. "Please make yourself right at home, my dear." After reaching down and lifting up Savannah's right foot, he removed her stylish red shoe. Antonio then tended to the left pump, removing it as well, taking great pleasure in doing so. "Is that better?"

Savannah smiled lazily, flirtatiously. "Very much so. Thank you, Antonio." Feeling safe and secure with this debonair gentleman, Savannah curled up on the sofa and shut her eyes.

Wiping the sleep from her eyes, wishing that the caller hadn't had the nerve to wake up a retired forty-five-year-old widow at 6:00 a.m., Savannah reached for the telephone. Tears sprang to her eyes the second she saw the familiar number. She had made up her mind before she'd gone to sleep that she wouldn't allow another day to pass by without her phoning her daughter. As she wiped the tears from her eyes, Savannah threw up a silent prayer of thanks to God.

"Mom, it's Kenya. How are you?"

Savannah sat up in the bed, resting her back against the coolness of the headboard. "I'm fine. How about you, Kenya?"

"I'm okay, Mom. I've been a little tired lately. Mom, I need a favor."

Savannah didn't like the tension-filled sound of her daughter's voice. However, she'd hear Kenya out before jumping to any conclusions. "What is it, Kenya?"

"I'd like to come up to Fontana and stay a couple of days. Cole has to go out of town. I don't want to stay here by myself."

Considering that Kenya thought her mother should always be alone Savannah found her daughter's request rather interesting. Although she wasn't keen on being in Kenya's company for more than a few hours at a time, she wouldn't deny her. "When is Cole due to leave?"

"Sometime next week, Mom. I'm not exactly sure of what day he's leaving town. Is it okay for me to visit with you while he's gone?"

No apology from Kenya for her bad behavior, no remorse whatsoever, Savannah mused. She'd allow Kenya to come stay with her, but certain conditions would be placed on the visit—her daughter would adhere to them. "Kenya, you already know that I'm friends with Mr. Delabay. You need to understand that I'm still seeing him despite your rude objections. If you are to be a guest in my home, you'll have to show the utmost respect to anyone and everyone that comes here to visit. Do otherwise, and you'll be asked to leave, immediately. Can you handle that?"

"You've already told me I have no choice in the matter,

Mom. But I think it's pretty sad that you have to give your own kids ultimatums. You're making me feel as if you're choosing that man over us, your own flesh and blood family."

"There is no 'us,' Kenya. No one but you is objecting to Mr. Delabay. Kevin does not share in your sentiments about me dating him, not in the least bit. I've said what I needed to say. No further dialogue on the subject is necessary. The decision to come or not to come here is up to you. If you do decide to visit, please call me the day before you plan to come."

"All right, Mom. Talk to you later."

Savannah shook her head from side to side as she hung up the phone. "That didn't go too well," she told herself. "Oh, well, it is what it is. Kenya can take it or leave it."

After sliding back down in the bed, Savannah pulled the comforter up over her and then closed her eyes. Although she didn't plan on going back to sleep, she felt that her body needed a bit more rest since she'd had such a late night. Time to reflect back on the previous evening's events would also be a nice diversion. Antonio had made her feel like she was the only woman in the world for him. He had such a fantastic way of wooing the opposite sex yet he'd come off as very sincere in trying to win her heart. Just the thought of seeing Antonio again made her smile and then giggle. Conjuring up his handsome face came easy for Savannah.

Antonio had set Savannah's hair on fire last evening and he had then taken his own sweet time in dousing the scorching flames. "What a lovely way to burn!" Savannah shouted.

Their first kiss had been phenomenal. It didn't matter to either of them that the kiss hadn't been deep and passionately invasive. That their lips had come together in a sweet, thrilling sensation had been enough for both Savannah and Antonio. The innocence of it all had actually made him and her look forward to the next time their lips met...and at that very moment they'd both seemed so sure that there'd be a next time.

The second kiss had come right out of the blue, smack dab in the middle of one of her sentences. The sensuality of this lip connection had landed her on a cloud far above the planet Earth. Antonio's eyes had then met with hers in a riveting gaze, right after the kiss was complete. Antonio had seemed to be searching for any indication that Savannah had liked the feel of his mouth on hers. Leaning into him for an encore had told him exactly what'd he'd been hoping for.

The third and final kiss from Antonio had come outside on Savannah's doorstep, when he'd dropped her off at home, just before the bewitching hour of midnight. The intimate gesture had had her wanting to ask him to come inside. Out of consideration for the lateness of the hour, and her reputation, she hadn't asked him to come into the house. Their last kiss had been filled with the kind of heady passion felt by a woman and man who deeply cared for each other.

Savannah had virtually floated into her house after the final encounter. As if the couple hadn't shared enough good times during the evening, Antonio had telephoned Savannah after he'd returned home. The late-night phone call had lasted nearly an hour.

Although Savannah had given a few minutes of thought to Antonio and Ms. Baker, she had vowed not to let it take her over. If and when anything suspicious happened with Ms. Baker over Savannah seeing Antonio, she'd decided that she'd deal with it then—and only then.

Savannah couldn't keep herself from laughing and shouting out a few hallelujahs. She felt really good this morning, better than she'd felt in a long, long time. Thinking that today would be a good day for her to begin volunteering her services at the Silver Wings Senior Center, Savannah dragged herself out of bed to begin her morning toiletry routine.

Chapter 7

As soon as Savannah completely filled out her application for volunteering and then read over the contract rules, she planned to take another short tour of the senior center, though this one was to be unescorted. Mrs. Anna Clifford was busy getting everything ready for the expected lunch crowd, which meant she wasn't able to show Savannah around again this morning.

"Since lunch is less than a half hour from now, Mrs. Richmond, why don't you stay and join us? That'll give you the opportunity to meet some of the other members."

"I'll do that, Mrs. Clifford. I'd love to meet everyone."

Before Savannah left the administrative office to start out the tour on her own, Mrs. Clifford had insisted on Savannah calling her Anna, just like all the other volunteers and members did. Savannah agreed and asked that the favor be returned.

The first stop for Savannah was at the picture boards that

hung on the walls inside the large game room. The majority of the photos were of trips taken and other special events that the senior members had attended as a group. She easily recognized how the women greatly outnumbered the handful of men. It was hard to tell the age of most of the folks in the pictures, but from what Savannah could see, many of these people looked to be a lot older than fifty-five. Age is only a number, she mused, and everyone wasn't photogenic. How many bad pictures had she taken? There was so many of them around that she'd lost count long ago.

Upon hearing footsteps on the tiled floor, Savannah turned to see whom they belonged to. It reminded her of the day Antonio had walked up behind her when she'd visited his senior center. It wasn't Antonio, though, but she really hadn't thought it would be.

The lady now facing Savannah looked to be in her early sixties, her face lined and cracked with more than its fair share of stress. The woman's body was rail thin, but she didn't look undernourished. Her entire head of hair was a steel-gray. Savannah thought she'd look much younger if she had it rinsed or added a temporary color in a softer shade of gray.

"Hello," Savannah said sweetly, extending her hand. "I'm Savannah Richmond."

Withholding her own hand, the woman checked out Savannah from head to toe. When her faded brown eyes reached Savannah's face, she rudely stared hard into it. "I'm Opal Redmond," she said gruffly, "one of the members of the center. Are you a new employee?"

Savannah laughed, shaking her head in the negative. "I

don't work here in an official capacity. I'm a volunteer. I just joined the volunteer staff today. Nice to meet you, Opal."

Opal muttered something under her breath, but Savannah couldn't make out what she'd said. Without uttering any sort of farewell, Opal turned and walked away, leaving behind a bewildered Savannah, who'd gotten the strangest feeling from this encounter. Meeting and making friends with members of the center might not be as easy as she'd imagined. Not wanting to be a pessimist, Savannah quietly convinced herself that all the members couldn't possibly be as unfriendly and rude to her as Opal had been.

Upon Savannah entering the dining room, she saw that the members were already going through the buffet line. As she looked around the room, trying to figure out where to sit, she saw that most of the tables were occupied. She then spotted a table where only one other person was seated, an older gentleman. Hoping he wouldn't turn her away, she started toward his table.

Smiling gently, Savannah stopped in front of the man's chair. "Mind if I join you, sir?"

The gentleman looked up at Savannah and frowned. Then his face suddenly lit up like stadium lights at night. "Not at all, young lady. There's one seat left…and it's all yours."

There were three empty seats left, but Savannah wasn't about to mince words with the handsome, silver-haired man, especially since he could turn out to be an ally. From the hard glares she'd received from some of the other women as she'd crossed the room, she thought she just might need a supporter. The ladies didn't look too happy with her presence. The fact that not one of them, including Opal, had summoned her to sit at their table was a good indication that she might be seen as unwelcome, or perhaps as even an intruder.

Savannah set down her purse on the chair she intended to sit in. "I'm going to get my lunch. Are you in need of anything else, sir?"

The man smiled broadly. "I'm just fine. I'm Noah Westfield. Who are you?"

Fearful of being rejected again, Savannah didn't extend her hand. "Savannah Richmond. We can get acquainted after I go through the buffet line. See you in a minute, Mr. Westfield."

"Just plain old Noah will do," he yelled after Savannah. "Mr. Westfield was my father."

Savannah turned around and acknowledged Noah's request with a bright smile.

After carefully selecting her food items, Savannah placed each one on the bright orange plastic tray. Her plate had more salad greens on it than anything else. To go along with the grilled skinless, boneless chicken breast, she placed on her plate a small amount of fresh green beans and a couple of tiny baked red potatoes. Savannah then filled a large plastic glass with ice and then raspberry tea. As she reached the table, she understood why Noah had said there was only one empty seat. There were now two other robust gentlemen seated at the table with him.

Savannah placed the tray down on the table. Before she could pull out her chair, one of the other gentlemen was Johnny-on-the-spot in taking care of that small task for her, grinning all the while like a Cheshire cat. Savannah groaned within. If these men were among the few eligible widowers that Anna had spoken of, she had probably gotten herself into big trouble.

Chester George and Irwin Lockett wasted no time in introducing themselves to Savannah. Although she was glad to make their acquaintance, their flirtatious stares made her feel as if she was one of the items on the lunch menu—the meat entrée to be more specific.

"Savannah," Chester said, "I can't believe you're a senior citizen. You don't look a day over thirty," he flattered knowingly.

Savannah laughed heartily. "So I've been told, Chester. But I'm not a senior citizen yet. Forty-five is my tender age. I'm here to volunteer my services wherever needed. How long have you guys been members here at Silver Wings?"

Chester ran his fingers through his thick head of silver waves. "My wife, Cordeilia, and I joined this center before her death four years ago. We were both fifty-five when we became members. She loved to come here and play cards despite the fact that some of these old biddies gave her a hard time. A real looker was my Cordeilia. As pretty as you are, I imagine you'll get a hard time around here, too. Competition is real stiff."

Irwin chuckled at Chester's comments. "I joined a year or so after my wife, Connie, passed away. Connie wouldn't have been caught dead in a senior citizens' center. No pun intended. Growing old was a difficult thing for her. She wouldn't tell a single person her age. Had I not met her in our youth, she wouldn't have told me either. She was a real vain girl."

Savannah was still stuck on Chester's warning remarks. He wasn't too far afield in what he'd said about the possibility of her receiving a hard time. She had already felt the distinct chill in the air. Because of her looks she had been given a hard time in high school as well. But she wasn't a teenager and she wasn't afraid to demand respect from others. No one would walk over her, she vowed. Working at a center like this one was supposed to be pleasurable, not painful.

Noah reached over and patted Savannah's hand. "You'll be fine, lass, as long as you stand up for yourself. Whatever you do, don't cower. You appear to be a strong young lady. Don't hesitate to put on the boxing gloves if the need arises."

Savannah raised both of her eyebrows. "Is it really that bad around here?"

"It can be," Irwin said. "You see, with there being a shortage of male members, some of these ladies think they have to fight for first dibs on us good-old boys." He chuckled. "It doesn't seem to matter whether we're interested in them or not. Just by sitting down here with us, you've more than likely made a few enemies already, Ms. Savannah."

"No," Savannah said, sounding shocked. Although she'd earlier wondered if she'd gotten herself into trouble by sitting with these men, having it confirmed for her was a little unsettling. She'd had no way of knowing that the other men would be seated at Noah's table when she'd first chosen to sit with him. Sitting off in the corner alone might've been a better choice. The women had probably labeled her as a loose hussy by now. The thought of that amused her.

Barely able to wait for the lunch hour to be over, Savannah halfheartedly listened to the three men's animated chitchat. Despite being widowers they seemed very happy and content. She was in no doubt that they missed their soul mates, but they seemed to have truly come to terms with their losses. These guys were prime examples that women didn't have a monopoly on gossiping. It sounded to her as if they knew the personal business of everyone in the Inland Empire. Savannah could clearly see that she and her female friends had nothing on these guys when it came down to spreading around all the 411.

"Are you going to stay for the monthly meeting, Savannah?" Noah asked.

Savannah shrugged. "Meeting? I didn't know there was one. What's it about?"

"Brainstorming new ideas for social events and educational programs and going over old business. It can get very interesting. It'll definitely be lively."

"That's for sure," said Irwin on a soft chuckle. "The meetings are where we find out who is who and whose agenda is what. Being a new volunteer and all, you should stay, Savannah."

The last thing Savannah wanted to do was attend a long, drawn out meeting, but if she was to be a part of this center, she should hang around just to see what was up. She might also get ideas on what kinds of things the members expected from the center. "You're right, Irwin. I'll stay." When Noah asked if they could all have her phone number, Savannah agreed to it.

Fifteen minutes into the meeting Savannah was appalled at what was happening in the recreation room. The appointed officers of the senior center were arguing among themselves and no one seemed to be of one accord. The treasurer had been accused of wasting money frivolously by using it on things that weren't necessities. Mrs. Olla Jackson, the treasurer, was clearly on the defensive as she shouted out her vehement denials of the charges. The president, Loretta Ames, was so angry about the monetary situation that she resigned her position right on the spot.

Seated between Irwin and Noah, Savannah kept glancing at each man to try and get a take on what they were thinking. The three men seemed amused by the whole thing. This was obviously what they'd meant when they'd told her things would be lively. Savannah had certainly learned who was who, but she hadn't figured out all the agendas yet. Wondering if she'd made a mistake by volunteering here, Savannah turned her attention back to all the hoopla.

It didn't seem that anybody was going to object to the president resigning. Once all the shouting had calmed down, the vice president, Miriam Preston, told the members that she'd act as interim president until a new one could be elected. It was up to the members as to when the election would be held. More shouting and disagreeing began right after that announcement.

By the time the out-of-control meeting was adjourned, approximately forty-five minutes after it had been called to order, Savannah's head was splitting. She had come up empty after rummaging through her purse for a couple of Tylenol. The small pillbox she normally carried in her bag was nowhere to be found, which had her moaning inwardly. Once she bade friendly farewells to all her male luncheon companions, Savannah made a beeline for the parking lot.

* * *

Right after Savannah let herself into the house, she ran straight into the master bathroom to get a couple of Tylenol for her headache. On the corner of the dressing table was where she discovered the pillbox. She'd obviously forgotten to put it back in her purse once she'd refilled it. Alka-Seltzer and Tylenol were the only two medicines that she'd ever taken. Savannah never forgot during her daily prayers to thank God for her excellent health.

Although Savannah thought a short nap might do her good, she decided not to lie down. There were a lot of things she could do before Antonio came over for a visit later in the evening.

The doorbell rang just as Savannah had finished changing clothes. She had exchanged her dressier duds for a pair of blue denim jeans and a purple-and-gold Lakers sweatshirt. Wondering who could possibly be at the door, since she wasn't expecting anyone, Savannah rushed out of the room and ran toward the front of the house.

Peering through the peephole gave her a clear vision of the African-American man and woman she'd never before seen in her life. The striking pair didn't look as if they were solicitors, but that still didn't help her out in determining just who they might be. "How can I help you?" she shouted through the closed door. Savannah never opened her door to strangers. Home invasion robberies were a common occurrence these days.

"We're your neighbors from a couple of doors down the street, Douglas and Inez Sheffield. We'd like to welcome you to the neighborhood."

Without giving it another thought, Savannah ripped

open the door, smiling neighborly. "Hello! Please come in." Savannah couldn't figure out why she hadn't seen the rectangular baking dish Inez Sheffield held until now. That might've given her a big clue, but she must've been too intent on peering right into their faces, Savannah thought.

The Sheffields quickly stepped into the foyer, smiling pleasantly.

Inez handed the baking dish to Savannah. "We baked you an apple cobbler. Hope you enjoy it. Doug and I own our own bakery. It's located in Rialto, the next city over."

Savannah accepted the baking dish. "Thank you so much, Douglas and Inez. I'm Savannah Richmond. Come on into the living room and have a seat. I've never met bakery owners before. I guess I should let you in on a little secret. I'm addicted to all sorts of pastries."

Douglas and Inez laughed heartily as they followed Savannah down the hall.

Savannah turned around to face her guests just before she reached the living room. "Since this cobbler smells so good, and it feels like it's still warm, I think we should go into the kitchen and have a bite of it," Savannah suggested. "I believe I have some vanilla ice cream on hand."

"That's okay by us," Inez said. "We still love to taste our own baking."

Doug nodded his agreement with Inez's statement.

Once Savannah's guests were comfortably seated, she went right to work on pulling out three bowls, a knife to cut the cobbler, spoons and napkins. She didn't even have a quarter of a carton of ice cream left, but she thought it was more than enough for each of them to have a scoop. Glasses of ice water were the last things she retrieved and then carried over to the table. Savannah joined her guests, smiling as she took a seat.

The first bite of cobbler had Savannah singing the praises of the two pastry chefs. According to the Sheffields, they did all the baking together. They were a team. The delicious pie melted in Savannah's mouth and the ice cream made it taste even better. "My son, Kevin, would walk a country mile to have a taste of this little slice of heaven. He loves pastries, too."

Inez stuck her spoon into the ice cream and just left it there. "I like my ice cream completely melted before I eat it. We're sorry we didn't get over here to see you before now, but we've been on vacation in Europe—Rome for one place. We must've moved in a week or so before you did, and then we were off and running a few days later. We just got home late last night. We're hardly settled into our new home. Boxes are still everywhere."

Savannah had gasped at the mention of the Sheffield's vacation destination. "Rome, the one place I've always wanted to visit." Geoffrey had promised to take Savannah to Italy once they'd both retired. The unfulfilled promise had died right along with him.

"Why haven't you ever gone there on vacation, Savannah?" Douglas asked.

Savannah looked morose. "My husband and I had planned to go one day, but it just never happened. It's too late for us to go there together now."

Inez gave Savannah a questioning glance. "Why's that?"

Wishing she didn't have to reveal bad news to her neighbors on their first visit, Savannah gulped hard. "My husband, Geoffrey, passed away over two years ago. It was sudden and totally unexpected. He hadn't been sick at all."

"Oh, my," Douglas breathed. "Sorry for your loss, Savannah."

Inez had grown deathly still. Her mocha skin had even paled. Then tears rolled down her cheeks unchecked. When Inez's hands began to shake uncontrollably, Savannah became terribly concerned. At a complete loss for words, she didn't know what she could possibly say to comfort her guest. She had no clue why Inez was even crying. Was Inez distraught over Savannah's loss, or perhaps a loss of her own? Savannah was left to wonder, because she was too scared to ask Inez what was wrong since she was already so distraught.

Inez sniffled, wiping her nose on a paper napkin. "I'm sorry for my outburst. I lost my husband, too. Frederick Martin has been dead a little over a year. He was a real good man. I miss him terribly. A day doesn't go by that I don't think of him and wish he was still here with me."

Though shocked at Inez's news, Savannah felt quite uncomfortable with the situation. Inez's comments had Savannah questioning Inez's relationship with the man seated next to her. Inez and Douglas had the same last name, but were they married? Perhaps they were brother and sister, she mused. Savannah couldn't help noticing how sad Douglas suddenly appeared; not to mention the discomfort displayed in his body language. Savannah could only imagine how he must feel if Inez was indeed his wife. She understood someone missing their deceased spouse, but to express it the way she had in front of her current husband, if he was that to her, had been extremely insensitive on Inez's part. It was obvious to Savannah that Inez hadn't gotten over her spouse's death. If that was the case, why had she married, if she had, so soon after his demise?

Savannah could hardly wait to find out if Inez and Douglas were in fact married.

The ice cream and cobbler was finished in complete silence. Savannah had actually lost her appetite, but she'd eaten her dessert anyway. She hadn't wanted to offend the Sheffields. It seemed as if a moratorium had suddenly been placed on them taking pleasure in getting to know each other. Savannah didn't know what to think about the awkward state of affairs. To ask specific questions would undoubtedly cause further trauma in an already traumatic situation.

"How'd your husband die, Savannah?" Inez queried unflinchingly.

Savannah had wanted the three of them to start conversing again, but she wasn't sure the topic Inez had chosen was a safe one, especially for Douglas, who still looked uncomfortable. But since Inez had asked the question, Savannah felt obligated to answer it. "A heart attack, Inez. It was over for Geoffrey in a matter of minutes." Savannah paused a moment. "I'd like to hear more about your Rome vacation, Inez and Douglas." Savannah felt desperate to redirect this conversation. Continuing to discuss Geoffrey's death would land her in a horrible funk. Savannah was feeling way too good to allow herself to fall back into the doldrums.

"Italy is a very beautiful country to visit. Rome is known as the Eternal City. To say it was fascinating would be an understatement. We were constantly mesmerized by what

we saw and experienced over there." Douglas had spoken
up first. He seemed happy that a lighter subject had been
introduced. The sparkle had come back into his eyes.
Savannah was glad to see that.

According to Douglas, he and Inez had visited Rome,
Venice and Florence. He went on to give a vivid description of all the famous landmarks they'd been privileged
enough to visit. The gondola ride in Venice was one of their
favored highlights. Seeing the leaning tower of Pisa was yet
another treat. Douglas and Inez considered their tour of
the Vatican as the most sacred part of the trip. The
Sheffields' eyes were alight with passion as they talked
about the romanticism of it all, which indicated to
Savannah that her neighbors were actually married.

An hour later Savannah walked her guests to the door.
The promise of them getting together for dinner real soon
had been made. Although there had been some very tense
moments during the visit, Savannah was eager to continue
both a neighborly and social relationship with the Sheffields. She particularly wanted to find out more about how
Inez had decided to marry only a year after her husband's
death, but without Douglas present, especially since it
seemed quite clear that Inez hadn't yet come to terms with
Frederick's absence in her life.

Seeing how much time had slipped away was surprising to Savannah. Practically the whole day was gone.
She'd spent much longer at the senior center than she'd
planned on, but it had all been worthwhile. She wasn't
fixing dinner for Antonio, but she did want to have a few
snack items prepared. There was also a lot of cobbler
left, so she could offer him that as well, but she'd have

to run out for more ice cream. There had been just enough left for the three scoops she and her neighbors had devoured.

Antonio had mentioned bringing over a couple of Tyler Perry's stage plays for them to watch, which were all on DVD. Savannah had seen a couple of the plays live, as well as the one that had been made into a movie. She hadn't viewed *I Can Do Bad All by Myself* nor had she seen the stage-play version of *Diary of a Mad Black Woman*. Antonio was to bring both.

After changing into loose-fitting attire, Savannah went into the kitchen to see what she could whip up for her and Antonio to snack on while watching the plays. Upon seeing all the fresh fruit she had stored in the refrigerator, she quickly decided on preparing a fruit platter. Once she'd pulled everything out of the cooling bin, along with a carton of Cool Whip, she took the fruit over to the sink and rinsed it off. Retrieving two glass sectional serving platters from the top cabinet shelf came next. Because of her short stature she had to use the handy stepping stool.

Savannah enjoyed cutting the white grape stems into small clusters and placing them on the platter. Leaving the greenery on the large ripe strawberries, she then arranged them in one of the three sections that were left. The Cool Whip would go into the small bowl that fit into the center of the large dish. Savannah popped a couple of the black-berries into her mouth to check them for sweetness; they were both ripe and sweet. The crisp Granny Smith green apples were peeled, sliced and arranged next. Before covering the platter with Saran wrap, she sprinkled onto the fruit a small amount of Fruit-Fresh to keep her goodies from turning colors. Satisfied with her handiwork, Savannah placed the platter in the refrigerator.

The second sectional platter was filled with salty snacks, such as mixed nuts, white cheddar popcorn, Ruffles potato chips, pretzel thins and large white-corn tortilla chips. The small center bowl was then filled with a spicy ranch dip. Savannah also planned to put out a bowl of fresh salsa when it came time for her to serve her guest. After also covering the salty snacks with the Saran wrap, she placed the platter on top of the microwave oven.

A glance at the clock revealed to Savannah that she could lie down for an hour or so. Then she'd get up and run down to the store to get the ice cream in case Antonio wanted to sample the cobbler. The sudden idea to call Antonio and see if he'd mind picking up the ice cream for her seemed like a good one. Savannah was sure he wouldn't mind. There were several grocery stores on the route to her home from his. She'd pay the money back once he got there. Savannah then made her way back to her bedroom to retrieve his number from her address book.

Savannah entered her bedroom and sat down on the bed. She then picked up her address book from the nightstand and thumbed through it until she came to Antonio's phone number. His voice mail picked up on the first ring. Not sure if she should leave a message or not about the errand she wanted him to run, Savannah paused for a moment. In the next second she decided to go ahead and tell Antonio what she needed. Nothing ventured, nothing gained.

Without bothering to take off her clothes, though she'd

already removed her shoes, Savannah pulled back the comforter and top sheet, and then she slipped into bed. The
firm mattress felt good beneath her slightly tired body.
Although she still had every intention of taking a short nap,
Savannah's mind went back to the strange events of the day.

The weird happenings at the senior center had
Savannah wondering if she should even go back there. She
certainly didn't want to spend her spare time in the middle
of controversies and ugly confrontations. Besides that, she
hadn't been made to feel very welcome there by the female
members, but her luncheon companions couldn't have
been any sweeter.

Savannah would never consider volunteering her time
as a loss, but she had the niggling feeling that she might
lose the opportunity to do something really important if
she stayed away. There was a definite need there for someone like her. She was sure of it. Not one to run away from
challenges, big or small, Savannah knew that was exactly
what she'd be doing if she allowed her volunteer service
contract to simply fall by the wayside down at Silver Wings.

The Sheffields had also left Savannah with a big question
mark at the end of their visit.

Inez's behavior and comments about her deceased
husband still had her puzzled. Douglas's response to it had
made her even more curious about their marriage. She had
learned a few interesting facts about their bakery and how
they'd gotten into the business. Inez had begun the
business by selling her homemade pastries to friends and
family during the holiday seasons.

Word of mouth had spread to others about Inez's delicious pastries, which had brought her many new custom-

ers. She had become an expert at cake decorating using the Wilton techniques after taking many classes. She had then been constantly commissioned by numerous clients to bake wedding, birthday and other special occasion cakes. Douglas had purchased the bakery for Inez as a wedding gift. The Rialto bakery had been open only six months.

No sooner had Savannah closed her eyes than the telephone rang. Thinking it might be Antonio she snatched up the receiver from the cradle. A quick glance at the caller ID revealed to her an unfamiliar number. Upon recognizing the caller's voice, she smiled gently. "Mr. Noah Westfield, what a pleasant surprise. How can I help you?"

Deep down inside Savannah hoped Noah wasn't trying to hit on her. He seemed like a very nice man, but she was only interested in Antonio at the moment. In no way did she ever want to hurt Noah's feelings, but if he had a romantic interest in her she'd just have to find a way to let him down easy.

Noah chuckled softly. "I'm glad you're pleased by my call, which is more of a business matter than a social one."

Savannah sighed a breath of relief. "What is it, Noah?"

"After you left the center today, several of us old folks continued to hang around and rehash and trash what had gone down at the meeting. That's when the haranguing started all over again. It appears that no one wants to be nominated as president, not even the vice president. Irwin, Chester and I then began to mull things over between us. After a bit of an animated discussion, we all came to the conclusion that you might be good at the job. The center needs some new fresh ideas and someone smart enough and upbeat to bring about some badly needed changes. The guys and me think you'd be a perfect fit for the presidency. What do you think?"

Both flattered and astonished, Savannah began to think over Noah's interesting proposition. Although performing an important job within the center was what she'd hoped for, she hadn't expected anything of this magnitude. Besides that, her age was definitely a negative factor. Also, the formidable female members had caused her to have second thoughts about trying to incorporate any of her ideas for making the center a huge success. Savannah still couldn't get over the fact that not a single one of them had welcomed her in as a volunteer.

"Noah, thanks for the vote of confidence, and I am flattered by the wonderful suggestion, but I'm sure we can't pull this off. I just can't imagine the members voting in a brand-new member as president, especially one my age. I think we'd have a very hard sell on our hands."

"At least you sound somewhat interested. That's a good start. If no one else wants to be president, I don't see why anyone would care that you're brand-new or not a senior citizen. If you'll consider taking on the job, let me worry about making it happen. Okay?"

"Well, yeah, I guess so. But what about you or one of the other guys running for office? I think any one of you would make a great president. I'm sure you'd get voted in with ease."

Noah laughed heartily. "Not in this lifetime. I'm too set in my ways to make any changes this late in the game. Trust me, the women would hate having me as president. The first mandate from me would be to throw out anyone who caused dissention among the members. More than half of the women would have to pack up and leave. Gossipers would get the boot next—that would include all the rest of the members, including me." Noah had a good laugh at that.

Another caller beeped in before Savannah could respond, which caused her to put Noah on Hold. This time it was Antonio. She promptly told him what she needed and then he promised her he'd take care of it. After telling Antonio she'd see him shortly, Savannah clicked the line back over to Noah so they could finish up their conversation. "Noah, are you still there?"

"Yes, I'm here waiting, lass. I know you're probably a busy lady, so I'm not going to hold you up any longer, but I hope you'll give some deep thought to my suggestion. You have my number. Please call me when you've made up your mind one way or the other."

"I'll do that for sure, Noah. Thanks so much for thinking of me for the presidency. I'm actually a little giddy that such a possibility may even exist. Talk to you soon."

Looking totally bewildered over what had just transpired between her and Noah, Savannah plumped her pillow and laid her head back onto it. Her as president of the Silver Wings Senior Center would be unbelievable. "What a hoot!"

Was this position in God's plan for her? Must be, Savannah mused, since the suggestion had come right out of the blue, coupled with the fact that she'd already entertained numerous ways of helping out at the center in some capacity. Her ideas were very innovative. The presidency certainly hadn't been so much as a thought, not with her age as a deciding factor. Volunteering in some capacity was what she'd had in mind. Then again, holding an office was also volunteer work since no pay was involved in the position. Her biggest worry was how the other members might react to Noah's suggestion, especially the female members.

Savannah then wondered if it would be out of line for her to run this situation by Antonio. As the director of Golden Age he probably could offer her a good bit of insight on things. Seeking him out for advice would more than likely be flattering to him than anything else. Savannah didn't want to come off as being a needy person, nor did she want to lean on Antonio too hard. But as she thought about it, she could see no harm in asking his opinion. She was sure that whatever he had to say would be helpful to her. With that issue settled in her mind, she set the alarm clock. Savannah then closed her eyes, hoping she wasn't too excited to fall off to sleep for a short spell. The possibility of another late night with Antonio warranted a brief nap.

Antonio brought Savannah into his warm embrace, hugging her with a strong but tender force. He kissed her gently on the lips, loving the way she fit so perfectly into his arms. He held her slightly away from him just to get a glimpse of her attire. No matter what she wore she looked good to him. She always managed to look so fresh faced and squeaky clean. Savannah's clothing was nothing less than chic. Her navy-blue casual slacks and navy-blue-and-white pinstripe camp shirt fit her petite frame to a tee. The white slip-on sandals she wore on her feet were cute rather than fancy.

Antonio was also casually dressed, wearing a pair of khaki Dockers, a short-sleeved autumn-gold polo shirt and a khaki linen blazer. Savannah's eyes openly roved his impeccable attire. His brown Italian loafers looked as if they'd been spit shined. In Savannah's opinion, he could wear a bunch of rags and still look like a million bucks. Everything Antonio wore had a way of accentuating his powerful physique. She also noticed that his beautiful silver hair had recently been cut and neatly edged. Savannah had a hard time tearing her eyes away from this debonair gentleman's tight body.

Savannah took hold of Antonio's arm before picking up the brown paper bag he'd placed on the counter of the hall tree when he'd first stepped inside the house. "Come on into the family room. We'll watch the stage plays on the big screen."

As the couple reached their destination, Savannah told Antonio to go ahead and have a seat. "Please excuse me for a moment or two, Antonio. I'm going to go and put the ice cream in the freezer and then pull out the snacks."

Antonio smiled sweetly. "Any reason I can't help you out?"

Savannah shook her head in the negative, smiling flirtatiously. "Can't think of a one."

Hand in hand Savannah and Antonio made their way down the hallway and into the kitchen, where Antonio removed the brown bag from Savannah's grasp and placed it on the counter. He then emptied it of its contents.

Upon seeing the boxes of Hot Tamales and Raisenets Savannah cracked up. Antonio had remembered her favorite movie-watching treats. Since the theaters practically charged an arm and a leg for the cinnamon-flavored and chocolate-covered candies, she made it a point to keep them on hand to take to the movies with her despite the "no outside food allowed" rule.

Savannah picked up one of the boxes. "Thank you, Antonio. You are just as sweet as what is inside this box. Thanks for always being so thoughtful." She stood on her tiptoes and gave him a big kiss. His lips were as soft as butter and every bit as sweet as his nature.

Although Savannah didn't want to rush the evening, she wanted to get on with it so there'd be plenty of time for her and Antonio to just sit and talk after the plays were over. With that in mind, she quickly retrieved the fresh fruit platter from the refrigerator and asked Antonio to grab the one off the top of the microwave. There were plenty of soft drinks and canned juices inside the small office-size refrigerator she'd recently purchased for the family room. She also kept foam cups, paper plates and plastic utensils in a basket on top of the fridge.

In a matter of minutes the couple was all comfortably settled in on the sofa and the first DVD was rolling. Savannah had chosen *I Can Do Bad All by Myself* for the first showing.

Since Antonio had seen all the shows, he really didn't mind the order in which they watched them. He just hoped Savannah enjoyed the lively entertainment as much as he had.

Minutes into the first show Antonio saw that he had nothing to worry about as far as Savannah liking the play. She was laughing her head off while tears of joy periodically ran down her cheeks. Savannah's obvious pleasure in what she was viewing made Antonio happy he'd suggested bringing over the incredible shows for them to watch together.

Tyler Perry was a comedic genius and a remarkable writer, director and producer. The inspirational spin he put on each of his plays made them even more appealing. The gospel singers and their golden voices were nothing short of amazing. The character Madea, played by Perry himself, was the finest portrayal of all, as she was completely insane, and funnier than any comedian he'd ever had the pleasure of seeing on the live stage or on television or in the movies.

Savannah had been moved to tears by the end of the second play, *Diary of a Mad Black Woman*. The heartbreaking finale had touched her deeply. That a woman could forgive a man who'd caused her so much pain was a real lesson in humility. The wife had had to humble herself completely in order for her to forgive the infidelities her husband had committed with her very own best friend. This particular stage play had been adapted for the silver screen, but neither Savannah or Antonio had seen the movie yet.

Antonio slipped his arm around Savannah's shoulder, pulling her in closer to him. "I don't have to ask if you enjoyed the plays, Savannah. It was evident to me throughout the viewing that you were having a tremendous time. It's one thing for a play or movie to be funny, but it's something else for it to be both comical and spiritually uplifting. Perry's plays are a perfect example of art imitating life. His story lines are so true to what happens in real life."

Savannah nodded in agreement. "I did have a blast. Thanks for bringing over the genius works of Mr. Tyler

Perry. I'm so impressed with him. I haven't had the opportunity to see all of his plays, but I'm definitely a fan. Please let me know if another one of his live plays comes to our area. I'd love to attend."

Antonio briefly touched his forehead to Savannah's. "And I'd love to take you. I'm on the Tyler Perry mailing list so I get e-mails about the upcoming events. You and I will have the best seats in the house. Perry sold out the Kodak Theater with *Meet the Browns*. Sometime during the week I'll check to see if it's still playing somewhere here in Southern California."

"That would be nice. I hope it is." Savannah reached up and gently touched Antonio's cheek. "How was your day?"

Antonio looked thoughtful. "A pretty decent day that went by very fast. I had several meetings, all of them lasting way too long. I have a hard time sitting still for long periods of time, especially when I'm bored to tears." He chuckled lightly. "All except for the times when I'm with you. I can sit and look at you and talk with you for hours and hours on end, Savannah. When I'm with you, I never lose interest. How did your day go?"

Savannah rubbed her hands together, wondering if she should replenish the snacks before getting into her day. Antonio politely declined her offer of refills, so that meant she didn't have to wait to give it to him straight. "So glad you asked about my day, Antonio. Boy, do I have a lot to tell you. I also need some sound advice."

Savannah launched right into the interesting things that had happened at the senior center and those which had occurred later on with her neighbors, the Sheffields. She could tell that she held Antonio's rapt attention by the ever-changing expressions on his face. That was a good sign.

Savannah's eyes were wide with wonder. "What do you think, Antonio? Should I take a convincing stab at trying to become the club president at Silver Wings?"

Loving Savannah's spirit of challenge, he thought her willingness to jump in headfirst was refreshing. Antonio eyed her intently, curiously. He didn't want to dampen her spirit, but he thought she should look at things realistically. Savannah needed to know who and what she was dealing with. Antonio went on to tell her just that. "Do you know what a bunch of clawing cats can do to a single free-flying butterfly, Savannah?"

Savannah nodded. "Claw it right out the of the air if its wings aren't quick enough. You're so right about those sisters down at the center having claws. Although I keep mine retracted, I have a sharp set of talons, too. I just don't want to ever have to unsheath them, Antonio. Why do you think the women refused to even acknowledge my presence today?"

Antonio hunched his broad shoulders. "I can think of a number of reasons why it happened, jealousy as the most prevalent of all. You're so beautiful and you don't come close to looking your age. When there are already too many hens and not enough roosters around the barnyard, the huffy hens don't want to see yet another rival bird entering the competition. You get my drift, Savannah?"

"With crystal clarity, Antonio. How do the already established women members react to new female members down at your center?"

Antonio laughed. "I've seen some downright wicked attitudes since I've been in this business, Savannah. I've even witnessed a few flying wigs. If you decide to run for president, you better make sure all the weapons in your arsenal are in excellent working condition. You *will* become a target, Savannah. Count on it. I don't understand why it's that way, but it is."

Savannah looked a bit weary. "So I've heard. But I'm up to the challenge. Since no one else wants to run for office, I may have a good chance of getting in. What I do with the office after I get in is what counts the most. I believe I have the necessary skills to make the center a burning success despite my age. Can I count on you to be there if I need you, Antonio?"

"Let me get this right, Savannah. You want me to help you kick my own butt in this rivaling business?"

Laughing, Savannah nodded. "Something like that, Antonio."

"Girl, you drive a real hard bargain." He kissed her forehead. "You should know by now that you can count on me, always, Savannah. That's what friends are for. Now that you know where my loyalties lie, please tell me why you're so concerned about your neighbors."

Savannah propped her feet upon the hassock. "After what I just told you about Inez, don't you think it was kind of strange for her to behave the way she did in front of her husband. The remarks she made about her late spouse were what gave me the willies. Douglas didn't look the least bit comfortable with her comments. How would you feel if that happened to you?"

Antonio took a couple of seconds to think about Savannah's question. He knew that constantly talking about a former spouse in front of the person they were now with could be awkward at best. That's why he hadn't talked too much about his wife to Savannah, who must've thought the same thing, since Savannah hadn't said a lot to him about her late husband. The comparison thing was definitely a no-no in his opinion, which they had talked over, but he didn't think it was healthy not to get into talking about their late spouses period. "Let me ask you this. We've both talked a little about our deceased spouses, but do you feel that you're betraying Geoffrey by not making him a part of our conversation every time we get together?"

Savannah was quick to shake her head in the negative. She guessed that Antonio needed her to answer this question before he could answer the one she'd already asked of him. "I don't see it as a betrayal at all. I think it would be rude of us to harp on our spouses at every turn. Besides, I still have my quiet moments when I talk to Geoffrey about how I'm doing. When I made the decision to move forward in my life, I had already come to terms with the fact that my old life was over, as I'd known it. You and I talked about the comparison thing. I don't ever want to do that with you or anyone else."

Antonio's eyes quickly lost their shine. "What's this *anyone else* stuff, Savannah? Are you dating someone else or are you planning on it?"

Had Antonio's expression not turned serious Savannah would've laughed. "We haven't talked about having an exclusive relationship, but no, I'm not dating anyone other than you, nor am I considering it. What about you, Antonio?"

Antonio took Savannah into his arms and kissed her

thoroughly. Once he released her, he entwined his hands in her hair, eyeing her with adoration. "I don't know about you, but I think I've found my second chance at happiness in you. I'd like us to become exclusive. That is, if you don't have any objections. I feel real good when I'm with you and I don't want that to change."

"No objections, Antonio. Not a one." Savannah then leaned into him for another kiss.

"To answer your question, I wouldn't feel too good about it if I were in Douglas's shoes. I'd probably be hurt by the strange behavior you've said that Inez has displayed."

Hearing all that he'd needed to hear from Savannah, Antonio held her tightly in his arms, silently thanking God for performing another miracle in his life. He felt certain that Savannah was the key to his happiness and that he was the key to hers.

Chapter 8

The hard, snooty looks Savannah had been receiving ever since she'd first sat down at one of the tables in the conference room at the Silver Wings Senior Center had her terribly nervous. Biting her nails wasn't an option since she didn't want these women to see how much they'd unnerved her. She had begun to believe that it just might be in her best interest to get up and leave the premises. Withdrawing her volunteer contract from the center was still a consideration. Being around unfriendly people wasn't Savannah's idea of having a good time.

Noah had phoned Savannah in the early hours of the morning to tell her that an emergency meeting was being called to order to discuss her possible candidacy for the presidency. She had begun to worry about how the women members might receive her immediately after the call had ended. What would happen next was anyone's guess.

There were fifteen women present and only five men.

According to what Noah had told Savannah she had the support of all nine male members. Noah, Irwin and Chester counted for three of the five men in attendance, which left four men unaccounted for. The other two men who'd shown up for the meeting had been introduced as Carlton Haynes and Jack Murphy. Both men appeared to be in their late fifties. It would surprise Savannah if she were to learn that they were any older than her estimation. The men seemed to be in a lot better physical shape than most of the women, which was somewhat surprising to her. Since a lot of the guys played golf, Savannah contributed their fitness to possibly walking the links.

The repeated pounding of the gavel by Loretta Ames, the resigning president, finally brought the meeting to order. An immediate hush fell over the crowd at the hard rapping sound. Looking as if she'd rather be anywhere but here in the center's conference room, Loretta peered out from around the podium, as she was too short to see over it.

Loretta cleared her throat. "Good morning. I thank all of you for coming to the center on such short notice. Since I have resigned my position as president, we're here to try and elect a new one. Miriam Preston, our current vice president, is not interested in running for the office, so we have to look elsewhere. Unfortunately no one else seems interested in the post either. However, our good friend Noah Westfield has recommended someone who may be interested in the office. I'll let Noah introduce us to his possible candidate."

Noah got to his feet and then walked over to Savannah, offering her his arm. Together they walked up to the podium. "Good morning, ladies and gentlemen. This young lady here to my right is Mrs. Savannah Richmond. She's a new volunteer at the center and a new resident of the Inland Empire. When I learned that no one was interested in the presidency, I called Ms. Savannah and talked with her about it. Once she expressed an interest in the office, I contacted Loretta and Miriam—thus, this meeting. I'm going to step aside now so you can pose your questions to Ms. Savannah."

Savannah was terrified of standing alone at the podium. Having Noah beside her had made her feel more comfortable. Although he'd only stepped a short distance away, she wished he hadn't moved at all. *What had she allowed herself to be talked into?* The cold stares had grown in intensity. Some of the women looked as if they were ready to rip right into her. Savannah wasn't feeling much love in this cavernous room.

Opal Redmond, the rude woman Savannah had met before the previous day's luncheon, got to her feet. "Exactly what is your platform, Mrs. Richmond? Since you hardly qualify as a senior citizen by age requirements, what makes you think you have anything in common with the members here who are all senior citizens?"

Savannah smiled weakly, praying for courage to face these formidable foes. "Well, I'd just like to be of service to my community. Since no one else was interested in taking on the job, I thought I'd like to try it. I'm retired now and could devote a good bit of my time to making the center a great place for the members to spend their leisure time. As for what I have may or may not have in common with seniors, I believe I can make a good case for myself."

Savannah went on to tell the club members that she'd spent a lot of time at the senior centers with her mother when she was alive and that she'd had the privilege of being involved with a lot of the activities that had taken place there. She also talked about the countless senior patients that she had provided health care for in her profession as a registered nurse. Savannah then spoke of her interaction with her elderly neighbors and the senior members of her church.

"What makes you think it isn't already a great place to spend one's time?" Miriam asked.

Seeing that no one was going to make this easy for her, Savannah squared her shoulders, ready to take on anyone who dared to try and embarrass her. "I haven't been a volunteer long enough to make that determination one way or the other, Ms. Preston. However, what I saw yesterday gave me an idea of the unrest that exists. I'm only interested in doing what no one else seems to want to do. Become the new president."

Noah stepped back up to the podium and gently took the microphone from Savannah's hand. "In talking with Ms. Savannah, I learned a few things about her abilities and special talents. I believe she can bring a lot to the table. She told me a few of her ideas for the center, and I think they're great ones. Instead of trying to be difficult here, why don't we give her the benefit of the doubt? No one else is willing to step up to the plate and take on this difficult task, myself included, so should we really be looking a gift horse in the mouth?"

"Hearing her ideas is what we're after," one lady shouted out. "So far she's given us nothing to go on. We'd like to know what you might do to improve the center, Ms. Savannah."

Savannah nodded her understanding to the tall woman who'd spoken. "Since I'm not sure of what all the existing issues are, I think it would help out if some of you told me what the center is lacking. Then I can tell you what I'd do to try and resolve the problem."

"Our membership numbers are low. What would you do to bring in more members?" one of the gentlemen inquired of Savannah.

"I'd first look closely at what the center already has in place to offer the senior public. Once I identified the needs, and made the necessary adjustments, even if it means cutting old programs and introducing more interesting ones, I'd then hold an exciting membership drive based on the new ideas. What I'd like to do is get the current members more interested in the programs already in existence. Getting the attendance up among the existing members needs immediate attention. We can't hope to bring in new members if we don't have full participation from all the current members. If you'll give me time to put together an effective proposal, I'd love to present one to you within the next week or so."

"As you can see for yourself, the women greatly outnumber the men. What would you do to try and bring in more male members?" asked a lady wearing a hat so big that Savannah could hardly see her face. "By the way, I'm Mable Grimes. I admire you for wanting to take on this unenviable task. I agree with what Noah had to say about looking a gift horse in the mouth. I don't know where we get the nerve to do so. Everyone wants to sit around and complain, but no one wants to get off their butts to try and make things better. Thank you for wanting to try."

Savannah smiled warmly. "You're welcome! In response to your question, I'd like to try and schedule some great activities to include some of the other area senior centers. It seems that women outnumber the men in all of the centers that I've checked out thus far, so that would still be an issue. But we can make a concerted effort to change things. Are we just talking about bringing in men or preferably single men, Mable?"

Mable cracked up. "You read me right, Ms. Savannah. As a widow of three years, single men are exactly what I'm looking for, lots of them. I really like your idea of getting together with members from other centers. Meeting new people is something I enjoy tremendously."

Savannah gave Mable the thumbs-up sign of approval. "Since our current vice president is also resigning her position, maybe you should consider running for that vacant office, Mable. If I'm elected, I could sure use the help of someone like you, someone who's not afraid to speak up and then walk the walk and talk the talk."

Miriam harrumphed loudly. "I'd think you'd try getting yourself elected before you start nominating folks for my job. Your age is a big issue, lady."

Mable rolled her eyes at Miriam. "Why should you care what she does, Miriam? You're not willing to stay in office to help get things back on track. When things get tough, the tough are supposed to get things going, not run away from them. In my opinion, both you and Loretta are cowards. At the first sign of trouble, you're ready to give up. I'm glad that I didn't vote for either one of you in the last election. Seems to me I had pegged you two peas in a pod just right. As for her age, she's certainly not old and bitter like most of you fast-on-the-jaw sisters. It's time for you all to start sharing new ideas for the center instead of showing us how loud your mouths are."

"As for things getting back on track, this train has been derailed for a long time," Chester said. "I say we vote in Ms. Savannah and get it over with. We need someone who's at least willing to give their best shot at running things. We can't do any worse than what we have now. If there's anyone else in the room who'd like to run for the presidency please raise your hand."

As Savannah looked around the room, she saw that not a single hand was raised.

"Just as I thought," Chester said. "You all want to run things from those chairs you're seated in instead of putting some real work into this center. We can go on like we have been, or we can start to make some positive changes. I'm all for Ms. Savannah as the new president! Who else has the guts to stand with me on this?"

Seeing Kenya's car parked on the street right out in front of her home was disturbing to Savannah, since she'd specifically asked her daughter to call and let her know exactly when she'd leave L.A. bound for Fontana. Kenya's behavior was puzzling to Savannah, but she wasn't going to make her daughter feel unwelcome in her home. However, she wasn't going to allow Kenya to make her feel uncomfortable either. After all, it was her own home, not Kenya's.

A fleeting thought of Antonio caused Savannah to flinch

inwardly. Talk about bad timing, she mused. In knowing how Kenya felt about her wonderful new beau Savannah was also aware that her daughter certainly wouldn't be able to appreciate the decision they'd made to become exclusive. Savannah didn't even know how to broach the subject with Kenya.

Then it suddenly dawned on Savannah that she didn't have to clue Kenya in, period. Whatever decisions she made for her life didn't always have to have a stamp of approval from her children. As long as she was satisfied with her life choices, she shouldn't worry about what anyone else thought. Savannah was more than satisfied with Antonio.

After pulling the car into the garage, Savannah killed the engine. She then stepped outside and made her way around to the front of her home, where she planned to wait on Kenya, who hadn't yet gotten out of her car. After several tense minutes had passed by, and Kenya still hadn't exited her car, Savannah grew anxious. Wondering why Kenya was still seated inside the car, Savannah started down the walkway to go and see what was going on, praying that everything was okay with her child.

The moment Savannah reached the driver's side of Kenya's car, she realized that her daughter was talking on her cell phone. She wasn't even sure if Kenya had seen her pull into the garage, since she still hadn't looked up. Whomever Kenya was talking to seemed to be getting an earful from her. That was indicated to Savannah by Kenya's jerky head movements. Savannah tapped on the glass to get Kenya's attention. When Kenya acknowledged her presence, Savannah gestured to Kenya her intention of going on into the house. She then stepped away from the car. After Savannah walked back through the garage, she hit the remote button mounted on the wall in order to bring the heavy door down. She then unlocked the entry door leading into the laundry room and stepped inside, dashing to the monitoring station to turn off her house alarm. Then Savannah rushed up to the front of the house and opened the door for Kenya to enter whenever she got through with her phone conversation, which she hoped wouldn't be too long. Savannah wasn't particularly fond of leaving the door unlocked.

A couple more Tylenol might help me out, Savannah mused, moving quickly toward the master bathroom. Upon reaching her destination, she opened the medicine cabinet and removed the familiar red-and-white plastic bottle. Once she poured a fair amount of warm bottled water into the small white plastic cup, she tossed down the pain reliever.

After what the haughty women at the senior center had put her through, Savannah was glad she wasn't suicidal. Someone a lot weaker than herself may have thought of taking the whole darn bottle of pills after that meeting. The downright rude women had riled her completely, so much so that she'd walked out on them, but not before telling them what she thought of their immature stall tactics. Savannah had then told them if they ever decided to give her a chance at the presidency she'd accept their phone call and a sincere apology.

Savannah heard the door close shut as she made her way up toward the front of the house. Hoping that Kenya didn't have her behind wrapped up around her shoulders, she picked up her pace. The sooner she got this greeting out of the way, the sooner she could sit back and relax. Since she'd already laid out the ground rules for her daughter's stay in her home, Savannah was happy they wouldn't have to get into that. The topic of Antonio would be off-limits to Kenya.

Still talking on the phone, Kenya set her large suitcase down near the end of the foyer.

The size of Kenya's bag concerned Savannah when she first saw it. Her daughter's traveling gear looked as if it held more than a couple days' worth of clothing. Well, Savannah thought, there were a lot of women who didn't know how to pack lightly. Having more than a few choices in one's wardrobe was important to some females.

Kenya finally ended the phone call, her eyes going straight to Savannah. "Hi, Mom. Sorry about that. I had a few important things to take care of. Some people just don't do what they say they're going to do. How are you?"

Even though Savannah had no idea of what Kenya was taking about, she wasn't going to ask for more information. Kenya would tell her what was up if she wanted her to know. "I'm fine, Kenya. Just surprised to see you."

Kenya looked abashed. "I know I was supposed to call, but I was halfway here when I remembered. I didn't call you on your cell because I've been on the phone ever since I got here."

Savannah smiled, looking relieved. "Good to know that you're the one who forgot. For a minute there I thought I was having a senior moment. Are you hungry? I can fix you something."

Kenya shook her head. "I stopped by the Wendy's on

Baseline. I had a salad and a burger. But thanks for the offer. If you don't mind, I'd like to lie down for a while. The drive was exhausting. Traffic was ridiculous on the 10 Freeway. I thought I was leaving L.A. early enough to avoid it. But there was a major accident in the center lane."

"I hope no one was seriously injured," Savannah said, looking concerned. "As for resting, your room is ready. All I did in there was dust and run the vacuum since you put fresh linens on before you and Cole left for home the last time you were here."

"The *only* other time we've ever been here," Kenya mentioned, laughing.

Savannah laughed, too. "Yeah, you're right about that. How is Cole? And where he's off to this time? The man stays so busy."

Kenya stared off into space for several seconds. "Cole's… fine," Kenya stammered. "I think he went to Vegas."

Kenya's long pause gave Savannah cause for concern. But that was only one of her worries. Her daughter's stammering was a clue that something unusual might be going on here, as well as the fact that Kenya didn't seem at all sure as to Cole's whereabouts. "You *think*, Kenya? You don't know where your husband is?" The painful look on Kenya's face had Savannah wishing she'd had the good sense to just let her daughter's response go unchallenged.

Kenya shook her head, as though she were trying to clear it of cobwebs. "I've had a lot on my mind lately, Mom. There's so much stuff going on in my life. Of course I know where Cole is. It's definitely Vegas. I don't know why I wasn't clearer with my initial answer." Kenya practically leaped to her feet. "The bed is calling me. See you later, Mom."

Savannah stood to receive her daughter's hug. The tension she felt in Kenya's embrace put her on a higher alert. Something was up. She was willing to bet on it. But what could it be? Savannah had no choice but to wonder. It was obvious that Kenya wasn't ready to share her problems, if in fact there were any. Savannah could only hope that she was overreacting.

Knowing she could use a good nap herself, Savannah started down the hallway, only to turn back around and head toward the kitchen. She was hungry. She hadn't eaten before she'd left the house to attend that sham of a meeting. Even though Savannah was almost sure they wouldn't call on her to act as president, she was going to prepare a proposal anyway. A woman without a game plan would surely get lost in such an unorganized shuffle.

The way the ladies had treated her had Savannah no longer sure as to why she even wanted the job in the first place. Then again, she did know. Offering a great service to her community would simply make her happy. It would also help her while away the hours of loneliness. Antonio couldn't fill all of her spare time or all of her heart's desires. He could only enhance her lifestyle. It was all up to her to make a life that would be pleasing and satisfying. Savannah was aware that no one but her was responsible for her happiness.

Age forty-five or the demise of a spouse wasn't a death sentence—and Savannah wasn't about to impose upon herself such a drastic form of punishment. She wanted to live the rest of her life to the fullest. No one knew when Jesus would send His angels to Earth to reclaim His children for Him. Although Savannah wanted to be ready for His return, she wasn't in a hurry to leave this world anytime soon.

Instead of preparing a cold sandwich, Savannah quickly decided on grilled cheese. After gathering all the ingredients, she went straight to work, since her stomach was growling something awful. Rarely did she allow herself to get this hungry, but messing with them folks down at the senior center had kept her away from her normal routine. Breakfast, the first meal taken, should always be eaten since it provided the fuel needed to help one get through the rest of the day, she mused, thinking of how she'd also instilled in her children healthy eating habits.

Savannah had to laugh at her thoughts. Grilled cheese wasn't the healthiest food choice.

The phone rang at the same moment Savannah laid her head on the pillow. Seeing her daughter's home number come up was rather puzzling. Cole was away and Kenya was in the other room asleep, so who in heaven's name could be calling from their home? With much hesitancy, Savannah finally answered the call.

"Mom, it's Cole."

"Hey, sweetheart! How are you?" Savannah had done her best to keep her voice light and airy, but Cole calling her from home had her filled with trepidation. In not knowing what was going on, she thought it best to let him do the talking so she wouldn't say anything that perhaps she shouldn't. Her initial thought had been to ask him how things were going in Vegas. Since it was obvious that he wasn't calling from Nevada, she had to keep quiet on that point.

"I'm trying to be cool, Mom, but it's hard when your daughter is such a trip."

"My daughter also happens to be your wife, Cole, but you didn't acknowledge her as such. Is there a specific reason for that?"

Cole chuckled lightly. Then a few seconds of silence came. Clearing his throat came next, followed by a couple more seconds of stillness. "You're right in what you're saying, Mom. But you know how it is. You want someone else to own what's yours when problems arise. Like when I was a child, my mother used to tell my dad what *his* son did wrong, instead of saying *our* son. That's how I'm feeling about Kenya right now. I'm seeing her as your daughter at the time and not as my wife."

Savannah got the distinct impression that Cole didn't know Kenya was there with her. Otherwise, she didn't think he'd be talking this way. He'd often share confidences with her, but never with Kenya anywhere in close proximity to either of them. How could she find out for sure what he knew or didn't know? *Just let him continue to talk*, said the little voice inside her head.

"Mom, I really don't like pulling you into our complicated stuff, but I have to talk to somebody. You're the only person I know of who can be objective, especially where their child is concerned. You always listen to both sides of the story and then tell it like it is, not what one or the other of us wants to hear you say. You never take sides either. Do you think it's right for a married woman to run off to Las Vegas with a bunch of her very single girlfriends?"

Aha! So the plot thickens. So that's the reason Vegas had suddenly come up. That Kenya would sit there and lie to her own mother right to her face was downright sinful, Savannah thought. She had the mind to go into the bedroom and shake Kenya until her teeth rattled, turning her every way but loose. Her daughter should be ashamed of herself, but that was too much to hope for. Kenya was too prideful for something as humbling as feeling shameful.

Since the weekend was still a couple of days away, Savannah wondered if Kenya planned on leaving her house to go there but tell Cole that she'd been with her mother all this time. It now made sense to Savannah why Kenya had such a large bag. Also, Savannah lived much closer to Vegas than Kenya and Cole did.

"I don't necessarily feel that it's wrong for a married woman to hang out with her single friends, but an entire weekend may be a different matter. And if the husband objects to the trip, then I'd have to view it differently. Am I right in assuming that you objected to the outing?"

"Vehemently!"

"I see. I guess it's also safe to assume that you two had a big fight over it."

"More like a war. We both said some pretty unforgiving things. I allow her to press all the wrong buttons, too often for my comfort. I thought I would've had her all figured out by now. I'm not even close to understanding what makes her happy. Do you have a clue, Mom?"

"Kenya is simply Kenya, Cole. She makes no excuses for the person she chooses to be, nor does she apologize for it. With that said, I thought you already knew that you can't make anyone happy. Happiness is all in the individual's state of mind. Neither you nor I are responsible for another human being's joy or sorrow, though we can cause others grief. One of the first things you need to understand when dealing with Kenya is that her happiness is her sole responsibility, not yours. So, is your wife going on the trip anyway?"

Savannah hated being deceptive this way, but she just couldn't go and tell things that really weren't her business. Although Cole was making it her business, Kenya hadn't done so.

"Going? It looks like the girl is gone. One of her suitcases is missing from the bedroom closet as well as several of her clothes. I've rung her cell phone repeatedly, but she won't answer it. I hate caller ID for that reason alone. That stubborn woman knows I'm the one calling. But I've made my last call to her. I keep forgetting to give her some space when she's like this. I wish I knew what was really going on. I believe it's something big. I just don't know what."

Savannah knew she had to hurry up and get off this phone. If Cole were to ask her if she'd heard from Kenya or knew of her whereabouts, she knew it would be hard for her to lie to him. Cole was so in love with his wife and he sounded so darn pitiful.

"Just be patient for as long as you can. Cole, you have every right to happiness. Just as Kenya's responsible for making her own joy, so are you. I've got to run. It'll all be okay."

"I sure hope so, Mom. I always feel better after talking to you. I'll be at home all weekend. It's one of the few that I've had off in some time, but Kenya's not here to share in it."

Savannah spoke a few more comforting words to Cole before disconnecting the line. She hated to see her son-in-law hurting like he was. He was a good man, handsome and very smart too. If Kenya didn't have Cole's back, someone else would surely be thrilled to cover it for him. Any woman in her right mind would want a good man who was a doctor for a wonderful mate. Kenya was crazy about Cole, which made it harder for Savannah to figure out all the dynamics.

Savannah had barely regrouped from Cole's phone call when a firm knock struck her bedroom door. She really wished all this unrest and these constant interruptions weren't happening. So much for her new life, which was supposed to have been a quiet, peaceful one. Reraising her children, after they had already become adults, was impossible. *Thank God no grandchildren were involved in this unbelievable mess.* "Come on in, Kenya," Savannah called out softly, keeping her eyes fastened on the opening door.

Kenya's puffy red eyes had Savannah's mind going crazy. Her child had been crying. That hurt Savannah's heart, but her hands were tied until Kenya dealt out the first hand. Unfortunately, Savannah had no ace hidden up her sleeve. This was one poker hand she couldn't win. Bluffing wouldn't work in this instance.

Kenya sat on the chair beside the bed, but what she really wanted to do was climb into the sack with her mother. She could use Savannah's arms wrapped tightly around her. Her life was suddenly a mess and Kenya saw no safe way out.

Seeing the look in Kenya's eyes, the same one she'd seen countless times over the years, had Savannah patting the spot right next to her on the mattress. "Jump on in, Kenya. It'll probably do both of us a world of good. You look like you need a great big hug and I could certainly use one, too."

Kenya loved that her mother had always been able to anticipate the needs of her children. Where her kids were concerned, very little got past Savannah. Although Kenya hadn't uttered a word about her personal troubles, she knew that her mother knew for sure that a few problems existed. As Savannah had done on so many occasions, Kenya knew that her mother would wait on her to make the first move. The only problem was that Kenya didn't know how to begin to tell her mother what was going on with her. Kenya was very much aware that Savannah would be terribly disappointed and hurt beyond repair if she knew what her only daughter was actually thinking of doing.

Unable to resist Savannah's invitation, Kenya climbed into bed and then went straight into her mother's open arms. Content to just lie there in silence with her daughter, Savannah nestled Kenya into her arms and then rested her chin atop Kenya's head. Although it was very peaceful at the moment, Savannah knew that Kenya's emotional storms were steadily building. The warning signs were all there for Savannah to see with crystal clarity.

For someone who'd just awakened, Kenya had fallen back to sleep within minutes of joining Savannah in her bed. Not a single word had passed between them, but both mother and daughter had felt the unending love they had for each other. Savannah shifted her position and then carefully laid Kenya's head back on the pillow. The urge to stroke her daughter's pretty long hair was overwhelming, but Savannah didn't want to risk awakening her.

As Savannah made herself more comfortable, Kenya's

wedding day suddenly sashayed into her mind. It was one of the most spectacular events Savannah had ever attended in her lifetime, her own wedding day included. Their daughter all dressed in white had been the most beautiful sight Savannah had ever seen. Geoffrey's chest had stuck out as far as it could go, his tears falling like a spring rain, as he'd proudly escorted down the red-carpeted aisle one of his greatest accomplishments in life, one of his most precious treasures, his lovely daughter.

The minister had then asked who gives this woman away. For several tense seconds it had appeared to everyone in attendance that Geoffrey couldn't bring himself to utter the words he needed to say or to place Kenya's hand inside Cole's. It was like he had been suspended in time, as if his mind might be reliving his and his daughter's entire history together. Then, with his hands shaking like a leaf caught in a windstorm, he had finally voiced the words, "As her father, I do." Geoffrey had then allowed Cole to take Kenya into his loving care.

Savannah had sighed a breath of relief at those telltale moments, only to find it wasn't over yet. Before she had even blinked an eye, Geoffrey had taken possession of Kenya once again, hugging her fervently, wishing he didn't have to let her go, his emotions continuing to burgeon out of control. Only after Geoffrey had placed a loving kiss onto Kenya's cheek had he been able to turn around and walk away, leaving her in the gentle hands of her husband-to-be.

As Savannah had dared to look around at all the guests, she'd seen that there weren't too many dry eyes in the house. When Geoffrey had slid into the pew to sit beside his wife, tears brimming in her own eyes, she had taken hold of her husband's hand, squeezing it tightly.

The phone bell suddenly intruded upon Savannah's wistful spin back in time. Before it could ring again, she quickly snatched it from the cradle, happy that it hadn't disturbed Kenya in the least. Upon hearing Antonio's voice, Savannah slid out of bed. Taking the portable phone with her, she left the bedroom and started toward the family room, talking to him all the while.

Once Savannah entered the family room, she stretched out on the sofa, pulled a soft down blanket from the sofa's back, and then covered herself with it. "I had been resting in bed," she said, responding to Antonio's question.

"I'm sorry, Savannah. I didn't mean to disturb you. You go ahead and get your rest. I can call you back later."

Savannah shook her head from side to side. "No, no, that's okay. I got out of bed and moved up to the family room so my chatting wouldn't disturb my sleeping house-guest."

Antonio grew silent. What was Savannah telling him? Did she mean to imply that someone was in her bed with her? His heart ached at just the thought of that. Then his common sense kicked in. If that were the case, Savannah was not the type of woman who'd flaunt such an intimate thing as that in another's man's face. At least he hoped not.

"Antonio, are you still there?"

"Yes, Savannah, I am. It's just that your last statement threw me for a loop. Did I misinterpret what you said, or did you really mention having a houseguest in your bed?"

Normally Antonio wouldn't have posed such a question, but he definitely needed clarification. This conversation couldn't go any further until he was satisfied that he'd heard Savannah wrong. Antonio desperately hoped that his ears had in fact deceived him.

Once Savannah thought about what Antonio had said, she couldn't help chuckling. "Yes, you did hear me right. Kenya's asleep in my bed. Sorry if you were misled. Not my intent."

Antonio didn't care one bit if Savannah had heard the loud sigh of relief he'd expelled. He was utterly relieved to know that he'd misinterpreted her remarks. Thank God it wasn't the other scenario he had briefly imagined. "Does Kenya being there with you mean that mother and daughter have finally made up?"

"It was only a matter of time, but Miss Kenya held out longer than I'd expected. When she called me, I was just about to phone her. My strength gave in to weakness. She'll be here for a couple of days. She may even be taking off for Vegas on Friday. She hasn't shared her plans with me. Although Kenya hasn't told me her problems yet, I just happen to know that there's trouble brewing in paradise. Cole called me earlier and he has no clue as to where his wife is. I'm glad he didn't ask me had I heard from her. It would've been hard for me to lie."

"I see. Why didn't you just tell Cole so he could have some peace of mind? I'm sure he's worried sick about Kenya."

"He is. I heard it in his voice. I have learned over the years to stay out of other folks' personal business. I happen to believe married couples should work out their own problems without any interference from the in-laws, or other family members, and friends. I'll only give Kenya advice when she comes to me to ask for it."

"Sounds like a good policy to live by. Since you have company, I guess I can't entice you to have dinner with me this evening."

Savannah laughed. "Who says? Where and at what time?"

Antonio was pleased as punch with Savannah's response. "Are you saying you don't want me to pick you up?"

"Under the circumstances it might be better if I just met you somewhere nearby. You already know that Kenya is having a hard time with me moving on. Nothing has changed."

"What about the Olive Garden in Ontario, about six o'clock? We'll make it an early night. Fair enough?"

"More than fair. You really love Italian food, don't you?"

"It comes in a close second to soul food. Do you know how to get to the restaurant?"

"I think so. Isn't it on Fourth Street?"

"That's the one. I'll see you at six. I can hardly wait, Savannah. If you can talk Kenya into coming with you, please do. I'm all for that. I'd really like to get to know your daughter."

"Thank you for making such a kind gesture. I'll closely monitor the situation before I ask. If she knows I'm going out to dinner with you, she'll more than likely have her say despite the rules I've laid down. If she doesn't react the way I expect her to, I'll then extend the invitation. See you later, Antonio. By the way, I'll be waiting anxiously to see you, too."

"Until then, Savannah."

Upon reentering her bedroom, Savannah saw that

Kenya was no longer in her bed. Sure that she'd gone back to the guest room, she went in search of her daughter. As she passed by the guest bathroom, Savannah heard loud sobbing. Since Kenya was the only other person in the house, she didn't have to guess at who was crying.

Savannah knocked gently on the door. "Kenya, can I come in?"

"No, don't come in here, Mom! I don't want you to see me like this."

As if she hadn't seen her daughter distraught before, Savannah mused, opening the door and entering the bathroom anyway. The sight before Savannah shocked her for a moment. Kenya's head was leaned over the toilet bowl, as she regurgitated violently. Savannah didn't know what to think, but she knew her daughter was ill. The mother/nurse flew into immediate action. After grabbing a white washcloth from the linen closet, Savannah wet it with cold water and then placed it against Kenya's sweating brow. "What *is* going on with you, Kenya? How long have you been throwing up?"

Kenya burst into tears. "For a couple of weeks now. I've been miserable. Mom, I'm afraid I might be pregnant. I'm not ready to become a mother yet. I'm still too young. If I'm with child, I'm considering having an abortion. I can't be that far along. Cole doesn't even know yet."

Knowing she couldn't have possibly heard Kenya right, Savannah stared openly at her daughter, as though she were looking into the tearful face of a total stranger. Had this been anyone other than her child, Savannah probably would've remained unbiased. But that wasn't the case. Her own flesh and blood was talking about taking the life of an unborn child. How could that be? Abortion went against everything Savannah believed in—and Kenya knew that.

God created life; therefore, He should be the only One to take it away.

Mustering up all the courage Savannah had within her heart came hard for her, especially when she felt so numb and weak. Then she realized she had to put her feelings completely aside. Her daughter needed her mother's strength right now. If they were going to get through this, Savannah knew that she had to remain objective. Kenya just wasn't thinking with a straight head; Savannah had to be there for her daughter in her time of dire need.

Seeing that Kenya's upheaval had finally ceased, Savannah guided her daughter back into the guest bedroom. After pulling the covers back on the bed, she prompted Kenya to climb in. Savannah then sat on the side of the mattress. "Will you be all right for a couple of minutes? I have to make a phone call, but I promise to come right back."

Kenya looked terrified. "You're not calling Cole, are you? Mom, please don't do that!"

Savannah shook her head. "No, I'm not. I had made a date with Mr. Delabay, but I'm going to cancel it." Savannah got to her feet. "I'll only be a minute."

"Mom, don't do that. I could use some time alone. I really just want to go back to sleep."

"I'm not leaving you like this, Kenya. Sleep all you want. I'll be right here in the house."

"Mom, I know I've been a butt about you seeing Mr. Delabay, but I also know I shouldn't have tried to interfere in your relationship with him. If you insist on staying home, why don't you have him come over here? He can just bring take-out food. I don't want to ruin your evening…and it's really time for me to stop being so selfish."

First of all, Savannah couldn't believe that she'd just heard Kenya suggesting that Antonio come over for a visit. Secondly, having an abortion was the most selfish thing anyone could ever do, so as far as Kenya calling a halt to being self-centered, Savannah wasn't feeling any truth in that remark. "Kenya, we need to talk. To do that we need to be alone."

"Not tonight, Mom. I don't want to talk about anything with anyone. I promise to talk with you first thing in the morning. We can discuss everything over breakfast. Okay? Please don't break your date. I'd feel worse than I already do if you cancel."

"What about Cole, Kenya? When are you going to talk to him? He has a huge stake in this, too, you know. If you're pregnant, you're talking about aborting Cole's child as well. It took both of you to conceive this baby. Your husband should definitely have some say in the matter."

Kenya shook her head from side to side, her eyes filling with tears. "I can't think about any of that right now. Please, Mom, just let it go until tomorrow."

Savannah knew when she'd lost the battle, knew how to concede the loss graciously. Although the war wasn't over by a long shot, retreating was the best option for now. "I'm going to leave you alone for now. Tomorrow you can expect me to come at you with both guns blazing. Make no mistake about that, Kenya. And if you honestly don't mind, I think I will ask Mr. Delabay to come over here. I could use the company."

Kenya shook her head again. "I really don't mind. I've got bigger things on my mind than you and your new boyfriend." Kenya even managed a half smile, making Savannah smile, too.

Spicy Popeye's chicken, coleslaw and French fries wouldn't have been Savannah's first choice for takeout, but she'd missed her chance at saying what she'd like to eat. It was her own fault because Antonio had certainly asked her to express her desires. It wasn't that she didn't like Popeye's; she actually loved it, but her palate really wasn't in the mood for it. Besides that, Savannah made it a point to eat spicier foods earlier in the day, not late in the evening. Because she wouldn't think of hurting Antonio's feelings, she'd eaten a good portion of what he'd bought. The next time they did takeout she'd be sure to tell him exactly what she wanted.

Although Kenya had said that she didn't mind Antonio coming there, Savannah still felt like she was on pins and needles. Her daughter's unpredictability hadn't changed one iota. Kenya could change directions in midstream and without a moment's notice. Savannah had also opted to sit in a chair rather than next to him on the sofa just to keep them a safe distance apart. She'd like nothing better than to be sitting right up under him, with his arm around her shoulders, but she was worried about Kenya suddenly popping into the family room. Savannah didn't like the distance she'd put between him and her, but she had to respect her daughter's feelings.

In Savannah's opinion Kenya was already going through enough trauma and drama.

Antonio was once again impeccably dressed, though his clothing was more casual than anything Savannah had seen him wear thus far. The blue denim designer jeans showed off his great physical attributes. A royal blue short-sleeved polo shirt spanned his broad chest, tapering into a perfect fit. Never without a jacket, Antonio's blazer was a close match to the jeans.

Antonio moved to the edge of the sofa. "Is there a reason we're sitting so far apart?"

Savannah looked slightly abashed, pointing toward the back of the house. "I'm trying to respect Kenya," she whispered. "If she was to come in here, I wouldn't want her to feel the least bit uncomfortable. I hope you understand."

Antonio smiled sympathetically. "Of course I do. How long is she going to be visiting?"

Savannah shrugged. "No clue. I wish I could tell you all that's going on, but I'm afraid she might hear me. That would cause an outright war between us. I sure could use some advice. This is a heavy burden for me to carry alone." Savannah made sure she'd spoken just above a whisper in case Kenya made an appearance.

Hearing the anguish in Savannah's voice was upsetting to Antonio. If he was to play a vital part in this woman's life, her problems had to be his to share in. Getting up from the sofa, Antonio walked over to where Savannah sat and then knelt down in front of the chair. "I feel your conflict, Savannah. Why don't we go for a walk so you can talk freely? I can tell that you need to have an outlet for release. It's a beautiful evening for a stroll around the block. You also have that great park across the street. We can stop by there on the way back here."

Savannah smiled brightly. "That's a great idea!" Even though she thought she shouldn't discuss her kids' personal business with others, Antonio wasn't just anybody to her. She was sure that whatever she shared with him would stay with him. Savannah truly trusted him.

It was times like this that made Savannah realize how much she had relied on her late husband to help her get through the tough times. But Geoffrey wasn't there for her any longer. Antonio could never take Geoffrey's place in her heart, but she had enough space left inside that soft spot for Antonio to create his own special space. He was well on his way to doing so. If Savannah hadn't felt that Antonio genuinely cared for her, she wouldn't share with him anything as personal as what Kenya was dealing with, which could eventually affect the entire family.

While dusk waited in the wings to complete its descent over the city of Fontana, the hot desertlike air of the day had begun to cool down. It was a beautiful evening, just as Antonio had said. Savannah couldn't wait for the first stars to appear up in the sky. Unlike the heavy smog that kept the stars hidden in the city of angels, Fontana's night skies were a dazzling light show.

So far Savannah and Antonio had been content to just walk around the block, basking in the comfort of each other's company. Since she really hadn't explored in depth the entire neighborhood in which she resided, Savannah was really enjoying the pleasurable tour.

New houses were still going up all over the place in the Inland Empire. Numerous homes were already finished, but there were that many more which were only partially built. The progress of the city's growth was astounding. Not so long ago there were only a few new houses sprinkled here and there, Savannah recalled, which were once just large plots of undeveloped land. Subdivision after subdivision was being constructed. A lot of work had been completed since the first phases had begun in the area. The one thing she enjoyed the most was the peace and quiet throughout the neighborhood. Savannah hadn't heard so much as a single dog bark.

As the couple neared the park, after walking around the neighborhood for nearly a half hour, Antonio removed his hand from Savannah's to put his arm around her shoulder. "Are you up to walking over to the lake in the park? It's only a short distance away."

Savannah nodded. "I'm up to it. There are several park benches over by the lake where we can sit down for a bit. I don't want to be gone too much longer, though. Kenya is probably awake by now. When I checked on her before we left the house, she was completely knocked out. I hope she sees the note I left her."

"I understand your concerns for Kenya, Savannah. Maybe you should go ahead and tell me what's going on while we make it over to the lake."

Savannah sighed. "Kenya thinks she's pregnant, Antonio, but she says she's not ready to become a mother. Feels she's too young yet." Savannah paused for a moment to try and keep her emotions under control. "The worst of this is that my daughter is considering an abortion."

Antonio's shrill whistle rent the air. "She actually told you she was planning that?"

"In plain English. I was mortified, Antonio, unable to

believe my own ears. I wanted to break down and cry, but I knew she needed me to be strong. I don't know how I'm going to handle this in the coming days. I won't know what to do if she really intends to go through with the abortion. Cole doesn't know a thing yet. Just the idea of it will probably kill him."

"Savannah, I know you realize that this is a very serious issue. I hope you don't take this personally, but I don't think you're dealing with this situation properly."

Savannah sharply raised an eyebrow. "Whatever do you mean by that, Antonio?"

Since they'd arrived at their destination, Antonio quickly directed Savannah over to one of the lakeside benches, where they each took a seat.

"Please let me explain how I see things." Antonio took hold of both Savannah's hands.

Savannah looked very fearful. "I'm willing to listen to you, Antonio."

Antonio explained to Savannah that she was helping Kenya practice deception against Cole. Harboring her daughter inside her home, when her husband didn't know her whereabouts, would probably make Cole feel that both his wife and mother-in-law had betrayed him. He then went on to say that she should make Kenya call her husband as soon as she got back to the house. It was not fair to have him worry himself sick about his wife throughout the night.

"Try to put yourself in Cole's place, Savannah. Then ask yourself how you'd want to be treated under the same set of circumstances. I know you said you'd prefer to stay out of their marriage issues, but you're not doing that by having Kenya staying with you when you know she isn't being on the up-and-up with her husband. If you don't take yourself out of the middle of this right away, before it goes any further, you could very well end up on the outside looking in. Worse than that, you may never be asked to come back inside their private lives again. I can guarantee you that Cole will see your part in this as unforgivable. He trusts you a lot."

Savannah was so close to tears. Antonio was absolutely right in his assessment of things. She had only halfway considered Cole's position in this matter. It certainly hadn't been her intent to become a coconspirator with Kenya against Cole, but that's exactly what had occurred. Geoffrey would've seen it the same way as Antonio saw it. If Kevin knew what was going on, he would probably be of the same mind. Savannah had unwittingly done the very thing she may've harshly criticized someone else for. It was solely up to her to rectify the situation.

"Thank you, Antonio. I see things so much clearer. I'll see to it that Kenya calls Cole as soon as I get back home. If she refuses, I'll call him myself. Since I'm already guilty of duplicity, though it was not my intent, I have to take myself out of the middle. Why do you think Kenya made Cole believe she only wanted to go off with her girlfriends? I'm guessing that was just an excuse she made up to get away to sort things out. There probably wasn't a Vegas trip at all."

"I think you're right." Antonio brought Savannah to him and gave her a loving hug and then a very passionate kiss. When she began to cry, he held on to her even tighter, rocking her in his arms. "Calm down, sweetheart. It'll be okay. Let me get you back home. I'm not coming in. You and Kenya need to sort all this out right away. Cole also needs to know where his wife is."

"Thank you, Antonio. I agree wholeheartedly."

Chapter 9

As much as Savannah had thought she was staying out of Kenya and Cole's private affairs, she had found herself right in the thick of things. Cole had shown up two hours after Kenya was all but forced to call him, which meant that he must've set his car on turbo pilot. The late-night hours up until the wee ones had brought much turmoil to bear for all concerned. Daylight had just made its entry into the skies, yet darkness had Savannah's home surrounded.

Still lying in bed, feeling emotionally worn down, Savannah had just finished doing her morning devotional to help restore her spiritual strength. Normally Kenya and Cole would've joined her in her morning Bible and daily devotional reading, but she hadn't dared to wake either of them. Husband and wife were in bed in separate rooms, but she couldn't help wondering how much sleep either of them had gotten. If how they'd parted company several hours ago was any indication, she knew that their time away from each other had been nothing short of fitful.

Antonio's theory had made perfect sense to Savannah, which had had her rushing home from the park to set things right. After sharing a few tender hugs and kisses with Antonio, right inside the door, Savannah had bid him farewell, wishing she didn't have to go through this alone.

Although Cole had been angrier than Savannah had ever seen him, he still didn't know the whole truth. Savannah had convinced Kenya not to mention anything about having an abortion since it hadn't been medically determined that she was with child. Savannah didn't think that Cole needed to hear from Kenya that she wanted to abort his child. She could only imagine what hearing something as devastating as that might do to his sweet spirit.

Cole didn't deserve that from Kenya. He loved her too much for her to destroy him in that manner. It would've been unconscionable on Kenya's part to tell him something she wasn't even sure about. Irreparable damage would more than likely occur. How was a man supposed to get over his own wife wanting to rid herself of their child, the very first? Savannah didn't think Cole would ever recover from it, which could possibly end in him seeking a divorce from Kenya.

Once Savannah had gotten that off her chest, her main concern then was for Cole to know exactly where his wife was hiding out. The call to Cole had eventually been made by Kenya, but only after she'd fought the idea tooth and nail. When Savannah had threatened to make the call to Cole herself, Kenya had finally conceded, but not before she'd nearly drained all her mother's emotional fortitude.

Kenya saw Savannah's interference in her private life as a definite betrayal. Savannah had quickly fired back, impatiently explaining to her daughter that she wouldn't have been in the middle of their marital problems if Kenya hadn't placed her there. Cole was also guilty of getting Savannah involved by the phone call he'd made to her earlier.

Savannah had later run out to the 24-hour pharmacy to purchase a home pregnancy kit for Kenya, but she had yet to find out the results. She wasn't sure if her daughter had even begun the testing or not, because Cole had called back while she was out to let them know that he was on his way up to the house. Right after Savannah's return from the drugstore, Kenya had spent at least the next half hour or so crying her eyes out, terribly fearful of the major showdown that was imminent between her and Cole. Kenya was as confused as anyone could ever be.

Upon seeing the red flashing light, Savannah realized she had phone messages. After retrieving the voice mail, she was surprised to learn that the one call had come before she'd even returned home from the senior center the previous morning. Even more astonishing than the call itself was the fact that she'd been offered the office of president.

It was made perfectly clear to Savannah by Loretta Ames that the offer was being made because no one else wanted the job, as if Savannah didn't already know that. She figured that she should probably be excited, but she wasn't. At the moment her kids' lives were in utter turmoil; their personal well-being was the most important issue in Savannah's life.

Nothing else really mattered to Savannah at this point in time.

Savannah quickly had to rephrase that statement. Antonio also mattered. He had been so tender with her last evening. It seemed to her that he really understood all that was happening. His sage advice had been right on the money and she couldn't wait to tell him how much she had appreciated it. The last thing she wanted to do was drop her family problems into his lap.

A budding relationship like theirs shouldn't be bogged down with serious issues such as Kenya and Cole's, but as a father himself, Antonio's kids had also had their share of serious downs. He had been quick to point that out to Savannah on their walk back to her place. He'd even gone as far as to ask her if she'd be there for him under similar circumstances. Before she'd had a chance to respond to his query, Antonio had told her he believed she'd support him in the very same way he was offering his support to her. Savannah had taken great pleasure in confirming for Antonio how right he was about her.

Loud shouting caused Savannah to jump out of bed and rush for the bedroom door. Realizing she was still in her silk nightgown, she quickly ran to her closet and grabbed an appropriate covering. The matching robe was as thin as the gown, which in her opinion was inappropriate attire to wear in front of her son-in-law so she put on a thicker cover-up.

As Savannah quickly made her way up to the front of the house, the voices sounded more heated with anger and had also grown much louder. Kenya and Cole were going at each other again, pretty much the same way they'd gone at it last evening. Since the kids were too busy arguing to notice her, Savannah's first thought was to go on back to her bedroom and let them work it out for themselves.

The thought of leaving the room had barely cleared Savannah's mind when she saw Kenya pick up one of her precious lead crystal vases and then hold it up at Cole in a threatening manner. Savannah wasn't that worried about the vase. Cole being hit upside the head with it was the bigger concern. If Kenya hit her intended mark, bloodshed would definitely occur.

Savannah shouted Kenya's name loud enough to grab her daughter's immediate attention. "Put that vase down right now, Kenya. You two are not going to come in here and tear up my place. You guys need to calm down so you can talk things through in a rational manner. Fighting like this isn't going to bring about any positive results. I don't want to be any more involved in this crazy mess than what I already am, but I'll mediate for you to keep you from killing each other. Can we please sit down and talk about what's happening between you two?"

Cole was hot under the collar, but he took a seat on the sofa. Of course Miss Kenya had to get in a few more cutting remarks before she finally sat down on a chair. Savannah sat in the other chair. Sitting on the sofa with Cole would be seen by Kenya as Savannah taking his side. Savannah was certain of that.

As Kenya and Cole sat there in stone silence, Savannah busily racked her brain, trying to figure out how to mediate this delicate situation. Since Cole still didn't know about the possible pregnancy, nor did Savannah know if Kenya had taken the home test, there wasn't any sort of real issue to present.

"What's this really all about, Kenya? I'm getting the impression that going off to Vegas with your girlfriends isn't the main event. Why did you leave home without telling me?"

Great, Savannah mused. Cole had taken the initiative to start the ball rolling, so all she had to do was sit there and listen and to make sure the conversations didn't go out of bounds.

Kenya rolled her eyes so hard at Cole that Savannah thought they just might pop out of her head. *Attitude personified*, Savannah deliberated. From where did her daughter get that mean streak? It surely hadn't come from either of her parents. Still, Savannah had to wonder, wishing she could give her daughter a good, thorough shaking.

"This is about you, Cole, being so insensitive to me. You're hardly ever home. You wanted me to be a stay-at-home wife, but you're not a stay-at-home husband. Why's that?"

Cole palmed his forehead hard, staring at his wife as if she'd lost her mind. "Kenya, why am I not home as much as you'd like? I know you know. I'm a resident, sweetheart. Before we got married, I told you my work schedule would be crazy for a few years. Do you honestly think I like being away from you? Well, I don't. If I'm to finish my residency, I don't have a choice."

"Resident or not, I don't believe you have to work as much as you say you do. We don't have a social life anymore either. Romantic dinners out for us have become extinct. Our fun times together came to a grinding halt not long after we got married. But you somehow manage to find time to hang out with your frat boys. I wouldn't be a bit surprised to find out that you have a chick or two on the side. You are gone from home way too much, Mr. Man."

Cole looked as if he'd suddenly been floored by Kenya's coldhearted accusations. The painful expression in his eyes was easy enough to discern. Kenya had attacked both his heart and his integrity. "Simply not true, Kenya. You are the only woman in my life."

Cole then moved to the edge of his seat, his shoulders slumping forward in a show of defeat. "I had no idea you felt that I'd be capable of hurting you in that manner. I guess you don't know me as well as I thought you did." He sighed hard. "In knowing how you feel, I really don't know where we go from here. Do you have any suggestions for us, Mrs. Standiford?"

So, there *are* other serious issues between Kenya and Cole, Savannah ruminated—quite a few of them. Kevin had been right when he'd suspected marital woes. Savannah had already known that Kenya had a gripe about Cole not having enough time for her, but this *chick on the side* thing was the first time she'd presented that awful theory, at least in front of her mother.

Savannah didn't believe for a second that Cole was cheating on his wife. There'd have to be hard evidence shown to the contrary before she could even consider such a thing. There was nothing about her son-in-law that might give her that impression. Coleman Standiford was a darn good man and had been a wonderful husband thus far. And whatever her daughter's reason, Kenya had deliberately made the reckless decision to hit him way below the belt.

Kenya appeared surprised that Cole had rolled the ball back into her court. It seemed to Savannah that Cole had given up much easier and much sooner than Kenya had expected him to. Although she hated to see her kids hurting this way, she was glad they were at least tabling the plaguing issues, all but the most important one—the issue of whether Kenya was pregnant or not.

Silence took over the room. Kenya didn't seem to know how to answer Cole's question. When she looked over at Savannah, as though she was seeking advice, Savannah only shrugged.

"Mom, Kenya and I both brought this troubling situation to you, so if you have any suggestions for us, please feel free to voice them. Otherwise, I'm afraid we'll remain hopelessly at a standstill." The emotional quaking in Cole's voice had come though loud and clear.

"Thanks for saying that, Cole. Your marital troubles obviously go much deeper than anything I could've ever imagined. In fact, I didn't even know you had any serious problems until shortly after Kenya had showed up on my doorstep. The only suggestion I'm willing to make is that you two seek marriage counseling from a professional."

Kenya sucked her teeth hard. "I'm not seeing no dang shrink!"

"In that case, Kenya, it's my guess that you're content in being a part of the problem rather than trying to be a part of the solution. If it's a divorce you're after, you're heading in the right direction, my dear daughter. If I dare to say so, and I do dare, your decision not to seek marriage counseling sucks." Savannah stood. "Let me know what you all decide. I'm going back to my room and get into bed. There are times when I do forget I'm a retiree."

Kenya looked horrified. "Mom, you can't do that! I need you."

Savannah posted her hands on each of her hips. "For what? To be a captive audience, while you continue to sit there on your high horse, remaining unwilling to compromise? I don't think so. And furthermore, I think you and Cole need to work this out in your own home. I don't see what else I can do to assist you all. Welcome to the game of life!"

"Are you telling us to go home?" Kenya shouted.

"*Us,* meaning you and Cole, has a real nice ring to it. Knock on my bedroom door before you guys leave so I can put on the alarm." With that said, Savannah left the room, sure that she'd confirmed for Kenya the intent of her comment.

Savannah was positively fuming by the time she reached her bedroom. As much as she wanted to slam the door shut behind her, after she entered the master suite, she didn't want to give Kenya the satisfaction of knowing she'd upset her mother once again. What Savannah had just done hadn't been easy for her, but she simply wasn't going to let Kenya and Cole come into her home and turn everything topsy-turvy. If they hadn't wanted her advice, they shouldn't have asked for it, shouldn't have brought their troubles to her, period.

Savannah once again told herself it wasn't possible to re-raise adult children.

After flinging herself across the bed, Savannah buried her head into a pillow, slowly inhaling and exhaling. As a teenager she had gotten into the bad habit of holding her breath when she'd felt anxious or fearful. Nearly fainting more than a time or two had made her see it as totally the wrong approach. The breathing exercises helped to keep her calm and in control.

That she was possibly being selfish with the kids was uppermost in Savannah's mind. But if she didn't look out for herself, who would? She almost felt sure that Kenya and Cole would work out their differences a lot faster if she stayed the heck out of it. It had seemed that her offer to mediate had been welcomed by the kids, but it obviously hadn't been used.

Cole had been more willing than Kenya to try and resolve things, more than likely because he didn't know the real deal. Savannah still felt that Kenya shouldn't discuss her physical condition with Cole until she was positive there was something to discuss. To do differently could possibly create a chasm too wide for her to cross back to the other side. Cole was an understanding person, but he had limitations, just like every other person in the world.

Putting Kenya and Cole out of her mind for now, Savannah reached for the telephone. Right out of the blue she had decided to go ahead and take the presidency challenge. Despite all the existing controversy among the members she was ready to take on this important job. A sudden knock on the bedroom door caused Savannah to put the phone back in the cradle.

"Mommy."

The endearing name had been spoken so softly, so sweetly by Kenya, causing Savannah's eyes to tear up. Although her kids had pretty much outgrown calling her Mommy, Kenya resorted to the use of it every blue moon or so. "You evil but sweet devil child," she said softly, shaking her head, wishing she could completely ignore it. Even if she didn't respond to that one weighty word, there was no way Kenya would do the norm. Most sane folks might think the person they wanted to see was resting and then decide to go away and come back later.

Not Kenya…

Knowing the door would pop right open within the next few seconds, Savannah sat up straight in the bed, crossing her arms against her chest. She then picked up one of the bed pillows. In the very next second, Savannah's prediction came true. The moment Kenya opened the door and stuck her head inside Savannah hurled the pillow right at her daughter, howling like she'd just discovered the great benefits caused by laughter.

Kenya was stunned at first, looking at her mother in total bewilderment. Then a few of her fondest childhood memories kicked in. Pillow fighting had been a favorite thing for her and Kevin to get into mischief with. Seeing how uncontrollable her mother's laughter was made her start laughing, too. Rushing over to the bed, Kenya grabbed up one of the fluffy weapons, hitting Savannah right upside her head with it. Then the pillow fight of all pillow fights was on.

Within a matter of only a few minutes it appeared as if every pillow in the bedroom had been tossed around between Savannah and Kenya, including the designer bolsters from off the microfiber covered settee and matching overstuffed chair. One down-filled pillow had burst wide open, making the room look like it was raining tiny down feathers. Ducking and dodging the flying head supports was of little use, since both Savannah and Kenya were excellent marks-women, hitting their target more often than not.

The boisterous laughter, loud screams and shrill cries finally brought Cole running headlong into the room. Upon seeing all the craziness happening before him, he tried to turn around and run to dodge the pillow sailing right at him, but he wasn't quick enough. The cushion hit him in the back of the head. Retaliation was all he could think of as he picked up the same pillow and hurled it back at the person who'd targeted him intentionally, his very own wife.

Joining in the melee of fun wasn't a problem for Cole, who was unable to contain his deep-throated laughter. He actually saw the pillow fight as a good way to relieve some of the tension they'd all been under. He and his siblings had also indulged in these types of battles as kids. In fact, he and Kenya had rolled foam bolsters at home, which they'd playfully used on each other as tension busters. Cole had to wonder if they could've kept their personal issues under better control had they used the soft plastic-handled bolsters during the past couple of months.

Cole also felt horrible for the way he and Kenya had involved Savannah in their battles of wills and wits, bringing about undue stresses for one of the sweetest women in the universe. His mother-in-law was an angel, a peace-loving woman, but he and his wife had declared war on each other, in her home, on the last two visits. Cole knew Savannah deserved better from them, deserved to have as good as what she always gave, which was the very best of herself.

The very moment another bed pillow burst open Savannah called an immediate halt to the ridiculous child-play. As she'd done so, she'd wondered if Antonio would've minded joining in on acting out such crazy nonsense. The thought of him and her having a similar battle just to have fun caused laughter to bubble inside her once again, believing he would've been game.

A completely exhausted Savannah collapsed in a heap atop her bed. She noticed that Kenya and Cole had already dropped down to the carpeted floor, each of their bodies stretched out fully. Savannah thought it strange that not one of them had spoken a single word since the pillow fights had first begun yet the presence of camaraderie was clearly felt.

Savannah smiled when she saw Cole cautiously throw his arm across his wife's abdomen. She gave a sigh of relief when Kenya didn't object to her husband's loving touch. Savannah knew that had she continued to interfere in their messy madness, when the couple was ready to make up, she figured the whole thing would've probably still had her upset. That could've also left her on the outside looking in. Life was one big mystery—one right after the other.

Savannah laughed heartily. "Guess what, kids?"

Kenya lifted her head to make visual contact with Savannah. "What?"

"Your mother's been selected as president!" Savannah shrieked, smiling broadly.

Cole peered up at Savannah, wondering what she was talking about. "President of what?"

"President of the Silver Wings Senior Center. Despite my age. Isn't that something?"

"It is, Mom. Congratulations! Why did you say selected instead of elected?" Kenya asked.

Savannah explained that no member had wanted to run for the office. Having already grown weary of telling the same old thing over and over again, Savannah was sure this wasn't the last time she'd have to give someone all the details.

Proud of his mother-in-law's accomplishment, Cole smiled warmly at Savannah. "Congrats, Mom! Can I convince you two beautiful ladies to let me take you out to lunch so we can celebrate the presidential appointment? That is, once we get this mess all cleaned up. These dang feathers are everywhere."

With Cole talking about lunch, Savannah glanced at the clock. Their frolicking had lasted a lot longer than she would've guessed at. The morning had somehow sprouted wings. "I can't believe it's after eleven already. Thanks for the offer of lunch, Cole. I'd love to go. If you don't mind, I'd like to give Antonio a call and invite him, too. Kenya, are you okay with my idea?"

Kenya frowned slightly, purposely wanting her mother to think she objected, even though she didn't. Giving her mother a hard time was one of her favorite things to do. Getting a rise out of Savannah was a hard thing for Kenya to do, which made the challenge that much sweeter.

Savannah sighed. "I can see by your expression, Kenya, that it's not okay with you. I understand, but I'd still like the three of us to have lunch. I can be ready in thirty minutes."

Kenya got up from the floor and then walked over to her mother's bed. "I was just kidding with you, Mom. Your idea is fine with me. Since you're not going to give Mr. Delabay up, I'd better start getting used to him being around. Mind if I'm the one to call and invite him?"

Savannah stuck her forefinger into her ear and gently turned it in a mocking gesture. "Either I have too much wax in my ears, and didn't hear you right, or I need to check you for any signs of a fever, child. You've definitely come down with a mysterious illness, Kenya."

Everyone cracked up.

Kenya covered the portable phone with her hand but didn't pick it up. "Please get Mr. Delabay on the line, Mom, before I decide to change my mind," Kenya joked with ease.

"Okay, Kenya, you win. But before we do that, I need you guys to listen up for a moment." Cole and Kenya directed their attention at Savannah as she sat up in the bed. "Guys, I know you're going through some really tough times right now. It's not that unusual for young married couples to experience a few serious trials. My favorite saying is *no rain, no rainbow.* If you remember nothing else, remember this— choose thy love and love thy choice. Whatever it took for you two to earn each other's love, the same things need to occur for you to keep it. You guys can work it out, but you have to be willing. Marriage is hard work, every single day."

Savannah went on to explain to her adult children that both of them were responsible for the state their marriage was in; that no one person should have to carry the burden of blame. They could work at their relationship or throw in the towel—marriage wasn't going to fix itself.

Savannah then expressed the importance of communication, telling Kenya and Cole not to expect each other to be a mind reader. Communicating was the best way to get their needs met. Not only did they have to talk, they had to become great listeners. Savannah couldn't say enough about how they needed to respect each other. Shouting at each other and calling names was totally inappropriate behavior. Savannah hoped she'd gotten through to Kenya and Cole.

Cole took hold of Kenya's hand and squeezed it affectionately. "Mom," said Cole, "we're sorry for getting you upset. We know how you love your peace. Thanks for putting up with us. Believe it or not, you walking out on us in the heat of battle has had a profound effect on me."

Cole then turned to Kenya. "I want you to come home with me. We can spend the rest of the day and night talking. We can continue to talk until we have it all figured out, but we can't ever stop communicating. I promise to listen. Will you please come home with me, Kenya?"

Kenya kissed Cole full on the mouth, brushing her knuckles down his cheek. "Yes."

As Savannah rushed around the kitchen to prepare lunch for her peers, she kept a close eye on the clock. In less than an hour Bernice, Janice, Marie, Madge and Clara were due to arrive at her front door. Savannah had even invited her neighbor, Inez, although Inez wasn't sure if she could make it, but she'd promised to give it her best attempt.

Now that Savannah had been all sworn in as the club president of Silver Wings Senior Center, the youngest one ever, Savannah needed some advice and support from the other women on planning her first major social event.

Savannah was determined to make a successful go of her new position.

The house was finally back to normal, all nice and quiet. Cole and Kenya had gone home a couple of days ago right after they'd returned from lunch. She hadn't heard from the kids since they'd called to say they'd made it safely back to L.A. Besides keeping Kenya and Cole in constant prayer, Savannah believed they'd eventually work everything through. Their love for each other was their biggest ally. Savannah also knew how love could turn into a deadly enemy.

The luncheon date Savannah had had with Kenya and Cole had turned out to be a very nice outing. Antonio had showed up at the Olive Garden within minutes of their arrival. Since they hadn't gotten to dine out there, as had been initially planned, because of all the stuff going on with Kenya, Savannah had chosen the same restaurant for the lunch date.

Things had been sort of awkward at first for everyone, as Kenya had obviously sized up Antonio, but his sense of humor had had Kenya laughing within just a short time. Antonio and Cole had seemed to hit it off from the start, pretty much the way Kevin and Antonio had become quick friends. Antonio was really an easy person to get to know.

What had later occurred at the popular eatery, not long after their food had been served, had totally blown Savannah's mind, not to mention Kenya's. If Kenya hadn't been completely sold on Antonio before, his loving gesture toward her and her mother had instantly won her over.

Antonio had had a dozen roses each delivered to the restaurant for Savannah and Kenya: red blooms for Savannah and yellow ones for Kenya.

Remembering Kenya's animated reaction to receiving the sweet-smelling bouquet had Savannah smiling. Emotionally full over the yellow roses, the young woman had barely been able to contain all the joyfulness she'd felt inside. Antonio's thoughtfulness had gone over in a big way with Savannah's daughter. Kenya hadn't been able to thank Antonio enough.

Not long after the flower delivery, it seemed that Kenya had suddenly developed an innocent crush on Antonio, just like little girls sometimes did with their single mommy's beaus. Kenya's eyelashes appeared stuck on flutter. Cole had also been impressed with Antonio's kind deed, which had also served as a very nice icebreaker for everyone.

Fully turning her attention back to the tasks at hand, Savannah hoped her friends would be pleased with the all-salad luncheon she had prepared in their honor. She had whipped up several kinds of salad, from pasta to plain garden and fruit. Her chicken salad was a favorite with Bernice so she'd included it on the menu as well. She had also made a large Greek salad, one of her own favorites. Savannah's pasta salad was favored most by her family.

The salad meal really hadn't taken all that much time for Savannah to pull together.

Savannah had also made a special punch of pink lemonade, cranberry juice and a few generous splashes of Sprite and 7 Up. Large strawberries were used as a garnish. For dessert Savannah planned to serve cheesecake with a choice of blueberry and strawberry glazes.

With all her kitchen tasks completed, Savannah rushed off to take her shower.

As Savannah looked around the table at each of her guests, about ten minutes after they'd all begun eating, she saw that everyone looked very pleased. She then glanced at the various bowls to see which salads had been the most or least favored. Savannah had this weird thing of grading the quality of her food by what was eaten or not eaten. By the looks of things, she might not have any leftovers. The Greek salad bowl was almost empty, but the pasta and chicken bowls had left in them a couple of servings. The fruit salad was practically gone as well.

Savannah couldn't have been more satisfied that her friends were enjoying the food. Then she realized that if Inez eventually showed up, she might not have anything left to serve her.

Bernice made direct eye contact with Savannah. "Everything is divine," she said, as though she'd read Savannah's mind. "The chicken salad is exceptionally good, as always. You really do have to let me know how you make it. That is, if it isn't a trade secret."

Savannah laughed heartily. "Honey, what in heaven's name are you talking about? The ingredients for my chicken salad are top secret. I could tell you…"

"But then I'd have to kill you," Marie chimed in, interrupting Savannah on a giggle.

Everyone laughed at that.

"Yeah, something like that," Savannah responded, laughing. "I'll give you the recipe, Bernice. And I promise that you won't have to die for it."

Laughter once again rang out among the ladies.

Madge waved her hand in the air. "You've invited us over for lunch, you've fed us, and I'm sure you have a delicious dessert of some type waiting in the wings. But what I want to know, Savannah, is what we did to deserve all this wonderful pampering? It seems to me you should be saving this kind of special attention for your new man."

There was something about Madge's question and her last statement that had rubbed Savannah the wrong way. It seemed to her as if this woman was always baiting her. Why did she feel the need to do that? Savannah wanted to ask Madge what she'd done to make her act as rude as she did, but she refrained. Madge was Bernice's friend. Savannah didn't want to offend her best friend over something that one of her friends were doing, something that made no sense to her. Savannah was aware that Bernice had no control over Madge's unruly lips.

Savannah batted her eyes in dramatic fashion. "Make no mistake about it, Antonio gets plenty of special attention from me, Madge. The man can never say he's being neglected by me." With that said, Savannah laid down her fork. "Well, since you guys brought all these gifts with you today, I can't use them as the reason for the pampering. Especially since this luncheon is not a housewarming event. But I can't wait to rip them all right open." Savannah paused a moment. "I actually invited you all here today to make a special announcement…"

Madge's eyes widened. "No, don't tell us! You're engaged to Delabay, aren't you?" Madge queried, having interrupted her hostess once again. "Don't you think it's kind of soon for that? You *really* don't know him that well, Savannah."

Savannah's expression grew somber, as she wondered how she was supposed to keep ignoring the barbed comments from Madge. Storing up anger and resentment wasn't a good thing. It seemed to Savannah that everyone else was feeling the tension, too. "Not even close, Madge! You and your over-the-top imagination," Savannah lightly scolded, when all she really wanted to do was spend her rage on her annoying guest. "I was elected president of the senior club at Silver Wings, ladies. But not by vote, mind you. I won by sheer default. No one else wanted the job." Savannah laughed before she went on to tell her guests all the things that had transpired before the election decision had finally been made.

Bernice shook her head in dismay. "Girl, I have to congratulate you, but I'm also going to have to move you further up on my prayer list. You sure enough got your work cut out for you. Those are some evil old women over at that center. Make sure you keep plenty of Tylenol on hand. I'll also keep a shoulder available for you to cry on. You might end up needing a shrink, since the majority of them chicks down at that center are plum crazy."

Clara nodded in agreement. "Especially that evil-behind Ames woman. She *was* their president. Did they vote her behind out? I wouldn't be surprised."

"Loretta Ames quit," Savannah said. "Right in the middle of a meeting. She was upset over the treasurer allegedly misusing some of the funds. There were a lot of catfights that day."

"Olla Jackson probably needed to borrow that money to buy her grandbabies some shoes," Janice said. "She's been having a hard time financially ever since her husband died. Her daughter, Rakia, is a totally messed up crackhead, so Olla's been raising them three babies on her own. I tried to help her out by offering her a few bucks, but Olla has insufferable pride."

"Friends, we've gotten way off the mark. Savannah was in the process of telling us specifically why she invited us here today," Clara remarked rather firmly.

Savannah was glad for the helping hand from Clara. Time had the tendency to get away from them before it was even realized. Since she had plans with Antonio later in the evening, she was eager to get the show on the road so she could rest before then. "Ladies, I invited you over here to solicit your help. After hearing some of what you've had to say, I know I'm going to need your support. I'm trying to get a lot of the senior club's business matters straightened out down at the center, but I also want to get started on planning a special event for my first big social activity. I'm thinking of a spring soiree of some sort, or perhaps a spring dance."

"So that's why we all get to sit in this fancy formal dining room. I knew you had something up your sleeve," Janice clowned. "Use of the good china, silver and crystal was just another indicator. If I didn't know better Savannah Richmond, I'd believe you were trying to butter up us girls, grease the skids so to speak."

Savannah grinned, feeling so glad that Madge hadn't been the one to make those same remarks. Coming from Janice they sounded perfectly innocent. There'd been no malicious intent in her tone. "Guilty as charged, Janice," Savannah sang out. "I guess I'm just not too good at hiding my ulterior motives. No, for real, guys, I need some serious help. Running this club effectively means a lot to me. I don't want the loose wagging tongues to have a thing to say."

Marie held up her hand to claim the floor. "The spring

soiree sounds like fun, Savannah. But I like the dance idea a lot better. As quiet as I keep it, I can still drop it like it's hot. You should see me keeping up with them the dancers on BET. However, if I get frisky like that out in public, I'd be fearful that I might not be able to pick it back up after I drop it."

The group laughed heartily at those comical remarks. Marie knew how to clown, though she didn't have a monopoly on it. All the ladies, including Savannah, had a humorous side.

"Inviting any exciting single men, Savannah?" Bernice inquired, batting her eyelashes in a suggestive manner. "If so, don't make them all too good-looking. You know how I am about that. I'd really like to find out if I can get my groove back. It's been missing so long I can't even remember what it was like."

"Never lost mine," said Madge. "Just don't have anyone to groove with. It looks like Savannah has come to town and stole away all our eligible bachelors. Those little hot numbers you wear, girl, are grabbing all the male attention. Maybe you should tone it down a bit so the rest of us can get something going on around this town."

Peals of laughter rang out yet again, but not so much as a giggle came from Savannah or Bernice. Savannah was too busy biting down on her tongue to keep from saying exactly what she wanted to. That Madge would continue to insult her, especially in her own home, had Savannah fuming inwardly. Bernice didn't know what was going on with Madge, but she didn't like the downright insulting things she was saying to their hostess.

Tamping down her anger, Savannah waved off Madge's

last cutting remarks. If she started saying some of the things that were on her mind regarding Madge, she wouldn't know when to shut up. "Come on, ladies, let's get serious. We all still have it going on. We just have to get back to using what we have."

Clara snorted. "What makes you think we're not serious, Savannah? We do all that social stuff down at the church, but this could be so different from those inspirational socials. A little innocent sinning might do all of us ladies some good."

Laughing, Savannah shook her head. "Clara, you're sweetly nuts. I just need a few good ideas to chew on. This event has to be off the hook. We're not that far behind on the times, ladies. Like I said, we still got it going on. Just 'cause some of us are widowed and divorced, that doesn't mean we can't go back to having lots of fun. Life is waiting on us to grab ahold of it."

Savannah cringed at her last remarks, hoping she hadn't offended anyone. The loud laughter told her that no one had been bothered by it, which had her sighing in relief. No offense had been intended on Savannah's part even if some of the ladies found it hard to move on.

Janice sucked her teeth. "You have lots of room to talk, Savannah, with your little cute, stylish self. Hardly anyone believes you're a day over thirty-five. You have a body most women would kill for. Besides that, you'll have a date for whatever event you eventually decide on, a gorgeous date at that. Maybe you ought to ask Delabay to invite a few of his old single war buddies. I'd like to get fixed up with someone before the event if possible. You feeling me?"

"I can't wear out a rug, or drop it like it's hot, but I can do 'off the hook,'" Marie said. "Whatever you decide to do, Savannah, you can count me in. You definitely have my support. I think you're onto something great with your plans for the senior center. You can also count on me to create any decorations or flower arrangements for your first event. I like the idea of the spring dance, too, but what about doing a black art show before the dancing begins?"

"How soon before the dancing?" Janice inquired. "Most of them tired old men that belong to the senior centers are in bed before eight o'clock in the evening. If you start the event too early, you might lose all the males before the dance even gets underway."

"Not the strong-looking, handsome men I met recently," Savannah offered. "There was nothing tired about that bunch of guys." She then told the ladies about how robust were Noah, Chester and Irwin—and how Noah had been the one to recommend her for the presidency.

Savannah saw that her description of the men sure had sparked a lot of interest among her small group of female comrades. "If each male reaches out to their single friends, we might have more men on our hands than you all can handle," Savannah teased. "No one will have to belong to a senior center to attend. But I could also use this event as a membership drive."

Marie gestured her desire to take the floor. "Okay, Savannah, get some paper and pens for us to use. We're going to throw out our ideas and then talk about the best way to put our plans into action. However, we need to get everything down on paper so we can see all that we've come up with at the end of this meeting. Before we get heavy into that, I'm ready for a slice of that heavenly looking cheesecake. A cup of coffee is not a bad idea either. I'll make it."

"If someone will be so kind as to serve the cheesecake, I'll get the paper and pens," Savannah said. "Thanks for offering to make the coffee, Marie. If anyone wants hot tea, just turn on the gas under the teakettle. I'm glad you all decided to help with my project. Be right back."

Bernice followed Savannah into her bedroom. Once there, she took hold of her dear friend's hand. "I'm sorry Madge has been insulting you like that. I don't know what's gotten into her. She's not normally that kind of person. She doesn't even know you that well yet she's saying things that make me think she's somehow formed an unfavorable opinion of you. I will straighten her out once we leave here, Savannah. You can count on that."

Savannah gave Bernice a warm hug. "Please don't mention a word to her. If there's any straightening out to be done, I'll be the one to do it. I'm the one Madge is insulting. I'm going to give her the benefit of the doubt for a while longer, since I'd really like to know her agenda. I promise that I won't let the resentment build so high that I end up verbally exploding all over her. Let's keep this between us. I don't think the others feel the full undercurrent just yet."

Bernice shook her head. "Savannah, you're some kind of woman. I wish I were that tolerant. I'd've been all over Madge by now. She's my friend, too, but you're my main girl. I won't stand idly by and listen to her tear you down. I just hope you put her in check before I do."

Savannah winked her right eye at Bernice. "You won't have to. I can handle it all."

* * *

For the next hour or so laughter came in abundance in between the exchanges of brilliant ideas for Savannah's social project. Her dear friend and fairly new acquaintances really wanted to see her plan work. These were women that Savannah had started out being cautiously friendly with; the last couple of hours had put her at total ease with everyone but Madge Jacoby. She had only come to know all these ladies through Bernice, who had brought their names up during numerous conversations between herself and Savannah. Savannah had started to feel very comfortable with the other three ladies who seemed so real and down-to-earth.

Although Savannah had only been in the presence of the women on a few occasions, she now knew that all but one of Bernice's close friends meant her no ill will. Savannah had truly come to understand that the other ladies were behind her all the way. During the course of the meeting Savannah was thrilled to learn that Bernice's friends wanted to have her as a close friend as well. Although Madge had voiced her support on the friendship part, Savannah knew better.

A sparkling-cider toast was celebrated among the six women once the meeting ended. A late spring dance had been decided upon. But not just any dance, a spring fling to celebrate the silver lining in all their lives. When Marie had come up with the fantastic idea, she'd made the statement that it seemed logical to her since they all needed to find joy in being single.

Bernice looked over at Clara. "Why don't you join Savannah's senior center? You just turned fifty. It's closer to your house than Golden Age."

Clara shook her head in the negative, fast and hard. "Oh, no, not me. I'm only forty!"

Bernice rolled her eyes dramatically. "Forty! Yeah, right. Forty plus ten, Clara."

"You got it wrong, Bernice. I'm only forty. I stopped counting ten years ago." Clara got up and twirled around in her spot, her hands sliding down her hips in a provocative manner. "How many women forty and over have swivel hips like these?"

All eyes turned toward Savannah.

"Well," Clara grumbled, "besides Savannah? We all know she has hips to die for. As for me joining a senior center that would be like me sitting around watching a marathon of bad episodes of *Golden Girls*. It's just not going to happen with this lively sister."

"Whether you know it or not, Clara, there are a lot of great benefits in joining senior clubs. Senior citizens get lots of discounts," Bernice explained patiently.

Clara pursed her lips, shaking her head vigorously. "I burned my AARP card the same day it arrived in the mail. They simply sent that devil's discount card to the wrong address. I love you all to bits, and I'm having a ball helping Savannah out with her social project, but I'm not willing to concede to senior-citizen status quite yet. If I sit in one spot for too long, arthritis might try to set in on me. I don't want to be mistaken for disabled. I'm still too young to settle into any type of daily routine. Savannah also said no one had to be a member to come to the dance." Clara stuck her tongue out at Bernice. "So there!"

"You're pathetic, Clara. Senior status or not, your tired, worn-out behind is still a half-century old." Bernice got to her feet. "Well, ladies, let's not wear out our welcome. This sister is bone tired, so let me chauffeur you all home so I can get into my bed and rest."

Janice poked out her lips in a pouting manner. "Can you please let me finish my punch? This stuff tastes so much like wine, it's got me over here romanticizing and fantasizing."

"Well if it's doing all that for you, Janice, maybe it'll help conjure up you a car to get your butt home in. While you're at it, have your imagination whip up a handsome driver for you, too. Girl, you been reading too many of them romance novels. You'd better come on here if you're riding with me," Bernice shot back. "I'm ready to go."

"Ain't nothing wrong with reading juicy stuff like that," Madge said, standing up. "I like the real steamy ones. You all think I'm joking, but I've had to get up in the middle of the night and take a cold shower a time or two, or maybe even three. You might want to try reading one. Janice, don't let this bunch of sinful saints make you feel ashamed. You know you always got a partner in transgression in me. We can even exchange love novels. I have more than enough to share." Madge had to laugh at her own silliness, causing the others to join in.

The bantering continued as Savannah walked her lively guests to the front door, very sincere in telling everyone how much she appreciated the help. She was pretty much told by the others not to worry, that it was their pleasure to be of assistance. Each woman had said she was looking forward to the next meeting, which would occur the very next weekend.

The warm hugs following all the farewells left Savannah

feeling great, as well as close to tears. Moving to a new city was a big achievement in itself, but making new friends in one could be a hard fought accomplishment. Savannah truly felt that she had been successful at both.

However, Madge presented an obstacle for Savannah, one she wasn't sure how to clear off her calendar. Still, she wanted to keep an open mind, preferred to remain optimistic.

Once the door closed behind her guests, Savannah dragged herself down the hall and into the kitchen, where everything was sparkling clean. Despite her objections the ladies had helped her restore order in the cavernous room. After pouring herself a tall glass of ice water, Savannah headed for her bedroom, hoping she could get in a short nap before Antonio's visit.

For a person who'd hardly ever taken a nap, up until recently, Savannah had to wonder why she suddenly felt so tired all the time. Every time she turned around it seemed as if she were climbing into bed or stretching out on the sofa. Did these bouts of fatigue have anything to do with her age? Although she didn't have an answer, she figured her body was probably making up for all the rest it had missed out over the years. Knowing she was due for a complete physical in a few weeks allowed her to dismiss her concern. Savannah set the alarm clock and then stretched out fully in the bed.

Antonio was due in two hours' time.

Chapter 10

Always the gentleman bearing gifts, the moment Antonio walked through the front door of Savannah's home, he handed her a beautifully wrapped gift box. The package was very tiny in size, which meant it could only hold one thing. *Jewelry*. Although she was absolutely giddy over what the box might contain, she waited until they were comfortably seated in the family room before opening it. Savannah's hands trembled as she carefully undid the wrapping.

As though Savannah were fearful of what she might find inside the box, she took her sweet time in flipping open the square-shaped velvet. Her eyes then lit up. "Ah, look at this exquisite piece of beauty," Savannah cooed, smiling up at Antonio. "Thank you so much."

The gold diamond-cut butterfly slide was simply magnificent, sparkling all over the place. All she needed to go with the slide was an Omega choker. Inside the jewelry box in her bedroom was the perfect one. Kevin had given her the Omega for Christmas last year.

Looking right into Antonio's eyes, Savannah brought her head close to his. She kissed him softly on the mouth. When his eyes closed slowly, she deepened the kiss, causing the passion to flare. Antonio and Savannah continued to share kisses for several minutes.

The second Savannah realized that their passion was on its way to reaching fever pitch, she pulled slightly back from Antonio. "Guess we'd better cool it down a bit, huh? I'm feeling a little heated over here, not to mention overwhelmed. Your kisses are deliciously potent."

Loving how open and honest Savannah could be, Antonio chuckled. She sure knew how to call a spade a spade. Although she was blushing like crazy, she wasn't a grown woman acting like a silly schoolgirl. She was physically turned on and she hadn't had a problem letting him know it. She wasn't into game playing. Antonio loved that about her. "That's really nice to know, Savannah. I'm glad you like how I kiss. Your sweet kisses are no less compelling." He gently pressed his forefinger onto the end of her nose. "I promise to keep the fire from fanning out of control, but I hope we don't have to completely douse the flames."

Savannah threw her head back and laughed heartily. "No, that doesn't have to happen, Antonio. We're both responsible adults." Waiting on no prompting from him, Savannah leaned into him for several more kisses, careful not to heat up his anatomy too much.

Once their little controlled session in passion was temporarily over, Savannah offered Antonio something to eat and drink. When he accepted her generous offer, she had him follow her into the kitchen, where she pulled out what few items she had left over from the luncheon.

While there weren't nearly enough salads for both of them to make a full meal, Savannah saw to it that Antonio's plate was fixed first. She then gave him the last scoop of chicken salad and what little was left of the garden salad. There was enough pasta salad for two, so she split it between them. After preparing Antonio's plate, she didn't feel there was nearly enough on it to satisfy a man his size, so she fixed him a triple-decker smoked turkey sandwich lathered with mayo. Not wanting a whole sandwich, Savannah placed two slices of the turkey on her plate.

The doorbell rang no sooner than Savannah had sat down at the table with Antonio. She looked at him and shrugged. "I'm not expecting anyone, but I guess I'd better see who it is. I hope it's not the kids again. They promised to try and work things out between them."

Savannah got up from her seat. Before leaving the room, she bent down and kissed Antonio atop his head. "I won't be gone long. At least I hope not. Go ahead and eat, though." Savannah's laughter rang out as she left the kitchen.

A couple of minutes later Savannah came back into the kitchen with Inez right on her heels. Before Savannah could introduce Inez and Antonio, Inez burst into tears, shocking the heck out of the other two folks present. Inez was sobbing terribly hard, sounding as if her heart was breaking. All Savannah and Antonio could do was exchange bewildered glances. Neither of them had a clue as to what had caused Inez's emotional outburst. Savannah then offered to call Douglas, but Inez vigorously shook her head in the negative.

Once Inez finally managed to calm herself down, she tearfully explained to Savannah and Antonio how much Antonio looked like her late husband. She went on to tell him that he even had the same build as her spouse and that the hair and eye color was the same. "It's like looking at a ghost, Savannah. I'm so sorry for the outburst, but for a second I thought you were my Frederick. It's Antonio, right?"

Antonio nodded. "Right." He looked fearful of saying too much more than that.

"Oh, my, you even sound like him. Frederick had a deep, mesmerizing voice, too. This is very uncanny. If Doug saw you in the flesh, he'd believe Frederick had risen from the dead."

Wondering who Doug was, Antonio raised an eyebrow, but he wasn't about to voice the question, fearing that whatever he did or said might once again remind Inez of Frederick.

Savannah was now even more curious than ever over Inez's relationships to her late husband and her current one. This woman could cry over her deceased husband at the drop of a dime. Savannah recalled being supersensitive over Geoffrey's death, but the majority of her outbursts had all been in private. She realized there were people who had no control over their emotions whatsoever. From all indications, Inez was one of them.

Savannah briefly patted Inez's hand. "So sorry for your grief, Inez."

Inez waved off the genuine sentiment, keeping her eyes fastened on Antonio. It was like Inez couldn't believe her own eyes. "It's okay, Savannah. Thanks. I popped over here to tell you how sorry I am for not making your luncheon. How'd it go?"

"We had a fantastic time, Inez! I'd have to say we indulged way more in pleasure stuff than we did in business. Got a lot accomplished, though. The ladies really came through for me. I wish you'd been able to make it."

"Me, too. I can't stay now. I have to get back home. I just wanted to drop in for a quick second." Inez got to her feet. She once again took a long, hard look at Antonio. "It was so nice to meet you, Antonio. I do hope we meet again. I promise not to become so shaken the next time." Inez then extended her hand for Antonio to shake.

"Nice to meet you as well." Antonio didn't know what else to say to Inez's remarks about her state of mind, nor did he want to take her hand. God forbid that his touch should also be like Frederick's. The last thing Antonio wanted to happen was another emotional moment for Inez.

As if Savannah had sensed what Antonio was feeling, she gripped Inez's extended hand and then directed her toward the door. "I'll walk you out, Inez. I'm glad you dropped by for a minute. Give Doug my best."

As Savannah walked back into the family room, she immediately noticed the troubled look on Antonio's face. She really didn't need to wonder why he appeared that way. Inez had probably shaken him up as badly as she'd rattled Savannah's own nerves. Although Savannah didn't know why Inez had so many emotional outbursts, she had gotten a clear view of how she herself could've become had she not finally managed to get a good grip on own grief. Inez's sorrow wasn't an attractive sight. Savannah felt both sorry and saddened for her neighbor.

Antonio reached for Savannah's hand as she sat down beside him. "Do you know what that was all about? The lady seems to be hurting something awful. My heart goes out to her."

Savannah frowned slightly. "I know what you mean. I wish I knew what was happening with her. I've never been alone with her long enough to ask. I think she needs to talk with someone. Maybe I'll get to see her by herself one day so I can find out. I really don't know Inez at all, but I'm worried about her, Antonio. This is the second time I've been in her presence and she's been emotionally unstable on both visits."

Antonio shook his head. "Grief can do strange things to you, Savannah. No matter how strong you think you are, there are some things that can zap your strength right out from under you. Hopefully you can find out what she needs. I know you'll help her out if you can."

Savannah nodded. "I hope so. I just don't understand why she'd marry so soon after her first husband's death if she weren't over it yet. That's what's so strange to me."

Antonio explained to Savannah that some people just couldn't stand being by themselves. Married people often became an extension of each other during the course of a long marriage. He understood how hard it was to live with someone for many years and then suddenly end up living alone. In his opinion loneliness was another one of the silent killers. He mentioned knowing a few male friends who'd married within a year of their spouse's demise. "They didn't care about the family objections or the gossip. These guys just didn't like living without a special woman. It may seem kind of selfish to some folks, but I can understand how they felt. They're also very happy in their current marriages. In some cases, happier than they were in the first one."

"That's very interesting," Savannah said on a sigh. Realizing the conversation had turned a tad morbid Savannah began talking about how she'd have to go about conducting herself as the newly selected president at Silver Wings. Since she hadn't yet told Antonio she'd gotten the position that had been her way of doing so.

Antonio beamed proudly at Savannah. He kissed her gently on the lips. "That's wonderful news! Nice work, Madam President. What's first on your agenda?"

Savannah enthusiastically shared with Antonio some of the ideas that she and the ladies had come up with during the luncheon, also telling him that she now considered those same women as friends. Although Bernice had been a longtime friend, and Antonio was already aware of that, she explained to him that she'd just thought of the ladies as peers since she'd only known them through Bernice.

"It sounds to me like you've become a big hit with all the ladies. I'm glad you're making a lot of friends, Savannah. There's nothing like having good friends around, especially since it's so hard to trust folks these days. I'm not surprised they want you as a friend. As you and I both know, I wanted you as more than just that, but I would've been willing to settle for friendship if that's all you'd wanted. I know I've said that to you before, but it's still so true."

With desire burning in her eyes, Savannah kissed Antonio's cheek. "I like the idea of us being more than friends. You're very special to me, Antonio. I think you know that already."

"I do know that, Savannah." He pulled her to him for a quick hug. "I'd like to hear all about the plans for your first social event. When and where?"

"We all settled on the idea of having a senior prom. Marie came up with the idea. Since we all liked the sound of it, we decided to call our event the Silver and Gold Spring Fling. What do you think of it, Antonio?"

Antonio chuckled. "It's very catchy. I certainly like it. I didn't get to attend my senior prom in high school. If you'll be my date, I'd love to escort you."

"It's a date, Antonio. Everyone won't have an escort, so I'm really lucky in that regard. We haven't decided on an exact date, but we're going to check on a few venues to see what we can come up with. Each of us promised to check out at least one venue. We hope to have it as an evening event. What about inviting some of your single buddies, Antonio? Is that a possibility?"

Antonio stroked his chin thoughtfully. "I can check with a few of my single frat brothers. I also belong to a retired military organization. Both officers and NCOs are members. Most of the single guys I know are divorced, but there are a number of widower members, too. We tend to throw a lot of summer social functions. The guys might find it a pleasure to do a little mixing and mingling with the female members at your senior center."

Antonio snapped his fingers. "The IE Country Club is a really great venue. I've got quite a few connections over there, including a great group of golfing buddies. The military-base club is another good place. I can probably get you good catering prices at both places. Savannah, I'd love to take you to check out these venues if you'd like."

"How soon can we go?" Savannah asked, laughing.

"Is tomorrow soon enough? We can also have lunch at the country club."

"That should be fun, Antonio. What time can you get away tomorrow?"

"Eleven o'clock to one o'clock is a good time for me. We should be able to see both places and have lunch within a two-hour time frame. We'll check out the base facilities first."

Savannah nodded. "The time is good for me, too. I'm getting excited already. I don't know how well the Silver and Gold Spring Fling idea will go over with the formidable ladies at Silver Wings, but I'm sure going to toss it out to them. I have a lot of people willing to help me out and I'm so grateful for that."

"Just give it to the members straight. You have to take charge of things from the onset. Don't start out taking any mess from them sisters either. Be firm and consistent. It might take the ladies awhile, but they'll eventually come around. Your compassion and winning personality will see you through it all. I know you're going to give it everything you've got."

"Thank you, Antonio. I suddenly feel empowered by your remarks."

"Anytime, Savannah. You can't possibly know how much you've empowered me."

"Since we've been on the subject of friends, and taking control and all, I've had a few unsettling moments with one of Bernice's friends, Madge Jacoby. I believe you know her and her late husband."

As Antonio shifted about in his seat, he suddenly looked a bit uncomfortable.

Savannah noticed Antonio's discomfort right away. The mention of Madge's name seemed to have set him off a bit. "Am I wrong about you knowing Madge and Branch?"

Antonio shook his head in the negative. "I do know them. Branch and I served in the military together. Good people. I'm just wondering why you're asking about them."

Savannah's expression was thoughtful. "Madge has been kind of rude and insulting to me. Since I really don't know her, it's been kind of puzzling. I thought you might be able to give me some insight into her behavior since you've known her a long time."

Antonio shrugged with nonchalance. "Branch is the one I really knew on a personal level. I wasn't around Madge all that much. I tried to be there for her when Branch passed away. I've not had too much interaction with her since then."

Savannah felt that Antonio might be leaving out something important, because he seemed so uncomfortable just talking about Madge and Branch. Since she didn't want to outright dispute him, she had no choice but to drop the subject. "I see. I guess I'll just have to wait until she exposes what I believe is a hidden agenda."

"I guess so," Antonio seconded. Pulling Savannah into his arms, Antonio kissed her, hoping to sweep all her uncertainties away.

Savannah looked up into Antonio's eyes and smiled. She couldn't believe how much he did it for her. Just sitting next to him had her feeling like she was on a cloud. He was so kind, gentle, and his constant tenderness made her want to weep with joy. His loving touch was always so warm and healing.

Although Savannah was aware that a physical coming together couldn't happen for them, not in the absence of marriage, that didn't stop her from wondering exactly what it would be like to have him make love to her. Savannah trembled and then shivered at such a delicious thought.

Believing Savannah might be cold Antonio wrapped her up in the warmth of his arms. She melted into him without hesitation. As her heart beat faster and faster inside her chest, she tried to calm herself down. Her body's untamed reaction to Antonio's physical closeness made her dizzy with longing. Savannah had to fear what might come next. With her body betraying her in this way she knew she had to remain in tight control.

Then Antonio's mouth suddenly claimed Savannah's. Forgetting her need to remain in control, she completely dissolved under the sweet manipulation of his soft lips all over hers. When he deepened the kiss, she received it as though it might be their very last. Her heightened desire for him frightened and excited her at the same time. This was such a fairy-tale moment for her, but it couldn't possibly have an enchanted ending, at least not this evening.

Savannah fought hard to turn off her physical desires. Although things weren't out of control, the potential was great. They weren't two adolescents who had no idea how to control the heat of the moment. *Then why did it feel that way to her?* She had to wonder.

Then Savannah reminded herself that they were actually two silver-age citizens acting like silly childhood sweethearts. The thought of that made her laugh inwardly. There were probably millions of people out there in the world who believed older folks had no clue about burning desire. Her kids could certainly be counted in among that group. Boy, would Savannah like to clue them all in on the truth of the matter. Age had very little to do with physical desires. The wick may flutter in the wind, but the burning flames of desire rarely died out.

Antonio was the one to bring the passionate-filled moments with Savannah to a halt. His breathing was quite labored, which told her a lot. He was still just as affected by their kisses as she was. That pleased her. Knowing she wasn't alone in her desires made her feel much better. Neither of them seemed to have a clue as to what to do with all the sweet, heady passion flaring between them. Doing absolutely nothing about it was obviously the right way to handle it.

Taking hold of Savannah's hand, Antonio looked deeply into her eyes. "Do you want to talk about what's happening between us?"

Trying to rid herself of the skittish adrenaline playing around in her throat, Savannah gulped hard. She hadn't felt this type of adrenaline rush since forever. "I don't know. What's there to talk about?" Antonio had opened up the crap game so she thought he should be the first one to roll the die. Savannah hoped her fear of the subject matter wasn't written upon her face.

Chuckling, Antonio leaned into Savannah and kissed the tip of her nose. "Don't look so scared, sweetheart. Talking about our feelings is not only natural, it's important. Do you agree? I know things are awkward for us in this stage of our romance, but this should pass with time."

Savannah wished she could come up with some clever response, a humorous statement that would ease the tension, but all she could do was shrug. "I agree with you, but I don't know what you're expecting me to say."

Antonio's brows furrowed. "This isn't about what I want to hear you say, Savannah. I want to know how you feel about the physical things going on with us. I know you have to be feeling what I am because your body language tells me so. Let me ask you this. How do you feel about us making love? Is that something you want to happen for us?"

Stunned beyond belief by Antonio's very pointed questions, Savannah wished she could suddenly disappear into thin air. Both of his questions were loaded with TNT. She hoped he didn't regret his queries, because she'd quickly decided to go ahead and let the bomb explode. There should be no mistake about her feelings on the issue, nothing left to chance. Her body might've been burning out of control, but she was very much in charge of her sanity. "In the absence of marriage our physical desires will never go any farther than they have already."

Even though Antonio had somewhat expected the direct response Savannah had given, he did his best to hide how much it had affected him. Her comments had touched him deeply, showing him she was everything he'd thought her to be. Savannah had clearly exposed her hand, leaving nothing for him to wonder about. Now it was time for Antonio to flip over his hole cards.

Antonio once again took Savannah's hand. "This might surprise you, but you and I are on the same exact page. It's only in this instant that I know exactly what I want for us. I'm not in this relationship to obtain physical conquests.

Since time is so very short, I don't want to waste a precious second on what might never be. I'm looking for love and marriage for us, Savannah. I don't want to live out the rest of my life alone. If you want the same things as I do, please let me know now. If not, it'll probably hurt a lot, but I'd be happy for us to remain just friends."

Talking about breathless, Savannah mused, more stunned than she was from before. *Wasn't she the one who was supposed to detonate the bomb?* Antonio had not only detonated the dangerous explosives, he'd dared to set off the TNT right in her face.

Savannah gently squeezed Antonio's hand. "If you thought I was at a loss for words with your initial questions, I'm totally baffled now. I can see that you have no problem getting right to the point. But I really like that about you."

Antonio rested his free hand on the side of Savannah's face. "Being right up-front with folks is the only way I know how to be, Savannah. Nothing else works for me."

Savannah looked down at the floor for a brief moment. "Love and marriage," she uttered in a low voice. "I could say so much on the subject of each. But I won't." She moved even closer to him. "Like you, I wasn't sure what I wasn't looking for, but I don't believe marriage had been dealt into the hand yet. But in this instant I too have learned what I want. I also know what I don't want—and that is to be involved in a physical-only relationship. Although I hadn't entertained the idea of marriage, I know now that I can't and won't settle for anything less. So I guess you could say that you and I are still on the same page. What do you say to that, Mr. Delabay?"

Antonio grinned broadly. "You've made me one happy man, Mrs. Richmond."

Antonio took Savannah into his arms and kissed her long and passionately. He couldn't seem to get enough of caressing and kissing her this way. He knew that she had no idea of how instrumental she'd been in helping his heart to heal. If what he'd had to say somehow scared Savannah away, he knew that he'd end up brokenhearted. Getting everything out in the open and letting Savannah know his intentions had been important to him. Antonio had been serious about not wasting precious time on a relationship that held no future.

Antonio gently stroked Savannah's hair. "I don't want you to think I'm rushing you into anything, Savannah, because I'm not. I know we have a long way to go before we make any final decisions, but I needed to find out if you wanted the same things I do. I had to make sure my mission was clear to you." Antonio picked up the bottle of water and then handed Savannah the one she'd been drinking from. "A toast to our future. May God continue to smile His saving grace upon us. We are a beautiful, blessed couple."

Savannah touched her bottle of water to Antonio's. "Amen to that!"

Savannah awakened to loud, earth-rolling-like noises, and a humongous headache. Her first thought was an earthquake. But then she didn't feel anything moving about, which did not indicate a California quake. As she lay very still, the sounds continued to drum out in her head. Then she suddenly realized what the noises were about. The pool company was starting the dig.

Although the loud commotion had been solved for her, Savannah couldn't understand why her head was hurting so much lately. The Tylenol no longer worked for her and she was cautious about asking her doctor to prescribe something stronger. As she thought back in time, she realized the headaches had been going on for over a month; they were only getting worse.

Knowing she had an appointment for a physical in less than a week she put the troubling thoughts out of her mind, but that didn't do anything to ease the horrific pain. Savannah climbed out of bed and trudged into the bathroom, where she took three Tylenol instead of the normal two. The regular dosage just wasn't cutting it for her. Savannah wanted the pain gone, instantly.

Later in the afternoon Savannah had to address the dreadful female club members and she needed to be totally fit. Even though some of those women were probably going to make her head hurt even worse, she knew she had to lay out her plans and then have a vote of approval.

The spring fling was such an appealing project and she didn't see how it could be voted down, yet she wouldn't be surprised if it was. There were several mean-spirited ladies in the club who seemed hell-bent on making her job in leadership a nightmare, but she had news for them.

Nothing or anyone was going to intrude upon Savannah Richmond's serenity. Just like the last president had done, she'd simply resign, yet she knew that would come very hard for her. She saw herself as a winner, one who loved a

great challenge. No doubt that working with these complicated women was to be one of the greatest challenges of
all time.

Showered and dressed in a beautiful fluffy white robe,
Savannah made her way into the kitchen to prepare a bit
of breakfast for herself. Thinking that the caffeine in coffee
might add to her aggravating pain, she decided not to
make any. Savannah opted to drink orange juice instead,
along with eating a small bowl of Special K and a banana.

As Savannah continued to sit quietly at the kitchen
table, after she'd consumed her meal, the roar from the
excavation equipment made it hard for her to think. The
pandemonium outside her window was loud enough to
prematurely awaken Rip Van Winkle. Since her head felt
like it was coming off her shoulders, and it was still just a
little after 7:00 a.m., she decided to lie back down for an
hour or so. The commotion wasn't half as bad in the back
of the house as it was up in the living areas in the front.

The doorbell rang just as Savannah was halfway down
the hallway. Sure that it had to be someone from the pool
company, a male someone, she didn't know if she should
rush back into the bedroom and pull on a pair of jeans or
just get the door. The bell sounding off again made the
decision for her. The robe covered her quite nicely. Or
perhaps she could even ask the visitor to give her a moment
to slip into something before allowing them entry, she
mused, hurrying to answer the bell.

Much to Savannah's surprise the visitor was her neighbor Inez. The smell from the pink pastry box Inez held in
her hands reached Savannah's nose before she even

opened the screen door. Savannah couldn't help inhaling the delicious scent of freshly baked goods. "Good morning, Inez. Come on in. You're up awfully early."

Inez handed the box to Savannah. "I hope I didn't awaken you, Savannah. I thought I'd bring along a bit of a peace offering just in case I did. Our apple fritters are demonically scrumptious. I really need to talk to you. Can you please spare this sister-girl a few minutes of your precious time? I haven't been able to sleep for thinking of the mess I made out of myself in front of your charming company. I am so regretful over how I behaved around Antonio."

The look of utter distress on Inez's face truly concerned Savannah. Although she wasn't sure she really wanted to know what was on her neighbor's mind, she had Inez follow her into the kitchen anyway. At Inez's acceptance of cranberry juice rather than coffee, Savannah poured the reddish liquid over a glass of crushed ice and then served it to her guest.

Savannah sat down at the table, prepared to listen to whatever Inez needed to talk about. She had to tell herself to keep an open mind, that perhaps Inez's issues weren't serious ones. *Why did it seem like everyone had suddenly pegged her as the one to come to for advice and problem solving?* Savannah was still reeling from Kenya's dilemma, which had yet to be resolved. Noah had also seen her as the one to take over the troublesome situation at the senior center, involving her in another tenuous state of affairs. *What did all these people take her for?*

Ten minutes into Inez's explanation about her strange behavior had already revealed to Savannah way more than she wanted to know. Inez was suffering from the worst case of guilt that Savannah had ever heard of. While married to Frederick, Inez had explained to Savannah that she'd had an illicit love affair with Douglas, which had eventually resulted in Frederick committing suicide. Finding out about his wife's infidelities had proved to be too much to bear for Inez's first husband. What came out of Inez's mouth next was the real shocker for Savannah.

For all Inez's tearful outbursts about missing her husband and wishing he were still with her, Savannah was astounded when Inez informed her that she couldn't stand to be around Frederick, that she had actually detested him. According to Inez, Frederick was very controlling and verbally abusive to her. He had also had numerous extramarital affairs, which was what had sent her flying right into the arms of sweet Douglas Sheffield, who'd treated Inez like a queen.

Douglas and Inez married a month after Frederick's casket had been interred.

"I know you probably find it interesting that I wasn't even happy with Frederick because of all the things I've said and done. It's almost like I created a new image for him after his death. His suicide was so hard to deal with— and still is. I don't know how to stop blaming myself for what happened on that fateful night. A couple of hours after Frederick caught Douglas and I coming out of a rent-by-the-hour motel together, Frederick was dead."

If there was ever a case of too much information, this was definitely it. Savannah's head was teeming with questions for Inez, but she didn't dare ask them. This woman was hurting so bad and the guilt had all but consumed her alive. There was no way Savannah could sit in judgment of Inez. It wasn't in her makeup to do so. Her desperate neighbor needed compassion, not condemnation. No one could heap any more guilt onto Inez's shoulders than she herself had already placed there. Savannah had no choice but to reach out to her neighbor with sympathy.

Knowing it was the right thing to do, Savannah brought the sobbing Inez into her comforting embrace. "Prayer is the only sure way to heal a broken spirit. God already knows every bit of your story, knew exactly what would happen in your life before it all unfolded. He is a kind, forgiving Father. His compassion is endless. Would you like me to pray with you, Inez?"

Inez lifted her head and looked into Savannah's eyes, so grateful for the empathy. "Oh, Savannah, if you only knew how much I've wanted to pray to God and ask His forgiveness. I couldn't dare to offer my sinful self to Him. I feel so unclean. How do I stand before His Highness cloaked in all this filthy shame and horrific guilt? My sins are simply unforgivable."

Savannah stroked Inez's hair. "I have to kindly disagree with you there, my friend. Jesus died so our sins would be completely washed away. *'He who conceals his transgressions will not prosper. But he who confesses and forsakes them will find compassion.'* Proverbs, 28–13."

Beautifully dressed in a red power suit and a white silk blouse, Savannah looked every bit the part of a professional as she stood at the podium inside the recreation center at Silver Wings. Her hair was impeccably groomed and her makeup appeared flawless. Savannah was one beautiful, head-turning woman, but she didn't seem at all phased by it. The men in the room were practically drooling over her, but she wasn't that flattered by so much male attention.

Wishing she had accepted from Noah the offered glass of water, she licked her dry lips. The speech she had just delivered to the senior club members had been riveting; at least she'd thought so. She'd covered everything from offering fashion, hair and physical makeovers to informative lectures on the grieving process. Then she had meticulously laid out her plans for the spring fling. Her gala ideas were vivid enough for anyone to imagine. Savannah was now impatiently waiting for the question and answer period. The voting would then take place.

Savannah had never kidded herself on the fact that addressing this group of women wouldn't be an easy feat, but she hadn't expected to deliver her presentation in such a hostile environment. The women in the audience were looking at her as if they hated her, as if they wanted to beat her down to a pulp. The hard glares and nasty stares had Savannah nervous.

How could these ladies be that mean-spirited when they didn't even know her?

Noah, Irwin and Chester had taken up seats right in the front row to cheer Savannah on and give her their staunch support. The men didn't really know her either, but for some reason they'd accepted her at face value from the moment they'd met her. Having the guys' support meant a lot to Savannah. She couldn't imagine how she would've faced this day without them.

Much to Savannah's surprise and dismay, Veronica

Baker was in the audience. Since she was a club member over at Golden Age Senior Center, Savannah had no idea why she was even present. Of all the hard looks Savannah had received, Veronica's were the most unsettling to her. At least Savannah knew Veronica despised her because of her relationship with Antonio.

Never in her life had Savannah been surrounded by such strong opposition. The enemy was as busy and as alive as ever. *God's in control*, she told herself. *This battle is already won.*

Loretta Ames stood up, her hat filling up most of the space in front and in back of her. "I like the idea of the dance, but I think calling it a Silver and Gold Spring Fling is a bit juvenile."

Irwin jumped to his feet. "Nothing juvenile about it. It has such a nice ring to it. It's spring and the perfect time of year for a nice romantic fling. Most of us are seniors and the dance will be like a prom, which is normally held in the spring." He then flashed the ladies a winning smile. "How many of you gorgeous creatures are with me on this one?" Upon seeing numerous delicate hands go up, Irwin stuck his chest out pretty far, as if to say: *I'm still the man!*

Savannah laughed inwardly. It looked to her as if the handsome Irwin had many of the ladies willing to follow him anywhere he led them. At the moment he was leading them to favor Savannah's ideas, which pleased her a lot. Savannah gave him her silent thanks.

After giving Irwin a petulant glance, Loretta turned her attention back to Savannah. "We're grateful that Irwin has given us his valuable input, but the question was directed at you, Madam President. Could you please respond?"

Madam President! Savannah had to try hard to contain her joy at hearing Loretta call her by that prestigious name, even if it had been delivered with a dose of heavy sarcasm.

Savannah stood up straight and tall. Nothing to be gained by slumping over this podium, she mused. *This meeting could turn into an all-out war; you can't be off-guard for a second.* "I really like the name and I love the beautiful idea behind it, Ms. Ames. My thoughts when the name was chosen are the mirror images of exactly what you just said. If you'd like, we can take a vote on whether to use Silver and Gold Spring Fling or not to." Savannah didn't like working so hard to appease this group of many grouches. However, she didn't feel that she had much of a choice. Savannah had an idea they couldn't ever be pleased simply because they weren't at peace with themselves. Putting another human being down was always the other person's way of lifting themselves up.

Looking highly perturbed, Noah practically leaped out of his seat. "I think many of us have already voted. Ladies and gentlemen, let's give another quick show of hands on keeping the name so we can move on to something more important. Things are starting to get real petty."

Far more hands went up than those who opposed. The name had won by a landslide.

Loretta had twisted up her face so hard with dismay she now resembled a dried-up prune.

It was obvious to Savannah that Loretta didn't like the men rallying around the new president. It was also apparent to her that some of the women who'd voted in favor of her ideas had done so at the prompting of the men. Savannah chuckled inwardly. These old girls were nobody's fool. They all knew in which direction the men's sails were blowing in the wind; they simply wanted to be caught up in the breeze.

Looking poised to succeed where Loretta had failed, Opal Redmond moved up to the edge of her chair. "You spoke of fashion, hair and makeup seminars, Ms. Richmond, which is all well and good. But how do you plan on paying for such an elaborate plan? I strongly oppose using funds from the club accounts. According to the minutes from the last meeting, we're already very low on money."

After taking a moment to consider the question, Savannah folded her hands and put them atop the podium. She then looked directly into Opal's face. "There won't be any expenses. I've run these ideas by many of my good friends and colleagues down in L.A. Without a moment's hesitation they each agreed to offer us their professional services for free. These highly skilled men and women will conduct informative and fun seminars for the senior center at no cost."

The look on Opal's face said she didn't like Savannah's response. "It won't be free. I can assure you of that. They're getting something out of it, if nothing but exposure for their business. We could end up paying a higher cost if we're not careful. Nothing is ever free in this world."

Savannah smiled brilliantly. "God's love is always free, Ms. Redmond."

By the look on all the faces in the room, not a single one dared to oppose such a fact.

Mable Grimes stood to her feet. "Despite all these petty issues being brought up, I think Ms. Richmond is going to make us an excellent president. I can tell that she has already put in a lot of time and effort on her presentation. I'm so impressed with her delivery. When was the last time we heard wonderful ideas like these for the center? I can tell you. Never! So let's stop working so hard against Ms. Savannah and try working with her. Can I get at least one amen?"

Several loud, supportive cheers came forth.

"One more thing before I rest my tired self back down on this chair, if no one else wants to run for the vice presidency job, I'd like to take Ms. Richmond up on her offer for me to do so. I think the two of us can turn this place into the hottest ticket in the Inland Empire."

"From all the immoral things I've been hearing about her, it seems to me that Ms. Richmond herself is the hottest ticket in town. At least the men all seem to think so," Veronica Baker said from her seat. "Do you fine ladies really want a man stealer operating among you?"

All eyes quickly turned on Veronica, but none burned brighter with disgust and outrage than those belonging to Savannah. *God, please speak through me. Don't let me blow it. Please stop me from reacting to this woman in a wicked manner,* Savannah prayed fervently. *I could easily strangle her with bare hands. Help me control my burning hands and acid tongue, Lord!*

The room came alive with the buzzing whispers of gossip and the loud gasps of shock.

Mable appeared incensed as she turned to face Veronica. "Who are you, anyway? As far as I know, you're not even a member at this senior center. You have no right to offer an ounce of input. This is not an arena for catfights, so please sheath your claws. You need to take that stuff on back to wherever you came from. We won't be having it up in here. This is our house, lady!"

To gain control of all the madness in the room Savannah picked up the gavel and pounded it hard. Everyone immediately redirected their attention back to the podium. Then she made the mistake of looking into Noah's eyes. The tears she saw swarming around his pupils caused her heart to nearly arrest. There was no doubt in Savannah's mind that he felt responsible and guilty for the position she was in, believing that he'd placed her right into the fiery furnace.

Savannah held her head up higher than she could ever remember holding it. No tongue was strong enough to take her down by force. "Mable, I can take it from here. Thank you. To address the scathing comments just made, I'm going to respond to it—and I need every one to listen up." *As if every ear in the room isn't fine-tuned into my voice already*, Savannah mused.

Savannah looked directly at Veronica. "If the lady who dared to air her ill feelings, or anyone else for that matter, has a personal beef with me, this is not the forum to settle it. Step to me in private or don't dare to step to me at all. With that said, let's quickly take a vote on whether or not to have the spring fling. The name has already been approved. After that, this meeting is adjourned. I'm sure we've all had more than we can take for now. I'd like to call a special meeting for next week. I'll personally phone each member with the details. Thank you."

A silent alarm went off and then a burning fear began to creep into Savannah's being as she drew nearer to her car. Leaning against her driver's door was Veronica, looking none too pleasant. Savannah slowed her steady pace, hoping that the woman blocking entry to her vehicle would come to her senses and just walk away. A physical altercation was something Savannah had no intention of involving herself in with anyone. She was too much of a lady for that. Fighting over a man at her age, or any age for that matter, was an utterly undignified practice. Savannah had far too much respect for self to allow something so primitive and crude to occur.

With Savannah knowing she couldn't move any slower than she was now doing, she took the final few burdensome steps that brought her within close proximity to her car. With her key already in hand, she disarmed the alarm, causing Veronica to make a sudden start. The sudden piercing noise had momentarily scared the threatening-looking woman, but not enough to make her move away from Savannah's automobile. It only took Veronica a moment to recover.

Savannah had to work hard to keep her laughter at bay. Veronica actually looked pretty silly to her. At least something had frightened this nutty woman, she mused. "If you will please excuse me, Ms. Baker, I'd like to get into my car so I can go home."

Veronica sucked her teeth with obvious intolerance, rolling her eyes at Savannah at the same time. "I'll excuse you all right, but only after you excuse yourself from this love triangle you've created for all of us. Before you came into the picture, he and I were enjoying an exclusive relationship." Veronica then flashed the large diamond she wore on her left hand by wiggling her fingers. "If this chunk of rock isn't a sign of commitment, I'll have to look up the meaning of *commitment* in Webster's. Do you always horn in on other folks' territory?"

Hiding her inner shock was extremely difficult for Savannah to pull off. It seemed to her that Veronica was suggesting that she and Antonio had been engaged, or perhaps still were. That was nothing short of downright unbelievable, yet it was still having an unsettling effect on her. She couldn't imagine him seating her and her family at a table with a woman he was engaged to, not without making that fact known to her right up-front. And if Antonio hadn't brought up the very nature of their relationship, she couldn't understand why Veronica hadn't done so.

This woman was either an outright liar or she suffered from delusions of grandeur.

Savannah smiled wryly. "I think this is something you need to take up with your man. If you two are in a committed relationship, then this is between you and him. This is really not about me, Ms. Baker, or between us. Not one little bit."

Savannah hadn't said Antonio's name simply because Veronica hadn't said it. She could just hear her later saying that she'd never mentioned him by name and that Savannah had drawn her own conclusions. Well, neither would she call out Antonio's name, Savannah decided.

Mable quickly approached Savannah and Veronica, after having assessed the situation for a couple of minutes. "Is everything okay with you all, ladies? Is there something I can do to help out? Is one of you having car trouble?"

Savannah breathed an inward sigh of relief. "Thanks, Mable, but everything here is cool. Ms. Baker and I were just having a minute chat. We're finished now. Aren't we, Ms. Baker?"

Veronica looked as if she wanted to slap Savannah silly, but she went on and moved away from the car instead. "Everything *is* fine, Ms. Grimes. Please take what I said under serious advisement, Ms. Richmond. It just might keep your fast behind healthy." Veronica had voiced her last comment low enough that only Savannah could hear her slightly veiled threat.

As soon as Veronica was out of earshot, Savannah grabbed Mable and hugged her, thanking her for interjecting herself into a bad scenario. "I don't know what would've happened had you not come along. I believe Ms. Baker would've physically assaulted me if she'd had the opportunity." It was then that Savannah first noticed how hard she was trembling inside.

Mable gently squeezed Savannah's hand. "I'm just glad I could be of help. Do you have any idea what's going on with her? She was so insulting to you in the meeting. There's nothing ladylike about her. This is so unreal."

Savannah shrugged. "This issue is very complicated, Mable. I really don't know for sure what's wrong with her, but I plan to get to the bottom of it. Pronto. I've never been in a physical fight with anyone, not even as a child. At any rate, thanks again. I've got to get on home now."

Mable gave Savannah a comforting hug. "You take care of yourself now. Just remember that I've got your back. You're shaking so badly, which is understandable. Is it okay if I call and check on you later? Your contact phone numbers are on the members' list."

Savannah smiled weakly. "I'd love to hear from you later, Mable. Talk to you soon."

* * *

After viewing the caller ID screen, Savannah chose not to answer the phone. Still emotionally reeling from the events of the earlier confrontations at the senior center, inside and outdoors, she had no desire to communicate with anyone, especially Antonio. Noah, Chester and Irwin had given her their deepest apologies after the meeting, along with her supporting encounter with Mable Grimes, but everyone else seemed to have avoided her like the plague. Veronica Baker had quickly disappeared once Mable had shown up in the parking lot, but Savannah was sure she had a few allies waiting in the wings to applaud her wicked behavior.

The moment the red flashing light signaled to Savannah that a message had been left, she picked up the phone to retrieve it. Her breath caught at the sound of Antonio's voice. He sounded so disappointed that she wasn't in, but what concerned her most was the distress she heard in his deep voice. His next sentence left her to wonder if he'd gotten wind of what had happened at the senior center during and after the meeting.

"I pray that you're not going to shut me out at a time like this, Savannah. I desperately need to see you. Please call me as soon as you receive this message. I'll be waiting."

Savannah winced hard at the pain striking her heart. Antonio's message had strongly indicated to her that he had heard the unsavory details of what had gone down. There was no way Savannah could talk to Antonio and not reveal how much she'd been hurt by what had been said to her by Veronica Baker. Antonio would know by the sound of her voice that she'd been mortally wounded.

Taking time to fully recover from the direct hits to her morality was the best course of action for now. Savannah's heart just wasn't into discussing the sordid matter, period.

Savannah reached over and turned off the lamp. With tears streaming down her cheeks, she scooted farther down in the bed and then closed her eyes. She didn't expect sleep to come easy or anytime soon, but she'd give it her best shot. "Good night, Antonio. Sweet dreams."

Chapter 11

Feeling much better than she had over the past week, Savannah looked forward to finally having a luncheon date with Antonio. He had suggested bringing along a picnic basket so they could spend a couple of hours in the park across the street from her home and also dine by the lake. The fact that it was an absolutely gorgeous day outside had Savannah very excited in spite of the trouble that silently brewed between her and Antonio.

Savannah hadn't seen Antonio since before the upsetting episode at the senior center, so she was eager to be in his company. After ignoring several of his phone messages, she'd finally returned his call to tell him that she wasn't prepared to talk about what had happened, but that she eventually would be. He had graciously backed off, promising to wait until she was ready.

It was now time for Savannah to discuss Veronica Baker in depth with him. In fact, she'd already put it off too long.

There were too many unanswered questions floating about inside her head for her not to start demanding some answers. If Antonio and Veronica were having a romantic relationship, or had ever had one, Savannah thought it was high time she knew about it.

How could she face an enemy totally unarmed?

After Savannah had taken to her bed that fateful night, she'd stayed there for several days, only getting up to take her meals, use the bathroom, and shower. The incident with Veronica had hit her hard enough to make her physically ill. Although she'd also been too emotionally ill to keep the doctor's appointment for her routine physical checkup, she had already rescheduled another one.

When Savannah hadn't been able to come up with any plausible reasons for the sudden headaches, she'd determined that it was probably all due to stress. A lot of stressful situations had occurred in her life since she'd moved from L.A. to Fontana, especially the serious problems between Kenya and Cole, not to mention the issues with the folk at the senior center.

The only phone calls Savannah had taken during that particular time frame had been those coming in from her kids, who were still unaware that anything was amiss. Savannah was not the type to burden her kids with her personal baggage.

Two days had passed before Savannah had called Antonio a second time just to keep him from worrying too much. Even then she'd phoned his house during his work hours so all she'd have to do was leave a message saying that she still wasn't feeling up to par and that she'd get back with him in a couple of days. The only other phone call she'd made had been to Noah to ask him to inform the other members that the special meeting would be held at a later time.

Standing in front of the full-length mirror, Savannah checked out her appearance from front to back. She liked how well the white capri pants still fit her hips despite the couple of pounds she'd recently lost. The brand-new lime-green-and-white striped V-necked tank top was also a perfect fit. Satisfied that she looked her very best, she walked across the room and sat down on the overstuffed chair, where she pulled on a pair of cute green-and-white sandals.

Seeing that she had at least thirty minutes to kill before Antonio was due to arrive, she sat back in the chair and then rested her feet upon the hassock. After picking up the notebook off the chair side-table stand, she began to look over the plans she'd come up with for the spring project. The senior prom had finally been approved by the members, which had come as a surprise and somewhat of a shock to Savannah.

After Veronica had thrown out her nasty little insults that day, during the meeting time, Savannah hadn't been sure that she'd ever be able to get any of her ideas voted in by the members of the senior center. A lame-duck president was what she thought she'd become until they'd find a way to impeach her. She still couldn't get over the way Veronica had confronted her out in the parking lot even though she didn't believe a single word of what she'd said. If Savannah had found truth in any of it, she and Antonio would not be picnicking in the park.

The sun couldn't possibly shine any brighter than it was. The outdoor temperature was just right: not too hot, not too cool. Every tree, plant and bush landscaping the charming neighborhood park looked as if it had sprouted millions of waxy green wings. Spring flowers in vivid colors and various types had popped up everyplace. Azure blue was the color of the shimmering lake that was clear enough to see one's own reflection.

Antonio never ceased to amaze Savannah. He always seemed to think of things that might never cross another person's mind. The old-style wicker basket he'd packed had held everything one would possibly need for casual dining in the park. Antonio hadn't forgotten to bring along his portable CD player so they also had music to help keep them entertained.

The shaved turkey on homemade rye bread was a big hit with Savannah. She couldn't believe he himself had blended the special dressing for the sandwiches and had also baked the turkey and the rye bread that very morning. His creamy potato salad was so delicious she thought it should be sold on the market. Fresh fruit cups with whipped cream had been served for dessert. Antonio had also created a nice fresh concoction of blended juices for them to enjoy over ice.

Antonio removed the Smokey Robinson greatest hits CD from the player and then popped in one made up of '70s golden oldies performed by various artists. He had re-membered the names of the '70s performers that Savan-nah had told him she loved the most, which had allowed him to create a CD that reflected her personal music pref-erences.

Staring into Savannah's eyes, Antonio took hold of her hand. "If you're ready, I'd like to hear about what happened to you at Silver Wings. I've heard this, that and the other, but I need to hear it straight from you. Only if you're ready to talk about it."

Although Savannah dreaded talking about it, it was a must for her to do so. She also thought it only fair that Antonio know the exact truth about what had happened. He shouldn't have to rely on what he'd heard through rumors and such, especially since the incident did directly involve him. Veronica would've had no reason to go on the attack against Savannah if Antonio hadn't been at the center of the controversy. With that in mind, Savannah began to tell Antonio everything that she'd remembered about the unsavory incident.

Antonio couldn't hide the outrage he felt over what Veronica had had the nerve to say to Savannah. It was no wonder that Savannah had refused to take his calls for several days. The audacity of Veronica was beyond his comprehension. Antonio was amazed at the great lengths Veronica had gone to try and ruin Savannah's fine reputation.

Savannah smoothed her palm across her brow. "Keeping in mind all that Veronica has said to me, I need to know, were you ever romantically involved with her? I don't think I've ever asked you this question directly."

Eyeing her sympathetically, Antonio brushed his knuckles down the side of Savannah's face. "Telling you I'm sorry will do nothing to heal the emotional damage inflicted upon you. Yet I feel deep regret over it."

Savannah was impatient for Antonio to get right down to the point. "The question I asked, Antonio. Please tell me if you've ever dated Ms. Baker."

Antonio sighed hard, deeply massaging the pads of his fingers into his forehead. "I'm sorry that I never told you this, but I did date Veronica, Savannah. The relationship was very short-lived. I don't think it lasted more than a couple of weeks. It never reached any level of intimacy. I've never done a single thing since then to indicate to Ms. Baker that I have any personal interest in her. You can rest assured of that, Savannah."

For whatever reason Savannah *had been* sure of that just before Antonio had confessed, which had obviously been a mistake on her part. Antonio had shown himself to be a man of great integrity, yet he had withheld important information from her about his dealings with this woman who hadn't gotten over whatever they'd had. He hadn't outright lied to her, since she'd never asked him that very question directly, yet she felt that she'd been lied to.

Time and time again Bernice and the majority of Bernice's close friends had told Savannah that Antonio hadn't paid any attention to the numerous women running behind him. Savannah had believed them. Now Antonio was telling her something altogether different. If he'd failed to tell her they'd once dated, could he have given Veronica the diamond ring she'd flashed that day? Veronica had made sure that Savannah had gotten a real good look at it.

As far as Savannah knew, none of the females in her newly created little circle were known for lying. Marie, Clara and Janice had already proved that they'd become as good a friend to her as they were to Bernice. Her new female comrades had already come to her rescue when she'd needed it.

Of course, Savannah wasn't the least bit sure about Madge, especially since the lady was still trying to give her the blues. Thinking of Madge suddenly made Savannah wonder if perhaps she also had had designs on Antonio at some point. Could a romantic interest in Antonio be the reason for the insults Madge was constantly hurling at her?

Savannah took hold of Antonio's hand. "I truly want to believe you, Antonio. I really have no reason not to, other than you withholding this important information from me. Ms. Baker is telling a different story about your involvement. She has offended me in a very vicious way and I don't think it's going to stop anytime soon. She never came right out and said you two had been engaged, but she did make a point of showing me the large diamond on her finger. Her malicious outbursts have hurt me terribly, but I'm hoping this pain will pass away, too."

"I sure hope so, Savannah." Antonio shook his head from side to side. "I never thought Ms. Baker could do something like this. But then again, the strange things she'd done around me were why I'd eventually backed away from her. As for that ring, she purchased it herself, showing it off the night she actually proposed to me. You can't even imagine how stunned I was. I'd never had a woman ask me to marry her, nor had I ever expected anything like that to occur. Surely not after only two or three dates, if that many."

Savannah looked stunned. "She asked you to marry her with a ring she'd purchased?"

Antonio nodded. "Afraid so. I really didn't get the chance to know her all that well. Her odd behavior had me running for cover, Savannah. She has left several phone messages for me down at the center. As the director of the senior center, I'm obligated to call her back. However, I'm not too comfortable with doing so. The minute the conversation turns personal, I'll have to end it. I feel that Ms. Baker has purposely trapped me in the middle of her messy madness. Too bad she doesn't know she's picked the wrong one to try and pull this off on."

"Do what you have to do, Antonio. I'm going to remain very wary of her, too." She would remain wary of Antonio too, but she didn't need to tell him that, not until he gave her just cause to do so. "I'm sorry you didn't think it was important to tell me about your involvement with her, but I don't see how I can really hold it against you since it was long before my time. However, I'm still bothered that you had us sit at the same table together."

"That was not intentional, Savannah. I'd invited you and the kids there before I learned whose birthday we were celebrating at the center. I would've never done that otherwise."

"I understand what you mean, Antonio. It might be better if you didn't even discuss with Veronica anything I've told you." Savannah didn't want him talking to Veronica, period.

"What if she brings it up, Savannah?"

Savannah shrugged. "I don't think she will. But if she does, you can just tell her you'd rather not discuss it. You just said that if it got personal you'd end the conversation."

"I see what you mean. Now let's get back to us. I've been trying to come up with something fun for us to do over an upcoming weekend. How would you like to take a drive up to Palm Springs with me in a few weeks? Separate rooms, of course."

Savannah laughed lightly. "That sounds like a nice trip. But I have to ask if this little outing involves eighteen holes of golf?"

Antonio chuckled. "Do you really think I'd be that selfish?"

Savannah swiped at him in a playful manner. "Not sure. Now answer my question."

"There's a golf tournament up there in a few weeks, but I don't plan to play. Just watch."

"I see. As I've told you before, I think golf is terribly boring, but I guess I can stay in the hotel and relax while you attend the tournament. I can also work on finalizing my plans for the senior prom. Being away from you doesn't sound like a lot of fun, though."

"I don't plan on us being apart. I want you to come along to the tournament with me. We'll just stay a short while if you're not enjoying it. I got a feeling that you just might start to like golf if you go and watch for a bit. At any rate, we can find a lot of other exciting things to do up in Palm Springs. I'm not a gambler, but I love to watch the high rollers do their thing."

"I think I can manage that, especially if it means a lot to you. I'm not selfish either, Antonio. It can't always be about just what I'm interested in doing. We agreed that we should always explore each other's interests. It wouldn't be fair otherwise."

"I promise to make it an exciting weekend for you, Savannah. The downtown stores carry great merchandise. We can check out as many of the quaint little shops as you'd like."

"Sounds interesting. Do you plan for us to leave on a Friday or Saturday?"

"I'd like to get up there by noon on that Friday. We can have lunch at one of the nice little cozy restaurants. The golfing tournament doesn't get underway until Saturday morning, very early. Does that schedule work for you?"

"Fine with me. It's not that long of a drive, so I can be ready by ten-thirty or so."

"That's perfect. I'll make all the arrangements for us when I get home. Do you prefer a king or queen-size bed, Savannah?"

"Would it be cheaper if we reserved a two-bedroom suite, Antonio?"

Savannah's question surprised Antonio. It also pleased him to know she trusted him enough to share the same quarters with him, just separate rooms. "Great idea, Savannah."

The week was a crazy one for Savannah. Much of her time had been spent on making more plans for the senior prom. She'd met with her friends twice during the week and they were also getting together over the weekend. As promised, Antonio had taken her to the country club and the military-base club. Both places were just fine for the dance, but Bernice and the crew thought the country-club setting was more appropriate as the dance venue. True to his word, Antonio had been able to secure decent discounts on the facility's catering services.

Savannah was in the process of looking for a live band or a DJ to handle the music entertainment. Madge was taking care of the floral arrangements and other decorating ideas. An abundance of balloons were also settled on as part of the décor. Lavender, pink and white had been chosen as the theme colors.

Marie had selected the themed ice sculpture—a pair of shimmering wings.

As for the members of Silver Wings, not much had changed there. Savannah was still receiving heavy opposition despite her many gallant efforts. Neither the outgoing president or vice president had offered any type of assistance to her, but Mable Grimes, a dynamo when it came to helping out, had finally been voted in as vice president. Mable was a great asset to the senior center. She had also come to Savannah's rescue on more than one occasion.

One of Savannah's young designer acquaintances was coming up from L.A. later in the afternoon to do a seminar on sensible, affordable but chic fashions for women. Thirty-one-year-old Cassandra Paige-Samms was a well-respected African-American clothes designer. Her label, Creations By Cass was quite popular among folks of all ages. Cassandra, also the exclusive designer for her own best friend, superstar recording artist Hillary Houston, was bringing along Trent Truveaux, a popular fashion designer for seasoned men. Savannah didn't know how well the fashion seminar would go over with the senior members, but she had high hopes for the best.

Antonio had also been invited to the fashion event, along with all the members from his senior center. This was the first joint venture between the local centers that Savannah had arranged. The fashion seminar was actually open to all Inland Empire senior centers. From the number of reservations that had been called in to Silver Wings she expected a great turnout.

To showcase Cassandra's brilliant work, Savannah had dressed herself in an elegant black-and-white pinstriped suit. The delicate white silk shell she wore beneath the double-breasted jacket had been embroidered in the center with her own initials: SRR. Her middle name was Raye. Savannah actually owned several suits of clothing designed by Creations By Cass.

Making sure she had all the important stuff that she needed to take down to the senior center, Savannah did a last-minute check of the bedroom she'd recently designated as an office. Since she'd made the programs on the computer right there in her home, with the help of Mable and Bernice, she scooped up the large white stationery box they'd stored them in.

Looking over her checklist, Savannah hoped that everyone else had done their assigned jobs as well. Although she hadn't become a member yet, Madge was in charge of the simple refreshments, which included hot tea, punch and freshly baked cookies. Much to Savannah's surprise and pleasure, Inez and Doug had donated the baked goods. The Sheffields had also promised to attend the fashion affair. Savannah and Inez had become prayer partners, praying together over the phone each morning at 8:00 a.m.

At the front door of her home Savannah slipped her feet into the brand-new pair of black patent LifeStride pumps she'd placed there earlier. Rarely did she wear anything but soft slippers in her new home, her way of preserving the light beige colored carpets. Most of the living areas in her place were done in ceramic tile with the exception of the bedrooms and both formals.

* * *

Much to her displeasure, Savannah bristled something fierce at seeing Antonio chatting with Veronica. It appeared to Savannah that the attractive-looking woman once again had her man hemmed up in the corner of the recreation room where they practically stood toe-to-toe. Veronica seemed to be doing all the talking while Antonio periodically nodded or shook his head from side to side.

Bernice slipped up beside Savannah and entwined their two hands. "Don't let that witch upset you. I've been keeping my eye on her. Veronica accosted Antonio the moment he walked in the door. If it's any comfort to you, he's not the least bit comfortable in that situation."

"Then why doesn't he just walk away from her, Bernice?" Savannah queried, her tone surly. "She doesn't have a gun held to his head, you know."

Bernice chuckled. "Maybe she does, Savannah, a very subtle weapon. I'm sure she knows full well that Antonio doesn't want her to cause any sort of scene in here today. I, for one, can't even believe she had the nerve to drop in here after that last drama-filled episode she created. We've all gotten a bitter taste of what she's capable of. Antonio will handle her in due time. Besides, your most loyal subject hasn't spotted you yet. When he does, it's over for her."

Savannah had to laugh at that. If nothing else, Antonio *was* loyal to her. Spouting off the numerous social plans he hoped for them to pull off in the not-so-distant future, he'd kept her on the phone until after midnight last evening. Antonio had even suggested that they take a drive up north to see Kevin and Madison. If they ended up doing all the activities he'd mentioned, their social calendars would be filled up for the next year or so.

The thought to walk up to Antonio and loop her arm through his was at the forefront of Savannah's thoughts. Knowing she couldn't be that rude she walked off with Bernice. Besides that, it was far from her to make a public display of herself. She'd leave that up to Veronica. At any rate, there was a lot to do before the senior center was filled to capacity, hopefully so, she hoped. Savannah prayed that her first event would be a huge success, knowing that it was important to the overall mission.

"Where are the other girls, Bernice? They are coming today, aren't they?"

Bernice waved off Savannah's concerns. "Of course they're coming. Marie, Clara and Janice wouldn't let you down for the world. They truly want to support you in all your endeavors, Savannah. My friends have come to like you a lot. Each of them has mentioned to me how real and down-to-earth they think you are. I still don't have a clue to what's going on with Madge, but she hasn't ever said a single bad thing about you to me in private or otherwise. I admit that I'm completely stumped by the rude things she has said and done."

Savannah smiled at Bernice. "I suppose I should be grateful for that. As I've mentioned to you before, I was cautious around all of them in the beginning. But the other ladies have put me at such ease. I'm sure whatever is going on with Madge will eventually come to light. I'm glad you were so willing to share your friends with me. Folks aren't always comfortable in doing that. Thanks, Bernie. You're the best, you know."

As the recreation room started to fill up with guests,

Savannah was quite pleased to see how many unescorted men had shown up, good-looking ones to boot. She couldn't help wondering how instrumental Antonio had been in getting the word out to his male friends. She was willing to bet that the majority of the men in attendance were somehow associated with the man she'd come to care so much about. Savannah's heart warmed just thinking about Antonio.

No sooner had Savannah's last thought passed through her head than Antonio suddenly appeared in front of her, kissing her lightly on the cheek. "Hello, Savannah." His eyes roved her stunning attire. "You look absolutely gorgeous, as always."

That Savannah had thought to wear the diamond-cut butterfly slide he'd presented to her as a gift made Antonio extremely happy. It looked so elegant and beautiful on the gold Omega she wore around her neck. He thought that she made quite the fashion statement all on her own. Antonio also thought that Savannah was beautiful enough to be one of the models for the event.

Savannah was so pleased to see Antonio, thrilled that he'd finally extracted himself from the widow Baker. As usual, he was impeccably dressed. The three-button, dark navy suit he wore was highly fashionable—more timeless than trendy. Seeing the solid lavender shirt and the silk tie done in various shades of purple made her smile brightly. If it wasn't the same exact tie she and Madison had convinced Kevin to purchase, the swirled patterns were very similar.

Antonio placed his hand under Savannah's elbow. "Are we sitting together, my dear?"

Looking uncertain, Savannah shrugged. "I'm not sure

I'll even get a chance to sit. I have a lot of duties to execute between now and the end of this event. In case I do get a chance to have a seat, will you please save me a chair, Antonio?"

Antonio grinned. "Not a problem. But from the looks of things, there may not be a seat left to save. You've got yourself quite a crowd, young lady. You've done a remarkable job, Savannah. I'm really proud of how much you've accomplished in such a short time."

Savannah graciously thanked Antonio for his kind remarks. Hearing him say he was proud of her made her feel especially good. She was proud of herself, too. Despite all the opposition she'd come up against, it appeared that her event would be a success. If the senior prom were as well attended as the fashion event, it would make Savannah extremely happy.

A light tap on her shoulder caused Savannah to turn around. In the next instant Savannah was pulling Kenya into her warm embrace. Then she hugged Cole, whom she was really pleased to see. Seeing Kenya and Cole together and looking very happy in each other's presence had Savannah's heart singing joyously. Savannah had talked on the phone to her daughter and son-in-law on a regular basis, but neither of them had brought up anything to do with their recent marital troubles. Savannah had respected their privacy enough not to make any such inquiries.

As if Savannah hadn't been surprised enough, Kevin slipped up behind his mother and wrapped his arms around her. Madison stood patiently by waiting on her turn to hug Savannah. Savannah did embrace Madison, just as warmly as she had done with her biological children.

"Oh, this is too much," Savannah gushed merrily. "I'm thrilled to see all of you." Savannah then hugged each of the adult kids again. "I'm so happy you four came to Fontana for the fashion show. None of you ever mentioned whether you planned to attend the event or not."

Kevin kissed Savannah on the forehead. "I made our airline reservations as soon as you told me about the event. Madison and I wouldn't have missed your debut event for anything."

Kenya took hold of Savannah's hand, squeezing her mother's fingers gently. "We also wanted to come up and support you from the moment we heard about the fashion seminar, Mom. However, we had to wait to see how Cole's monthly schedule panned out."

Cole smiled at Savannah. "Once we saw we could make it, we wanted to keep it as a surprise." He looked around the room. "Looks like your first event is a winner. Although you consider the senior prom as your first big social event, this one is none too shabby, Mom."

Before Savannah could respond to Cole's statement, Antonio joined the small circle of family members, offering warm, sincere greetings to each of Savannah's children. Savannah was so pleased when Kenya reached out to embrace Antonio with a tender hug. Madison followed Kenya's lead by giving Antonio a great big hug. Antonio then shook hands with the two guys.

"There are several seats left in the row I'm seated in," Antonio offered. "We'd better grab them up before someone else does."

After Savannah's family told her they'd see her once the fashion show was over, the striking couples followed Antonio to the row where his seat was located.

Several minutes later, after everyone had found a seat, Savannah took center stage, from where she'd eventually introduce the attendees to Cassandra Paige-Samms. Savannah first gave a brief personal bio on Cassandra, as well as a short history on the designer's label.

As Savannah left the podium, she spotted Inez and Douglas. Her smile grew even brighter. Everyone who'd promised to attend the fashion event had done so thus far. Seeing all her family members and friends in attendance made Savannah very happy.

Then, when Savannah heard that all the models, both male and female, were of senior age, she nearly broke down and cried. It was a brilliant idea—and Savannah could only wish that she'd been the one to come up with it. Using senior citizens as models for the fashion event was a great concept, one that Savannah was sure would be a huge hit with everyone in attendance.

The spring fashions were unbelievably fresh, classy and stylish. Pastel shades in every color were seen in the attire worn by the models. Although the female senior citizens weren't professionals, they each exuded confidence. The attractive, youthful-looking ladies had the maniacal twists and turns down pat. As young as they all looked, it would be hard for anyone to guess their exact age. The ageless complexions were practically flawless, just as was the light covering of makeup the women wore on their faces.

Savannah couldn't stop smiling. The fashion seminar was more than she'd ever hoped for. Before the show had begun Cassandra had talked about fashion sense and how important it was to accessorize. She mentioned what fashions were in and the ones that were out. Colorful seersucker was big in this year's fashion market and the Capri pants had survived yet another season, she'd informed them. Cassandra had also enlightened the large intently listening group on the difference between trendy clothing and timeless attire. *Timeless* was never out of season.

As Cassandra introduced one of the handsome male models, the room came alive with loud gasps and contented sighs. All eyes were trained on the tall, smoky-complexioned man with the satiny salt-and-pepper waves. Whispers began to run rampant when the senior gentleman began to proudly strut his tall, dark and handsome self up and down the makeshift runway.

Savannah chuckled under her breath when she overheard one woman tell another one that the male model didn't have on a wedding ring. The same lady went on to say that if the model was indeed single, she hoped he was going to stay on a bit after the seminar and enjoy the grand reception to take place immediately after the special program ended.

The elegant formal wear worn by the models appeared to excite the crowd the most.

Paired off in twos, the ladies took to the runway wearing stunning full-length gowns fashioned in colors from bold fire-engine reds to subtle basic blacks. The striking-looking men were decked out in full-dress tuxedos, featuring tails and top hats—and both black and white formal jackets.

While some of the males wore fashionable vests with their formal attire, others wore the traditional cummerbund and bow tie. Some of the male accessories were also done in colorful African prints, which complemented a couple of the tuxedos. Two of the women also wore full-length African-designed attire, along with amazing, beautifully wrapped headdresses.

The touching mock wedding ceremony was held last, that featured all the models. The important members of the wedding party sashayed out first. Then the lovely bride and the handsome groom sauntered onto the stage looking as if they owned the entire world and all that was in it. By the way the bride and groom looked at each other, no one would've ever guessed that they weren't truly in love. Lots of tears were shed as the grand finale signaled the end.

There were so many seminar attendees, both male and female, who came up and offered Savannah their sincere congratulations on the success of the fashion event. Then there were the others—the ones who wouldn't even think of giving her the time of day, yet they'd showed up. Savannah's feelings were somewhat hurt by the blatant snubs, but she had made a conscious decision to delight in all the compliments rather than allow herself to wallow in the ignorance and rudeness of the same group of grumpy women she'd encountered time and time again.

Judge Marlton Townsend had participated as one of the models in the fashion show, the finest black man who'd taken to the runway, the breathtaking one. Several minutes after a group of women flocked around him, he excused himself to go and speak with Savannah. The look on his face indicated that the judge, who was still active on the bench, might have a personal interest in her. Several of the women whispered comments to each other as the good-looking, silver-haired gentleman made a beeline to where Savannah stood talking quietly with her children.

Judge Townsend extended his smoky-colored hand to Savannah, verbally introducing himself to her at the same time. His smile showed off beautiful even, white teeth. "I understand from Mrs. Paige-Samms, the fashion designer, that you were the one to come up with this brilliant idea. I'm so glad I was able to participate in such a worthy cause. I'm surprised that you weren't one of the models. You would've made a stunning addition to our group."

"Yes, she would've, Marlton," Antonio said, coming face-to-face with the judge. "The beautiful Savannah would've caused quite a ruckus among the male populace." Antonio then offered his hand to Judge Townsend. "Long time no see, Marlton. Where've you been hiding?"

Judge Townsend firmly shook Antonio's hand. "You're the one who's been hiding out. I've only seen you a few times since you moved up here from L.A. How are things going?"

Upon putting his arm around Savannah's shoulders, Antonio gave her a knock-dead smile. "Things couldn't be better, Marlton. This young lady here has helped to make me a very happy man. We're now dating, exclusively." Antonio squeezed Savannah's shoulder.

Judge Townsend had received Antonio's message loud and clear. Although Antonio had clearly misread Marlton's intent toward Savannah, he respected Antonio for making his verbal claim on one of the most beautiful women in the room. Marlton didn't think his old friend could've told anyone in any nicer way to *back off* from his woman.

Antonio then took the liberty of introducing the judge to Savannah's family members despite the fact that Marlton had pretty much taken care of that himself. It seemed to Savannah as if Antonio wanted to make sure Marlton knew that Antonio was in cahoots with her family as well.

Savannah thought it was kind of cute the way Antonio had clearly staked his claim on her. She was so pleased that Antonio didn't mind letting everyone know they were an exclusive item. She only wished the widow Baker would get a clue about their relationship. Savannah was so much into Antonio that she just wished there were no obstacles for her to contend with.

As if Savannah's brief thoughts on Veronica had somehow conjured her up, the woman in question sauntered up to Antonio and softly asked to speak with him in private. When Antonio actually stepped away with Veronica, Savannah had a hard time hiding her dismay. Savannah knew they'd never get rid of Veronica if Antonio didn't stop encouraging her in this way.

Although Savannah figured that Antonio was just trying to be polite, she still wished he'd consider her feelings before taking off with a woman who was obviously trying to cause trouble between them. It wasn't like he didn't know all the vulgar things Veronica had said about her.

The group of attendees appeared to enjoy partaking of the delicious freshly baked cookies and the tea and punch provided for them as refreshments. Savannah couldn't thank Inez and Douglas enough for the generous contributions. She also thanked Bernice, Marie, Janice, Clara and Madge for all the help they'd given her on the project. Mable had been a big help also.

For her being the newest kid in town, Savannah believed she'd done a good job, and that she'd been blessed with a bunch of great new friends, the most loyal kind. She didn't have to worry about who had her back, because she already knew who was behind her and who wasn't. Smiling sweetly, Savannah approached Cassandra, who looked as if she was ready to take her leave. "Cassandra, the seminar was the very best. I really didn't know what to expect, but you sure gave me more than I'd imagined. Using seniors to do the modeling was brilliant. I think women and men alike were quite enlightened by the informative presentation. I'd like to have you come back before the fall arrives. In fact, I think we should do a seminar for every season. Calling it a seminar seems like an understatement. We received so much more."

Cassandra took hold of Savannah's hand. "Thank you for saying that. Feedback means a lot to me in my line of work. I'd love to do a seasonal presentation. That's a great idea. As I mentioned to you before, my friend Hillary Houston is a recording artist. Maybe we can get her up here to perform the next time. Doing something charitable for the seniors would be right up her alley. As for me, I can't wait to return. I hate to run, but I must. Thanks for making everything so wonderful for me, Ms. Savannah. The hospitality has been magical."

"I'm glad you're so willing to come back. We'll be looking forward to it. I'll call you at the end of July to start making plans for early September. Thanks again, Cassandra!"

* * *

Savannah's home was filled with company. Antonio, Kevin, Madison, Kenya and Cole had come back to the house with her. She had also invited along Bernice, Madge, Marie, Janice, Clara, Noah, Chester and Irwin. Antonio had asked the judge to join them, but Marlton had to get back to L.A. Kenya and Cole would also be returning to L.A. within the next hour or so. Kevin and Madison were staying on with Savannah for a couple of days.

Kevin handed Savannah a cup of hot tea before seating himself next to her on the sofa. "How're you doing, Mom? You look very tired."

Savannah's head was hurting something awful, but she didn't want to make an issue of it. She *was* extremely tired, so she wasn't surprised that she looked like it. "I can keep up a little longer, Kevin, but I have to admit that I'm looking ahead to falling into bed as soon as the house is emptied. Pulling this event together has been hard work. I'm glad it was such a success."

"It was extremely nice, Mom! I didn't know older folks could have so much fun. It appeared to me as if everyone was having a grand time. The up-tempo music selections were the bomb. 'I Believe in You 'n Me' was a great song for the wedding portion. I'm sure it brought back sweet memories for you since it was the same song sung at your wedding."

Savannah smiled gently. "I did get a little emotional, son. It was hard for me not to. Where are Madison, Kenya and Cole? I haven't seen them for a few minutes."

Kevin pointed at the French doors. "I saw them go out on the patio. They're probably checking out the progress of the pool. It's coming along nicely. Can't wait until it's finished. Kenya and Cole seem a little more relaxed since the last time I saw them. I can't believe Kenya's actually behaving herself. Have you found out what their personal issues are yet?"

Knowing she couldn't dare to break Kenya's confidences to her son, Savannah shrugged. "That's something you'll have to ask them, Kevin. But this evening might not be a good time."

Kevin nodded. "I agree, Mom. It's rare to see Kenya smiling and acting nice to everyone. Don't want to ruin those Kodak moments. She also seems to be getting along well with Mr. Delabay. By the way, how are things between you and him?"

Savannah put her arm around Kevin's shoulders. "For the most part, they're wonderful. There is a little trouble in paradise, but it isn't terribly serious, though it has the potential to become so. There's another lady involved in our relationship. She's also a widow."

Kevin scowled hard. "Is he seeing both of you at the same time?"

As Savannah pondered Kevin's pointed question, she looked over at Antonio, where he stood talking animatedly to Bernice and her crew of close friends. She noticed that he held everyone's rapt attention. Since Antonio was such an interesting, intelligent person, she understood the ladies' fascination with her handsome beau. Savannah was just as fascinated.

Savannah smiled softly. "Antonio's not a cheater, Kevin. Far from it. He wouldn't still be around if he were, unless we'd agreed to see other people." She went on to tell her son how the widow Baker was in hot pursuit of Antonio even though he had ended any involvement with her.

Kevin laughed heartily. "I can't believe this kind of drama goes on with you folks. Who would've ever thought that women your age would be fighting over some man and vice versa? I saw the way Mr. D. let the judge know he was trying to pitch his tent in the wrong campsite. I thought that was really funny."

Laughing, Savannah playfully cuffed Kevin's head. "I beg to differ, boy! I'm not fighting over anyone. If it were to come down to that, Veronica Baker could have Antonio all to herself. I wouldn't think of going there with her. And you'd better get back to watching your mouth! Despite the body-wash trend, I still stock several bars of soap in every bathroom. If you're not careful, son, you might just find a bar or two stuffed into your sassy mouth."

Kevin laughed, giving his mother a playful hug.

Upon seeing Antonio coming toward them, Savannah told Kevin they'd resume their conversation after everyone had gone home. Antonio and Kevin immediately began to easily converse with each other. Neither of them was at a loss for words or an interesting topic. Savannah liked the fact that the two men got along so well.

Antonio showing a genuine interest in Kevin and what was going on in his life was a good thing. Kevin missed Geoffrey and the good fatherly advice he used to give him. Geoffrey could never be replaced in Kevin's life, nor would she want that, but Savannah was glad he had Antonio to talk to about things he might not be able to or even want to discuss with her.

Several minutes after Antonio joined Savannah on the

sofa, Bernice and her friends came over to Savannah to tell her they were leaving. As it was her duty to do so, Savannah got up to walk her guests to the front door. Noah, Chester and Irwin had also decided it was time to leave, so they walked out with the others.

At the front door lots of warm hugs were exchanged between Savannah and her male and female friends. She was once again congratulated on a job well done by all her departing guests. Noah told Savannah for the umpteenth time how proud he was of her and how he'd known from the start that she was the one to light a fire under the members at Silver Wings Senior Center.

After bidding everyone safe travels and a good evening, Savannah returned to her family and Antonio, the only remaining guests. It had been a long day, but she was so pleased with the outcome. As she reclaimed her seat on the sofa, she told the others how delighted she really was, thanking each of them for showing up to help make her event even more special.

"Mom, we wouldn't have missed your event for the world," Kenya said, smiling sweetly. "I just hope we're not too old to attend the Silver and Gold Spring Fling."

Savannah looked puzzled. "Too old?"

Kenya giggled. "Mom, some of you guys act and look so young. A few of you guys made me feel really old. I need to get back into the swing of things so I can keep up with my moms!"

Everyone had a good laugh at Kenya's comical remarks.

Cole brought Kenya to him for a quick kiss. "I have no complaints, sweetheart. I love you just the way you are."

Instead of rudely blowing off Cole's remarks, like she

normally did, Kenya kissed him back. "Thank you, Cole. That was music to my ears. Speaking of music, I'm ready for us to turn on the radio or the CD in the car and make our way home. It's getting late."

Cole looked down at his watch. "Yeah, it's close to seven o'clock, sweetheart. Mom, we hate to run, but duty calls early for me tomorrow. I'm glad we could make it, though."

Savannah immediately got to her feet and ushered her family out. Kevin, Madison and Antonio walked to the front door with her, each of them bidding Cole and Kenya safe travels. The warm embrace between brother and sister nearly brought their mother to tears. Kenya even gave Madison and Antonio toasty hugs, causing Madison's eyes to well up.

Savannah didn't know what was happening in Kenya's life, but it seemed as if she and Cole had turned things around. They looked happier than Savannah had seen them looking in a good while. Though very curious, Savannah was content in waiting until Kenya enlightened her.

Cole and Madison remained standing once Savannah and Antonio sat down on the sofa. Savannah could tell just by looking at Kevin that he had something on his mind. "What is it, son? What's on your brilliant mind?"

Kevin grinned. "I'd like to borrow the car, Mom. We want to take in a movie."

Savannah pointed at the end table, where her evening bag was. "The keys are in my purse. You can get them. What movie do you plan to see?"

Kevin shrugged. "Don't know. We'll see what's playing when we get there. We'll go to the big one out at Ontario Mills Mall. I saw the theaters the last time we were here. I think there's like thirty theaters housed in that one complex." Kevin picked up his mother's purse. Instead of rifling through it, though he had permission to do so, he took it to Savannah.

"I remember how huge the movie building was," Madison added.

"You're right," Antonio said. "AMC 30 is the name of the movie complex. There's also a Lowe's theater complex out there. At least twenty-two screens are in that particular building."

Kevin smiled broadly. "Looks like we'll have lots of choices. Something should just be starting by the time we get there. Would you guys like to join us?"

Savannah stretched her eyes. "Heavens, no! I'll be lucky if I can make it down the hallway to my bedroom. This has been a full day for me already."

With the keys in his hand, Kevin bent down and kissed Savannah. He then gave Antonio a hug. "Don't wait up for us," Kevin said on a chuckle. "We'll more than likely see you in the morning. Mom, go ahead and set the alarm when you go to bed. I remember my security code."

Following Kevin's lead, Madison gave Savannah a kiss and Antonio a hug. "See you guys later," Madison said sweetly. "We'll be sure to be quiet when we come back in."

Once Antonio heard the door close shut, he slid his arm around Savannah's shoulders. A sweet, passionate kiss from his lips to hers came next. "Hmm, that was so sweet," he murmured against her mouth. "I've been dying to taste your lips all day. Mind if I have a few more?"

Savannah blushed. Closing her eyes, eager for more, she offered up her mouth to him.

For the next several minutes no one but them existed in Savannah and Antonio's world.

The fires were still burning hot, but both Savannah and Antonio pulled out their own brands of flame retardant. It was time to cool things down, considerably. The couple laughed as they backed slightly away from each other.

Not ready to fully concede to less passion, Antonio leaned in for one more kiss. "Boy, this is getting harder and harder. You have no idea how much I want us to be together."

Savannah smiled smugly. "We *are* together, Antonio."

Antonio rolled his eyes to the back of his head. "Don't be coy, Savannah. You know exactly what I meant."

Savannah chuckled. "I do, but I thought I'd have a little fun at your expense. Are you mad at me now?"

"Mad about you is more like it! What are we waiting for, anyway? We're both adults. We already know what we want."

Savannah looked a bit upset. "I think we'd better back up a bit. I'm confused. What are we talking about now?"

Antonio turned slightly to the side so he could look right into Savannah's eyes. "What do you think we're talking about, Savannah?"

Savannah held her hand up in a halting position. "Oh, no, mister. You're not turning this around on me." If anyone were going to do any clarifying on the matter, Antonio would have to be the one. She wasn't about to step into something she wasn't sure about. He had to be talking about either sex or marriage. Since Antonio had brought the subject up, Savannah thought that he should be the one to make things clear.

Antonio's expression grew somber. "Savannah, we've had this conversation before. I don't know why you're so confused, since I already told you I was looking for a permanent relationship. I've been trying to give you the time you need to make sure you want to marry me."

"So, this isn't just about sex?" Savannah could've bitten off her tongue the second after that stupid remark had left her mouth. Not only was her comment dim-witted, she felt the same way. "I'm sorry. I don't think that came out right. It's just that things had gotten a little heated between us which made me unsure of what you were referring to."

Antonio felt as if all the air had been let out of his sails. He couldn't understand how she could've misinterpreted his remarks, but then again, he'd also misinterpreted a few of hers, he mused, his mind taking him back to when he thought another man was in her bed. "I see. Well, now that you know I'm not talking about anything physical, how do you feel about us going on and tying the knot? I'm ready for it, Savannah. I'm ready for us to live together under one roof."

Savannah's mind was in a tizzy. Now that Antonio had clarified his position she wished that he hadn't. There were still so many things for them to talk over. Marriage wasn't something she was willing to step into with so many stones left unturned. Veronica Baker was one of those stones, but she was more like an obtrusive boulder than any little old rock. "What about Veronica Baker, Antonio?"

Antonio looked puzzled. "What about her, Savannah?"

"You're the only one who can answer that question, Antonio. Despite the recent conversation we had on this very subject, in spite of the way she disrespects me, every time I turn around I see you off in some corner with her. She calls out your name and you go running at her command, even when you're somewhere with me. What's that all about? What kind of hold does she *really* have on you, Antonio? Are there other skeletons that you haven't cleaned out of your closet yet? I'd really like to know."

The emotional pain was visible in Antonio's eyes as he jumped to his feet. How had things gone from him suggesting they go ahead and get married, though in a subtle way, to getting himself downright insulted by her? "If you have to ask me those kind of questions, Savannah, then I guess we're not on the same page after all. I thought I had made my honorable intentions toward you very clear from the start. Perhaps not. I never saw you as the jealous, insecure type, but that's not the impression I'm getting right now. If you'll excuse me, I'd better go on home before we say anything else we might live to regret. I can find my own way out. I hope you're feeling much better in the morning. Good night, Savannah."

Savannah immediately jumped to her feet to follow after Antonio, hoping she could get him to stay so they could talk things out and hopefully clear everything up.

Minutes later, sad and disillusioned, Savannah went back into the family room. Just as she was about to reseat herself, a sudden barrage of pain tore through her head, stopping her cold. Believing she was about to black out, Savannah eased her way out of the family room and gingerly made it back to the bedroom, where she turned on the alarm and fell into bed.

Seconds later Savannah slowly got up from the bed and went into the bathroom to retrieve a couple of Tylenol.

Knowing that she'd be seeing her doctor first thing in the morning helped her to rest a little easier. As if Savannah didn't already have enough headaches, this one was more real and much more painful than any she'd ever experienced.

Chapter 12

All during her meager breakfast Savannah had sat quietly as a church mouse. As worn out and tired as her entire body had been, she'd gotten very little sleep the previous night. She was still having a hard time believing what had happened between her and Antonio. She now knew that she had offended him terribly. After giving it much thought, she realized she would've been insulted too had the shoe been on the other foot.

Still, Savannah thought it was only fair that she should find out what Antonio intended to do about Veronica. The way she'd asked him about it was more than likely the problem. Although she'd rephrased the same question out loud to herself a dozen times or more, she still didn't see how she could've come off any less offensive to get right to the point.

After running behind Antonio, as he'd stormed his way to the front door, she had called out to him, but he'd totally ignored her pleas for him to come back and talk with her. She had also thought he might've called her once he'd reached home and had had a chance to think about everything, but she had yet to hear a word from him. The pain of that was almost as unbearable as the excruciating headaches she'd suffered with all during the night.

Was it over for them already? Savannah could only wonder.

The loud construction noises compelled Savannah over to the French doors, where she looked out at the work in progress. The construction crew had come a long way. The hole had been dug for the pool and spa, the plaster had also been poured, and the grayish-mauve colored tiles were in the process of being laid.

Savannah had opted for the crystal stone surface over the plaster material. The crystal stones carried a lifetime warranty. Unlike the plaster, the crystal surface would never have to be replaced. She had also chosen pea gravel for the decking, which would take up a good portion of the backyard. Savannah wanted very little grass to upkeep. The patio would be constructed from wood and brick and the cover would be done in tinted fiberglass blocks. The fiberglass would allow in natural sunlight to keep the patio from being too dark.

The majority of the guys on the crew were very young. There were a couple of older guys, the veteran pool builders, which made Savannah breathe a little easier. She was sure the younger guys were pros at what they did, but she liked the idea of them having a few seasoned supervisors. All in all, Savannah was very pleased with the progress of the project. The pool should be up and running within the next few weeks. As hot as it was getting, Savannah would welcome the time when she could take a dip or just lounge in the cooling waters.

Hoping it was Antonio, Savannah quickly reached for the ringing telephone. Since Kevin and Madison were still asleep, she didn't want the ringer to awaken them. They'd been out late the previous evening, well after 1:00 a.m. Savannah had glanced at the clock upon hearing the alarm.

"Mom," Kenya called out cheerfully, "how are you this morning?"

"Okay, sweetie. How about you?"

"Great! I just wanted to call and tell you what a good time we had at the fashion event. You really did a great job. It was nice seeing everyone. Cole enjoyed himself, too. He sends his love. What're your plans for the day?"

"Thanks again, Kenya. As for plans, I'm going to the doctor for a checkup and then probably rest for the remainder of the day. I'm bushed from all the activities. I'll be here hanging out with Kevin and Madison later on. We may do lunch or something. They took in a movie last night and didn't get in until late. They're both still asleep."

"I see. When are they leaving?"

"Tomorrow, Kenya, a late-evening flight. Kevin has to get back to work."

"I was hoping they'd get down to L.A. before they leave. If you weren't so tired, I'd asked you all to come down for dinner this evening. I could whip up something really great."

Wondering how she could make things happen for Kenya, Savannah chewed on her lower lip. "Kevin and Madison could come. They can take the car. Would that work for you?"

"Yeah, but I really would like it to be a family affair. I guess I want to make up to everyone for how badly I behaved when they were here before. Maybe another time."

"No, Kenya, I can come, too. If Kevin drives down, I can just relax in the backseat. Can I get back with you after we talk it over? I don't want to wake them. So as soon as they get up, I'll check things out with Kevin."

"Check out what with me?" Kevin asked from the doorway.

Savannah held up her finger to Kevin in a waiting gesture. "Your brother just popped into the kitchen. I'll talk to him now and call you back in a few minutes. Bye, Kenya."

"Okay, Mom. Talk to you then. Bye."

The second Savannah hung up the phone she jumped up to fix Kevin a cup of coffee.

When Kevin realized what Savannah was doing, he took her by the hand and led her back to her seat. "I can get my own coffee, Mom. You need to just sit and relax. What was the phone call all about? What's on the unpredictable mind of the Princess Kenya?"

"Your sister wants to fix dinner this evening for you and Madison. Of course she wants me to come, too. What do you think of the idea, Kevin?"

Kevin's expression was one of open skepticism as he sat down. "Kenya, cook for us? Please! What's her real motivation? I know she has to have something up her sleeve. You better have your daughter see a doctor, someone other than her husband. The girl's definitely ill."

"Oh, Kevin, be serious now. Kenya is trying to atone for her past behavior and we should probably let her. If she is ill, we'd better go ahead and take advantage of whatever ails her before she fully recovers and goes back to her old self," Savannah joked.

Kevin cracked up. "I know what you mean. But what about you, Mom? I have to tell you, old girl, you look like you could use a day or two off. Are you really up to it?"

Savannah shook her head. "Thanks for the compliment, but I got your 'old girl'! However, I think we should try to do this for Kenya. As I told her, I can rest while you drive. That is, if you're feeling up to it. What do you say?"

"I'm game. Maybe we can go down to L.A. early, right after your doctor's appointment. That way I can check out the old hood. I'd like to see Sean and Robert. I haven't talked to my best homies in a minute. They used to be permanent fixtures in our house. Those guys were at our place so much I used to wonder at times if maybe I was at the wrong house. Madison is showering right now, but I'm sure she'd love to go down to L.A. Kenya and her seemed to hit it off much better this time. They would've been okay the last time we visited if it had been up to Madison. What about Mr. D.? Are you going to invite him since Kenya seems to have taken a sudden shine to him also?"

Savannah's heart thundered. How was she to answer that question without revealing the recent troubles in paradise? Honestly, she quickly decided. "Mr. D. is a little miffed at me at the moment. I offended him last night when I asked him what he planned to do about Ms. Baker. The question had been put to him while he was talking about our plans for the future, but I wanted to make sure the future included only the two of us."

"Marriage? Was he asking you to marry him, Mom?"

"Something like that, at least the suggestion of such," Savannah said, her tone bland, her heart full of regret. "The subject of marriage has come up a time or two before, but I think he wanted to know if we're possibly ready to see if we could etch out some definite plans."

"And you asked about the other woman amidst something as important as that? Wow! I think I would've been offended, too. Bad timing! How did you know he was upset with you?'

"The old coot actually walked out on me," Savannah said on a nervous chuckle, hoping to lighten the heavy burden on her heart. Laughter was always a good remedy for lifting the spirit. "Can you imagine him doing something like that? I haven't heard from him since."

Kevin shook his head. "I'm afraid I *can* imagine. I probably would've done the same thing as he did. As far as you not hearing from him, it hasn't been all that long. I'm sure he'll call today. It's not even seven yet. Mr. D. more than likely regrets this incident as much as you do. You do regret it, don't you?"

"Kevin, I feel regret, but I'm not sure that it's over the question as much as it is over how I phrased it. This woman has been up in his face every time I turn around. If he goes off with her every time she beckons him, should I not be concerned about what's going on? I can't imagine marrying someone who's constantly at the beck and call of another woman. I understand that he has to use professional courtesy since she's a member of his center. But this is a personal matter, not a business one. There's no room in our relationship for a third party, plain and simple. Delabay has to get rid of Ms. Baker if we're to have any kind of future together. He also said he now sees me as insecure and jealous. What do you think of that one?"

Kevin howled, but he quickly changed gears upon seeing the admonishing expression on Savannah's face. "Mom, I don't mean to make light of this, but I'm just having a hard time believing people your age act like this. You and Mr. D. are acting like this is the first stage of puppy love. Come on. Get real. You guys are nearly a half a century old. This situation seems like it's right out of the soaps. Somebody in this relationship really needs to grow up. Hello!"

"And whom do you think that someone should be?" Savannah asked rather pointedly.

Before Kevin could respond to Savannah's question Madison popped into the kitchen, looking all cute and fresh-faced, with her hair piled loosely on top of her head. Dressed in blue jeans and a simple white tank top, Madison looked like an innocent little teenybopper.

Acting like a man madly in love, Kevin leaped from his seat and gently pulled Madison into his arms for a good-morning kiss. "Hey, honey, you look great! All ready for a cup of coffee? Mom has some freshly baked pastries, too, compliments of her friendly neighbors, the Sheffields. If she doesn't quit accepting these deadly goodies from them, we may just have to roll her out of this house one day."

Savannah and Madison laughed at that remark.

Madison swatted playfully at Kevin with an open hand.

"If that's the case, why would you want me to eat any of them, Kev? I'd think you'd want me to keep my figure intact, too."

As soon as Madison let go of Kevin, she bent over and kissed Savannah on the cheek and then hugged her warmly. "We need to check him, don't you think?" Madison had whispered into Savannah's ear. "The boy is out of control," Madison said, loud enough for Kevin to hear.

After Kevin set down a cup of coffee before Madison and a peach Danish, he nibbled at her ear. "I'm always out of control with you around. You're trouble with a capital *T*, you know."

Madison responded by dipping her finger in the icing on the Danish and smearing it over Kevin's lips. "And you love all of me, roly-poly or slim and trim!" She kissed the icing away.

Although Savannah thoroughly enjoyed the loving exchange between her adorable son and his charming girl-friend, seeing Madison looking like the beginning of a bright new day had her wanting to get herself all dolled up for her doctor's appointment so she wouldn't appear too pitiful. She had showered before she'd come into the kitchen, but she had only put on lounging attire. Savannah got to her feet. "I'm going to get dressed now for my appointment. Kevin, please talk to Madison about L.A. Let me know if we're going, as soon as you can."

Madison bounced up and down in her seat. "L.A.! I'd love to go. I've never been. Can we do it, Kevin, please?"

As Kevin's mind went completely off the road map with Madison's question, he actually blushed. "Girl, it seems like you and my mom both need to watch how you phrase things. But, yeah, we can go. But I have to tell you this. We're going to Kenya's for dinner. Still want to go?"

Madison looked puzzled. "Of course I do. Why wouldn't I want to? Kenya's cool."

Kevin grinned. "Enough said. Mom, it looks like you have your answer. L.A. is a go. Can you be ready within the next hour so we can get to your doctor's office a little ahead of schedule? Since you're his first patient maybe he can see you earlier."

Savannah doubted that. "I can be ready in thirty. How's that on timing for you?"

"Perfect. That'll give us plenty of time to get down to L.A. and hang out a bit before dinner at Princess Kenya's castle. On second thought, that's if your doctor doesn't keep you waiting all day. We'll be ready soon. See you in a few, Mom. Love you."

"I love you, too, Kevin. Be good to each other. See you later, kids."

As lonely as Savannah felt, she knew she needed this time alone. Kevin and Madison had only been gone two days, but it felt much longer to her. She could call Antonio to come over, and he probably would oblige her, but she probably shouldn't do so. Much to her surprise, Kenya had also invited Antonio to dinner at her home when her Kevin and Madison had gone there a couple of evenings ago. What had really surprised her was that he'd actually shown up there despite their current circumstance. Savannah could only imagine the look on her face when Antonio had first walked into Kenya's living room.

Deep down inside Savannah had been very pleased to

see Antonio, but, unfortunately, she'd given him an under-cover freeze-out and a discreet silent treatment for well over twenty minutes. Then she had remembered Kevin saying that someone needed to grow up. Savannah knew that that someone had to be her since Antonio had probably staved off his ego to be there.

Kevin had later sworn to his mother that he'd had nothing to do with the dinner setup.

The dinner engagement had gone over very well. The Standifords had been great hosts, though no one had expected any less from them. Kenya had Cole grill fantastic boneless rib-eye steaks and spicy barbecued chicken for the meat entree. Cole's mother had made the potato salad, greens and baked beans.

It turned out that Kenya had only been able to take credit for the roasted corn on the cob.

Kevin hadn't let Kenya live down her minor part in the dinner for the entire visit. So much for her cooking for them, he'd told everyone. He'd also told Kenya they should've known better than to think she'd be preparing the meal with her own two hands, that spoiled brats rarely thought of others first. Once again Savannah had thought an outright battle might ensue between her two kids, but Kevin had kept things in a light, joking manner. Kenya had seemed to take the good-natured ribbing from him very well, much better than she had done in the past.

After picking up the remote control, Savannah turned off the television. She wanted complete quiet when she gave thought to the rest of the time she'd spent with Antonio. Once she'd gotten over giving him the cold shoulder, she'd talked quietly with him while the kids had

played a game of Taboo. With all the shouting and anima-
tion going on in the room by the others, she had figured
that no one would overhear their very personal conversation, though it had been kind of hard for them to hear
each other.

Antonio had apologized to Savannah for his part in what
had happened between them. Savannah had accepted
Antonio's apology, but she hadn't said she was sorry
because she thought it was hypocritical of her. But she had
apologized to him for how she'd come across. He'd then
gone back into the things they'd discussed about marriage
before the upset.

Although Veronica Baker hadn't come up during the
conversation, she had definitely been on Savannah's mind.
When Antonio hadn't offered any suggestions on what
he'd planned to do about their nemesis, Savannah hadn't
said anything on the subject either. Before she would ever
think of agreeing to marry him that issue had to be settled.
If Antonio thought it could be any other way than that,
Savannah was afraid that he was sadly mistaken.

Then, when it had been time to go home, everyone had
insisted, with Antonio remaining neutral, that Savannah
ride back to Fontana in the same car with him so he
wouldn't have to ride home alone. Not knowing anything
about their earlier rift, Kenya had insisted on it the most.

Savannah, not wanting to make waves, had conceded
before things had gotten way out of hand. She hadn't
wanted to draw any more attention to their personal
troubles than what she'd already shared with Kevin. Kenya
had been left totally in the dark, but there were just some
things that Savannah couldn't talk to Kenya about. Her re-

lationship with Antonio was one of them, especially since Kenya had been so opposed to them as a couple in the very beginning.

Savannah had been giving remarriage a lot of serious thought—the pros and the cons. Although it was countless years away, she would be eligible for Geoffrey's social security benefits once she turned sixty-two, which would more than likely garner her more money than the monetary benefits from her own account. At any rate, Savannah could only collect on Geoffrey's account since he was deceased, once she met the age requirement.

Senior citizens and widows and widowers really had a lot to think about when considering remarriage, Savannah considered. She knew of a lot of folks who'd opted to live together because one or the other had been in danger of losing their pensions had they married or remarried. It was a shame that people were forced to make those kinds of choices, all because they'd fallen in love again after losing a beloved spouse or being in love for the first time ever.

Then there was the property factor to consider. With California being a community property state, she needed to look into how her property would be affected, since she planned to leave everything to her children, equally. There were other insurance policies as well as bank CDs, stocks and bonds. When Geoffrey died she'd had to change the beneficiary on all the accumulative assets. Kevin and Kenya were her only beneficiaries.

There were a lot of things for Savannah to think about. So just standing at the altar and saying "I do" wasn't as easy as it sounded. Antonio certainly had a lot of tangible assets also. Although their children wouldn't be eligible for either of their retirement pensions, they had a right to everything else. How to broach these important things with Antonio was one of her biggest concerns, yet they had to be discussed in great detail. Savannah knew she couldn't decide on marriage until these issues were settled. Was a prenuptial agreement needed in this instance?

Savannah now knew that it was more than likely past time for her to consult with her sisters on her personal problems. The women talked several times a month, but when trouble brewed, they were known to keep up with each other on a daily basis, if not more frequently, until all issues were completely resolved.

The matter of her sudden health issue was also a big concern for Savannah. While her internal medicine physician, Dr. Russell Eddington, hadn't given her a definitive reason for the excruciating headaches, he had suggested that they needed to keep a close watch on the onset of the pain and how long each episode lasted. If the painful headaches continued, he'd said that further diagnostic testing should be done. The word "migraine" came up, but he couldn't be sure of that either, not without a more thorough medical workup.

"Yeah" by Usher was blaring loudly from the speakers mounted on the walls inside the Silver Wings' spacious exercise room. Sweating bodies were trying to keep up with the fast-paced music. Some senior members were moving rapidly, as others moved slowly, with many of the folks in tune and some completely out of sync to the funky rhythm of the popular song.

The workout outfits worn by the senior members, both

male and female, ran from serviceable, to cute, to classy, to simply outrageous—and then on to downright ridiculous. Having the majority of the members participating in the workout had been the goal of Savannah and the exercise instructor she had commissioned. The fitness class really wasn't about what the members wore on their backs, despite the recent fashion seminar held at the center.

Smiling at the great efforts being made by the group, Karen Butler, an exercise guru with twenty years experience, wanted the members to get in shape, but she desired them to have a good time more than anything else. She had promised Savannah she'd make the class fun and interesting for her participants. Karen was a delightful person with mega energy.

Savannah had called on Karen to teach the class because of her experience and her near senior status. At forty-eight, Karen's slender, medium-framed body was in excellent shape. She ate extremely healthy and lived and breathed the art of movement, a perfect example of how women over forty could actually look if they really worked at it. Karen was also a perfect role model for those wanting to get back into shape and begin leading a healthier lifestyle.

"Move it, ladies and gents. Roll those hips and keep those feet moving. This is about movement, people. Don't think of what we're doing as exercise. Just think movement. If we get a little tired, don't be ashamed to slow it down. We don't want to burn ourselves out. We're here to have fun, lots of it, as well as get into good shape. Work those derrieres, guys and gals, as much or as little as you're comfortable with. Do the 'Tighten Up,' people. You all remember that fabulous song from when the good times were rolling by Archie Bell and the Drells."

Karen smiled brightly, laughing and joking playfully, as she took the members through a range of modern dance moves, always careful to keep the group moving at an easy pace. Attitude was everything for the instructor. Confidence was a must. A great personality was a major asset. If she didn't appear as though she enjoyed herself, Savannah knew how easily she'd lose her group. The fact that Karen really enjoyed herself tremendously was half the battle.

The songs now playing were from the '70s. "Brick House" was rocking the place. Since that old-school song happened to be one of her favorites, Savannah smiled happily.

"Think about all those groovy dances we attended as teenagers. Those were the good old days. Now let's do the dance moves we liked to do best back in the day. Everyone doesn't have to do the same steps. We can even come up with something completely original if we'd like. *Movement* folks, simply *movement!* Ten more minutes of the faster paced music and then we'll slow it down with some of those golden oldies. You know the ones. The slow jams we used to groove to with the blue lights on downstairs in the basement or upstairs in the den. When we slow it down, we can pair up with partners or just use make-believe ones. Whatever we like."

Smiling all the while, Karen continued to enthusiastically move to the music. "Let's whip it all in shape and have loads of fun getting down. By the time we're through with this four-week session, I expect us to be able to stop traffic whenever we're out and about the city."

Everyone laughed at that. Then the loud moans and groans of disbelief came next.

"Okay, so I exaggerated a bit. What the heck! Take your frustrations out on the dance floor. Imagine that it's my head we're doing the boogie on," Karen joked, laughing up a storm. "That vision should put some fire in your fannies, not to mention your feet. 'Skin Tight' by The Ohio players is coming up next. Then we'll slow it down a bit with 'If You Don't Know Me by Now' by Harold Melvin and the Blue Notes. Teddy Pendergast's 'Turn Off the Lights' will play also. The last cooldown number is 'For the Love of You' by the incomparable Isley Brothers."

The members all seemed excited about the upcoming music selections.

Once the exercise class was over, Savannah asked the members for their undivided attention. She had come up with a few other great ideas for the center and needed some input. After everyone in attendance had taken a seat, Savannah walked to the front of the room, microphone still in hand. "Did everyone enjoy Ms. Butler's workout routine?"

The majority of hands went up. Once again, as was expected by Savannah, the holdouts were Opal and her group of sinister friends, including the past official office-holders. Selling her new programs wasn't going to be easy but Savannah knew it was necessary.

"Thanks for the show of hands. Now let's get on to the other business. I've been thinking of what we could do with all the great space we have here at the center. There are so many more activities we could offer which would utilize a number of the idle rooms. I understand this is a senior center, but I'd like to see us open up the center to other age groups. I've heard a lot of women over forty say they hate going out to clubs to meet men and other new friends."

Savannah went on to say that perhaps the center could provide a fun environment for other age groups to come to Silver Wings and socialize and fellowship with their peers. She then mentioned the many teens residing in the area that could also use a safe haven. It was her belief that if the center were made accessible to other age groups that the memberships would soar and they'd have plenty of extra revenue to handle all the business fees. Savannah even thought it might be good idea to hold weekly Bible study classes for the community to attend.

Savannah looked out over the audience. "I'd like to have some feedback, please."

Opal jumped to her feet. "This is a center for seniors! What are you trying to turn this place into? The neighborhood youth will have this center torn apart in no time. Being president doesn't give you the right to change the rules and take away what rightfully belongs to the senior community. You have some nerve coming in here and demanding to have it all your way."

An elderly lady, one that Savannah had never seen at the center before, slowly got to her feet. After introducing herself as Marcia Grimes, she raised her hardwood cane and shook it at Opal. "I resent your comments about the youth, young lady. I'll have you know that my three beautiful grandchildren live in this community, very respectful children. They often complain to me that there are not enough fun things to do after school and during the summer. As a retired schoolteacher, I think the idea of a good program for teens is right on. Maybe you should listen sometime, Opal, and not do so much talking." With that said, Marcia reclaimed her seat.

Opal looked as if she wished the floor would open up and swallow her whole, but that didn't stop her from shouting out a few expletives aimed directly at Savannah.

Miriam Preston, former vice president, got to her feet. "I agree with Opal. This center was not created or opened up for anyone other than the seniors. We're definitely not here for forty-and-over women to meet men. This is not a brothel of some sort. We voted you in and we can vote you out," Miriam threatened.

Mad as a wet hen, Savannah posted one hand on her hip. "What you've said is all well and good, but I am the acting president. No longer will I back down from the trouble you bring on, nor will I continue to try and be the diplomat. You cantankerous ladies are not going to run me out of town. And if you hadn't noticed, there are many people who are behind my ideas. I'm going to get my programs through one way or the other. You all can be sure of that."

"I can only imagine how you're going to get them through," Loretta said, "and in the disrespectful ways I believe you're capable of resorting to."

Savannah gave a soft chuckle. "Loretta, perhaps you can discuss with me later what you imagine. If I think it'll work, I just might try it. Can we now please hear from the folks who are interested in making positive changes?"

Even though Noah was chomping at the bit, he remained seated. "I don't agree with either of you three ladies," Noah stated strongly. "We could do a lot of good in this community if we opened this center up to realize its full potential." He looked at Miriam, Loretta and then Opal. "If you're so interested in what happens here at the center, why'd you hightail it out of here like you did? You three cronies have been nothing but bad news since this center first opened. Ms. Savannah, I suggest that you call a special business session and take up a vote. We're not going to get anywhere fighting back and forth among us. I'm sure everyone in here would like to voice an opinion. Let the vote represent the voices of all the members."

Savannah nodded. "Good idea, Noah. We can have the meeting early next week. Mable and I will notify everyone by phone of the date and time." Savannah shook her head in dismay when Opal knocked over her chair in her hasty retreat. When she didn't bother to come back and pick it up, Savannah could only consider the source.

Feeling as if she had to say a bit more, Savannah lifted the microphone to her lips once again. "Listen, folks, I'm only here to try and make the center all it can be. We have so much unused space that we could put to darn good use. If we can help our youth, among others in our area, let's do whatever we can to make this center an integral part of the community."

Freshly showered and dressed in clean clothing—simple jeans and a T-shirt—Savannah was stretched out on the sofa in the family room, a colorful caftan thrown loosely about her body. She couldn't have been more pleased with the first workout session, though it had left her worn-out. Karen had won over most of the members, especially the males, but of course.

Savannah was determined to see all her proposed programs through to the very end.

As Savannah had just gotten off a conference call with her sisters, Meredith, Jacqueline and Royal, a quick glance at the clock told her she didn't have very long to rest. Bernice, and her other newly acquired girlfriends, Marie, Janice and Clara were coming over to go over the final arrangements for the senior prom, which was to take place in a couple of weeks. No one was sure if Madge was coming over or not. If she was, Savannah hoped she'd leave her sarcasm behind. Mable was coming by to help out Savannah also. The two women worked so well together.

The entire group of women had worked hard on this special project and they all had high hopes for it to be a huge success. The other women hadn't done much with their secret singles club; they'd been too busy helping Savannah out with her social events. Once the senior prom was behind them, Savannah vowed to help her friends get their secret society of women going.

Savannah was really excited that her three sisters were coming into town for the major event, as each of them would offer her even more support than she already had from the other wonderful ladies. She was also eager for them to meet the dashing Antonio even if their relationship was still kind of up in the air. Savannah didn't know if her brother, Eugene, and his wife, Arlene, were coming to California or not, but they were definitely trying to make arrangements to do so.

This little get-together could turn out to be a family

reunion as well, Savannah mused. In fact, she was going to insist that the family make a pact to see each other at least once a year from now on, if not more. Mostly all of her other siblings had reached senior-citizen status, with Savannah being the youngest child. No one was going to get any younger. That was for sure.

Savannah giggled inwardly as she thought of some interesting news. She couldn't wait to tell Bernice what Antonio had recently told her. Bernice was going to be very surprised and hopefully very pleased, just as Savannah had been. Marie and Irwin and Janice and Chester had decided to double date for the prom just for the heck of it and it also looked as if Clara and Noah might even hook up just for the one special evening. Madge wasn't interested in having an escort. At least that was what she'd been advertising, but Savannah wasn't so sure about that.

Of course that bit of juicy news about the double dates had already made its way onto the ever-winding grapevine. The latest in gossip hadn't set too well with the grumbling female members at the senior center since Savannah had been accused of stealing their men for her girlfriends, women who weren't even members of Silver Wings.

A nasty note had also been left on Savannah's windshield, citing all sorts of unkind things, even going as far as to call her out of her name. Since her car had been parked in the senior center parking lot at the time, she had to assume that one of the members might've done it. However, Savannah definitely hadn't ruled out Veronica as one of the prime suspects. Anything that unpleasant woman might do wouldn't surprise her in the least. Veronica was downright evil.

As Kenya came to mind, Savannah frowned slightly. She'd had the opportunity to spend a short time alone with her daughter, which had allowed them a chance to have a mother and daughter heart-to-heart. Kenya and Cole were working through their problems, but there hadn't been much he could do about juggling his very busy work schedule. Cole knew that he had to be dedicated to his profession or fail. Kenya was trying to be more understanding, realizing that it wouldn't always be this difficult. She loved Cole and simply craved his undivided attention.

Kenya still didn't know if she was pregnant or not. After she'd checked the calendar, Kenya had realized she wasn't quite as late with her cycle as she'd initially thought, but that she was nonetheless late. Because she still wasn't sure if she could commit to having a child under the present state of their marriage, Kenya hadn't taken the home pregnancy test. She had told her mother that she planned to give her cycle a couple of more weeks before she'd take up any measures. Cole still didn't know that she might possibly be pregnant with his child.

That Kenya hadn't taken any steps toward discovering the status of her health issues had grieved Savannah something terrible. She had hoped that her daughter had worked everything out, especially after having seen her and Cole looking so happy at the fashion event.

Although Savannah hadn't wanted to overlecture her daughter during their brief social visit, she had once again been adamant in informing her that there'd be dire consequences should she go against God's will for the sanctity of life if she were in fact pregnant. Savannah pleaded with Kenya to seriously think everything through, paying close attention to all the issues, all the players, telling her daughter to leave no matter unattended.

Kenya had definitely been made to know that her mother would be there for her and that she could call on Savannah no matter the day or the hour. Savannah had even told Kenya that if she were with child that she'd keep the baby for her until she was ready to fully take on the responsibility. Under no circumstances did Savannah want Kenya to have an abortion. That would be such a sad chapter in all of their lives and it would more than likely become the end of Kenya and Cole's fairy-tale love story. Just revisiting the thought of how horrible Cole would feel about everything made Savannah sick inside. Kenya just couldn't hurt her husband like that.

As the doorbell pealed, Savannah laughed lightly. So much for a short nap, she mused. How many times had she lain down to rest in the past month to no avail? Many times. Until the senior prom was over and done with Savannah had finally realized there'd be no rest for her.

When the ladies had suggested doing an early potluck dinner in conjunction with the meeting, Savannah was all for it, which meant she hadn't had to worry about pulling an entire food menu together on her own. Chinese dishes had been decided on so everyone was bringing their very own favorites. Egg rolls were warming in the oven and curry chicken simmered in the Crock-Pot, filling the air with the delicious mixed scent of Indian curry and Chinese spices.

As usual, enthusiastic greetings were exchanged among the ladies—including Madge—all of whom were very animated. After trooping through the house and on into the kitchen, everyone placed the tightly packaged food items on the counter. A bunch of new delicious scents were about to fill the air.

Each of the ladies began unwrapping what they'd brought along to eat: sautéed garlic green beans and veg-etables, sweet and sour chicken, beef and bell peppers, hot and sour soup, Chinese chicken salad, chicken chow mein and lo mein noodles. Someone had even brought along a medium-size Tupperware bowl filled with colorful foil-wrapped fortune cookies.

Savannah told everyone they could help themselves to the curry chicken right from the Crock-Pot, after she pulled from the oven the aluminum pan of egg rolls and placed them on the counter. "Shall we eat first and then work, or what?" Savannah asked.

"Let's eat while we work here in the kitchen," Marie sug-gested. "Savannah, did you take my hint about making our favorite white cranberry punch?"

"I sure did. I'll get it out of the refrigerator. As you can see, the plates and utensils are on the far end of the counter. Let's go ahead and get started, ladies. We don't want all this delicious-looking food to get cold. I asked my neighbor, Inez, to join us, but like always, I'm not sure she'll make it. I haven't heard from her since our prayer session early this morning. The bakery takes up so much of her time, but she'd like to start hanging out with us from time to time."

Before the ladies began eating, Savannah passed the blessing. She also thanked the Lord for once again bringing them together safely, asking Him to bless their meeting, and then garnering safety for the groups' return travels. Everyone said amen at the finish of the prayer. Savannah then said a silent prayer for her and Madge to get along.

"That was a real nice supplication, Savannah," Bernice praised. "After I heard you talking about Inez being your prayer partner, I thought it would be great if we could all get a conference call going early in the morning and do the same thing. Who's up for the idea?"

All hands went up, including Clara's, who normally played the devil's advocate. Bernice called it just being plain contrary, an addiction to controversy.

Bernice grinned. "Okay, we'll get that project started once this one is over with. We still have to get cracking on a few things for the secret singles club. We're going to stay real busy."

"I like busy," Marie said. "Keeps this lonely divorcee from getting depressed."

Savannah saw her opening. "Speaking of busy, I know of a gentleman who wants to keep one of us ladies real busy," Savannah said, smiling wickedly. "Anyone care to know who at this table has a secret admirer?" Savannah asked, taking the first bite of her food.

All eyes connected with Savannah's, curiosity burning brightly in each set of orbs.

Madge rolled her eyes to the ceiling. "The answer can only be *you*, Savannah, since you attract the opposite sex like rats to cheese. You're the only one of us who seems to ever get any social action. It's not that the rest of us are un-attractive, so why don't you let us in on your secret? How do you attract all these men? What's your secret weapon? Sex, perhaps?"

Bernice saw red. "Wait a minute now, Madge," Bernice said, jumping to her feet.

So much for my prayer, Savannah thought, blowing out a shaky breath. Since Bernice was in arm's length of her, Savannah quickly reached for her friend's hand, prompting her to sit back down. "I've got this, Bernie. Please let me handle it."

With a dreadfully worried look on her face, Bernice slowly resumed her seat.

Once Bernice was settled back in her chair, Savannah instantly turned her attention to Madge. In doing so, she could see that the others appeared to be holding their breath. "I need to understand something, Madge. Not long after you started coming to my home, you suddenly began insulting me. Since I have no clue as to why, I'd like you to tell me your reason for doing so. If you have a specific problem with me, I can't address it if I don't know what it is."

Madge looked stunned, as if she never would've expected the soft-spoken Savannah to call her out, especially in front of all the others. After a few moments of Madge squirming about in her chair, she finally made eye contact with her hostess. "I don't think I've been insulting to you. What's wrong with me calling it like I see it? You should only wear the shoe if it fits."

Savannah raised an eyebrow. "And just how *do* you see it?"

Madge pushed her chair slightly back from the table, as though she wanted to be in a position to defend herself if she had to. "Savannah, I've run across far too many women just like you. You come off as having this supersweet personality, but deep down inside of you lays a character of a totally different color. I personally think you're a phony."

Savannah was clearly astonished by Madge's succinct remarks, as was everyone else. Sensing that Madge was far from through having her say, Savannah gestured for her to go on.

"Men don't love women like you just because you're beautiful and stylish. There has to be more to it than that. Even if you're not aware of it, I see a lot of flaunting and flirting dished out by you. Ladies like us," she said, encompassing her friends in her steady gaze, "always get lost in the background when flirtatious women like you turn on their indelible charms, false or otherwise. You all seem to drown men in your sultriness, and your sexy attire, which makes me wonder how far you all are really willing to go to get what you want. Why is it that you women have to be the center of attention no matter where you are? Why can't you ladies give the rest of us a chance with the fellows, Savannah? It would be nice if you all had the spirit of sharing."

Savannah licked her lips, taking time to choose her words carefully. It surprised her that she wasn't super angry by the unfair attack on her character. She had been hurt by it, though. But she actually understood where Madge was coming from. Savannah had actually encountered the type of women Madge had described; she just wasn't one of them. "I'm simply going to take your advice, Madge. Since the shoe you just described doesn't come close to fitting my foot, I'm not going to even bother to try and put it on. However, I'd like to suggest that you really get to know my shoe size before you try it on my foot. You should also get to know me before you try to define who I am. One other thing before I let go of this, Madge. If you have to continue to insult me like this, I'd rather you not come back to my home. Thank you."

Audible gasps permeated the room, but no one said a single word, including Madge.

Savannah turned her attention away from Madge and then looked dead at Bernice. "I probably shouldn't tell you this before we finish eating, but our food is already cold. Even though you have an aversion to handsome men, I can't keep it in a second longer. Judge Marlton Townsend asked Antonio to find out from me if he could have your phone number." Savannah paused a brief moment, eyeing her friend closely. "What do you think, Ms. Bernie?"

With all the prior drama taking second place to Savannah's news, chattering among the other ladies had already gone wild. As for Bernice, she sat in stunned silence, unbelieving of any of what Savannah had just said, though she knew her dear friend would never joke about something like this. Nor would she lie to Bernice. Savannah would see both as plain cruelty.

Janice nudged Bernice with her shoulder. "Girl, hurry up and say something. Otherwise, we're going to think you're in a state of shock. Are you?"

Bernice shook her head from side to side. "Savannah, I know you wouldn't joke about this, but are you serious? And are you talking about the finest black man in the fashion show?"

Savannah cracked up at the expression on Bernice's face. Bernice had said she believed her and then she'd turned right around and asked if she was serious, Savannah mused. "Of course I'm serious. I'm not joking or telling a story. Judge Townsend has a personal interest in you."

Madge drummed her fingers on top of the table. "Not to make waves, Savannah, but I had gotten the impression on that day that the judge was interested in you. I guess I was wrong."

Bernice's statement had lent some credence to what Madge had said about how Savannah was able to attract men, but Bernice knew her friend was nothing like the women Madge had described. Bernice couldn't wait to later set the record straight with the widow Jacoby.

"Both you and Antonio were wrong. Antonio had thought the same thing. But the judge was making his way over to me to find out whom Bernice was. Since I was the one in charge of the fashion show, he assumed I knew Bernice, according to Antonio's account of things."

Bernice still had a bewildered look on her face. "I don't know about this, girlfriends. Good-looking men like that carry around all sorts of curses to put on us females. I know that fine brother's capable of putting down a serious mojo on me. Help me, you all! You know I'm scared silly of men like the judge. Do you think he was just pulling Antonio's leg, Savannah?"

Savannah shook her head in the negative. "If I thought that, I wouldn't be telling you what Antonio said to me. He seemed to think that Marlton was more than just a bit curious about you. He apparently asked Antonio a lot of questions about you after he learned you were both members of the same church. Bernice, do you really think it would hurt for you to explore it?"

Bernice hunched her shoulders. "I don't know. I have no clue."

"Maybe you could just look at this as a possible date for the senior prom, Bernice," Clara said. "There should be no harm in doing that. I understand your reluctance to get involved with Judge Townsend, considering your history with handsome men, but that was a long time ago, Bernice. Don't you think it's time to get over it, time to give another handsome guy at least a chance to prove that all pretty men aren't just alike? If you don't go into this thing expecting a fairy-tale ending, you should be okay," Clara urged.

"I agree with you on that, Clara. We ladies have to learn to enjoy the beginning of a relationship instead of always worrying about it ending badly," Janice remarked.

"And why do we always think it has to become a serious relationship?" Madge asked. "What happened to just dating for fun? We're no longer in high school. If we don't at least give things a try on for size, we'll never know if it might fit. We won't know the outcome period."

Bernice held up a flattened palm. "I'll tell you what, ladies. Let's finish eating and then finalize our business for the senior prom. We can revisit my issues after the meeting. I know we've been eating while talking, but I really want to enjoy this good food without interruption. I lost my appetite to fear there for a minute. Think we can all agree to discussing this later?"

All heads nodded in agreement.

In spite of the unscheduled interruption, everyone was pleased with the outcome of the meeting, which left nothing else to do until all the plans were put in action. The ladies were now cleaning off the table and picking up after themselves.

Madge was busy at the sink washing the containers the food had been brought in so each person could claim their bowl or dish before leaving Savannah's home. Unsure as to whether she'd ever be welcomed in Savannah's home again, Madge had no desire to stir up another hornet's nest. Keeping quiet was the best way to stay in her place, which was exactly where she felt that Savannah had put her.

When Savannah had earlier mentioned that she'd taped the last episode of *Desperate Housewives*, Bernice had suggested they watch it, somewhat motivated by wanting to steer the conversation away from her situation with the judge, once the meeting was adjourned. That scenario would eventually get resolved and Bernice hoped for later rather than sooner.

Since the ladies always liked to mix a little fun in with their business gatherings, Bernice thought that watching such a controversial television program, and the later discussion of it, was a great note on which they could end their evening. However, with the way Madge viewed so-called "women like her," Savannah was no longer sure it was the best line of entertainment. The women on Wysteria Lane just might fit the M.O. Madge had referred to.

As Savannah's guests moved into the family room, she went into her bedroom to retrieve the DVD disc from the television in her room. After she ejected the disc from the DVD player built right into the television set, she took a quick bathroom break before rejoining the others.

Just as Savannah made her way over to the television set in the family room, her ears suddenly started to ring. Her legs began to wobble all over the place. The room began to spin, causing her to feel totally unstable. Then the floor swiftly rose up to meet her.

In the next second the shadows of darkness had Savannah completely surrounded.

Looking up into the anxiety-ridden faces of her friends had put the fear of God into Savannah. Wondering what in the world was going on with everyone inside her family room, she tried to lift her pounding head from the sofa pillow. A severe bout of nausea gripped Savannah's stomach ferociously, causing her to double up in sheer agony.

Bernice quickly grabbed the plastic-lined trash can and placed it at Savannah's side. "Honey, an ambulance is on the way. Try to relax now. We're all here for you."

Savannah looked terrified. "Ambulance? What's going on, Bernie?" Savannah then looked to the other ladies. "What's happening?"

Marie, also a retired registered nurse, came hurrying over to where they had laid Savannah down, after they'd picked her up from the floor. Marie hadn't ever seen the poised Savannah looking so terribly frightened. Having heard Savannah's question, she quickly knelt down beside the sofa. "That's what we're trying to figure out, Savannah. You suddenly blacked out on us. Do you know what happened to you before you lost consciousness?"

As if Savannah didn't quite understand what had been asked of her, she looked totally confused. Then her eyes filled with tears, which only caused her head to throb even harder. Her eyes connected with Marie's for a brief moment, then she quickly closed them. The incredible pain in her head was agonizing, near blinding in intensity. To try and keep the throbbing from getting any worse Savannah decided to just keep her eyes shut.

Seeing how much agony Savannah was in had all her friends exchanging worried glances. After Bernice swapped places with Marie, she gently placed Savannah's hand in hers, gently stroking her hair. "Don't worry, Savannah. Marie knows how to take real good care of you. Like you, she hasn't been retired that long from nursing. The paramedics should be here momentarily. Hold on, dear friend."

No sooner than the comforting words had left Bernice's mouth did the loud sirens pierce the night. Then the screeching of tires could be heard coming to a halt outside Savannah's home.

Marie rushed outside to meet the arriving medical team. Savannah's skyrocketing blood pressure had her quite worried. Knowing that Savannah owned a blood pressure cuff, Bernice had found it inside the linen closet in Savannah's bathroom. The sooner the paramedics got inside the house to assess her condition, the better off things would be.

Marie was in no doubt that her new friend would be transported to the hospital. In fact, she would insist on it. Marie knew that no one could get any rest until they knew what had caused their new friend to suddenly black out, without any kind of warning whatsoever. While Marie articulately informed the paramedics of what was going on, she had them follow her into the house, talking and walking at a rapid pace.

Once the highly skilled medical team invaded the

house, Savannah's friends, other than Marie, stood help-lessly by as the paramedics quickly took control. It was quickly decided that Savannah needed to be transported to the nearest hospital, which was located in San Bernardino.

Madge couldn't feel any worse than she did, wondering if she'd stressed out Savannah to the point of causing this sudden blackout to come down on her. The attack had been unjustified.

"Should I call your daughter?" Bernice asked, wondering if she should also call Antonio.

Savannah pointed down the hall. "My phone book is on the bedside table," Savannah had struggled to say. "It's under their last name, Standiford. Cole's work number is right under their home number..." Savannah began to gasp for air, as though she couldn't breathe too well.

Marie instantly recognized Savannah's new symptoms as more than likely the onset of a panic attack. "Don't try to talk anymore, Savannah. We'll get it all figured out."

Bernice wasn't sure who Savannah's new doctor was, but she'd flip through her personal phone book until she found his or her name and number. She was aware that Savannah had been to the doctor only a couple of days ago, but as far as Bernice knew the visit had only been for a routine physical checkup. Savannah had made mention of her appointment being at the San Bernardino Medical Center. Bernice had figured that her doctor was probably on staff at the hospital nearest the medical center, the one where Savannah was to be transported.

Once Bernice made the announcement that she'd ride in the ambulance with Savannah, the others agreed to meet her in the E.R. waiting room. Since Marie had come over to Savannah's home in Bernice's car, Marie would now drive Bernice's car to the hospital.

Chapter 13

Savannah had spent another couple of days in bed after the thorough examination she'd received in the emergency room at the Inland Empire Medical Center, which had turned out to be closer than the hospital in San Bernardino. Cole had known that by calling the E.R. doctor on behalf of his mother-in-law, that his medical credentials would help her to receive the very best in medial care. However, Cole didn't believe that the kind of care anyone received should ever be based on someone in the family being a doctor. Unfortunately, status mattered, which was often chalked up as simply a professional courtesy.

Kenya and Cole had been fussing over Savannah ever since they'd arrived up in Fontana, shortly after Bernice had called them to inform them of the blackout that had occurred. They were supposed to have left for home two days ago, but they'd stayed on in Fontana so they'd be able to go with Savannah to her next doctor's appointment for a follow-up. Because of his medical duties, Cole had been commuting back and forth between L.A. and Fontana.

The trio had already eaten breakfast and was now getting dressed for the doctor's visit.

Deciding to go with something simple, Savannah was dressed in crisp white jeans and an apricot-colored sleeveless top fashioned from a lightweight gauzy type material. The sandals she wore were the same color as the top. Savannah loved to match from head to toe. Although she didn't resort to it that often, there were times when her fingernails and toenails matched up with her attire. The lip gloss she'd chosen to wear today was also apricot in color.

Kenya knocked on her mother's bedroom door and then waited for her response.

Instead of calling out to the person on the other side of the wall, Savannah just opened the door. Seeing her children always brought joy to her heart and a smile to her lips. "I guess you were wondering what's taking me so long, huh?"

Kenya grinned. "I just wanted to make sure you hadn't taken ill again. You look very nice. Are you about ready to go?"

"As soon as I grab my bag and my medical cards. What about Cole? Is he ready?"

Kenya nodded. "He's been ready. He's sitting in the family room reading some sort of medical journal. I'm going to go on and have Cole take the car out of the garage. Don't forget to set the house alarm, Mom."

"I won't forget. Go right ahead, Kenya. I'll be outside in a couple of minutes."

After Savannah took her medical cards from the metal

fireproof box she kept them in, she put them in a zipper pocket inside her purse. One more glance in the mirror left her satisfied with her overall appearance. A quick jaunt into the bathroom came next.

As Savannah reached up to open the medicine cabinet, she wondered if she should take any pain medication before her appointment. She had been taking the medications as prescribed for her headaches, but it really hadn't been helping all that much. The diagnosis for what ailed her had been severe migraine headaches. It had been recommended by the emergency room doctor that she see a neurological specialist for further diagnostic testing.

In looking at the white casual pants Kenya wore, it suddenly occurred to Savannah that Kenya might like white clothing as much as she did. Kenya had been dressed in white on the last few visits. The royal-blue top with white polka dots and a sailor collar was so cute. The straw hat Kenya held in her hand had a strip of the same matching polka-dot material as her top wrapped around the band. Savannah already knew that Kenya was also into matching from head to toe.

After Savannah and Kenya once again exchanged smiles, warm hugs, and then traded compliments on each other's attire, Kenya opened the front passenger car door for her mother.

Savannah nudged Kenya slightly forward. "No, you sit up front with Cole. I'll be fine in the backseat. I'm just so happy that you two are here to go to the doctor's office with me."

Kenya wrinkled her nose. "Are you sure, Mom? I really don't mind sitting in the back."

"Positive, sweetheart."

"Okay, but let me get the door for you, Mom."

Once Savannah and Kenya was buckled in for safety, Cole, already snug in his seat belt, started the engine and then slowly backed the car out of the driveway. Mindful of children outside playing and watching for any ball or other toy that might suddenly roll out into the street, he drove through the neighborhood with extreme caution.

Kenya was worried about her mother, but she tried hard not to let it show too much. She also knew that Savannah had tried to wear a brave face for both her and Cole, but during her painful ordeal in the emergency room her vulnerability had been highly visible. Kenya couldn't ever remember her being this ill. She recalled her mother having had a couple of colds and sore throats, but there'd been nothing that had come close to bringing her to her knees in sheer agony.

Kenya twisted her body slightly so that she could converse with Savannah. "When I talked to my girlfriend, Loni Jones, this morning, whom you haven't met, I told her all about the success of your fashion event. Loni wished she could've been here and she also sends you her sincere congrats and feel-better wishes. She's currently taking classes at one of the top modeling schools up north. She was once a teacher in Inglewood. Fifth graders."

"That was so nice of her, Kenya. Any chance that I'll get to meet your friend, Loni?"

"I'm sure, though she's living up north right now, near San Francisco. Cole and I are looking forward to visiting Madison and Kenya as soon as he gets a long break. I heard Kevin say that Mr. Antonio might come up to his place with you. That would be nice if we could all go at the same time. How's Mr. Antonio doing, anyway? He was so upset over your illness. I found myself really worrying about him, too. He was a nervous wreck out in the E.R."

Cole vigorously nodded his head up and down. "Yeah, I was also concerned about Mr. Delabay, Mom. I'm sure you already know it, but he cares a great deal for you. He may even be head over heels already. I thought he was going to break down and cry when he saw you lying in that hospital bed. I agree with Kenya. Mr. Delabay really did have a hard time of it."

Wearing an odd expression on her face, Savannah pressed her lips together. "I'm aware of how distraught Antonio was. I keep wondering if he'd been reliving some part of his late wife's illness, but I wouldn't think of asking him that. Sylvia died of colon cancer. I can't imagine him wanting to deal with something as serious as that ever again. He's so darn vibrant. His wife's illness hit him just as hard as your dad's death hit me, Kenya. Recovery didn't come easy for him either."

Kenya thought about Savannah's comments. She then tried reading between the lines of what her mother had just said, sensing that there might be an underlying meaning. It sounded to Kenya as if her mother wasn't sure Antonio could stand strong against another devastating illness to a loved one. If Savannah's headaches turned out to be more than just treatable migraines, Kenya got the impression that her mother didn't think Antonio would be able to endure yet another life-threatening situation.

Kenya also thought Savannah was dead wrong about Antonio's staying power.

What Kenya had witnessed that night in the E.R. was a strong black man, physically and spiritually, one who cared for and deeply loved the small, fragile woman who'd suddenly fallen ill with an unknown malady. Kenya had seen a valiant man, one who wasn't a stranger to challenges, adversity and pain, a man who wasn't afraid to take on anything thrown his way.

After she and Cole had first arrived at the hospital, Kenya had also observed Antonio's respectful, caring treatment of Savannah's distraught female friends. Before they'd gone into the E.R. cubicle to see Savannah, Antonio had prayed fervently for Savannah with Kenya and Cole and the other women. Those emotionally telling moments had defined for Kenya who Antonio was as a man and as a wonderful humanitarian. Antonio had unwittingly proved that he was a man whom Kenya and Kevin could be proud of as a personal partner for their beloved mother.

Dr. Walter James, a nationally renowned neurological surgeon, had carefully laid out his findings for Savannah. At her request he had discussed her medical issues in the presence of Cole. Kenya had stayed behind in the waiting room even though Savannah had asked her to come in with them. Being a very emotional person, knowing she'd have a hard time controlling herself if the news wasn't good, Kenya had decided it was best for her to opt out.

"Once we get the results of the MRI, Mrs. Richmond, we can take it from there. But getting the MRI done is what I recommend as the first step. Since the E.R. doctor prescribed the same medications I would have, we're okay there. However, I'm going to up the dosage a bit on the pain meds since it sounds to me like they're not giving you maximum relief. Are there any other concerns that you or your son-in-law would like to have me address, Mrs. Richmond?"

Feeling slightly anxious, Savannah rubbed her hands together. "How long will it take to get the results after the test is administered?"

Dr. James ran an open palm across his forehead. "Not long at all, Mrs. Richmond. Perhaps in the same day, depending on what time the test is performed and how many cases the radiologist has to review. If we schedule the test in the early morning, by the end of the day we could have results. However, there may be up to a two-week wait for an MRI appointment."

"The fainting spells," Cole said, "should we expect them to reoccur?"

"I'd have to say it's probably a safe bet. Mrs. Richmond, it'll be very helpful for you to recall what you're doing and how you feel physically if another spell happens. What leads up to the blackouts may help us determine the cause. You also need to try and avoid stress at all cost. Stress sometimes can cause blackouts. I'm sure you drive, so you have to be careful there as well, at least until we find out what's really going on inside your head. Do you live alone?"

Savannah nodded. "Totally alone. My daughter and son-in-law live down in L.A."

Dr. James stroked his chin thoughtfully. "Can you get someone to come in and stay with you until we get a definitive diagnosis, which should occur not long after the testing?"

Cole nodded. "I'll check with my wife to see if she can

stay on with her mother a few more days. I won't even mind the commute awhile longer. Someone will definitely be in the house with my mother-in-law. I can assure you that we can work out the living arrangements."

Dr. James shook his head. "We can't have her in any stressful situations or even in a stressful environment. But I'm sure you all will work that out. Mrs. Richmond, I'll see you back in my office after you have the tests. The receptionist will schedule the appointment for the MRI and our next visit. She'll call you once she has everything taken care of." Dr. James then shook the hands of both Savannah and Cole, telling them it was nice to have met them.

Kenya was a bundle of nerves by the time Savannah and Cole reappeared in the waiting room. She jumped up from the chair as soon as she spotted them coming out the office exit. Close to tears from all the nervous anticipation, Kenya nearly fell into her mother's arms.

In the hours and days leading up to this important doctor's appointment, Kenya had begun to realize how much her mother truly meant to her. Savannah had always been there for her children and now Kenya knew that she, Kevin and Cole had to be there for Savannah. Kenya had committed herself to taking care of her mother's every need, no matter how big or small.

In that instant Kenya had also realized that she had room in her life and in her heart for her own child. If she were pregnant with Cole's child, Kenya would embrace it wholeheartedly.

"Are my two girls up to going out for lunch?" Cole asked.

Kenya eagerly nodded her head. "I'm very hungry, but

my stomach is still nervous. Maybe it'll be calmed down by the time we stop to eat."

Savannah brought Kenya to her for another hug. "I'm hungry and nervous, too."

The last person Savannah wanted to deal with was Veronica, who was seated behind Savannah's desk, as if she belonged there. Savannah's first thought was to walk right back out the door, but that wasn't going to get this agitating woman off her back. After closing her office door, Savannah took one of the chairs near her desk. "What can I do for you now, Ms. Baker?"

Veronica twirled a pen around between her fingers. "I've already told you what you can do for me, but you don't seem to be listening. Why don't you understand that I'm not going away? I still want Antonio Delabay and I won't stop until I get him, even if it is by default. When are you going to pound that matter of fact into your thick skull, Ms. Richmond?"

A firm knock suddenly struck the door, causing both Savannah and Veronica to look toward the entry. Without any sort of prompting from Savannah, the visitor just opened the door and stepped in. Seeing Antonio standing there had Savannah exhaling a deep sigh of relief. On the other hand, Veronica looked as if she'd seen a ghost.

"Hello, ladies," Antonio said, stepping farther into the room. "How are you both?"

Making a quick recovery, Veronica got to her feet. "I'm fine, but I'm not so sure about Ms. Richmond." After walking over to Antonio, Veronica lazed her thumb across his cheek. "I'm sorry your friend isn't able to get it, Antonio. You need to tell her how determined I am."

Antonio looked puzzled. "Determined about what?"

"About us," Veronica breathed. "There is an us, Antonio. It's destined. It's time you come clean with the lady here before she gets in too deep. I don't want to see her hurt."

Savannah was out of the chair so fast that Antonio only got a glimpse of her flashing by. Thinking she was going to lay Veronica out, he tried to get in between them. When Savannah only opened the door fast and furious, he let loose with an audible sigh.

Savannah pushed the door farther back. "It seems to me that you're the one that's not getting it, Ms. Baker. I'm filing a restraining order against you today, lady, so you'd better be aware of the consequences the next time you come near me. How's that for coming clean? I'd hate to see you as a guest of the county jail, but I'll be happy to reserve your stay for you. Now get out of my office, Ms. Baker!" Savannah shouted at the top of her lungs. "Get out right now!"

The minute Veronica cleared the door in a rapid-fire manner, Savannah turned to Antonio. "You need to go, too. It's past time for you to handle your business, Mr. Delabay."

Antonio started to protest, but something about the odd look in Savannah's eyes had him quickly changing his mind. He wanted to kiss her goodbye, but that didn't seem like a good idea either. "We'll talk later, Savannah."

Savannah looked straight ahead. "I'm sure we will, but not until after you set that crazy lady straight. This is starting to get dangerous for me. You have some serious clarifications to make. Ms. Baker is your problem, not mine. I repeat. Handle it, Antonio, if you want me."

Savannah suddenly had a change of heart, which had her calling out to Antonio who'd only gone a few steps. As he came back into her office, she asked him to have a seat. Savannah then propped herself on the corner of the desk. "I guess I should say something if we're ever going to get this situation resolved once and for all. I'm getting mixed signals here, Antonio. I don't know what to believe anymore. Where do things stand with you and Ms. Baker? Are you or are you not still involved with her?"

Antonio didn't so much as blink an eye. "Not! She's a difficult woman, Savannah. You've seen what she's capable of. I can't control her impulses anymore than you can. What is it you want me to do? I've told you the truth about our brief involvement. It's been over for me."

Savannah really wanted to believe Antonio. He seemed so sincere, but it was hard for her to accept that a woman would run after a man like a crazy person without any encouragement from him whatsoever. *Did women really do insane stuff like that?* Well, she considered, Veronica surely was making a darn fool of herself, and she was doing it in front of a lot of people.

Antonio got to his feet and came to where Savannah was perched on the edge of the desk. "Savannah, I don't know what else I can say or do to convince you that I'm faithful to you, have been so since our first date. You either believe in me or you don't. I can't make you have faith in me if you're unsure of what we have." He leaned down and kissed her cheek. "I love you."

Savannah sighed hard. "I believe that you love me,

Antonio, but you have to find a way to get Ms. Baker off your shirttail. We can't have a happy ending if you don't finalize things with her. Either you're not convincing enough for her, or she's just plain ignoring all the signals. Either way, you've got to find a way to handle it. Until that's done, I think we should cool it."

"Whatever you wish, Savannah." Having said that, Antonio walked away.

After closing the door behind Antonio, Savannah locked it. She then sat down and lowered her head onto her desk. Her body began to shake as her sobs came hard and jagged. Moving up to Fontana had not been the wonderful experience she'd had such high hopes for.

It seemed to Savannah as if many of the people in and around her new area of residence wanted to make her life as miserable as possible. For a woman who was now financially stable, having been able to retire at the age of forty-five because of it, she wasn't happy with her present circumstances. Trouble had sought her out at every turn. This was supposed to have been a joyful time for her, a time to get on with making the rest of her life one delight after another.

It appeared to Savannah as if so many people wanted a little piece of her, but she was all pieced out, tired of being torn in every direction, mainly by strangers. There were the evil women down at the senior center, women like Opal Redmond, Veronica from Antonio's past, and now Madge Jacoby, Bernice's friend, had all joined the "destroy Savannah" bandwagon.

Now faced with the new puzzling medical problems, Savannah had more on her plate than she knew what to do with. It was far too much there to swallow whole. Something had to give—and it needed to happen pretty quickly. Otherwise, Savannah felt as if she was headed for a nervous breakdown. If relief was only an instant away, she needed it to make a quick entry.

"God, please help me. This is not how I want to live out my remaining years, however short or long they may be. I pray for the renewal of my spirit and salvation of my soul." Tears continued to roll down Savannah's cheeks as she asked the Lord to roll away her heavy burdens.

After Savannah lifted her head, she wiped her eyes with the back of her hand. Taking a tissue from the holder atop her desk, she blew her nose.

Savannah then raised her eyes toward heaven. "Geoffrey, if you're tuned in, you know how much I'm hurting. If you were here, you'd tell me exactly what I needed to do. I know what I'm *not* going to do. No longer will I be the whipping girl for these folks. Tell them all to bring it on," she cried out, managing to have a really good laugh. "I've got something for all of 'em."

With Savannah knowing full well that she had to take total control of her life from this point on, she vowed to pull it all together. Being sad and upset didn't feel good and she desperately wanted to feel great. The only way she was going to have a happy life was to take it. No one was going to give her anything. That much was apparent to Savannah Richmond.

As Savannah waited in the treatment room for Dr. James to come in and tell her the results of the MRI, she wondered if it was wrong for her to be doing this all alone.

Kenya had gone home to check on things and would be back at day's end, but had she known about her mother's medical appointment she probably would've stayed on until afterward.

In making her decision to take the appointment on her own, Savannah had taken into consideration the fact that Kenya hadn't been able to come into the office with her on her first visit to see Dr. James. Kenya had opted to stay outside in the waiting room because of emotions.

It's best this way, Savannah told herself. If it's good news, no one will be upset with me. If it's bad news, she thought she'd like to have some time to get used to the results before sharing the findings with her family and friends. Savannah quietly prayed for a favorable outcome.

Wanting to think only pleasant thoughts, Savannah's mind drifted to the senior prom, which was to occur only a short time from now. There were instances when she'd thought she wouldn't be able to attend her own event because of her illness, glad that she'd been able to hold on and work through the pain.

Time had certainly gotten away from Savannah recently, but her and her friends were all prepared for the big night. Everything was in place for the gala affair. It was now time for the execution of duties. If everything went as planned, Savannah expected everyone to have one incredible evening.

Savannah looked right at Dr. James when he came into the room. The somber look on his face immediately put her on edge. His facial expression didn't indicate that he was about to deliver good tidings. She then steeled herself for what might not be such good news. Closing her eyes for a brief moment, she prayed to God for strength and courage. Savannah already knew that the heavenly Father wouldn't put any more on her than she could bear.

"Well, I guess I don't have to ask how you're feeling, Mrs. Richmond. The results of your MRI tell me everything I need to know. Unfortunately, what has been revealed to us isn't at all what we'd hoped for…."

A couple of days after Savannah had received her final test results, she had convinced Kenya and Cole that she'd be okay alone for a while, that they should at least go back to L.A. and check on the house again. However, Kenya was coming back later in the evening and Cole would return in a day or so. Savannah had had no choice but to accept the arrangements since the doctor had said she shouldn't be alone.

Bernice had assured Kenya that she'd keep a close eye on her mother and Inez had promised her she'd do the same. The two women had come over to Savannah's after she'd called them to inform them of her diagnosis. Before the end of the conversation, she had asked them to stop by and talk with Kenya and Cole, just to reassure them that they'd be there for her.

Proving Savannah's theory that wonderful friends and good neighbors were invaluable, the two women had agreed to come over right away. Janice, Marie, Clara, Mable and even Madge had eventually shown up at Savannah's also, once the word about her diagnosis had trickled down from one friend to the other.

With everyone seated in Savannah's family room, Madge asked Savannah if the two of them could go out into the kitchen. Madge stated that she had something to say to her host, but she wanted to do it in private. Although reluctant to be alone with one of her nemeses, Savannah agreed to Madge's request anyway.

Bernice cleared her throat to get everyone's attention. "My feeling on you two going off alone to talk is this. Savannah already has enough to deal with. She needs no more drama. Since you didn't mind insulting Savannah in front of the rest of us, and in her own home, I think we should all hear what you have to say now, Madge. Savannah doesn't need to be alone with you if you're going to continue being nasty and rude to her. I won't stand by for that to happen again."

Savannah agreed wholeheartedly with Bernice, which kept her from protesting her friend's very reasonable suggestion. If Madge was bold enough to do her dirt in public, then she should be willing to say whatever she had to say in the same forum.

Madge folded her hands and placed them in her lap. "I see your point, Bernice. But I have no intention of insulting Savannah. Just the opposite." Madge then turned slightly and made direct eye contact with her host. "I wanted to speak to you alone so I could apologize, Savannah. My jealousy of you has been quite obvious. I'm glad you refused to put on the shoes I handpicked for you personally. You were right. They don't fit."

Madge went on to tell Savannah and the rest of her friends that she'd once had high hopes of her and Antonio getting together after both their spouses had died. She had been terribly attracted to him even when Branch was alive. Antonio had outright rejected the idea of them as companions. He thought it would be offensive to his late friend's honor. Antonio didn't think Branch would've given his blessings for them to become anything more than friends.

Madge wrung her hands together, her anguish obvious. "I think that was the way Antonio had chosen to say that he simply wasn't interested in me romantically. He wouldn't have wanted to hurt my feelings. So my ill-treatment of you has been all about that. I couldn't stand the fact that he was interested in you and not me. I hope you can forgive me, Savannah. I am truly sorry."

Savannah couldn't believe what some women were willing to do and then put somebody else through just to win the affections of a man. She'd known from the start that Veronica and Madge's bad behavior toward her had nothing to do with anything she'd ever done to them, because they hadn't ever met each other prior to her move to Fontana.

All of this madness was so amazing to Savannah. It was hard for her to believe that these women would continue to pursue a man who'd already made his intentions toward them very clear. If Antonio had wanted either Veronica or Madge, he'd be with one of them. Why weren't these two women able to comprehend that? Savannah couldn't help wondering.

Savannah eyed Madge with deep curiosity. "I could sit here and play the devil's advocate, Madge, but that's really not my style. Although I'd really like to know if your sudden change of heart has come about because of my illness, I won't ask. If guilt is at work here, please know that I don't need or want your pity. There are so many people who genuinely love me and who will be in my corner through the good, the bad and the ugly…"

Savannah took a couple of seconds to effect composure. She then reached over and took hold of Madge's hand. "I *do* accept your apology, Madge, only because I believe you really are sorry. I can also use all the allies I can get during this difficult time in my life. I really don't like having enemies. Thanks for having the courage to say what you needed to say in front of all of us. I have some rough road ahead of me and I'd really like your prayers and support."

Madge posted her hand on Savannah's shoulder. "You'll have both my prayers and support, Savannah. Don't hesitate to let me know if you need anything. Anything at all."

Bernice wiped the tears from her eyes, as did the other ladies. "I think a group hug is in order." Without a moment's hesitation, the ladies all came together in a warm embrace.

Now that Kenya trusted Antonio without question, he had been called by Savannah and invited over to the house, but Savannah had wanted to wait and tell him the bad news in person. All of Savannah's friends had taken their leave shortly after Antonio had arrived, knowing that she was in very capable hands until Kenya returned from L.A.

Looking rather anxious, but more concerned than fearful, Antonio was seated next to Savannah on the sofa in her family room, a place where he'd certainly come to feel right at home. Savannah had just finished relaying to him that she needed to have a tumor removed from her brain, a large growth believed to be benign by Dr. James, her neurosurgeon.

Antonio's heart was beating fast and furious with his

concern for her overall well-being, but he knew he had to remain relatively calm. It wouldn't do Savannah any good for her to witness him coming apart at the seams. Antonio repeatedly reminded himself that Savannah was in God's unchanging hands.

Antonio took Savannah's hand and squeezed it gently. He hugged her, planting tender kisses in her hair. Although his tears threatened to come, he bravely held them back. "In that case, Savannah, I think we should marry right away, rather than waiting any longer. We've cooled it long enough. I want us to exchange marriage vows as soon as possible, before you undergo surgery, not afterward. That way, we can deal with all the medical issues together, as man and wife. When two people love each other as much as we do, we shouldn't waste another minute apart from each other. Will you marry me now, Savannah?"

Savannah simply couldn't believe her own ears, yet she'd heard Antonio loud and clear. How she responded this time around would probably make or break them up for good. Antonio wasn't likely to again accept her rejection of the idea of them getting married like he had before.

Yes, she loved Antonio, loved him dearly, but they still hadn't discussed any of the important issues she'd been muddling over in her mind since their major spats. The timing for bringing it up had never seemed right. *But what better time was there than right now?* This was the perfect time, she thought, knowing she wouldn't consider marrying him until everything was out in the open regarding their assets and such. The time for clearing the air was here and now.

Savannah blew out a stream of nervous breath. She then went right into the matter of laying out her concerns to

Antonio in painstaking detail, leaving nothing to misinterpretation.

Chuckling inwardly, Antonio brought Savannah to him for a bear hug and a few passionate kisses. Holding her slightly away from him, he looked deeply into her eyes. "Communication is everything, Savannah. I recall telling you that right from the very beginning of our friendship. Do you remember me saying that to you?"

Looking a bit sheepish, Savannah nodded. "I do. Clearly. I'm sorry I've failed to communicate my concerns to you before now. But there's something else I want to discuss with you. It's a very important issue for me, Antonio."

Antonio nodded. "Whatever is important to you is important to me."

"I've heard what you said here today and I believe you, but I have to ask if you're not just a little bit fearful of what I'm faced with. Any surgery is serious, but a brain operation is even more so since it's so dangerous. I can only imagine what you went through with Sylvia's illness. With Geoffrey's life coming to an end so quickly, I wasn't a caretaker like you. So many things could go wrong in this instance of surgery. I don't want to see you saddled with a sick new wife if things don't turn out favorably. While the doctors believe the tumor is benign, no one can be sure until after it's removed and then sent out to pathology."

Wishing he could wipe all of Savannah's fears away, Antonio kissed her forehead tenderly. He knew how hard it had been for her to say all that she had said with her facing such danger. If it was in Antonio's power, he'd do all he could to allay Savannah's every fear.

Antonio cupped her face between his two large but

tender hands. "Nothing in this life is a certainty, Savannah. If I lived my life based on what-ifs, I'd probably be crazy by now. And that would be such a sad way to live. I want to marry you regardless of your current medical status. I don't fear it and I don't compare it to anything I've been through before. This is here and now, which is where I prefer to live my life, not in the past. I'd rather spend a few minutes as your husband than never to have had the honor of having you as my wife. God is in control, Savannah. Only He knows the beginning and the end. Let's leave it in His loving hands."

Savannah lowered her lashes, wishing she could control her emotions. Antonio hadn't said what he thought she might want to hear. Antonio Delabay had simply spoken his heart.

"All the other things you've talked about are also a nonissue for me. If you want a prenuptial agreement, Savannah, fine by me. As far as I'm concerned, we can leave things just as they've been set up for years. Your children get whatever financial holdings you have and my kids get what I have. However, my kids aren't eligible for my pension in the event of my death, nor are they eligible for my social security or retired military privileges. Those things would all go to you and I'd definitely want you to have each of them. What do you think about that?"

Savannah released a huge sigh of relief, happy that Antonio had made things so easy for her to openly discuss all her concerns with him. That she hadn't met his children yet was a bit unsettling for her, but she was sure that that would be taken care of very soon.

Besides, they weren't marrying each other's children.

Savannah lazed her finger down Antonio's cheek. "I think you're wonderful, Antonio. I thank you for all that you've said. My children can't get my pension either, so you'd be eligible for mine, too. I don't think either one of us should sell our homes. If we get married, we can decide which home to live in and then lease the other one. That way, we can move back into our own home when one of us leaves this earth, which will free up the vacant home for the children to have as part of their inheritance. Can you live with that sort of arrangement, Antonio?"

Antonio grinned. "I can and I will, simply because I love you with all my heart. We should have the legal papers drawn up as soon as possible so that we can get on with our lives. I don't want you to have anything to worry about when you go into surgery. I know you haven't said 'yes' to marriage yet, but I wanted you to know exactly where I'm coming from. Is everything cleared up for you, Savannah?"

Tears swarmed in Savannah's eyes. "Very much so. However, there's one more thing. The last time I brought this up to you it sent you running for the front door, resulting in our first fight. Then we had a problem in my office when Veronica…"

Antonio had silenced Savannah with two of his fingers to her lips, something she wasn't unfamiliar with him doing when he wanted to squash her anguish. "Ms. Veronica Baker has never been an important part of my personal life, Savannah. She never will be. Ms. Baker is just a troubled member of the Golden Age Senior Center, one who has no life," Antonio remarked strongly. "She'll never be anything more than a business acquaintance to me. I've already made that quite clear to her in the kindest way possible after we left your office. I know it's illegal, but I taped a later phone conversation with her so you could hear it if you needed proof. Do you need to hear that proof, Savannah?"

Savannah felt badly for the entire situation involving Ms. Baker, but she'd never insult Antonio by asking him for proof that he'd settled it. His word was his bond. She knew for a fact that he wasn't a liar, wished she had trusted him to handle Ms. Baker from the onset. Savannah now knew that his way had not been harsh. Antonio wasn't the kind of man to lash out callously at a woman or anyone else, even a person who had terribly hurt him and someone he loved.

No response to the question regarding her needing proof was the best response.

Certain that her future was secure with Antonio, Savannah wrapped her arms tightly around his neck. "My answer to your proposal is a resounding yes! I love you so much." She kissed him softly on the mouth, touching her forehead to his. "But we can't marry until after the surgery, Antonio. It wouldn't be fair to either of us or to our families to do it any other way. Will you still marry me despite that one important condition, Antonio Delabay?"

"Savannah Richmond, I'd marry you under any condition. Yes, I'll marry you!"

Chapter 14

Over orange juice and wheat toast, Savannah reread all the get-well cards that had been sent to her over the past few days. Mable had come over to help Savannah address the thank-you notes she'd written to all those who'd sent flowers and other forms of well wishes. Mable had brought along with her a bunch of notes written to Savannah from several of the members down at the center. The cards that really surprised Savannah were from a couple of members who had voiced the strongest opposition against her, those from the former president and vice president.

Savannah handed one of the handwritten notes to Mable. "Check this one out."

Mable read the note and then chuckled. "I know you find it hard to believe, but I believe Opal Redmond means what she's written. People have finally started to see all the great things you've done for the senior center. You not being around the place for a good while has opened a lot of blinded eyes. Savannah, you are genuinely missed by so many. It's too bad a serious illness had to happen to you for some of them to see you for who you really are. I'll be glad when you can come back to us. The center hasn't been the same without you."

Overwhelmed by the good wishes, Savannah wiped the moisture from her eyes with a paper napkin. This kind of empathy wasn't something she would've ever expected from the majority of folks down at the center. This was an unbelievable moment for her, one that she'd cherish forever. It felt so good to be cared about—and by so many.

Savannah reached over and briefly touched Mable's hand. "Thanks, Mable. All the get-well notes I've received have thrilled me—and I haven't even had the surgery yet. The flower deliveries have been nonstop. I'm also overwhelmed by the numerous phone calls. When you're down and out, you sure find out in a hurry just who your real friends are. Mable, you've been super. Thanks for all the support you've given me. I'm so blessed to have you as a friend."

Mable reached over and patted Savannah's hand. "To have a true friend you have to know how to be one. I learned that bit of sagacious truth a long time ago. I knew you were special the first day I met you, Savannah. I feel just as blessed as you do."

A knock at the French doors caused Savannah to look over in that direction. Upon seeing Inez standing there, she quickly scrambled from her chair and ran over and opened the door. With her arms full of small to medium-size pink boxes, Inez rushed over to the counter, where she put down her stack of delicious-smelling parcels.

Knowing that more pastries were the last things she needed, Savannah groaned inwardly.

Inez acknowledged Mable with a warm verbal greeting and then she embraced Savannah as though she were a long-lost friend. "Good to see you feeling much better, kid. You had us worried. I don't know what I'd do without you around here to keep me grounded. I know you're having lots and lots of company, so that's what all the baked goodies are for. Doug will bring over more later on this afternoon. What time does your family arrive in Ontario?"

After drawing a blank for a moment, Savannah laughed out loud. "Six o'clock this evening. I can't wait to see everyone. My brother is coming, too. We're all going to attend the senior prom together. I'm glad that surgery isn't scheduled until two days after the event, but in the meantime I have to be careful not to get too excited or too fatigued. As for all the delicious pastries you brought over, I thank you and I know my family will thank you, the moment they feast their eyes on all those pink boxes. If we're not careful, you and Doug are going to fatten up the entire neighborhood. The sweets are so delectable, irresistibly tempting."

Inez smiled, grateful for the complimentary remarks. "You're welcome, Savannah."

The front doorbell rang, causing Savannah to throw up her hands. "It's like Grand Central Station around here this morning. If this keeps up, I just might be able to win a popularity contest. That'd be nice since I've been so unpopular for the past couple of months. I wonder who that could be at the door. No one else has called to say they were coming by."

"I have to leave, anyway, Savannah, so I'll get the door. Should I send the new arrival back here?" Inez inquired. "Or do you want me to come back and tell you who it is first?"

Savannah got up from her chair. "I'd better come see for myself. Can't have you letting a total stranger into my house," Savannah joked, laughing lightly.

Mable stood up, too. "It's also time for me to move along, Savannah, so I'll walk up front with you. It was good to see you, Inez. Hope you can join us for a meeting in the near future."

"Thanks, Mable. I hope so, too. It's not like I haven't been trying."

Upon Savannah seeing her family standing at the front door, it was impossible for her not to get overly excited. Since she hadn't expected them until later in the evening, their showing up in the early morning hours came as a total shock to her. Tears flooded Savannah's eyes as she looked from one sibling to the other. Each of them was a sight for sore eyes.

After flinging herself into Eugene's arms, and encompassing his wife, Arlene, at the same time, Savannah hugged them tightly. She then warmly embraced her sisters and brothers-in-law one at a time. Royal was married to Martin Barrett; Jacqueline belonged to Thomas Simpson; and Meredith and Theodore Drexler had been joined at the hip since forever.

With Kevin and Madison coming back into town for the senior prom, Savannah didn't know at the moment where she was going to house everyone, but she'd find a way even

396   *Linda Hudson-Smith*

if she had to pay for hotel rooms. Some of her family could probably stay with Kenya, but that was too far of a commute since everyone was staying over for her surgery. Savannah didn't know why she hadn't thought of housing arrangements before now, but she hadn't.

Savannah's four-bedroom home was suddenly looking very small to her.

Alone, lying down in her bedroom, Savannah had had to take a time-out from all the excitement and craziness. She had later learned that her family's flight had been an early morning one from the very beginning. They had merely wanted to surprise her. Her family had rented a van because they'd known that Savannah would've had to make at least a couple of trips to transport all of them and their luggage from the airport. Savannah thought that it had all worked out quite well, even without her being in control.

Kevin and Madison would be in later in the evening and Cole and Kenya were expected to arrive back in Fontana around the same time. Kevin had also wanted to rent a car, but Savannah saw no sense in him having that kind of expense since he'd have exclusive use of hers. Once Kevin had agreed to allow Antonio to pick them up at the Ontario airport, Savannah had been pleased, glad that everything had fallen into place.

As for the sleeping arrangements, that had been figured out, too. Everyone had decided to make the best of the accommodations in Savannah's house even if it meant pallets on the floor. Antonio had informed Savannah that his children would also be coming in for her big event.

Unexpectedly, Savannah's memory took her back to the

moment Dr. James had first told her she had a brain tumor, an operable one. Fear had filled her from head to toe. Tears had sprung to her eyes. Her heart felt as if it were going into cardiac arrest. Shaking uncontrollably outwardly and the vicious trembling inwardly had hit her at the exact same time. Choking back her screams had come hard, especially when all she'd really wanted to do was yell her head off.

Savannah's first sober thought on that fateful day was of how unfair life was. How many folks had worked hard all their lives just to reach retirement, only to die suddenly or come down with some serious illness that prevented them from living life to the fullest? There were many victims of such outrage that she knew personally, Geoffrey included.

It was as if their life's work had all been for not.

On the ride home all Savannah had been able to do was think about her terrible misfortune, wallowing around in the woe-is-me syndrome. Of all the people in the world, how could this have happened to her? What was God punishing her for now? Hadn't she been a good enough Christian? Why was he testing her again, and so soon after her husband's death? What message was God sending her this time? What lesson did she need to learn?

After much soul-searching, and wailing and gnashing of her teeth, Savannah hadn't been able to think of a single thing that she'd done that was so terrible to cause her to be cursed with a brain tumor. Then why was this happening to her in the prime of her life?

No sooner than Savannah had gotten downright sick and tired of pitying herself and questioning God's motives for this horrible malady, it had suddenly dawned on her that Dr. James had said her tumor was operable; many growths were inoperable. More than likely the tumor was benign, she'd recalled him saying. The odds were definitely in her favor there, she'd figured. Of course there was the danger of losing her life on the operating table, she'd thought, not to mention death from anesthesia, but that wasn't a given. Something could go wrong during the surgery, but that wasn't a certainty either, Savannah had realized.

As Savannah had begun to look at the positive side of things, rather than continuing to focus on the negative, her courage had begun to return. She had started to feel a renewal of hope. She had then begun to see things in a totally different light. There were people all over the world in a much worse physical state than she was. Who was she to question God, anyway?

Right after Savannah had left the doctor's office, she'd driven down to L.A., and had gone back to the hospital where she'd used to work. The doctor had forbidden her to drive until after she'd had the surgery, if she in fact decided to have it, but she'd done so anyway.

Once inside the hospital, Savannah had visited the AIDS wing, then the rehabilitation area, where stroke victims were housed. She'd then gone on to the pediatric ward, where babies and older children were literally fighting for their very lives. Because practically everyone at the hospital knew her from when she'd worked there, she'd been allowed to visit the various critical patient-care areas without any hassles whatsoever from the staff members. The experience had been a major eye-opener for her. It had completely changed Savannah's way of thinking.

Unlike a lot of people, Savannah knew that she had the sheer will to live. And live she would, God willing. If not, then that was God's will for her also. God's will be done had been her fervent prayer before she'd finally left the health-care facility. The decision to go through with the surgery had been made on her drive home. After she'd taken a stroll through her forty-five years of life, she had come to the conclusion that she'd already lived a full, happy existence. Savannah had then accepted the fact that she'd been very blessed all through her life.

As Savannah closed her eyes, hoping to take a short nap, she thanked God for helping her to see the light. She also thanked Him for bringing all her family together under one roof, and for their safe arrival. Last on the thank-you list, she thanked God for Antonio's undying love for her and for his unyielding commitment to her and to their relationship.

Savannah then asked God to keep her safe within the hull of His hands.

Amazed by the beautiful decorations gracing the President's Ballroom at the Inland Empire Country Club, Savannah felt like she'd just stepped into a fairy-tale setting. The soft lighting was both romantic and alluring. Her heart was beating like someone who'd just won the California lottery. Even the bandstand had been decorated with flowers and balloons and a large banner that read: Silver and Gold Spring Fling. Everything was simply magnificent.

At the last minute the theme colors had been changed from lavender, white and pink by a unanimous vote from Savannah and her cohorts. Gold and silver better represented the Fontana community of the liveliest middle-aged folks and senior citizens in the Inland Empire.

Fresh spring blossoms with silver and gold-glittered ribbons, decoratively threaded around large candles, served as the centerpieces for the beautifully silver and gold-skirted tables. Hundreds of silver and gold balloons, also inscribed boldly with Silver and Gold Spring Fling, hung from the cathedral ceiling. Madge, in charge of the decorations, had done a marvelous job.

All this extraordinary beauty far exceeded Savannah's expectations.

The podium was decorated the most amazing of all. Adorned with silver-and-gold-lame-draped high-back chairs for the Inland Empire King and Queen of Silver Wings, the podium was positively fit for royalty. The lucky winners, voted on by all the members of the Silver Wings Senior Center, were to be announced sometime during the gala festivities. There weren't going to be any long, drawn out speeches tonight. Savannah had made sure of that.

The Silver and Gold Spring Fling was to be a purely entertainment event. Tonight was all about the young and older members getting their groove back!

As Savannah viewed her dream come true, she fought hard to hold back her tears. Stunning in all white, Savannah looked as if she were dressed for her wedding day. The formal length chiffon tiered dress hugged every curve and caressed every inch of her fantastic body. One shoulder was completely bare; the other was elegantly draped with a billowy wisp of chiffon, a designer's work of perfection. Savannah's gold shoes sparkled like yellow diamonds.

Antonio slipped up behind Savannah and gently placed his hands on her waist. "Are you as astounded by this place as I am, sweetheart? You and your friends have done one incredible job. I hardly recognize the place and I've been here for several formal events. Are you happy?"

Savannah turned around and then slowly snaked her arms around Antonio's neck, careful not to get her makeup on his white tuxedo shirt. Looking into his eyes was like seeing a bright reflection of love, crystal clear and dove pure. "I couldn't be happier. All of my programs for the center have been voted in, which gives me even more to look forward to. In a couple of days they'll be drilling around inside my head, but tonight belongs to our friends and us, Antonio. Let's make it a very special night, one we'll never forget."

Nuzzling her ear with the tip of his nose, Antonio inhaled deeply of Savannah's tantalizing perfumed scent. "Anything your heart desires, Savannah. Special is what it'll be, very special." Astounded by Savannah's courage, not to mention her beautiful spirit, Antonio kissed her gently on the lips. "Tonight is definitely ours, sweetheart."

Antonio then slipped his hand into his jacket pocket and brought out a small velvet box, flipping it open for Savannah to see its brilliant content, a three-carat trillion-cut diamond. "Will you marry me, Savannah?" he asked, slipping the ring onto the third finger of her left hand.

Although Savannah had already agreed to marry him, Antonio wanted to make it official.

Savannah responded to Antonio's question in a positive

way by giving him an unforgettable kiss, which spoke volumes. After looking down at her finger, marveling at the sparkling beauty resting there, she smiled brightly, and then looked back up at Antonio. "I can't wait to marry you. I feel like a young girl all over again, Antonio. Thanks for helping to make this middle-aged girl feel that way. I love you."

Antonio lifted her hand and kissed the ring he'd placed upon Savannah's finger. "I love you, too, sweetheart. Now we'd better go get the rest of the clan and usher them to the reserved tables. How do you feel about us announcing our engagement sometime during the event?"

"I think that's a wonderful idea. Since I've now met your lovely Antoinette and handsome Sylvan, I think you should take your children aside and tell them first, before we make the public announcement. Kenya and Kevin already know I've agreed to marry you after the surgery, and they couldn't be happier for us. I wouldn't want to spring our engagement on them either. The rest of my family will be surprised but they'll also be very happy for us."

"I've already enlightened my kids. We had a good, long talk right after they arrived. Antoinette thinks you're so beautiful. She also helped me decide on the ring. Both of my children are very happy for us, Savannah."

"Thank God! I want us all to be one big happy family. I can't wait for our first holiday celebration together. I just love big family gatherings. Oh, Antonio, I feel wonderful!"

With the Silver and Gold Spring Fling now in full swing it appeared to Savannah that everyone was having a marvelous time. Each of her sisters wore exquisite evening gowns and their husbands looked equally as handsome. Kenya was gorgeous in her white designer gown and Madison looked too charming for words in her formal attire. Savannah, Madison and Kenya had all chosen to wear white, making for a stunning group of lovely women.

Savannah was very impressed with how wonderfully all of her family members had presented themselves. She was also very proud. With everyone all dressed up, tonight would've been a perfect time to have a family portrait made. Since there was a hired photographer on board for the event, Savannah wondered if they might actually be able to pull it off.

Upon spotting Bernice and Marlton, Savannah had to smile. They were a striking couple. Since they appeared to be all into each other, she couldn't help wondering if a budding relationship was in progress. With Bernice looking happy and content, Savannah sure hoped so.

Getting Bernice to come to the event with the judge had been like pulling teeth. Bernice had resisted the very idea of it for days. Marie had been the one who'd finally gotten to Bernice, when she'd told her she was going to dry up and end up dying as a lonely, miserable old woman if she didn't start taking risks. Marie had also told Bernice to look at it as one date, not a life sentence. If she didn't like the judge, she never had to see him again. It wasn't long after that spirited conversation that Bernice had agreed to the date.

For all Madge's carrying on about not wanting a date for the event, she had one, a very nice one to boot. Antonio had hooked her up with one of his military buddies, Aubrey Reynolds.

Madge and Aubrey had had one date prior to this one. She had later said she really liked him. Savannah was happy that she and Madge had been able to put their differences aside.

As originally planned, Marie and Irwin and Janice and Chester had come to the prom together—and Noah and Clara had also decided to go for it. At the moment everyone was just friends, but Savannah envisioned more in the romance department for each of her good buddies. The best in relationships started with a solid friendship. She and Antonio were a testimony to that. Savannah couldn't wait to share the news of her engagement with all the others.

As it was time for Savannah to open the event with a warm welcome and a few words of encouragement, she slowly made her way to the podium, smiling, speaking and nodding to the folks sitting at the tables she had to pass by. Just as Savannah reached for the microphone, everyone got to their feet and began to applaud her and cheer enthusiastically.

The standing ovation surprised Savannah, causing her emotions to erupt. Never in her wildest dreams would she have imagined such an uplifting welcome. If she didn't know how much she was loved and had been missed by many of the club, staff and volunteer members down at the senior center, she knew it now. Savannah's heart was full.

After Savannah took a few seconds to try and compose herself, she raised the microphone to her mouth. "Good evening, ladies and gentlemen! I must say I'm completely overwhelmed by the ovation and the warm, rousing welcome. Thank you and welcome to the Silver and Gold Spring Fling!

I am pleased to announce we've decided to make this event an annual one."

Another round of applause broke out and Savannah waited for things to calm down.

"It's such a pleasure and a blessing to be able to stand before you this evening," Savannah said. "Your prayers, notes and phone calls to wish me well are so appreciated." Emotionally filled to the brim, Savannah placed her hand over her heart. "Thank you so much for allowing me to lead the Silver Wings Senior Center as your new president. I am so honored. I'd also like us to give our vice president, Mable Grimes, a huge round of applause. She has been super in every way imaginable. Thank you all for attending this very special event."

Mable stood in front of her chair until the applause died down.

Savannah went on to acknowledge the distinguished guests from other local senior centers and to also give them a warm welcome. She also thanked the Sheffields for their sweet contributions. She then introduced her family members and Antonio's who were seated at two of the five head tables. The pride flowing over in her sisters' eyes was not lost on Savannah.

The look of love on Kenya and Kevin's faces truly made all of Savannah's days. Although disappointed that Kenya wasn't pregnant, that she wasn't going to become a grandmother, Savannah still felt relieved. Her daughter wasn't emotionally prepared to have a child, but Savannah was pleased by how much Kenya had grown through this real life experience. Kenya and Cole were still very young and had plenty of time to start a family.

Savannah nearly broke down as she thanked Bernice, Marie, Madge, Janice, Clara and Mable for all their hard work and dedication to the project. "Ladies, this special evening would not have happened without you. Thank you for your tireless contributions to this wonderful event. As promised, no long, drawn-out speeches. With that said, let the festivities begin. We're all here to have a good time and to try and get our groove back. Dinner is now served."

Savannah then asked Antonio to offer a word of prayer.

Right after dinner the king and queen of Silver Wings were announced. Not a single soul was surprised when Savannah and Noah's names were called as the winners. Noah was their king, the one who had had the good sense to reveal to them their queen, long before the members became aware that Savannah possessed a heart of gold.

As the crown and tiara were placed on the heads of the king and queen, another standing ovation occurred, along with another thundering round of applause. The king and queen then had their ceremonial dance, which opened up the entertainment portion of the event, featuring a great band from the seventies era. The band began to softly play "Lean on Me" by Bill Withers.

Minutes after the ceremonial dance was complete, Savannah and Antonio dashed up on the stage. Taking up the microphone, Antonio asked to have everyone's attention. He then pulled Savannah closer to him, resting his arm around her shoulder.

As expected by Savannah and Antonio, the ballroom was all abuzz with speculation.

Happy to share their good news with family and friends,

Antonio was grinning from ear to ear and Savannah's bright smile had her eyes aglow. "Savannah and I are extremely proud to announce our engagement. We're going to be married."

Antonio held up Savannah's hand to show off her sparkling engagement ring.

"No wedding date has been set yet, but when we have one you all will be the first to know. Please keep us in your thoughts and prayers as we bravely face Savannah's surgery next week. Savannah and I are so in love and can't wait to be married."

Without any prompting from the crowd, Antonio took Savannah into his arms and kissed her breathless, causing the audience to once again erupt into applause and loud cheering.

Savannah held up her and Antonio's entwined hands. "How's this for a silver season!"

Postlogue

Savannah surveyed her stunning new look as she peered into the bathroom mirror inside the honeymoon suite at the Jamaica Grand Hotel in Ocho Rios. The cute, short-haired wig wasn't half bad in her opinion. Antonio had said he liked the great new look, too. Until her own hair grew back, she planned to experiment with several different kinds of human hair wigs to see what lengths and styles she liked best. Although she never dreamed she'd ever have to wear a wig, she had to admit that it was kind of exciting. Savannah had the clever idea that she could be a different woman for her new husband on a regular basis. The thought of that thrilled her silly.

Savannah laughed heartily. "Yes, I can have lots of fun with this until my own beautiful tresses grow back." Then Savannah suddenly closed her eyes and fell down on her knees.

"Thank you, Jesus, for blessing the spiritual union

between Antonio and me. Thank you for bringing me through all the dark storms in my life. I'm still here only because of you and your unyielding grace. Thank you, Lord, for allowing me to live, when you could've easily taken me away to one day abide with you in your many mansions. Father, may these lips of mine, the ones you've formed so thick and so beautifully, never cease to give you all the glory. Amen."

Upon reentering the room, the first thing Antonio saw was Savannah down on her knees. Wondering if she'd fallen ill, panic arose in him. He rushed to her side, kneeling down next to her. Seeing the tears streaming down her face caused his internal alarms to go crazy. Antonio quickly drew Savannah into the comfort of his arms. "Savannah, what is it? Are you ill?"

Savannah hugged Antonio fiercely. "No, darling, no. I'm just fine. I was just giving thanks and praise to the Savior, my Redeemer, for the gift of life. That tumor could've been malignant and inoperable, but it was neither. He has seen me through the worst of the worst and I can't help falling on my knees to praise His name every chance I get. He has seen fit to bring us here to this beautiful place and to have all our children join us. There is no end to His mercy and His grace, Antonio. I love you, heavenly Father," she cried out with a joyous heart.

As Antonio looked into the watery eyes of the woman he loved, moisture quickly formed in his own. He then took hold of Savannah's hand. "Let us exalt Him together, Savannah. He is so worthy of our love and praise. Let us lift up His holy name. As John 4:24 says, 'God is spirit, and those who worship Him must worship in spirit and truth.

For God did not send the Son into the world to judge the world; but that the world should be saved through Him.' John, 3:17."

"God is so good," Savannah enthused.

Antonio wrapped his arms tightly around Savannah. "Yes, He is indeed!"

Dear Readers:

I sincerely hope that you enjoyed reading from cover to cover A SILVER SEASON. I'm very interested in hearing your comments and thoughts on the inspirational and romantic story of Savannah Richmond and Antonio Delabay, who find love with each other after losing their lifelong spouses. I love hearing from my readers and I do appreciate the time you take out of your busy schedule to write.

Please enclose a self-addressed, stamped envelope with all your correspondence and mail to: Linda Hudson-Smith, 16516 El Camino Road, Box 174, Houston, TX 77062. Or you can e-mail your comments to LHS4romance@yahoo.com. Please also visit my Web site and sign my guest book at www.lindahudsonsmith.com.

Linda Hudson-Smith